THE BLEEDING CHALICE

THE SISTER SWUNG away from Sarpedon, reversing the swing of her axe and trying to bring the butt of it into his ribs. He raised a leg and deflected the blow but the leg's joint folded under the impact and he lurched to one side. Sarpedon rolled with the motion and lashed out with two legs, catching the Sister with a glancing blow, and knocked her back a pace. There was a pause, a fraction of a second, as the two sized one another up and tried to anticipate the next move.

'Traitor,' hissed the Sister, hefting her axe from one hand to the other, her pistol holstered and forgotten.

'No traitor,' said Sarpedon levelly. 'Just free.'

More Ben Counter from the Black Library

SOUL DRINKER

DAEMON WORLD

A WARHAMMER 40,000 NOVEL

THE BLEEDING CHALICE

Ben Counter

To Helen

A BLACK LIBRARY PUBLICATION

First published in Great Britain in 2003 by
BL Publishing,
Games Workshop Ltd.,
Willow Road, Nottingham,
NG7 2WS, UK.

10 9 8 7 6 5 4 3 2 1

Cover illustration by Adrian Smith.

A CIP record for this book is available from the British Library.

ISBN 1 84416 054 8

Distributed in the US by Simon & Schuster
1230 Avenue of the Americas, New York, NY 10020, US.

Printed and bound in Great Britain by
Cox & Wyman Ltd, Reading, Berkshire, UK.

See the Black Library on the Internet at
www.blacklibrary.com

Find out more about Games Workshop
and the world of Warhammer 40.000 at
www.games-workshop.com

IT IS THE 41st millennium. For more than a hundred centuries the Emperor has sat immobile on the Golden Throne of Earth. He is the master of mankind by the will of the gods, and master of a million worlds by the might of his inexhaustible armies. He is a rotting carcass writhing invisibly with power from the Dark Age of Technology. He is the Carrion Lord of the Imperium for whom a thousand souls are sacrificed every day, so that he may never truly die.

YET EVEN IN his deathless state, the Emperor continues his eternal vigilance. Mighty battlefleets cross the daemon-infested miasma of the warp, the only route between distant stars, their way lit by the Astronomican, the psychic manifestation of the Emperor's will. Vast armies give battle in his name on uncounted worlds. Greatest amongst his soldiers are the Adeptus Astartes, the Space Marines, bio-engineered super-warriors. Their comrades in arms are legion: the Imperial Guard and countless planetary defence forces, the ever-vigilant Inquisition and the tech-priests of the Adeptus Mechanicus to name only a few. But for all their multitudes, they are barely enough to hold off the ever-present threat from aliens, heretics, mutants – and worse.

TO BE A man in such times is to be one amongst untold billions. It is to live in the cruellest and most bloody regime imaginable. These are the tales of those times. Forget the power of technology and science, for so much has been forgotten, never to be re-learned. Forget the promise of progress and understanding, for in the grim dark future there is only war. There is no peace amongst the stars, only an eternity of carnage and slaughter, and the laughter of thirsting gods.

ONE

THE YEARS LAY so heavily on the corridors of the Librarium Terra that the very air was thick with age. The endless tottering rows of bookcases and verdigrised datastacks seemed chained down by the weight of the thousands upon thousands of years of history. The librarium was deep within the planet's crust but even som the indistinct hum of activity droned through the labyrinthine corridors, just as it did everywhere else on the holy hive world of Terra. It was the sound of billions of souls grinding their way through the bureaucracy that kept the Imperium of Man together.

Even the captain of the deletions unit felt the sheer importance of the information that filled the librarium. He had lived on Terra all his life, immersed in the endless repetition of the myriad tasks that made up the government of the Imperium. He had done his job since birth, just as his forebears had done, and the shadows beneath Terra comprised his whole world.

But even he, after the decades spent performing his thankless task, had some instinctive understanding that the Librarium Terra held a repository of particularly pure, dangerous history.

The captain glanced around the next corner. The gallery he saw was lined with shelves of books so old they were little more than banks of rotting paper, lit by yellowed glow-globes that picked out the faint silver spider's webs that had been there, undisturbed, for as long as some of the books.

No one knew the full layout of the Librarium Terra. Estimates of its size varied, as no one had been to its furthest extents and returned – the deletions team had taken three days of forced marching to get this far. But, by the best estimates of the adepts who gave the unit its orders, the objective was close by.

The captain waved his ten-strong unit forwards. They wore black bodysuits with hoods that left only the eyes visible, rebreathers built in to keep aeons of dust out of their lungs. Their gloved hands held narrow-nozzled flamers connected to fuel canisters on their belts. But the captain carried a silenced autogun with a flaring flash suppressor. They moved quickly and almost silently, each one covering the other. They had always been members of the same unit, just as the captain had always commanded them. The captain didn't need to actually give them orders – they just did as they had always done, as generations had done in the endless predator's game beneath Terra.

The captain hurried down the gallery until it opened onto a landing overlooking a tangled knot of bookcases and datastacks. The cases held huge leather-bound volumes, tarnished infoslates, crumbling scrolls and reams of parchments, crammed onto shelves that had collapsed here and there into drifts of tattered paper. The datastacks, blocks of smooth black crystalline material that could store remarkable amounts of information, ranged from sinister glossy black obelisks to elaborate info-altars covered in filigree decoration and crowned with clusters of statues. Several of them bore images of the Adeptus Astartes, the armour-clad Space Marines who formed the elite of the Imperium's armed forces, battling aliens and corruption across the distant stars.

The captain peered into the gloom that flooded the labyrinth below. He spotted movement – a scholar worked in an alcove formed by the cases. Surrounded by discarded books he was leafing rapidly through another. His face was incredibly wizened and his arms had been replaced with jointed metal armatures that flicked through the book's pages with incredible speed. The scholar could have been a servitor, a mind-wiped automaton that was human only in the sense that it was formed from a rebooted human brain. Or it could have been a sentient human, a loyal servant of Terra like the captain himself, acting out some task that was probably redundant and meaningless but which represented the loyalty of everyone on Terra to the immortal God-Emperor.

The captain raised his autogun close to his face and focused on the hairless, tight-skinned skull of the scholar. The autogun coughed once and the scholar's skull crumpled suddenly as if paper-thin. The body slumped and fell, sprawling against the shelf behind it and disappearing beneath a cascade of books.

There were to be no witnesses to a deletion. That was the way it had always been done. Had the scholar been aware of it, he would have understood why he had to die.

The captain vaulted from the balcony down into the shadows below. The rest of the unit followed him, their feet padding on the tarnished wood of the floor as they landed. Down here the air was so heavy with age and knowledge that moving around was like walking through water. The faint, sickly glow from the electro-lanterns dotted here and there served only to make the shadows harder. The captain spotted some titles and dates on the volumes on the shelves. These books held details of the Imperium's armed forces, regimental histories of the Imperial Guard and accounts of long-forgotten battles. The deaths of billions of men were glossed over in those pages, and the captain could almost hear them screaming from the same pages that praised their sacrifice to the Emperor.

A simple hand signal, and the deletions team spread out, each taking a section of bookshelf and pulling out volumes at random, glancing at the covers and contents and then casting them to the floor. A servitor appeared without warning, its deformed splay-fingered hands spinning along the floor in a fruitless attempt to keep it clean. The nearest of the unit turned, sprayed a lance of flame through its vulnerable soft human core, and turned back to his work as the servitor shuddered and died in a burst of sickly smoke.

Another unit member hurried up to the captain. He was holding a book of red leather, its pages edged in gold. On the cover was a raised symbol of glittering black stone – a chalice surrounded by a spiked halo. It was the symbol they had been ordered to look out for.

The captain tapped the nearest deletions trooper on the shoulder. The trooper then tapped the nearest to him, and the signal passed through the whole team in a heartbeat. They dropped whatever they were holding and drew their flamers.

They fired plumes of flame into the bookshelves, filling the power-charged air of the Librarium Terra with the stink of flame and smoke. The protective clothing of the team reflected the worst of the heat but the labyrinth was still a furnace, with walls of superheated air billowing between the burning cases.

The captain removed the magazine of his autogun and replaced it with a single round picked from his belt. He aimed at the closest datastack, which was shaped like a three-panelled altarpiece with its mem-crystal worked into heroic images of battle. The gun fired again, with barely a sound, and the explosive round shattered the crystal into a flood of broken black glass.

Wordlessly, with an efficiency born of generations of toil, the deletions unit moved through the whole section of the library, burning and shattering anything that might hold the information they had been ordered to destroy. Already the energy suppression drones were hovering in from around every corner, projecting dampener fields that held back the heat of the fires and kept them from spreading. When the team left, the drones would move in and their overlapping fields would smother the flames – but not before the books and datastacks were reduced to smoke and ash.

Centuries of history were lost. Whole planets and military campaigns vanished forever from the Imperial memory. But more importantly by far, the deletion order had been carried out, and all official record of the Soul Drinkers Chapter was erased from the history of Mankind.

* * *

LIKE MOST OF the rest of the Imperium, no one really knew when Koris XXIII-3 had been settled. The grey-green, mostly featureless world had supported continent-spanning grox farms for longer than the Administratum could accurately record. The agri-world supported barely ten thousand souls, but was a subtly critical link in the macro economy of the systems that surrounded it, for grox formed a commodity as vital as guns or tanks or clean water.

Grox were huge, lumbering, reptilian, unsanitary and foul-minded. Crucially, however, they were almost entirely edible, each producing a mound of colourless, tasteless, stringy but nutritionally sound processed meat. Without the grox that were lifted from Koris XXIII-3 in vast-bellied cargo ships every three months, the billions of workers and gangers on the nearby hive worlds would starve, riot, and die. The shipyards of half a segmentum would find their human fuel faltering.

The Administratum knew how important the grox were. They administered the agri-world directly, circumventing tax-dodging governors and grafting private enterprise by keeping their own adepts as the sole power and, indeed, the whole population.

Very little of interest happened on Koris XXIII-3, a situation the adepts of the Administratum had worked hard for. The roaming herds of grox and the small islands of adept habitats went centuries with scant incident, the passing years marked only by the arrival of the huge dark slabs of the cargo ships and the occasional desultory deaths, births and promotions amongst the handful of humans.

So when a ship actually landed at the planet's only spaceport at Habitat Epsilon, carrying something other than another adept to replace a stampede death, it was a rare event. The ship was small and very, very fast, mostly composed of a cluster of flaring engines that tapered to a sharp wedge of a cockpit. There were no markings and no ship name, whereas an Administratum ship would bear the stylised alpha of the organisation. Adept Median Vrintas, the highest-ranking adept in the habitat, guessed that the ship carried someone or something important. She quickly donned her black formal Administratum robes and hurried across the meagre, dusty streets of the habitat to greet the ship's occupant.

She didn't know how right she was.

Habitat Epsilon, like every other structure on the planet, was formed of gritty brown rockcrete, premoulded and dropped from low orbit. The buildings were ugly and squat, the architecture featureless and windowed with dark reflective glass that kept the glare of the orange evening sun from the offices, workrooms and tiny living quarters. The spaceport was the only feature that made Habitat Epsilon remarkable, a prefabricated circle jutting from the edge of the habitat. There was a small unmanned landing control tower and a few unused maintenance sheds, indicative of how very few ships landed there.

A section of the ship's hull lowered with a faint hiss of hydraulics. Feet tramped down the ramp and three squads of battle-sisters marched out. Soldiers of the Ecclesiarchy, the church of the Emperor and the spiritual backbone of the Imperium, they wore ornate black power armour that clad them from gorget to foot and carried enough firepower in their boltguns and flamers to reduce the habitat to smoking rubble. Their leader was more stern-faced than the rest of the Sisters, and old in a way that suggested she was a damn good survivor. She bore a huge-bladed power axe. The armour of the Sisters was glossy black with white sleeves and tabards – order and squad markings had been removed.

The sister superior said nothing to Adept Median Vrintas as the Sisters of Battle filed out onto the spaceport's ferrocrete surface. They flanked the ship as an honour guard, weapons readied – as if anything in Habitat Epsilon could threaten them. Adept Vrintas had heard of the Sisters of Battle, of their legendary faith and skill at arms, but she had never seen one of them in the flesh. Was this some priestly delegation, then? The Missionaria Galaxia, or a confessor come to see to the planet's spiritual health? Vrintas mentally congratulated herself on having the habitat's small Ecclesiarchy temple swept out just three days before.

The next figure to emerge from the ship was a man. He was not particularly tall but his considerable presence was aided by the carapace armour that covered his torso and upper arms and the floor-length blast-coat of brown leather lined with flakweave plates. His face was long and lined, his jaw pronounced and his nose slightly lumpy as if it had been broken and set a few times. His eyes were a curious greyish blue, larger and more expressive than eyes set in that face had a right to be. His black hair was starting to thin. Subtle implants in one temple and behind the ear were for neuro-jacks, simple as far as augmetics went, but far beyond the means of any planet-bound adept. His hands were gloved – one held a data-slate.

He strode past his honour guard of Sisters, glancing at the sister superior with a barely perceptible nod. The watery sunlight of Koris XXIII-3 glinted off the rings on his free hand, that he wore over the black leather glove. The stiff breeze fluttered the hem of the blastcoat.

'Adept?' he asked as he walked up to Vrintas.

'I am Median Lachrymilla Vrintas, the chief adept of this habitat,' said Vrintas, tingling with the realisation that this visitor must be far, far more important than anyone she had ever met before. 'I oversee the planet's second most productive continent. We have five hundred million head of grox in nine…'

'I am not interested in the grox,' said the stranger. 'I ask only a few hours of your time and access to one of your adepts. There need be minimum disruption to your important work here.'

Vrintas was relieved to see a subtle smile on the man's face. 'Certainly,' she said. 'I shall need to know your name and office, for the records. We can't have just anyone wander around our facilities. And of course you and your colleagues will need to walk through our disinfectant footbaths. There will be quarantine protocols if you wish to leave the habitat as well, so once I know under whose authority you are acting…'

The man reached into his blastcoat and took out a small metal box. He flipped open the lid of the box and inside Vrintas saw a stylised 'I' of gleaming ruby in a silver surround. 'Authority of the Emperor's Inquisition,' said the man with the same smile. 'You need not know my name. Now, you will kindly direct me to Adept Diess.'

INQUISITOR THADDEUS was an extraordinarily patient man. It was this quality, above all others, that had kept him doing the Inquisition's work when men more violent, or brilliant, or strong-armed had found themselves lacking. The Ordo Hereticus, the branch of the Emperor's Inquisition that rooted out threats amongst the very men and women it was sworn to protect, needed all those qualities. But it also needed the understanding that the Imperium could not be healed of all its sicknesses at once.

It needed men who could see the enormity of a task that stretched well beyond their own lifetimes, and not give way to despair. Thaddeus knew that, as just one man, even with the magnitude of the resources he could command he could do but little in the grand scheme of the Imperium and the divine Emperor's wishes for mankind. At present he had a full company of Ordo Hereticus storm troopers and several squads of battle-sisters under Sister Aescarion, but he knew that even with their guns he could not hope to end the corruption and incompetence that threatened the Imperium from within – just as aliens and daemons threatened from without. The whole Inquisition had that responsibility. If the task was ever to be finished, it would be finished by men and women of the Ordo Hereticus, many generations distant.

Thaddeus understood all this, and yet was willing to give his life to the cause, because if he did not, who would?

It was precisely because of his patience that Thaddeus had been given his current task. The first inquisitor to have taken on this mission, a bloody-minded and morbidly stubborn soul named Tsouras, had been selected because he happened to be the only one available at that time. He had failed because he had no patience, only a burning determination to win visible triumphs to terrify and amaze those around him. Tsouras, and inquisitors like him, had their uses, but that mission had not been one of them. When there was time, the lord inquisitors of the Ordo Hereticus had selected Thaddeus to take over, because Thaddeus could succeed by picking away at the layers of lies and confusion until the truth was uncovered before its captors realised.

At that moment, Inquisitor Thaddeus wished he had not been given the mission at all. Though the higher purposes of the Inquisition were burned into his remarkably resilient mind, he was still ultimately just a man, and he knew a dead end when he saw it. The few available leads had dried up, and the man now sitting across the untidy desk opposite him was, grim as it sounded, possibly his last hope.

'I do hope I am not inconveniencing you,' said Thaddeus, who never saw any reason to be impolite no matter what his state of mind. 'I understand the importance of the work done here.'

'The numbers aren't important,' said Adept Diess. 'I just stamp forms all day.' Diess had, until recently, been a fit man, middle-aged but wearing well. Now he had given up on himself and was putting on weight, though he still looked sharper than anyone on this planet had a right to be.

Thaddeus cocked an eyebrow. 'You sound as if the Emperor's grox farms do little to inspire you. Median Vrintas would be discouraged to hear that.'

'If you had spent as much time as I have balancing the books for this place, you would know that Median Vrintas can hardly count. She can have her opinions but I keep this planet making the Administratum tithes.'

Thaddeus smiled. 'You speak freely. A rare thing, believe me. Refreshing, in a way.'

'If you have come here to kill me, inquisitor, you will do it no matter what I say. If you have not, you won't waste the bullet.'

Thaddeus sat back in the uncomfortable chair. The other adepts had shown the sense to leave the office before Thaddeus had to ask for them to be removed, so the only sound was the grinding of a cogitator somewhere in the back of the low-ceilinged room. Dust motes floated in the thick light from the setting sun outside.

The office was home to maybe thirty adepts, each at a partitioned workstation. Every wall and surface was covered with paper – statistical printouts, graphs, charts, graphic depictions of the many diseases that plagued the common grox, and grim notices reminding the adepts of the ceaseless sacrifice they were compelled to make for the Imperium. The Administratum tried to foster the same atmosphere whether it was running a palace or a workhouse – its members dedicated their lives to the work that kept the Imperium running, the unending mundanity of jobs without which the macro economy of the Imperium would collapse.

'You are an intelligent man, adept. Not many men of your station would know an inquisitor when they saw one. Median Vrintas certainly didn't. I have heard men swear blind we don't exist, or that we're all fighting evil gods and don't bother with the likes of mortals such as yourself. But you seem to know rather more than them. Am I right, consul?'

The adept smiled bitterly. 'I am glad to say I no longer hold that office.'

'I think we understand one another, Consul Senioris Iocanthus Gullyan Kraevik Chloure. You know what I am here to talk about.'

'It's been a long time since anyone called me that.' Chloure seemed almost nostalgic. 'I could have had command of a whole sector, if I'd just toed the line for a few years more. But, I wanted too much too fast. You've probably seen it before.'

'You understand,' said Thaddeus without changing his tone, 'that Inquisitor Tsouras condemned you to death in your absence.'

'I assumed so,' said Chloure. 'How many of the others got out?'

'Not many. Captain Trentius was spared, although he will never pilot anything larger than an escort. A few menials that Tsouras decided were sufficiently minor to be incapable of true incompetence. But most of the rest were executed. I must say, though Tsouras is not the subtlest of my colleagues, you have showed great resourcefulness in evading him for as long as you have.'

Chloure shrugged. 'I planet-hopped for a while. Faked up some references, I talk the talk so there weren't too many questions. I got posted here eventually, and I wasn't intending to go anywhere else. Not many people look on a place like this for a wanted man. At least, I thought so until you turned up.'

'You should know, consul, that you don't do anything in the Administratum without someone writing it down. Your paper trail was long and winding but I have associates who could follow it.'

'Well,' said Chloure. He looked more exhausted than frightened, as if he had always known this day would come and just wanted it over with. 'The Soul Drinkers.'

'Yes. The Soul Drinkers. In light of your coopera-tion, I shall let you begin.'

Chloure sat back and sighed. 'It was three years ago, you know the dates better than I do. Anyway, we had been detailed to take over the Van Skorvold star fort. We knew Callisthenes Van Skorvold had some alien trinket that was particularly valuable. We fed it into a couple of databases and found out it was the Soulspear.'

'The Soul Drinkers artefact?'

'The very same. It was a legend the search turned up, some poem about how it could level cities and kill daemons and such like, and how they'd lost it.' Chloure sat up sharply and leaned across the desk. 'I am a greedy man, inquisitor. I am ambitious. I could have let the Imperial Guard do it but I wanted it finished quicker and cleaner. I know I could have left the Soul Drinkers out of it entirely. If I had just played it by the book I would have saved us all a lot of grief. But like I said, I'm greedy. I mean, we all want something.'

'There are far graver sins, consul,' Thaddeus said, with a veneer of understanding that surprised many. 'You let the word go out that you had found the Soulspear. The Soul Drinkers would arrive, eliminate all resistance, and take the item, leaving you to march into the star fort unopposed. Is that the case?'

'If it had happened like that I wouldn't be shovelling grox dung for the rest of my life. But you know all of this.'

'What can you tell me about Sarpedon?'

Chloure thought for a second. 'Not much. I only saw him on the bridge screen. We had an Adeptus Mechanicus ship with us. They sent a teleport crew into the star fort and snatched the Soulspear right from under Sarpedon's nose.'

Thaddeus could imagine what Sarpedon must have looked like to the gaggle of naval officers and Administratum adepts – a Space Marine commander, a psyker, an angry man burning with betrayal.

Chloure was calm, having imagined his final reckoning with the Inquisition for some time, but even so the fear he must have felt when he first saw Sarpedon played briefly over his face. 'Were you able to judge his state of mind?' asked Thaddeus. 'His intentions?'

Chloure shook his head. 'I wish I could help you more, inquisitor. He was angry. He was prepared to kill anyone who got in his way, but you know that. You haven't found them, have you? That's why you're here. Not for me.'

Thaddeus's face betrayed nothing. 'The Soul Drinkers will be found, consul.'

'You must be desperate to have gone to the trouble of tracking me down. I was just along for the ride, Inquisitor Tsouras was calling the shots and presumably he couldn't help you. What did you think I could tell you?'

Chloure was a sharp man. In many ways he was the first decent adversary Thaddeus had encountered for some time. It was difficult to threaten a man who was perfectly resigned to his death sentence. He had guessed what Thaddeus was loathe to admit – the Soul Drinkers' trail had turned cold. There were barely any leads left from the debacle at the Cerberian Field when Tsouras and the battlefleet, nominally under Chloure's command, had been outfoxed and eluded by the fleet of the renegade Space Marine Chapter. Sarpedon and his Chapter numbered less than one thousand men, and such a force was barely a speck in the vastness of the Imperium, almost invisible against the boundless galaxy.

Chloure was, in a very real sense, one of Thaddeus's last hopes.

'You are one of the few surviving individuals to have had any contact with the Soul Drinkers,' continued Thaddeus. 'There is a chance you picked up something that Tsouras did not.'

Chloure smiled, almost in triumph. 'To think that a humble agri-world adept should cause the mighty Inquisition such woes! I can only tell you what you already know. Sarpedon won't give up, not ever. He cares for his honour more than his life or those of his men. He'll run if you make him and attack whatever the risks if there's a principle at stake. That's all I know. From the sound of it, that's all anyone knows.'

Thaddeus stood up grandly, letting his blastcoat sweep around him. 'The Inquisition knows where you are, consul. You do the Emperor's work much better here than if you had attained a higher rank, I feel, and for this reason you can consider your execution indefinitely stayed. But should your standards fall, I can ensure the sentence is carried out. We will be watching the tithes with great care.

'So, until then, consider my presence here nonexistent. Continue the work of the Administratum, Adept Diess.'

The man who had been Consul Senioris Chloure, gave a sardonic salute and returned to the thankless task of sifting through the mountain of forms on his desk.

Thaddeus swept out of the office, down the darkened stairway, and out into the grim exterior of Habitat Epsilon where the evening sun was now setting and the endless rolling fields beyond the habitat were dark with the herds of sleeping grox.

The Sisters were still waiting by the ship.

'Prepare for takeoff, sister,' said Thaddeus to Sister Aescarion.

'There is nothing here?' she asked. Sister Aescarion talked to Thaddeus as if she was his equal, for which Thaddeus was grateful.

'Nothing. Tsouras left us precious little when he put half the Lakonia Persecution to death.'

'Have faith, inquisitor. The Soul Drinkers have committed blasphemy in the sight of the Emperor. He will guide our hand if need be.'

'I am sure you are right, sister. But I imagine the Emperor does little to help those who cannot prove their worth and we have proven very little so far.'

Thaddeus and Aescarion walked up the ramp and into the body of the ship. The Sisters trooped in behind, filing into the personnel compartment. The ship was clean and new, requisitioned by the Ordo Hereticus from the shipyards of Hydraphur and a rare example of craft both small and fast, with the manoeuvrability and firepower to look after itself. The inside was simple: glossy, black and bare metal, decorated with devotional texts to the Emperor that the Sisters had pinned up on bulkheads, walls and small shrines. Thaddeus had kept the trappings of faith from the cockpit, but gradually the Sisters had taken over everywhere they were stationed and had turned it into a mobile chapel to the Emperor.

Aescarion joined her battle-sisters in the grav-couches inside, and the Sisters murmured a prayer of respect as she took her seat beside them.

Thaddeus headed for the cockpit, which he had upholstered with dark maroon tharrhide. His co-pilot's seat nestled next to the installed pilot-servitor – once human, its facial features had been replaced with an array of scanning devices. One of its hands was now a set of gold-plated compasses that scritched out trajectories and geometric shapes on the data-slate jutting from its ribcage. The other hand was hard-wired into the instrument panel of the cockpit, and sent messages from its once-human brain into the ship's cogitators and engine controls.

'Launch,' said Thaddeus to the servitor. The remnants of its brain recognised the command and the ship lurched as the thrusters on its underside kicked in. The featureless landscape of Koris XXIII-3 yawed and was replaced by the clear bright sky. Suddenly, the ship's primary engines roared, and Thaddeus was thrust into the deep upholstery as the ship tore through the planet's atmosphere.

Thaddeus didn't know if anyone else would go to the trouble of hunting down Consul Senioris Chloure. He hoped they didn't – Adept Diess was doing far more for the Emperor's flock than Chloure ever would have done.

Finding him, and letting him live, passed for a small victory, and Thaddeus anticipated few enough of those. The Soul Drinkers were tough and resourceful, and their intentions were unknowable. Though a Space Marine Chapter could conquer just about anything, it still consisted of just a thousand men, and the Soul Drinkers probably numbered significantly less. Thaddeus's own staff numbered more and he did not wield the massive household armies of some inquisitor lords.

The Soul Drinkers could disappear, if they wanted to.

But they would not. That was Thaddeus's best hope. Sarpedon was still, in many ways, a Space Marine, and he would not just sit tight in some far corner of the galaxy waiting to be forgotten. He still believed in something, no matter how twisted, and he would keep on fighting. The Soul Drinkers would do something to make themselves visible again. Thaddeus would be there, and he would find them. He would trap them and kill Sarpedon, if he could. Then he would coordinate whatever resources he needed to shatter the remnants of the Soul Drinkers Chapter for good.

He had faith, like Sister Aescarion. And even if that was all he had, for an inquisitor, it was enough.

THE SOUL DRINKERS Chapter had disappeared in its entirety at the climax of the Lakonia Persecution, when the Chapter's fleet had fled through a long-forgotten warp route leaving Inquisitor Tsouras's battlefleet grasping at nothing. The events leading up to the Persecution had been enough to mark the Chapter as rebels of the most dedicated and dangerous sort – an attack on the Adeptus Mechanicus, the destruction of the Lakonia Star Fort, the refusal to submit to Inquisitorial examination, and the killing of the interrogator sent by Tsouras to deliver his ultimatum.

When the smoke cleared, the Soul Drinkers had vanished from the face of the Imperium.

Well over a year later, salvage crews in the far galactic east reported a huge find: a massive graveyard of ships, some battleship-sized, that had all been destroyed by scuttling. The investigating Imperial authorities soon ascertained that this was the Soul Drinkers' fleet, including the mighty battle barge *Glory* and a shoal of strike cruisers and support craft. Of the Soul Drinkers themselves there was no sign. No one knew where they were or how they were travelling, but the fact that they had destroyed their own fleet – one of the most powerful independent forces for some sectors around – indicated that they were determined to make life difficult for anyone trying to follow them.

The fleet could have been tracked. But these mere thousand men could not be tracked – not when they had the immeasurable vastness of the Imperium to hide in.

And so it came to Inquisitor Thaddeus of the Ordo Hereticus. There was no question of letting Tsouras carry on with the task of hunting down the

Soul Drinkers – he had let them slip by once and that was once too often. Thaddeus had few leads left to follow from the wreckage of the Persecution and the burned-out remnants of the fleet. Chloure was the last to be exhausted and like the others – Archmagos Khobotov of the Adeptus Mechanicus, killed in a generatorium explosion on the Forge World Koden Tertius, Captain Trentius of the Cardinal Byzantine and a few others who had survived Tsouras's enthusiasm – he had yielded nothing to indicate where the Soul Drinkers were or what they were planning. But Thaddeus did not despair at the magnitude of his task. He was reliable and thorough. He would get the job done eventually.

He knew hardly anything about the Soul Drinkers. He had studied their history in great detail, of course, and it indicated a zealously loyal Chapter, independent of will but ready to throw its valuable Marines against insane odds in the Emperor's name. There was barely a taint on them. But that was not the Chapter he faced now – the Soul Drinkers had broken so violently with their faith in the Imperium that their heresy left nothing of the Chapter's previous personality. Thaddeus knew that Sarpedon, who had taken command of the rebellious Soul Drinkers, would be the primary force behind the Chapter's new, blasphemous existence. Sarpedon was a psyker, one of the Chapter's Librarians and highly decorated throughout his seventy-year service. He would be tough to crack. Probably impossible.

Thaddeus knew he would have to kill him. Sarpedon would have to die before the Chapter could be broken. Thaddeus might be unable to do it himself and might have to call in other inquisitors with their own resources, perhaps agents of the Officio Assassinorum or even the planet-scouring Exterminatus, once he had located the Soul Drinkers and driven them into a corner.

Messy and costly. But every drop of spilt Imperial blood would be worth it. A rebel Space Marine Chapter was a danger too great and unpredictable to forgive.

All these thoughts, as they often did, occupied Thaddeus as he sat in the darkened navigational chamber on the *Crescent Moon*. The circular chamber formed an auditorium of upholstered reclining couches that could have held a couple of hundred, but Thaddeus was usually the only one there, silent in thought as he sunk into the deep padding. The seating was reclined because the navigational display was projected onto the vast glowing disk of the ceiling, shining down on the chamber like a full moon.

The *Crescent Moon* was Thaddeus's own ship, a ribbed gunmetal-grey cylinder with vast particle scoops like the fronds of an anemone sprouting from the bow. These fuelled the four enormous engines just behind them, leaving the rest of the ship to house the bridge, living quarters, cargo holds, machine-spirit chamber, and all the rest of the many places that a spaceship needed to function. Thaddeus' own quarters, and those of his Interrogator, Shen, were armoured sections in the heart of the ship. The inside of the ship was furnished to Thaddeus's taste – simply and darkly. The ship was a rare creature, the sort of craft the shipyards of the Imperial Navy couldn't make any more, assembled centuries before from parts millennia old by one of Thaddeus's mentors. It was fast and comfortable, and it only needed a crew of a few dozen, which gave Thaddeus some valued privacy. However, with the storm troopers and Sisters occupying the refitted cargo sections, the ship was feeling rather more crowded of late.

'Sector map,' Thaddeus said, and the vox-sensor switched the star map from the shining star field to a map of the sector, with the many star systems and planets flagged with names and coordinates. The *Crescent Moon* was still orbiting around Koris XXIII-3, and Thaddeus had to give some thought to where he would head next – probably towards the nearest Inquisition fortress or subsector headquarters to relate the paltry scraps of information he had found to the Ordo Hereticus. The cluster of agriworlds was surrounded by a ring of populous hive worlds and manufactoria planets, many of which had their own permanent Inquisitorial presence. Thaddeus was trying to decide which one would be the least grim place to explain his lack of progress when the vox-casters chimed in alarm.

An incoming transmission. The astropathic choir, the half-dozen telepaths who received and transmitted messages between Thaddeus and the rest of the Imperium, spoke in unison over the vox, their voices whispering and raspy. 'From subsector command Therion, sector Boras Minor, Ultima Segmentum. Ordo Hereticus naval liaison staff report rogue space hulk, possible Adeptus Astartes activity. Report to follow. Have faith lest your unbelief consume you.'

Thaddeus pulled himself upright and walked through the darkened auditorium towards the door that led towards the bridge. To tell the truth, he had held little hope that the requests he had made of the Hereticus command – that he be informed via astropath of any unusual discoveries that matched certain criteria, including the possible presence of Space Marines – would bring in much information of value. Now a space hulk had been found by the Imperial Navy, and the find had become known to the section of the Ordo Hereticus that kept watch on the fleets of the Ultima Segmentum. For whatever reason they had suspected the superhuman warriors of the Adeptus Astartes were involved. It was a thousand to one shot that the Soul Drinkers were the Marines in question (literally, for they said there were a thousand Chapters of Marines, though Thaddeus suspected the true number could be anything), but it was a better lead than anything else he had.

The bulkhead slid open and instead of the corridor beyond, Thaddeus was confronted with the sight of the Pilgrim.

Tall and shrouded and surrounded by a cloud of thick, sickly incense, the Pilgrim's face was hidden by the tattered dark grey hood of his robes. His hands were wrapped in heavy bandages. Thick cables ran from within the hood down to the quietly humming respirator clipped to the leather belt at his waist, to assist whatever was under those robes to breathe. The bulky power pack on his back, which ran the Pilgrim's portable life support systems, gave him a crippled and hunchbacked look. The ever-present incense was billowing from the twin censers that topped the pack, and a faint glow burned through the rents and frays in the shroud as if the Pilgrim was fuelled by a furnace.

Thaddeus permitted the creature to be referred to as the Pilgrim because he professed to be an utterly devoted follower of the Emperor, and he served Thaddeus as an expression of this fervour.

Although Thaddeus valued him greatly, the Pilgrim had a habit of acting in the most sinister manner, occasionally seeming to anticipate Thaddeus's movements.

'Inquisitor,' it said with a heavy, monotone, half-mechanical voice. 'The hulk. Will we go?' The

Pilgrim turned and followed Thaddeus as he headed past it towards the bridge.

The Pilgrim must have been monitoring the information Thaddeus was receiving. Thaddeus knew the upper echelons of the Hereticus must be spying on him most of the time, but he was not happy that the Pilgrim was doing it too. Still, Thaddeus knew better than to risk a rift with the creature. 'Perhaps,' said Thaddeus. 'We are duty-bound to follow up any clues. But the chances of the find being relevant are...'

'It is them.'

'Unless you have some intelligence I have not received, Pilgrim, it would not do to get our hopes up. We have received more promising leads than this before.'

'Think on it, inquisitor.' In the Pilgrim's voice, the rank sounded like an insult. 'One craft is more difficult to track than a fleet. A hulk is large enough to house a whole Chapter. And what loyal Chapter would sink to taking up residence on a space hulk? The perversion of such an idea would suit Sarpedon perfectly.'

The Pilgrim knew the histories of the Soul Drinkers in depth, and had read of the many great victories they had won in the Emperor's name, from the dawn of the Second Founding to the eve of their heresy. It had instilled in him a hatred of what the Chapter had become; it was a hatred that rivalled Sister Aescarion's religious faith. The Pilgrim was a profiler, and expert in the means and beliefs of the Soul Drinkers, and he could be the most valuable individual in Thaddeus's entourage if it all came down to guessing which way Sarpedon would jump.

'We can't be sure,' said Thaddeus. 'The Ordo Xenos was tracking more than seven hundred hulks and suspected hulks at the last count, and they were only the ones they were willing to mention.'

'You are right of course, inquisitor,' replied the Pilgim. 'One ship amongst hundreds gives us long odds. Perhaps you are pursuing a better lead at the moment? One strong enough to negate the value of optimism in our mission?'

Thaddeus had decided long ago not to rise to the Pilgrim's baiting. If he wasn't so useful, Thaddeus would have refused to accept him into the strike force when it was first assembled by the Ordo Hereticus. But the feel the Pilgrim had for the soul of the renegade Chapter was one of the few edges Thaddeus had.

They came to a bulkhead in the form of a massive set of bronze double doors. Thaddeus spoke a code-word and the doors swung open. Thaddeus and the Pilgrim stepped through into the cavernous space. The bridge of the *Crescent Moon* was suspended above the engineering decks, so the navigational consoles and command pulpit looked down on the massive spinning plasma turbines that churned away a hundred metres below. The engine-gang, pale-skinned red-eyed men who rarely emerged from the depths of the ship's engines, could be seen scuttling between the turbines, making adjustments in anticipation of the *Crescent* leaving orbit and putting into the warp.

Thaddeus had no flag-captain. He commanded his own ship. Servitors were slaved into most of the consoles so they could relay his commands directly. The platforms of the bridge held only the servitors, Thaddeus and the Pilgrim, Sister Aescarion, and Colonel Vinn of the Hereticus storm troopers.

'Sister, colonel,' said Thaddeus briskly. 'Our course is for the Subsector Therion. Have your troops make ready for warp travel.' At his words the servitors twitched as they fed his commands into the *Crescent's* machine-spirit. 'A space hulk is an environment not to be taken lightly. You may be required to put your troops at considerable risk.'

'We have chased ghosts for too long,' said Aescarion. 'My Sisters will give thanks for the opportunity to bring some purity to the place.'

'The men of the Hereticus Storm regiment will be ready,' said Vinn. Vinn had been mindwiped several times owing to the things he and his men had seen as they fought the Hereticus war against witchery and corruption. He had been forced to learn the ways of fighting several times in the course of his life and the result was a wealth of experience and battle instinct that he did not remember receiving but which made him an effective leader and an unquestioning Imperial servant. His bland features hid utter ruthlessness and beneath the black and red storm trooper fatigues he was covered in scars from the many near-suicide missions he had led.

The regiment, actually a vast body of men dispersed across uncountable Inquisitorial retinues and fortresses, had been seconded to the Ordo Hereticus for so long that they now had nothing to do with their parent Imperial Guard at all, instead being raised at Hereticus's request and trained in Inquisitorial facilities. Thaddeus had five platoons, over two hundred men, in the *Crescent Moon's* cargo holds, every one of them rigorously conditioned to face any horror with their assault-patterned lasguns, and perform the most gruesome of tasks at Thaddeus's request.

Thaddeus ascended the short flight of steps to the command pulpit that overlooked the banks of servitor-manned consoles and monitors. He tapped the subsector code into the glowing lectern display and a line of coordinates flashed up, streaming into the half-minds of the servitors as they in turn input the commands that would have the *Crescent Moon's* machine-spirit direct the ship through the warp. The ship's lone Navigator, a recluse named Praxas who had not left his cramped quarters in the ship's prow for months on end, would even now be preparing to gaze onto the warp and guide the ship through its treacherous currents.

'Has he had some insight?' Sister Aescarion enquired. She was standing by the pulpit and watching the Pilgrim, who was looking down on the rumbling engines as the engine-gang got them started.

'He seemed confident the hulk has something to do with the Soul Drinkers,' replied Thaddeus. 'I have reason to trust his judgement.'

'I understand that I am under your command, inquisitor, and that he and I will be called upon to fight the same battle. But it makes me uneasy that I have so little idea of who or what he is.'

Thaddeus smiled. 'Sister, do you think me a radical? You should not believe the rumours you hear. We are not all daemon-baiting madmen in the Inquisition. The Pilgrim is not a monster.'

Sister Aescarion did not return his smile. She had gained a reputation as a dependable commander of battle-sisters working alongside the Inquisition, and she would have heard more than enough rumours. Many of them were true – Thaddeus had himself been involved in clearing up the mess left by the Eisenhorn heresies and the destruction of the rogue Hereticus cell on Chalchis Traxiam. 'The Sisters wonder, inquisitor,' she said. 'That is all. They must be certain they are commanded by those who have the same depth of faith as they do. Idle chatter undermines the purity of faith and it would be better for me if you were more open about your companions.'

'The Pilgrim can be trusted, Sister. You have my word on that and this is all you need. Now, you should make sure your Sisters are prepared for departure, we will be in the Empyrean for some weeks.'

Sister Aescarion nodded curtly and strode off the bridge, the boots of her black lacquered power armour clacking on the metal floor of the bridge. Colonel Vinn followed her, stepping smartly as if on the parade ground.

The preparations took little time. Thaddeus valued the *Crescent Moon* partly because the procedures for beginning a major warp journey, which on an Imperial battleship could take days of tech-priest ministrations, could be handled in hours. Soon the massive engines roared and lit the bridge from beneath with the bright orange plasma glow. The flaring particle scoops folded into the cylindrical body of the ship and blue-white bolts of energy arced off the hull. The *Crescent Moon* drifted out of high orbit and the warp engines fired.

The inhabitants of the agri-world looked up to see a tiny bright star winking suddenly in the sky and then disappear. One of them, Adept Chloure, sighed a prayer of gratitude to the Emperor that the visitors had not taken him with them, and turned back to the never-ending mountain of paperwork.

TWO

THE SKY HAD turned dark over Eumenix. The whole hive world was locked in a perpetual twilight, lit only by the weak orange glow of the heatsink exhausts and the flickering, dying lumospheres that were winking out one by one as the planet died. Over Hive Quintus, home to a rapidly decreasing population of almost a billion, it rained greasy ash as the pyres of the dead begin to tower over the looted palaces of the nobles. The hive city's screams could be heard for kilometres around – wailing sirens of Arbites riot control tanks, the shriek of collapsing tunnelways as hordes of citizens tried to flee the latest hotspot, roars of explosions as looters tripped booby-traps or overladen tramp shuttles crashed on takeoff from makeshift pads.

And the smell. Burning, certainly – it could hardly be otherwise when fire was the only thing that could keep anything clean any more. And spilt fuel. And panicked sweat. But there was something else, sweet but caustic: a smell that made noses wrinkle and eyes water. It steeped the entire city from the pleasure-galleries to the underhive, to the endless maintenance warrens and the gold-plated halls of trade. It seeped out into the barren wastes between cities. Even in the wilds outside the city, those who tried to flee by land could smell it, and just before the seething pollution flats claimed them they knew it was the stink of death. And not just the ordinary death that wandered Hive Quintus constantly – this was the stench of the plague.

Some had called it the white death, or the underhive pox, or spirit rot. The doctors who tended to the city's ailing aristocracy invented long, complex High Gothic names for it. But by the time old Governor Hugenstein had succumbed, his body a mass of seeping welts, along with his family and most of his staff, it was known simply as 'the plague'.

No one knew how to cure it. Everything from full blood transplants for the super-rich to folk remedies, devised when the city was young, were tried and failed. In desperation, the people looked for a cause – and scores of innocents were burned as pox-spreading political agents or witches. By the time the pyres of plague dead broke the city's skyline, even being uninfected was a death sentence. But no one could tell where the infection came from. And trying to understand it just made it kill quicker.

Some got out. The Administratum offices cut through enough red tape to get the higher echelons to safety. Some of the manufactorium owners made the most of their razor-sharp business sense to buy themselves passage out of Hive Quintus as passengers on fleeing pleasure-yachts or human ballast on smugglers' scows.

Others could have run but did not – the governor had done the most noble thing of his reign and presided over the death of his city. The Adeptus Arbites decided without debate to stand their ground and preserve the Emperor's laws even as the city fell apart. The preachers of the Adeptus Ministorum stayed, and bellowed the Emperor's praises from temples crammed with desperate infected citizens. But the hundreds of millions who filled Hive Quintus's thousands of layers all wished they had the chance to flee in one of the pitifully few craft that were escaping. Any craft large enough to carry a significant number of people was shot down by orbital defence lasers maintaining the quarantine order against Eumenix – those who escaped did so in a tiny trickle, barely a dent in the massive, doomed population.

That, of course, did not stop larger ships from taking off and being turned into long burning streaks in the sky – more omens of death for the people below. But there were some smaller ships in the city that might run the quarantine blockade. Some spaceports were still operational, and whenever word went round that there was a ship about to launch, hordes of half-dead victims piled up around the launch pads and ship hangars.

Most of the time there were no ships. But as the plague reached its height, on Ventral Dock 31, Cartel Pollos managed to salvage a small research vessel just spaceworthy enough to get the House patriarch and his immediate family off Hive Quintus. Sure enough, masses of plague victims swarmed against the walls around Ventral Dock 31, held at bay by the private army of Cartel Pollos. Shotgun blasts ripped down into the crowds as the ship fuelled and prepped for takeoff. It was perhaps the last hope for anyone to escape the plague.

Hope was the rarest commodity of all. But when a massive explosion tore out a section of the east wall, all hope disappeared.

THE AUTOSENSES IN Sergeant Salk's helmet snapped his pupils shut as the glare of the explosion burst across the east wall. From his squad's vantage point in the ruins of a hab-block like an island in the centre of the heaving plague-infected crowd, he could see chunks of ferrocrete hurled into the air with a massive thunderclap. Pollos's guards were thrown off the battlements and a ripple ran through the crowd as the front ranks were blown backwards by the force of the explosion.

Karrick's demolition charge had done the job. Separated from his squad, Karrick would be lucky to survive to meet up with the rest of the squad, if any of them got inside the spaceport at all. But that didn't matter now. Captain Dreo was dead and Salk was in charge. The squad had secured their target and he understood that if he had to cash in the lives of his battle-brothers to complete his mission, then he would do so.

'Go!' he yelled into the vox and the six remaining Soul Drinkers vaulted from the burned-out windows of the shattered hab-block. They landed in the thick of the crowd and Salk felt festering limbs pushing against him as he sunk into the crowd as if into an ocean. He clambered to his feet and saw the rest of the squad battling against the human tide – Space Marines were a clear head and shoulders taller than the tallest unaugmented man and Salk easily spotted the Marines of his squad: Krin with the plasma gun, Dryan, Hortis, Aean and big Nicias hauling the squad's sole prisoner.

Nicias had been forced to abandon his missile launcher after the mission's bloody early stages, where Dreo was lost, and had fought on with knife and bolt pistol. He had accepted responsibility for hauling the prisoner, head covered and wrists bound, with his free hand.

Salk forged a way through the heaving crowd. Lolling-mouthed, mad-eyed faces loomed from the masses and hands grabbed at him. They were lit by

the fires that burned in the hive-spires rising all
around like mountain ranges, and the searchlights
directing the fire of the soldiers on the breached
walls of the spaceport. There must have been ten
thousand crowding up against the east wall alone,
and Salk could see where they were piled up, living
and dead, against the barricades beneath the walls.

Salk pushed through them, his power armoured
body barging bodies aside. He picked up and threw
those in front of him. He didn't want to hurt these
people – they could not help the madness of the
Imperium into which they had been born – but if
they put themselves in his way, he would crush
them underfoot. This mission had turned ugly from
the outset, and it would end ugly, too.

The crowd surged forward as the front ranks
recovered from the blast and began to pour into the
breach. Gunfire stuttered from up ahead as the Cartel Pollos troops poured their fire into the plague
victims that clambered over the rubble onto the
landing platform of the spaceport.

A missile streaked down from the closest watchtower and blew a hole in the surging crowd. Salk
pushed against the crowd and burst out into the
smouldering crater, ringed with blackened bodies,
a short sprint from the yawning breach in the wall.
The wall was twenty metres high and several thick,
but the charge had torn a huge section out of it.
Autogun fire was already spraying from behind the
fallen chunks of masonry, with shotgun blasts

barking beyond the rubble as Cartel Pollos troops hunted down the plague victims that had got through.

'Nicias, Krin, with me!' voxed Salk as he fired a couple of bolter shots at the gaudily dressed Pollos troops ducking behind the masonry. 'The rest, covering fire!'

The huge form of Nicias tore out of the crowd beside Salk, followed by Krin. Already some of the troopers had spotted the massive purple-armoured Marines and were directing their fire towards them, rightly singling them out as the biggest threat to the east wall. Autogun fire spanged off Salk's shoulder armour and he returned fire, almost blind, as he put his head down and ran across the open ground towards the cover of the rubble in the breach.

The two Space Marines back in the fringes of the crowd opened up on full auto with their boltguns, spattering the walls with miniature explosions. Troopers on the walls jerked and fell, some tumbling over the lip of the wall onto the barbed wire and barricades below, their bodies mingling with those of the fallen plague victims.

Salk slid into cover as a heavy stubber in the watchtower stitched fire all around him. Nicias was seconds behind him, firing up at the watchtower. There was a missile launcher and a heavy stubber up there, and by now the Pollos troops would have marked Salk and his Marines as priority targets.

And with good reason. A spear of white heat ripped up from the open ground behind Salk and the top of the watchtower billowed open, the blast of the plasma impact compressed within the fire-point and incinerating whatever men and munitions were inside. Krin, plasma gun shimmering with haze as the heat rose from its charging circuits, stumbled under the impact of autogun fire from the walls but slid into cover beside Nicias.

Nicias's prisoner had given up struggling by now. Dressed in simple rust-red coveralls, blackened with grime and the residue of bolter fire, the prisoner simply hung on as Nicias hauled the rag-doll figure around with one hand while his other held his bolt pistol.

Salk ducked to one side to see what lay within the breach. A sergeant of the Pollos troops was organising his men into a firing line across the breach, most of them armed with autoguns, but there were a few shotguns mixed in. There were about twenty men, all dressed in the emerald green of Cartel Pollos with bright gold buttons and buckles and shiny black knee-high boots. Most of the time they were used by the cartel for show, hence the garish uniforms, but the cartel had built itself on the intimidation value of a private army and these were well-trained and motivated men.

Salk nodded at Nicias and Krin, then cast a handful of coin-sized frag grenades past the slab of rubble he lay against. A series of low whumping explosions sounded and Salk scrambled up the slope of rubble towards the firing line through the falling dust kicked up by the grenades.

His first few shots were sprayed on full auto to keep the troopers' heads down. Then he switched to semi-auto and fired as he ran, bolts kicking up crimson spray as they snapped back heads of those soldiers firing back. Shells impacted all around him, a couple registering as flashes of pain as they penetrated the ceramite of his armour. Salk ran through the bursts of pain and leapt into the heart of the firing line.

This was how the Soul Drinkers fought. Cold and fast. A Space Marine was safest at the very heart of the battle, face-to-face with his enemy where his armour, weapons, physical strength and valour were magnified and the resolve of his enemy could be shattered. As Krin's recharged plasma gun burst liquid plasma over the far end of the line, Salk clubbed the stock of his bolter into the first face he saw. Streaked with grime and lined with fatigue, the trooper stared in disbelief at the three-metre killing machine that reared over him even as Salk's gun cracked into the side of his head. Salk pulled the body beneath him, drawing his combat knife and slashing at the trooper behind the first.

Salk's second victim fell, clutching at the deep wound across his torso scored by the monomolecular edge of the knife. Nicias's bolt pistol spat shells into the troopers along the line and many were already running, to be cut down in turn by Nicias.

Nicias was still hefting the prisoner as if the quivering body weighed nothing. If the prisoner died, the whole mission would fail. But Nicias was using his massive, barrel-chested body to shield the prisoner from incoming fire. He was a huge man even for a Marine, which was why he was one of the Chapter's few heavy weapons troopers, and the few shots that hit him burst against his armour in showers of sparks.

Salk pulled a third body off his knife and pumped half a magazine of bolter shells through the breach, showering the threshold of the spaceport with fire. The troopers' officer was trying to rally them into a new firing line on the smooth surface of the spaceport itself – Krin vaporised him with a gout of superheated plasma and the Pollos troopers broke and ran.

'Squad Salk, report in!' voxed Salk hurriedly to the Marines who had stayed behind to cover his assault. 'Aean, Hortis, Dryan!'

The only reply was broken fragments of speech cut up by static. Whichever of them was still alive was swamped by the masses of the crowd so heavily that his vox equipment had been damaged. Since the receiver was implanted in the ear and the transmitter in the throat, that meant a fractured skull at least. It was no way for three good Marines to die, pulled down by a baying, half-mad mass of dying civilians. No way to lose Soul Drinkers, who in their entirety were down to about seven hundred battle-brothers. The mission was a costlier one than the Chapter could really afford, but if it succeeded Commander Sarpedon had assured Dreo and Squad Salk that it would be doing the Emperor's work in an immediate and valuable way.

Salk didn't know what Sarpedon's plan was. Dreo had, but he was dead, far beneath Hive Quintus. But Salk believed in Sarpedon, the mutated, visionary Librarian who had rallied the Soul Drinkers against the evils of Chaos and the blindness of the Imperium alike. If he had to die here to ensure the prisoner was delivered as Sarpedon commanded, then Salk would die.

Salk waved the two Marines with him forward as he slammed a fresh magazine into his bolter. They had to move now, while the troopers in front of them were scattered and the crowd had yet to surge forward behind them. Even now he could hear the masses pouring towards the newly cleared breach. Three men, even Space Marines, could drown in the human tide.

Salk clambered over the crest of the rubble and saw the Ventral Dock 31 spread out before him. Lit by makeshift landing lights of burning fuel drums, it was a wide expanse of blast-stained ferrocrete with landing zones marked out all over it. Massive maintenance sheds and building-sized docking clamps broke up the surface, and many of these had been transformed into firepoints by Cartel Pollos. Emerald-uniformed troopers manned heavy stubbers and artillery pieces, nervously waiting for the hordes to burst in.

There, several hundred metres away, was Salk's immediate objective. An ugly, crouched craft, like a huge metal fly, squatted on one of the launch zones. Bulky servitors lugged thick fuel lines towards the craft as the maintenance crews tried frantically to prep it for takeoff. A gaggle of exotically dressed men, probably the leaders of Cartel Pollos, were being escorted across the spaceport by shotgun-wielding troops with crimson as well as emerald on their uniforms. Household troops, bodyguards of the cartel heads. No match individually for Space Marines, but they could be guaranteed not to give up.

The ship was the only way off Eumenix, and the Soul Drinkers had to ensure they were the ones who took it. They had been dropped onto the planet what felt like a lifetime ago by drop pod, because the risks from the orbital batteries were too great for a Thunderhawk gunship to bring them down. The plan had been for Dreo to lead them out into the barrens outside the city so they could be picked up later, maybe months afterwards, but the risk from the plague extended even there and the prisoner would not have survived. Ventral Dock 31 was the only choice left.

Salk ducked back down beyond heavy stubber fire from the closest hard point. A pair of two-man teams was hiding amongst the huge metal claws of a docking clamp, covering the breach.

Salk charged again, sending a volley of shots tearing into the heavy stubber position. Heavy chains of fire ripped into the ground all around him, one catching him on the greave and almost pitching him onto his face. He spotted Nicias out of the corner of his eye, taking shots to the torso as he tried to shield the prisoner. A plasma blast washed over the docking clamp and a couple of the gunners were turned to bursts of ash, but the fire kept coming, pinning down Salk and Nicias on the edge of the spaceport concourse.

A sudden explosion ripped the docking clamp apart, sending chunks of metal spinning, split sandbags fountaining the earth, broken bodies flying. Stubber rounds cooked off like chains of firecrackers. From the wreckage a single black-clad figure ran, gun in hand. Salk was about to open fire when he realised that the figure was as tall as he was, in power armour charred black but still with the chalice symbols picked out in bone on one shoulder pad.

'Good work, Brother Karrick,' voxed Salk.

Karrick crouched into a firing position, keeping troopers away from the firepoint. Salk sprinted to his side, Nicias behind him, and another plasma blast burst amongst the next firepoint along the line as Krin broke cover behind.

Fire rattled over the Marines' heads and Salk realised the fire from the spaceport was being drawn into the crowds now swarming over the rubble behind him. 'Now!' he voxed, and the surviving Marines outran the approaching edge of the crowd, charging towards the lone spacecraft. Salk sprayed bolter fire at any glimpse of emerald and Krin ripped a plasma shot into the ground by the Pollos heads' entourage, forcing them to delay embarkation as they scattered from the incoming fire.

Salk felt small arms fire impacting against the ground all around him as he ran, ringing off his armour. He switched to semi-auto and flicked shots off at the bodyguard trying to drag the dignitaries towards the ship. Two fell, and another spasmed as bolt pistol shots from Nicias tore through him. Karrick sprayed shells around the rear of the ship and the bodyguards fell back, trying to put themselves between the incoming fire and the dignitaries.

Salk could see the heads of Cartel Pollos now, clad in impractical aristocratic dress with so many layers they looked corpulent and farcical as they scrambled around the rear of the ship, trying to shelter behind the sternward landing gear. The bodyguards were opening fire at the Marines and the crowds spilling over the concourse, but they didn't have the range of the Marines' disciplined bolter fire. A quick volley of snapped shots from Salk took one man's head off and knocked another off his feet like a punch to the gut. Karrick kept the rest pinned down and Krin vaporised a handful of troopers trying to bring a missile launcher to bear.

Salk reached the prow of the ship, firing all the time, switching magazines as Nicias covered him with pistol fire and then sniping at the bodyguards through the landing gear.

'Get aboard!' voxed Salk to Nicias. Covered by Karrick, Nicias ran round the side of the ship and threw the prisoner over the extended boarding ramp and into the passenger compartment. A spray of fire sparked off his armour, tearing chunks from the ceramite as he vaulted his huge form into the ship.

Krin was next, then Salk and Karrick firing a full-auto volley as they clambered into the ship.

Inside, the small compartment was luxuriantly upholstered in the deep, clashing greens and reds of Cartel Pollos. There was room for about a dozen back here, and seemed cramped when filled with the bulk of four Space Marines and their single prisoner. Salk glanced at the remains of his squad – Karrick's armour was charred and the purple paintwork had almost all blistered off. His helmet was gone and one side of his face was badly burned. Krin's gauntlets were smoking from the overheated plasma gun, and Nicias's armour was riddled with bullet scars. Many of Nicias's wounds were bleeding, his blood clotting almost instantly into dark red crystals.

The prisoner was slumped on the carpeted floor, motionless except for shallow breathing.

Salk turned and saw the hatchway leading into the cockpit of the shuttle. It was shut. He slung his bolter, dug his fingers into the edge of the door and ripped it clear out of its frame, metal shrieking. In the cockpit were two pilots in emerald uniforms, young and terrified, shivering with fear. They had neural jacks plugged into sockets in the backs of their shaven heads. Salk glanced at the readouts on the instrument panels in front of them – the shuttle was fuelled up and ready to go.

Salk removed his helmet, feeling sweat running down his face. The smell of gun smoke from his bolter, burned skin from Karrick and the ever-present miasma of hive city pollution, flooded his senses.

'Launch,' he said. The two pilots paused for a second, mesmerised by the immense armoured figure that had just torn its way into the cockpit. Then they turned to the shuttle controls and, almost mechanically, began switching on the main engines and direction thrusters. The rumble of the main engines cut through the background noise of gunfire and screams.

Salk turned back into the passenger compartment. Past the closing boarding ramp he could see the crowd swirling just metres away, emaciated plague victims dragging down Cartel Pollos bodyguards and the heads of the cartel themselves. Krin lined up a shot into the crowd but Salk pushed his plasma gun aside – there was no need. Within a few seconds the shuttle would be aloft. There was nothing these people could do to them now.

The boarding ramp swung shut and there was a hiss as the interior pressurised. Salk looked through to the cockpit and saw, through the frontal viewscreen, the spires of Hive Quintus burning and the smoke-laden clouds boiling up ahead.

The primary thrusters kicked in and the craft lurched forward, away from the burning nightmare of Eumenix and Hive Quintus. Salk was leaving many good Soul Drinkers in the hive city, including Captain Dreo, none of whom the Chapter could easily afford to lose. But as long as their prisoner survived and was brought off the planet, any losses were ultimately acceptable. Commander Sarpedon had made that very clear to Captain Dreo, and Salk had been compelled to carry out those same orders when Dreo was lost.

Salk returned to his squad. Karrick and Nicias both needed medical treatment and Salk had been apprenticed to the Chapter apothecarion as a novice, before he had been selected as a squad sergeant and then taken into Sarpedon's confidence after the terrible Chapter war. More importantly, the prisoner was in shock and would have to be properly looked after.

They would have to search the shuttle for supplies. It would be some time before they could expect pickup and they would have to keep the prisoner alive. But for the time being, he would have the squad enter half-sleep and take turns watching the prisoner, and settle into the routine that would keep them alive until they could return to the Chapter.

Salk didn't know the details of Sarpedon's plan. But he knew enough to guess that this mission was only the start.

SUBSECTOR THERION WAS a near-empty tract of space, notable only for the scattered asteroid fields that yielded rare minerals to the hardy prospectors who mined them. It was these prospectors who first had alerted the Imperial Navy salvage teams to the presence of something strange and truly immense that appeared without warning, as if cast randomly out of the warp.

It was huge. There were parts of it that were still recognisably Imperial warships, aquiline prows jutting from the mass of twisted metal. Smaller ships, fighters and escorts, were welded into nightmarish starbursts of jagged steel. Other parts were completely alien, with scythe-shaped hulls or bulbous organic engine pods. No one could hope to count how many spacecraft were mashed into the space hulk, only that there were craft from every era and from civilisations that could not be identified. The hulk had clearly been in the wars, and recently – there was a new scar, silver and raw, where an enormous section of the hull had been torn open as if by a giant claw. The hulk was one of the ugliest things even the Imperial salvage crews had ever seen.

Inquisitor Thaddeus agreed with them. The monstrous space hulk was huge even from his vantage point on the bridge of the *Crescent Moon*, where the bridge holos projected a curved viewscreen several stories high above the engine room. The wide slice of space that Thaddeus looked out on was dominated by the grey-black mass of the hulk. The light of Therion, the subsector's primary star, picked out jagged metal edges and left the corners of the hulk in pitch black shadow. A few bright slivers hovering around the hulk were Imperial Navy salvage craft, which were transmitting their comms signals to the nearby escort cruiser *Obedience* and then on to the *Crescent Moon*.

The captain of the *Obedience* had accepted Thaddeus as the commander of the salvage operation without having to be asked. From the logs of the first few days of the operation, it seemed seventy-four salvage engineers had boarded the space hulk so far. Thirteen had got out.

The survivors had reported that the craft seemed devoid of the dangerous organisms that normally inhabited space hulks, but was instead rigged with well-hidden booby traps. Bundles of frag grenades were wired to bulkhead hatches. Gun-servitors guarded intersections. Airlocks opened into hard vacuum.

But there had been glimpses of what was beyond. There were areas partitioned into monastic cells, and a library crammed with leather-bound books.

One man reported a deck of fighter craft and vehicles. That had been before the news of the hulk's recovery had been passed on to Thaddeus, and the exploration of the hulk had been halted at his request until he arrived to oversee it personally.

Space hulks, ships which were lost in the warp and drifted after centuries back into realspace, were frequently home to savage aliens, insane cultists, and worse. But this hulk, enormous as it was, did not seem to contain any such monstrosities. Rather, it appeared to have been inhabited until recently.

Thaddeus's fingers ran across the controls of the navigation pulpit and several inset images appeared on the viewscreen. They were jerky, low-res transmissions from cameras mounted on the shoulders of salvage team officers, who were now waiting with their men in Navy landing boats attached to entry points on the near side of the hulk. There was no hope that they could explore anything like the whole mass of the hulk – such a task would take years given its size – so Thaddeus had ordered them into some of the more stable-looking, recognisable areas, like an early-pattern Imperial hospital ship and an escort destroyer from the time of the Gothic War.

Imperial Navy salvage teams were hard-bitten veterans of some of the most dangerous environments deep space could offer. They knew men had died on the hulk, but they were prepared to go that bit further in than anyone else to make sure their crew got credited with a find that could be spent in the dives of the next port they put into. Armed with shotguns and sheer guts, most of them would be pirates or black marketeers if the Navy hadn't press-ganged them from the hives and frontier worlds. It would be a shame to have to mindwipe them if they found anything they shouldn't know about, but they understood that risk, too.

'Captain?' said Thaddeus.

'Lord inquisitor?' replied the clipped voice of the captain of the *Obedience*.

Thaddeus couldn't claim the status of a lord inquisitor, but he didn't correct the man. 'You may begin.'

The transmissions from the *Obedience* filtered through a film of static that came from the bridge speakers. The images on the viewscreen juddered as the salvage crews, each a dozen strong, moved from their landing boats into the outer body of the hulk.

One team moved past the devotional plaques and shrines of the hospital ship, now dark and empty where once Sisters of the Orders Hospitaller had tended to the wounded from some unknown Imperial battlezone. Another was in the cavernous entrails of a starship's engine room, keeping their weapon-mounted torches probing into the shadows beneath the plasma generators. The corridors were dark and deserted; the only sounds the footsteps and orders of the salvage crews and the creaking of the hull. Transmissions from the crews informed

Thaddeus that the hulk seemed to be empty and, sinisterly, far too clean. The gravity was working and the atmosphere, most remarkably, scanned as safe on the teams' crude auspexes. The youngest member of each team was ordered to remove his respirator and the fact that he didn't drop dead meant that there were no airborne toxins.

Moving further into the hulk, one team found a brig that looked like it had been used recently, with new locks and cells with devotional High Gothic texts on the walls. A ship's bridge had been opened up and the complex electronics of the cogitators and comm-links spilled out across the deck, with monitoring devices hooked into the workings. The plasma generators encountered by the team in the engine decks had been restored to working order. Someone had lived in the hulk, cleaned up the useable parts and even, it seemed, tried to make the hulk spaceworthy. If they had succeeded, the hulk would have been a formidable weapon indeed, a fortress capable of carrying a massive number of personnel, along with the firepower of several of its constituent ships.

Thaddeus was now seriously entertaining the possibility that the Pilgrim was right.

'Coming up on Leros's crew,' came the voice of one of the team leaders. 'What's left of them.' The corresponding image showed the bloody remains of several men, blown apart as if by explosives or large-calibre gunfire, spattered around the corridor.

'Keep your wits about you, team seven,' ordered the *Obedience's* captain. Team seven, Thaddeus thought, probably didn't need reminding.

Thaddeus pressed an icon and the image from team seven was magnified on the viewscreen. They were in one of the warships, one with Low Gothic mottos scratched into the walls by a devoted crew. Leros's crew was scattered: an arm here, a head there, a weapon broken and thrown aside.

Something moved up ahead, a glint of metal.

'Halt!' barked the team's leader. 'Fall back! Lorko, you cover…'

A sheet of stuttering gunfire ripped down the corridor. The image swung wildly and a gauze of static shivered over the scene. Thaddeus could make out a man thrown back against a wall, the chest of his dark grey coveralls shredded and sodden with blood. Another man fell backwards, the upper part of his body blown apart.

Shotgun fire ripped back. Bright trails of an automatic gun spattered across the corridor. The team leader was yelling orders to fall back to the next junction.

Thaddeus caught sight of what was shooting at them.

'Team seven,' he said calmly, knowing his voice would be relayed directly to the team leader. 'It's a gun-servitor. What explosives do you have?'

The leader was running back with his squad. 'Just signal flares,' he said breathlessly.

'Use them. It will be blinded.'

Thaddeus heard the team leader gathering a handful of flares from his men. The screen burned scarlet as they were lit and thrown back down the corridor behind them.

The shooting stopped. The image filled with thick red smoke from the flare as the team ran towards the blinded servitor. A volley of thudding shotgun blasts came a second later.

'It's dead,' said the team leader. He had doubtless lost many men from his team on previous missions and his voice did not sound shaken in the least.

'It was never alive,' replied Thaddeus. 'Show me.'

The leader kicked the closest flares down the corridor and waved some of the smoke away. Thaddeus could make out, on the floor, the remains of the servitor – its lower half was a hover unit. Its arms had both been replaced with twin-linked autoguns connected to large cylinder box magazines. Its face was just a jutting mass of sensors. Presumably it would have been difficult to make and would have been set to guard something important – a task it had succeeded in with the first team to come across it.

'Proceed,' said Thaddeus.

The squad moved past the junction the servitor had been guarding. The leader glanced about, but Thaddeus saw that one of the corridors led to an arched doorway.

'That one,' he said.

The team assembled at the threshold. The room beyond was large and unlit, and nothing could be seen past the doorway.

'Auspex?' asked the leader.

'Nothing,' came the voice of one of his surviving crewmembers.

The leader shone his weapon torch through the doorway. The light played across a floor laid with smooth black marble veined in white, and across the foot of a bookcase. As the squad moved in they could see more in the light of their torches – cases of books that reached right up to the high ceiling. The shelves were full of books, most of them small volumes that could fit into the palm of a large man's hand, but there were a number of larger books, scrolls, and even stone tablets alongside them. A pulpit of stone stood before several rows of hardwood benches.

'Team seven, are there signs of habitation?'

'No, sir,' said the leader.

'Movement!' came a shout from behind. The leader spun around to bring his gun to bear and his camera showed a squat shape drifting along the floor – another servitor, but not a combat pattern this time. It was an autoarchiver, its legs and arms replaced with long, thin jointed metal manipulators which removed and replaced volumes from the shelves as it moved along on the wheels set into its back.

It was still functioning. That meant this place – this library – had been used recently and had probably been abandoned in a hurry.

'Leave it alone,' said Thaddeus. 'I want this place intact.'

'Understood,' said the team leader. 'Don't shoot it!' he yelled to his men. 'And don't touch anything. The bosses want it clean.'

A faint mumble of discontent from the other men indicated that they had been looking forward to seeing what they could loot.

Thaddeus glanced at the other images. One inset screen was blank – the team had stumbled into an explosive booby trap in the hospital ship, a set of tripwires strung across the entrance to one of the surgery theatres. Another had lost three men when a gantry over an engine room gave way under their weight. The team in the brig were rifling through the contents of an armoury locker – they were taking out wicked combat knives the size of short swords, power mauls and large-calibre ammunition for which the corresponding guns were missing. Gradually the teams were moving further into the hulk, and most of them were finding signs of a recent, organised and presumably human presence. One or two had reached parts of the hulk evidently of xenos design. But here their orders were to halt.

Thaddeus looked back at team seven. The library seemed huge – several bulkheads had been removed to form a large enough space. Mem-slate blocks stood like glossy black monoliths in rows between the bookshelves.

'Get me one of the books,' said Thaddeus.

The team leader took one of the small volumes from the nearest shelf.

'*Catechisms Martial*,' read the team leader from the gold lettering on the book's cover.

'Thank you,' said Thaddeus, and switched from the team back to the officers on the *Obedience*.

Thaddeus was a well-read man – an inquisitor had to know a great deal about the various histories and philosophies of the Imperium to be able to root out the heresies that infected it. But he had only recently become acquainted with the *Catechisms Martial*, a work of tactical philosophy that espoused a swift, shattering form of warfare where speed and overwhelming focused strength were the primary weapons.

It was written by the philosopher-soldier Daenyathos. Daenyathos of the Soul Drinkers.

The Pilgrim had been right, again. The Soul Drinkers had made the hulk their home but they had left suddenly and recently. The hulk was the single biggest clue Thaddeus could reasonably have hoped to find, but it was still just a clue and not a part of the goal itself. The Soul Drinkers were somewhere else in the galaxy, pursuing some perverse plan while Thaddeus took tiny steps towards them.

'Captain,' Thaddeus transmitted to the *Obedience*, 'have your crews secure a landing zone. I shall oversee the exploration from the hulk.'

By the time the captain replied to object that the hulk was still not safe, Thaddeus was already gone from the bridge.

THREE

THE FIRST SIGHT of the enemy was a scarlet streak through the upper atmosphere, glimpsed from the porthole of the Thunderhawk gunship as it plummeted from orbit towards the landing zone.

'Gunners, can you lock?' voxed Captain Korvax as the xenos craft flashed past.

In response the Chapter serfs who manned the gunship sent lances of heavy bolter fire chattering through the air, the report of the heavy weapons sounding through the hull and over the din of the ramjets decelerating the Thunderhawk. There was a flash of orange as the alien craft broke apart at speed, scattering a black drizzle of debris behind it.

One down. The serf gunners were good; the Soul Drinkers had trained them well. But the fact that the

*alien fighter had closed with them at all indicated that
the Marines were coming to the battle late. These aliens
were fast, and the outpost could be lost in minutes if the
Soul Drinkers weren't faster.*

'Fleet command, how's our landing zone?' voxed Korvax to the strike cruiser Carnivore, in high orbit far above the force of six Thunderhawks.

'Contested,' came the reply. 'Vox-traffic indicates xenos landfall of light troops, three hundred plus.'

'Understood,' replied Korvax. He knew that for this particular variety of heathen alien, the eldar, 'light troops' meant lightning-quick, skilled, and well-armed specialist soldiers.

'Prepare for rapid deployment,' ordered Korvax as the Thunderhawk's deceleration ramped up a notch and the G-force kicked in.

The engines flared and the Thunderhawk was hovering about thirty metres above the ground. Korvax glanced out of the porthole – he could see two of the other gunships alongside. The shape of the outpost – a low building set into the hard frozen earth of the tundra – was broken by the Adeptus Mechanicus troops firing from the roof at the eldar moving rapidly towards it. Small arms fire from the strange eldar shuriken-firing weapons spattered against the Thunderhawk's hull.

The rear ramp of the Thunderhawk opened and the sound of the engines flooded in, punctuated by explosions and gunfire from below. Cold air rolled in, too, for the outpost was on a planetoid of frozen tundra too far from its parent sun to be hospitable. The restraints on the grav-couches snapped open and with practiced speed the ten-strong squad of Soul Drinkers Space Marines dropped out of the ship on rappel lines, bolters slung.

Korvax was amongst the last to drop out of the Thunderhawk. He saw Marines from the force's other gunships doing the same – he counted five ships in total and a small black shape trailing smoke and heading upwards, meaning one of the Thunderhawks had sustained damage and was heading back to the Carnivore. That still left fifty Space Marines making landfall.

Fifty against three hundred plus. Though pride was sinful in the eyes of the Emperor, Korvax still admitted to himself that those were the kind of odds he liked.

The battlefield yawed below him, and as the rappel line hissed through the clip he grasped it with his right hand. The outpost was surrounded by smoke and gunfire. Tech-guard on the roof had formed fire points and were firing at the eldar now moving to surround it.

The Mechanicus had access to the most advanced of weapons, Korvax saw a form of rapid-firing missile launcher send volleys of frag missiles into the eldar lines, and glimpsed the unmistakable liquid fire of a heavy plasma gun bursting amongst the aliens. The eldar were in many forms – as was the way of this heathen species – some wore bone-white bodysuits with tall masks which shrieked horribly as they cartwheeled through the gunfire to use their power swords against the tech-guard up close. Others had plumed helmets and shuriken weapons, and were covering green-armoured eldar with buzzing heavy chainswords and masks with mandibles *that spat laser fire at the tech-guard manning the forward defences. The first wave of eldar had easily swarmed over the first lines of sandbags and barricades and, though many of their number lay broken and burned by the tech-guard fire, several hundred of them were surrounding the outpost and moving in for the kill.*

Korvax hit the ground in the centre of his squad. A quick hand signal told them all they needed to know – advance and engage. The safest place on the barren battlefield was toe-to-toe with the eldar. The aliens were quick and skilled, but pile on enough pressure and they would break. Korvax had fought them before on Quixian Obscura and broken them, too.

The squad rapid-fired as they ran, spattering bolter fire into the defences. Blue-armoured eldar, seeing this new threat landing behind them, turned to man the defences they had just overrun. Their shuriken guns spat volleys of shining silver at Korvax and his squad, studding the Soul Drinkers' purple armour with razor-sharp discs. One Marine – Solus, the squad's flamer-bearer – went down, crimson spurting from the disk embedded in his knee joint. The bolter and shuriken fire met in a storm of metal, the Soul Drinkers closing quickly as the other squads did the same along that whole side of the defences.

The night sky above was clear and cold, and through it streaked a missile from Squad Veiyal, cracking in a flash of fire into the centre of the eldar sword-bearers. Two of them died, blown apart. Bolter fire ripped into them as they tried to regroup, and by the time Squad Veiyal reached the defences the xenos manning it were dead.

Korvax's squad hit the eldar on their section of the line. Korvax tore up the edge of the sandbag parapet with full-auto fire and deftly drew the power sword from its scabbard on his armour's backpack. The power field jumped into life as his gauntlet closed around the hilt and it shrieked as he brought it down towards the first eldar he saw. Eldar reflexes were notoriously quick and the alien jinked to the side, but the blade still caught its shoulder and sheared the arm clear off. Korvax vaulted into the ditch behind the parapet, kicking the eldar to the floor as he did so and bringing his bolter, like a club, cracking into the side of its skull.

Bolter fire spattered like rain into the ditch. Eldar died, or stopped firing to scramble out of the way. The ditch was deep but the far edge had collapsed into a crumbling slope where the frozen earth had been pulverised by explosive fire – the eldar retreated up this, attempting to fire as they went.

One of them moved with sudden, supernatural speed, seeming to flip over trails of bolter fire. It had a sword that looked like it was made of bone in one hand and a shuriken pistol in the other – the pistol flashed and a shuriken took Brother Brisias through the eye.

Korvax crunched through the body of the eldar he had killed and drove up the slope towards the eldar with the sword – part of their leadership caste, he guessed. They said eldar followed many paths of war, each type of soldier the result of a different path – those who became trapped on those paths became their leaders on the battlefield. They were considered priority targets in assaults.

The eldar saw Korvax approach, and fixed the black glass of its helmet eyepieces on him for a moment. As if acting on some warrior code, the alien paused for a split second, raised its blade, and somersaulted towards him.

Korvax followed no code save that of the Emperor and the sacred place of the Soul Drinkers in his plan for the Imperium. In the shadow of the beleaguered outpost he duelled with the eldar leader, matching the alien's speed with his own strength. Many times the eldar struck home with a blow that would have killed a normal man, but Korvax knew the protection that power armour offered and he knocked each blow aside with a shoulder pad or an armoured forearm.

The alien tried to flip away from him, but Korvax reached out with his free hand, grasped the plume of its helmet, pulled its head down and slammed his knee into its faceplate. The eldar reeled and Korvax slashed a deep gouge across its torso, cutting through the armour plates set into its deep blue bodysuit. He felt its thin ribs give way and drove forward, hacking at it as each parry from its bone sword became weaker. With one final slash Korvax brought the blade down through the eldar's guard and the power blade cut right through the alien's torso, shearing the spine. The alien froze for a moment, then fell limp. The sword dropped from its hand.

The power field around the blade burned away the tissue it touched and the corpse slid off the sword with a flick of Korvax's wrist. The blue-armoured eldar were dead. The Soul Drinkers had taken the aliens by surprise, catching them as they themselves were trying to storm the outpost with speed and skill. Korvax saw Squad Veiyal was almost at the outpost's front blast doors – he also saw that the doors were wide open and smoking. The xenos must have got inside.

The Adeptus Mechanicus Biologis outpost was a crucial research station. The experiments it housed were vital to the Imperium. Korvax did not know the exact nature of the work done here, but for the Adeptus Terra to ask the Soul Drinkers to defend it from alien raiders must mean that the work was of the greatest importance. If the eldar got inside and destroyed – or, worse, stole – the Mechanicus research, the consequences would be great.

They were too late. The heathen xenos had breached the outpost. It was time to make amends.

Korvax quickly voxed round his squads. Veiyal was the furthest forward while two other squads were busy pinning down the eldar reinforcements landing nearby. Assault Squad Livris was on Korvax's flank, clashing chainswords with the green-armoured eldar. They had lost a couple of Marines but they had cut their way through most of the eldar. That left Korvax three squads for the assault, with two more keeping the emerging eldar support units at bay.

'Veiyal, Livris, rush the doors!' voxed Korvax on the all-squads channel and he waved his squad forward, the Tactical Marines firing volleys sweeping across the defences in front of them as they advanced. More blue-armoured eldar tried to dig in and hold off Korvax's squad, but he led his men charging into their flank and drove them against Squad Livris. Many more eldar died between Korvax's bolter fire and Livris's chainswords.

That was how the Soul Drinkers fought. Hard and fast, never stopping.

Korvax saw Squad Veiyal at the doors, using the massive plasteel construction of the blast doors as a firepoint, as they gave covering fire to the two squads approaching. Explosive fire suddenly streaked over from the eldar heavy weapons units trying to reach the outpost. Bursts of fire and shattered earth fountained up where they hit, and several Marines were thrown off their feet. The autosenses of Korvax's helmet cut out for a second then juddered back. A warning icon flashing on his retina told Korvax the pict-recorder on his backpack was damaged, and was no longer recording the view over his shoulder for the mission's debriefing.

Korvax would have to survive. He ran on through the pall of falling earth as a rune winked out, indicating Brother Severian's lifesigns had ceased in the midst of the barrage. Korvas ducked into the doorway and his squad barrelled in behind him. Blue-armoured eldar fired shuriken shots after them but were shredded by Livris's charge, and the Assault Marines joined the rest of the spearhead at the outpost entrance.

Korvax checked the runes on his retina display. There were about half a dozen Marines down, maybe dead, but definitely out of action. Not bad losses. But the eldar had

got inside the outpost and could even now be wrecking
research vital to the Imperium.

Korvax slammed a new magazine into his bolter and
heard half his squad doing the same. He glanced at
Sergeant Veiyal – his helmet had been damaged and he
was bareheaded, his breath coiling white in the cold.

'The others have our backs,' said Korvax. 'Sergeant
Livris, your squad has the point. Veiyal, with me.
Advance.'

Korvas levelled his bolter and followed the Assault
Marines as they charged into the darkened heart of the
outpost…

THE IMAGE WINKED out to be replaced by static.
Thaddeus frowned and tapped the controls on the
data-slate, rewinding the recording past the point
where the feed cut out. It was the view over the
Space Marine commander's shoulder from a
recorder on his backpack, showing a screen full of
showering earth and sharp white lines of gunfire.
The recording rewound and the Soul Drinker commander's charge played out in reverse. Implosions
sucked Marines back onto their feet.

The holomat was set up in the centre of the librarium. Salvage teams and tech-priests from the
Obedience had carefully swept the librarium and lost
several men rooting through trapped bookshelves.
Once it had been established that the librarium was
that of the Soul Drinkers Chapter, Thaddeus had
ordered the salvage teams to be confined to the

hulk and to secure the immediate area. Corridors had been sealed off with rockcrete to prevent decompression traps from emptying the librarium sector of air. The teams slowly spreading out into the hulk were locating dormitories and meditation cells, weapons lockers and infirmaries, all converted from ancient, empty sections of Imperial ships welded into the mass of the hulk.

The datacubes recovered had mostly been wiped. The truly crucial information had probably been portable enough for the Soul Drinkers to take with them before they abandoned the hulk. But there was some residual information in the glossy black monoliths of data-slate and the cogitators of the various intact ships. The Soul Drinkers had referred to the hulk as the *Brokenback*, and had clearly adopted the craft as a home after the scuttling of their fleet. There were records of journeys across the galaxy, often to apparently dead sectors, and hints of massive Marine losses in a battle on some unnamed world.

And then, there was the pict-file that Thaddeus had just played, showing the assault.

'It had been accessed repeatedly,' came a voice from across the library. It was Interrogator Shen, a tall and handsome man who still carried an air of the tribal warrior about him in spite of the archaic carapace armour he wore and the inferno pistol holstered at his waist. His voice was clipped and somehow artificial, for he had been sleep-taught

Imperial Gothic relatively late in life. 'Whatever its significance, the Soul Drinkers scrutinised this file extensively before they left. That was why the tech-priests were able to piece it together from the various cogitators.'

'Do they know what it depicts?' Thaddeus was cycling slowly backwards through the file, watching the assault unfold in reverse.

'We presume it is some former operation. The location is uncertain. It could be the event that cost them so many of their own, but the Adeptus Mechanicus were the first organisation they turned against and here they are helping them.'

Thaddeus shook his head. He pointed towards the weapon now sucking bullets back out of the eldar aspect warriors. 'That's a Centauri pattern bolter. The Soul Drinkers' equipment was well up to date when they turned, this file must have been shot a decade ago at least. Before their heresy. We need to find out where this is, have the tech-priests begun forensic scrutiny?'

'They have begun, Master Thaddeus,' replied Shen. 'But there is little to work with. The outpost building is apparently a common STC construction and there are no landmarks. It is a Mechanicus outpost and the world is one of tundra, but there are thousands such. And if the events are as old as you say, it may not even be there any more.'

Thaddeus paused the image. The recorder captured the instant when the tactical squad had

leapt over the first barricades into the Dire
Avenger defences. Dire Avengers were the most
disciplined of the eldar aspects, diligent and
dependable, the mainstay of the eldar elite. But
the Soul Drinkers had smashed through them and
other aspects alike, though outnumbered and
unsupported. They had been most admirable in
their time, thought Thaddeus. Great warriors, and
fearless, but they had been proud. Their pride had
led them to a terrible heresy, to break with the
Imperium itself. It was a shame that they would
have to be destroyed, but Thaddeus would see that
they were.

'If it was important to them,' said Thaddeus, 'then
it is important to us. If we find the location of this
recording we may well find the Soul Drinkers. Shen,
you may have to follow up other leads on your own.
It is no little responsibility.'

'I accept, Master Thaddeus.' Shen had served
Thaddeus for seven years, the latter few as a solid
interrogator. Unlike Thaddeus, Shen was a warrior
first, but Thaddeus had put most of his efforts into
training the man's mind, and Shen could be trusted
to look after himself.

'Good. Bring the astropathic choir aboard the *Brokenback* and have them take up their vigil again. I
want to hear of any further sightings of the Soul
Drinkers, no matter how trivial or unlikely. We may
be able to use them to pin down this location. Take
some of the *Obedience's* astropaths, too. Use my

authority. The *Brokenback* will be our base of operations until I say otherwise.'

Shen bowed neatly to the inquisitor, and strode off to fulfil his duties. Thaddeus wondered if Shen ever really thought he would be an inquisitor one day. In truth, Shen didn't have the patience or imagination to hunt down the enemies that threatened mankind from within. Thaddeus knew his own strengths, and Shen didn't come close. He was, however, as fine an interrogator as Thaddeus could wish for – loyal, diligent, and able to summon a deadly streak of violence in a tight spot.

Thaddeus looked once more at the holo image, where purple-armoured giants charged fearlessly into a storm of gunfire. He had never truly understood how Space Marines, particularly the assault-oriented Soul Drinkers, could make a tactic of a headlong, suicidal attack and somehow attain victory after victory when mere men would be cut to pieces. It was as if their conditioning and sheer faith carried them through when physics and logic should bring them low.

And now that faith had been perverted until a whole Chapter of such giants had declared themselves the enemies of the Imperium. Thaddeus found it difficult to imagine a more dangerous enemy.

IT WAS A beautiful day. It was always beautiful in House Jenassis. The dome under which the habitat was built had been constructed of electroreactive materials that always created a flawless blue sky overhead no matter what the conditions on the planetoid outside. The atmosphere was permanently stabilised at an even summer's day, allowing the impressive alien plants of the gardens to flourish. Phrantis Jenassis always made time every day to walk the gardens, until he lost sight of the palace's golden minarets between the spreading boughs of imported alien trees.

House Jenassis was a colony several kilometres across, housed in an atmospheric dome and consisting of the palace itself, the grounds with their lakes and greenhouses, a cluster of simple rustic habs for the retainers, and the temple-like complex that housed the Grand Galactarium. House Jenassis was also the name of a Navigator family that had served the Imperium for more than ten thousand years, since before the Horus Heresy. Phrantis Jenassis, the current patriarch of the House, had himself taken the Emperor's starships through the warp where only his warp eye could see the way, but had returned after a long career to take over the House. It was a good life, especially considering how so many less fortunate billions suffered to survive. But it was a life deserved, of that Phrantis Jenassis was sure, for without the Navigators the Imperium would be no more than a vulnerable collection of isolated star systems at the mercy of its enemies.

The duties for the day were many. Phrantis had to negotiate with the Departmento Munitorum to contract Imperial Guardsmen to guard the many scions of House Jenassis on their travels. There were reciprocal arrangements to make that bound Navigators to particular individuals or Imperial organisations. New births would have to be registered and Phrantis would have to sign the examiners' reports to confirm that the new bearers of the Navigator gene were free from corruptive mutation. The House's accounts were due to be reviewed and a long and tortuous process that would become. Yes, the House retainers would doubtless thrust many sheets of parchment under his nose to be read or signed or acted upon, but that was for the rest of the day. The morning would be spent enjoying the gardens, for why else would Phrantis Jenassis have worked so hard if not to earn some deserved leisure time in old age?

Past the old summerhouse was one of the habitat's prettiest lakes, where crested devilfish swam between trailing branches of silver-barked fingertrees.

Phrantis wandered across the quaint little bridge that spanned the lake and watched a captive flock of jewelbirds wheeling beneath the clear blue dome.

The jewelbirds scattered as if in fright. Then the sounds reached Phrantis – reverberating booms like some huge hammer striking the surface of the dome. Ugly black cracks suddenly ran across a section of the dome and, with a sound like thunder, the section shattered.

Huge sheets of glass like giant knife blades fell, embedding themselves in the ground within sight of the lake. There was a growl of rushing wind as the heat within the dome rushed out into the cooler atmosphere beyond. A massive tear had been gouged out of the dome and Phrantis saw with horror the roiling grey-white clouds of the planetoid outside. The trees shook and the water rippled. Phrantis's jewelled robes ruffled in the wind and he felt a sudden cold wash over him.

A tiny black shape dropped from the storm clouds towards the tear in the dome. As it plummeted closer Phrantis could see that it was like a bulb of metal, ringed with restraints, segmented like the unopened bud of an ugly grey flower. Bright flares ripped from its underside to decelerate it but when it landed, maybe three hundred metres from Phrantis, it still hit the manicured lawn in a fountain of earth. Two more followed, then a fourth, and Phrantis realised the last one was heading for the lake.

He turned to run, but his old frame had barely lurched a few steps when something massive thudded into the lake, drenching him in a wave of spray. He turned to see the metal seed pod bursting open and the purple-armoured soldiers inside – ten of them – snapped off their restraints and waded out into the water of the lake. The lake was quite deep but their heads still showed above the water, indicating they must be a good metre taller than Phrantis himself. Phrantis knew of the Adeptus Astartes – he had occasionally come across those superhuman warriors in his career – and he had no doubt that Space Marines were invading House Jenassis.

The House had been loyal. It had served the Imperium with all its energy, asking only gratitude in return. Why would Space Marines be attacking a House that had helped the Imperium maintain its grip on the galaxy?

The Marines were already clambering up the bank, each with a pistol in one hand and an out-sized chainsword in the other. Each wore the emblem of a chalice on his shoulder pad. One had some kind of attachment for a hand – Phrantis realised with a start that it was not a bionic but the grotesquely warped hand itself, with long muscular multi-jointed fingers gripping the haft of a power axe. The helmetless Marine wielding it was a grizzled veteran, face battered and scarred, and he had spotted Phrantis.

Phrantis didn't run. He was old, and they would easily outpace him. Either that, or his long and distinguished life would end with a bolter shell in the back. The closest Marine clambered up the bank, covered the distance in a few long strides, and dragged Phrantis to the ground by the scruff of his neck.

The sergeant with the mutant hand ran over. The power field around the blade of his axe was activated and droplets of water were hissing on the metal.

'You. What is your name?'

'Patriarch Phrantis Jenassis of House Jenassis.' Phrantis was amazed he had been able to answer.

'A Navigator?'

Phrantis nodded.

'Bind his hands,' said the sergeant to the Marine holding Phrantis down. 'Don't let him take his turban off. His warp eye'll kill you.'

Phrantis's hands were pulled behind his back and a plastic restraint tied around his wrists.

'What do you want?' gasped Phrantis. 'We are loyal here. We have been loyal since the days the Emperor still walked amongst us! Our warrant of binding was signed by his hand! We are loyal!'

The sergeant grinned, showing broken teeth. 'We're not,' he said.

Phrantis was hauled to his feet. Not loyal? Phrantis had heard dark tales of Space Marines who fell from grace and joined the great enemy, the powers of Chaos that could not be named by righteous lips. Chaos Marines, all the pride and vigour of Space Marines turned to cruelty, bloodlust and desecration.

A warzone, where the Chaos Warlord Teturact was carving out an empire, was only a couple of subsectors from House Jenassis. Phrantis had been assured

that the warfleets massing on the border of the warzone protected House Jenassis from Chaos raiders,
but perhaps those raiders had found a way through.
Had these Marines come from the Teturact's
hordes? What could they want with House Jenassis?
Navigators for their fleets? Slaves? Or just the
despoiling of somewhere beautiful?

Phrantis saw other purple-armoured giants moving away from the other pods that had fallen, taking
up firing positions amongst the trees. With the
breach in the dome the sky was darker and a chill
wind was blowing down from above. Beautiful
House Jenassis was already imperfect.

'Commander?' the sergeant was saying into his
communicator. 'We've taken the patriarch. I'm
heading to your position now. No other contacts.
Over.' There was a pause as someone made a
reply Phrantis couldn't hear. 'I see you. Graevus
out.'

Phrantis followed Sergeant Graevus's gaze, and
saw a nightmare.

COMMANDER SARPEDON, Chief Librarian and Chapter Master of the Soul Drinkers, was a half arachnid
mutant renegade. His eight legs – seven chitinous
limbs and one bionic – skittered rapidly as he
moved with Squad Hastis across the rolling lawns
towards where Squad Graevus was advancing with
their prisoner. The boots of Hastis's Marines
churned up the manicured grounds.

Sarpedon met up with Graevus in the shadow of a spreading alien tree with scarlet leaves that cast a dim shadow beneath the darkening sky. Graevus, like most of the Chapter, was a mutant – his hand had deformed to give him greater strength and reach with the power axe he carried. Squads Hastis and Krydel were setting up a perimeter in case the planet's Arbites or Navigator House retainers arrived quickly. Techmarine Solun, the Marine whose machine-skills would make the difference between success and failure here on Kytellion Prime, was with Squad Krydel, the mem-plates covering his armour glinting black.

Phrantis Jenassis was a grey-haired, thin-faced slip of a man in ruby-red robes embroidered with gold and gemstones. A turban wrapped around his head concealed the third eye, the warp eye, in the centre of his forehead. It could look out on the warp itself but also, they said, kill a man with a glance.

'He's unhurt,' said Graevus. 'We found him alone.'

'He will not be alone for long,' said Sarpedon. He turned to the shivering patriarch. 'Where is the Galactarium?'

Phrantis looked up blankly for a moment. 'I will not yield, Chaos filth,' he stuttered.

Sarpedon reached down and grabbed Phrantis by the chin. 'Do not waste our time, old man. We do the work of the Emperor. Where is the Galactarium?'

'The… the Arbites will be here, we have a precinct dedicated to our protection…'

Sarpedon cursed the fragmented intelligence he had been able to muster on House Jenassis. The Soul Drinkers knew the Galactarium was here – one of the wonders of the Imperium, by all accounts – but there had been no map of the house environs to plan the assault properly. 'We will kill them all if we have to,' said Sarpedon, knowing they would if it came down to it. 'That does not have to happen. All we want is access to the Galactarium, then we will go. House Jenassis can run back to the Imperium in safety if you just give us what we want.'

Phrantis Jenassis closed his eyes and whimpered, trying to shut out the cold, dangerous place his home had suddenly become.

'We have no time for this,' said Sarpedon, irritated. Time was an enemy here, as were so many factors. He switched to the all-squads vox. 'Squads Hastis, Krydel, spread out and find me the Galactarium building, then report back and hold tight. Squad Graevus, hold this location with me. Post forward troopers to spot contacts. Move out.'

HOUSE JENASSIS WAS located on Kytellion Prime, a planetoid with a superdense core (and hence Earth-standard gravity). Other settlements, undomed and exposed to the planetoid's cruel weather, dotted the barren landscape, mostly isolated trading settlements that had been founded by retainers released from House service. One of them, however, was a massively built compound with walls of sheer ferrocrete and watchtowers on every corner. This was the Kytellion Prime Adeptus Arbites precinct, where several squads of Arbites judges and suppression units were responsible for the protection of House Jenassis. Their presence next to the habitat was one of the many ways in which the Navigator House was repaid for its diligent service to the Emperor's fleets.

There were several events that would cause the Arbites to be mobilised. The breaching of the dome over House Jenassis was one of them, signifying as it did a potential meteorite strike or other disaster, or even an almost unthinkable direct assault on the House. Within minutes of the alarm going up, a column of riot control vehicles and APCs, loaded with heavily armed Arbites officers and judge commanders, was snaking rapidly along the short road towards the entrance to the dome ready to defend the estate of the Navigator House they had sworn to protect.

The precinct astropath, as per the protocols that had been in place since House Jenassis had come to Kytellion Prime, transmitted the distress call across the ether, alerting the highest authorities that the ancient and holy House Jenassis was violated.

A few scant minutes afterwards, it was answered.

Squad Hastis had come across a few retainers with hunting rifles, and scattered them with a volley of bolter fire before moving into the palace itself. Without engaging the palace's automated servitor defences, the squad ascertained that the palace contained plenty of marbled galleries and lavish quarters, but no Galactarium.

Squad Krydel, heading the other way, had located the low building of marble with deep crimson lacquered panels and battlements plated with gold. It was located in a shallow depression in the landscaped gardens, surrounded by a ring of trees and with a marble-paved road winding to its collonnaded entrance.

The Soul Drinkers' enhanced senses had picked out handfuls of retainers from families bound into service by House Jenassis, straggling from their picturesque village on the other side of the grounds. They would be little more than a nuisance if any of them proved brave enough to attack, but they were not the ones Sarpedon was worried about.

'Ready to secure the structure,' said Sergeant Krydel. His squad was crouched by the columns at the front of the building. Techmarine Solun was beside the sergeant.

'No time,' replied Sarpedon. 'We'll go in together.'

Sarpedon, Squad Graevus and the captive patriarch moved rapidly through the trees and up to the threshold of the temple-like building.

'Squad Hastis,' voxed Sarpedon to the squad by the palace, 'advance to this position and maintain a perimeter.'

An acknowledgement rune flashed on Sarpedon's retina. Hastis was a good, solid soldier, and

Sarpedon feared the assaulting squads would need backing up soon.

With a gesture, Sarpedon sent the three squads into the building. It was dark and cool inside, and with the breach in the dome there was a new chill in the air. The walls were of huge blocks of multi-coloured marble bordered with plated gold and shiny lacquered panels. Banners representing the branches of the Jenassis family hung from the ceiling, which got higher as the floor sloped downward. Most of the building was beneath the level of the surrounding landscape.

Sarpedon skittered on his altered legs close to Sergeant Krydel. Krydel was a tactical squad sergeant whose squad had distinguished itself when the Daemon Prince Abraxes had manifested on the *Brokenback*, and he had a reputation for utter unflappability. From the front Sarpedon could see the huge marble architecture opening up into a central gallery, exposed to the darkening sky and surrounded by elegant columns of jade. The open space was several hundred metres across, and in the centre was a raised circular structure of white stone.

'Solun?' voxed Sarpedon.

'The auspex reads plenty of activity,' replied the Techmarine. 'There's a lot of electronics beneath us. This place must have its own power source.'

Sarpedon led the Soul Drinkers across the stone, leaving a handful of Marines as a rearguard. Graevus hauled Phrantis Jenassis to the front alongside Solun.

'Open it,' demanded the Techmarine.

'What do you want with it? What are you?' gasped the patriarch.

'Permission to do this the old-fashioned way?' said Graevus, unclipping a handful of anti-armour krak grenades from his belt.

'Granted,' replied Sarpedon. Phrantis was hauled away as Graevus planted the grenades at seams between the blocks of the circular structure, then fell back.

The grenades went off with a sound like a string of gunshots, kicking a haze of marble splinters into the air. Phrantis whimpered as the stone shell of the Galactarium, wonder of the Imperium, fell away.

The Galactarium was an extremely complex construction of strange dull grey metal and glistening black psychoplastics, nests of concentric circles and spinning globes on delicate armatures. Slowly it unfolded like the legs of a spider, rings spinning, sections rotating, like a huge armillary sphere that blossomed to fill almost the whole courtyard. Beneath the gathering clouds the rings and armatures spun faster and faster until points of light began to shimmer in the air as if conjured. Strange shadows played around the assembled Space Marines as stars and constellations bloomed into existence above them.

'Hastis, secure this structure,' voxed Sarpedon. 'Solun, get to work.'

The Techmarine ran beneath the spinning mechanisms towards the centre of the Galactarium. Already the map was solidifying in the air – a star map, the largest and most comprehensive ever constructed. The Imperium was too vast to ever be properly mapped, and no one had ever managed to even catalogue its inhabited worlds. But attempts had been made, and the Galactarium was the closest thing to success the Imperium had. There were few places not represented on the immense stellar map now spherically projected around the Galactarium.

The Galactarium was the pride of House Jenassis; it was spoken of with reverence amongst fellow Navigators and the Adeptus Mechanicus Explorator commands alike. It was a dangerous target because taking it left the Soul Drinkers momentarily visible and vulnerable, but it was the Chapter's only hope.

'Commander?' came a vox. It was Sergeant Hastis, leading his squad back across the grounds from the palace. 'We've got contacts. Arbites, coming in from the dome entrance. I count seven vehicles heading for the palace and five moving towards your position.'

'Understood. Do not engage, get back here and help maintain our perimeter.'

'Acknowledged. Hastis out.'

Sarpedon did not want to kill anyone here. There was no need. But if he had to, he would, and he knew his battle-brothers would do the same.

Solun drew threadlike cables from the interfaces in his armour and plugged them into the base of the Galactarium. The huge map display was flickering and a new image was ghosting over the starscape. It showed a low building set into frozen tundra, obscured by gun smoke and ringed by ditches and barricades. It moved jerkily as the recorder moved closer, explosions flashing, armoured alien figures returning fire and spasming as silent bullets hit them.

Purple-armoured Marines moved across the battlefield. They were Soul Drinkers, from the lost days before the break with the Imperium. The Marine carrying the recorder glanced up at the night sky…

…*The night sky above was clear and cold, and through it streaked a missile from Squad Veiyal*…

Solun paused the image. The night sky of the planet was transposed over the Galactarium map to form a smeared mess of stars. The Galactarium stars suddenly whirled and Solun's eyes went blank as the mem-plates on his armour filled up with stellar data and his mind was flooded with star maps.

Solun would have to be quick. Sarpedon didn't even know if he could do it. Techmarine Lygris was one of Sarpedon's most trusted companions, and Lygris himself couldn't have done it. He had recommended Solun for the mission instead, knowing the younger Techmarine was an expert in information and its manipulation. If Solun's mind was unable to cope with the storm of information flooding through it, he would be reduced to a drooling infant in a Marine's body.

'Taking fire,' came a vox from Hastis. Light automatic fire chattered in the background.

'Squad Krydel will cover you from the temple,' replied Sarpedon.

'I see them,' voxed Krydel from amongst the columns at the front of the temple. 'We've got a hundred plus, Arbites riot officers with five riot control APCs and light vehicles.'

Sarpedon grabbed the cowering Phrantis Jenassis and hauled him with him as he sprinted towards the sound of bolter fire, the seven chitinous talons and single plasteel bionic clattering on the marble.

He saw them through the columns, a dark line of Adeptus Arbites lining the crest of the depression, spread between the trees. Adeptus Arbites officers maintained the laws of the Imperium and were equipped with fearsome anti-personnel weaponry and body armour. They were well drilled and ideologically motivated. They could not just be broken, they had to be thoroughly defeated.

Gunfire flashed down towards Squad Hastis, the ten-man tactical squad running down the tree-lined path towards the temple. Sergeant Krydel yelled an order and his squad's bolters opened up as one, sending lances of fire stripping leaves from the trees and keeping Arbites ducked below the ridge.

Squad Hastis reached the temple and added their fire to Krydel's. An Arbites APC, based on the Rhino APC pattern, rode over the crest and opened fire with twin heavy stubbers. Bullets kicked fragments from the marble columns and rang off Marines' armour.

Sarpedon watched as a command APC emerged from between the trees, a large antenna dish revolving on its roof and twin banners flying – one for the Arbites, one for House Jenassis. The top hatch opened and a judge emerged, eagle-crested helmet silhouetted against the grey sky.

'Cease fire!' yelled Sarpedon. The gunfire stopped.

A vox-caster was brought out of the APC and mounted on the vehicle's roof. The judge took the handset.

'Intruders!' boomed the voice from the vox-caster. 'Cast down your weapons, release your captives, and surrender to the Emperor's justice!'

Sarpedon glanced back into the temple. The Galactarium map was pulsing, closing in on one star system at a time and then wheeling to show a different one. Solun was twitching as information seethed through him. The battle-brothers had to buy him more time.

Sarpedon strode out from between the columns. He knew what he looked like – the Arbites would see a mutant. And they were right. He wore the gold-chased armour of a Space Marine Librarian and carried a nalwood psychic rod in one hand, with an artificer-crafter bolt gun and the Imperial eagle still emblazoned across his chest – but Sarpedon was still a mutant. He hoped the Arbites wouldn't open fire on principle alone.

He motioned for Squads Hastis and Krydel to stay in cover as he moved into the open, still dragging Phrantis. He counted about thirty Arbites sheltering in the trees, with many more doubtless waiting on the reverse slope. Another APC rumbled into sight, this time with a breech-loader that would fire a shell large enough to leave even Sarpedon a smouldering crater.

'We will fight you if you make us,' called Sarpedon, his voice booming through the heavy silence. 'Every single one of you will die. Or you can turn around and leave. You have no business with us, we are no longer beholden to Imperial law.'

'Release your prisoner and come out unarmed,' replied the judge on the vox-caster.

'Graevus?' voxed Sarpedon quietly. 'Do we have a match?'

'Solun's close,' replied the assault sergeant. 'He's got a lock on three stars.'

Sarpedon glanced over his shoulder. He could just see the whirling circle of stars that filled the Galactarium chamber. Turning back to the assembled Arbites, he dragged Phrantis Jenassis out from behind him and held him down on the ground in front of him with his front two legs. He took his boltgun from its holster and pressed the tip of the barrel against the back of the Navigator's head.

'This man is worth more than all of your lives put together,' called Sarpedon. 'If we leave, he will survive. If you bar our way, he will not.'

The judge did not reply. He ducked back into the APC for a moment before the hatch opened again. This time, it was not the helmeted judge who appeared but an astropath, one of the powerful telepaths who provided faster-than-light communication across the Imperium. Sarpedon's enhanced sight picked out the man's blind, sunken eye sockets and the puckered, prematurely aged skin of his face.

The astropath's voice wavered as he spoke into the vox-caster. It was clear from the artificiality of his tone that the voice he spoke with was not his own.

'Commander Sarpedon,' spoke the voice. 'Do not end it with such futility. These men are under my authority and will kill you at my order. You and your battle-brothers are under arrest by the authority of Inquisitor Thaddeus of the Ordo Hereticus.'

FOUR

FOR ALL THEY cared, Teturact had always been there. There had never been anything else. If they had any recollection of their lives before the plague took them, it was just a washed-out memory, whereas now their lives were illuminated by the light from Teturact, the saviour, the way.

On a hundred worlds he had come to them, and saved them from the ravages of disease. He had taught them not to fight it but to accept the plague, to make it a part of themselves and draw on its power. The agent of their death had, with Teturact's word, become the foundation of their life. To forge worlds, hive planets and feral worlds he had come and saved them all. And they would follow him to the end of the galaxy. Because of him they were no longer dying but brimming with life, so full of seething vitality that it wept from their pores and seeped from the cracks in their skin.

Teturact had first appeared to them on the Imperial Navy dockyard world of Stratix. Now, all those who could be spared made the pilgrimage to the seat of his power. It was a world of gargantuan spaceship docks supported on great stone and metal columns riddled with hive settlements, and now followers poured from the cultist-held spaceports towards the throne plaza of their saviour. Millions passed his throne in a seething pestilent throng, gazing up with their cataracted eyes to the top of the black stone pillar that lifted him above the masses. Teturact looked back down from a palanquin held aloft by four massively muscled bearers, immense muscles rippling, their bodies subsumed to Teturact's will. The brute-mutant bearers contrasted with Teturact's own frail, wizened body, and yet power seemed to flow from him. His thin, ancient-looking face radiated wisdom and his long, fragile fingers reached down benevolently as he bestowed his blessing on the masses.

Teturact ruled an empire a dozen systems across, and he ruled them utterly. His servants carried orders to whole worlds of the faithful, who obeyed as one, without question. The Imperium, who had betrayed and abandoned them, was trying to reclaim their worlds but Teturact, in his awesome wisdom, was calling upon his followers to mire the

Imperial armies in planet-wide battlezones and give up their lives for the glory of their saviour. The fleets of warships docked at Stratix had been turned into groups of fast raiders and fireships, breaking up the Imperial Navy spearheads. The Imperial armouries were stripped and used to turn hordes of grateful infected into loyal armies that rose up to slaughter the Imperial Guard that approached their cities. With their deaths, they would keep the empire of Teturact inviolate. There was no better way to die.

The empire included the Stratix system itself, and the forge worlds of Salshan Anterior and Telkrid IX. It encompassed the mineral-rich asteroid fields that circled the blue dwarf star Serpentis Minor. From naval shipyards, to agri-worlds that produced enough to feed those of his followers who still needed to eat, Teturact controlled enough resources and manpower to force the Imperium into a war that could last for centuries. The empire of Teturact was not due to fall for a very long time.

THE EMPIRE OF Teturact flickered by on the grand Galactarium, its diseased star systems whirling around the superimposed image from the pict-recording. Gradually individual stars locked in place over the image, until the star map and the night sky recorded over the outpost were identical.

Sergeant Graevus ran over to Techmarine Solun, who was reaching feebly for the wires plugged into the back of his head. Graevus unplugged the wires and Solun's eyes flickered back into focus.

'Did you find it, brother?' asked Graevus.

'Stratix Luminae,' said Solun. 'Outlying the Stratix system. It's still there untouched, it was never settled.'

'The Arbites have caught us up. Can you fight?'

'Always.'

'Good. Follow me.'

Sergeant Graveus and Techmarine Solun were still heading from the Galactarium chamber towards the front of the temple when the gunfire began.

SARPEDON HAD KNOWN the Inquisition would find them eventually – the Soul Drinkers were excommunicate, and Sarpedon had personally killed the Inquisitorial envoy who had delivered the sentence to the Chapter. But if the Ordo Hereticus could only have stayed off the scent just a little while longer, instead of finding the Chapter at their most vulnerable.

But they were implacable and intelligent. Inquisitor Tsouras, who had been outwitted by the Chapter in their escape at the Cerberian Field, had been little more than an enforcer, a thug who used his authority to bully and coerce. Thaddeus, though, must be a subtler and more patient man. It was an enemy Sarpedon did not need, not now when the whole Chapter needed to act with speed and secrecy. But Sarpedon had always known he would have to face the Inquisition again.

The first shot was from an Arbites sharpshooter, a cold-blooded killer and a good officer. His sniper-fitted autogun sent a bullet through the right eye of Phrantis Jenassis, blowing the back of the old man's head apart and leaving him a dead weight in Sarpedon's hand. The order had probably come from Inquisitor Thaddeus himself – the hostage represented Sarpedon's sole advantage, and that advantage had to be removed. The authority of the Ordo Hereticus exceeded even that of the Navigator House to which the Arbites precinct was bound.

Now the other officers had no reason not to open fire on the mutant who faced them. The pintle-mounted weaponry on the APCs sent shots raining down and Sarpedon scuttled to the side just in time to miss a cannon shot that ripped a hole in the ground and nearly blew him clean off his talons. The Arbites were mostly armed with short-ranged shotguns designed to break up riots, but those with longer range used them – sniper fire and shrapnel from grenade rounds spattered off his armour and lacerated the skin of his legs as he dropped the twitching body of Phrantis Jenassis and ran to the cover of the temple.

The body of Phrantis Jenassis flopped to the ground. His ragged turban fell off and his glossy black warp eye, now blind and harmless, stared blankly at the sky.

'Thin them out and fall back!' Sarpedon ordered Hastis and Krydel as he headed back towards the Galactarium.

Gunfire ripped out of the front of the temple and scoured the slope as the Arbites advanced. Their shotguns were useless over open distance but once in the temple they would be ideal for blasting around cover, so the riot details advanced through the bolter fire coming from the two Soul Drinker squads. Sarpedon had given his Marines time to pick their targets, but a cannon shot blew one of Squad Krydel to pieces and volleys of small arms fire from the sharpshooters and APCs soon made it impossible to size up targets at will. As the first shotgun blasts sent splinters of marble showering from the pillars, Hastis and Krydel yelled at their men to fall back into the body of the temple, following Sarpedon towards the court-yard.

The Galactarium was frozen, its sphere now showing only the night sky of Stratix Luminae. It was strange to finally give the place a name. But if the Soul Drinkers could not get that information off Kytellion Prime, it would mean nothing.

Graevus's squad was at the edge of the courtyard, with Solun alongside them. Solun was apparently alive and capable of fighting, which was just as well. If the Arbites judge had any sense he would send officers with grenade launchers onto the roof of the temple to rain frag and krak grenades onto the Soul Drinkers as they fought the Arbites coming in through the front. And in a spot like that Sarpedon needed all his battle-brothers fighting.

'We will defend this space and try to break them. Hastis and Krydel will be the front line – Graevus, you are our reserve.' Sarpedon pointed towards the machinery of the Galactarium. 'Destroy it.'

Graevus yelled an order and an Assault Marine ran towards the Galactarium, unhooking a large metal canister – an anti-armour melta-bomb – from his backpack. Squads Krydel and Hastis were assembling at the entrance to the courtyard, shotgun shrapnel following them as Hastis stopped his squad, turned them, and began to direct their fire against the Arbites storming in between the columns. Sarpedon added his own fire, snapping a shot into the stomach of one officer and sending others ducking back behind the columns with a volley of bolts.

A series of massive explosions ripped from the front of the temple, throwing a cloud of earth and marble dust into the interior. Squad Krydel was caught in the storm of shrapnel and fell back, purple armour chalked with the white dust.

'Demolition charges,' voxed Hastis. 'They've brought down the front of the temple.'

'More cover for the advance,' replied Sarpedon. 'We have no fields of fire. We'll have to fight them toe-to-toe. Graevus?'

'Commander?'

'Counter-attack on my word.'

'Understood.'

There was a pause as the dust cleared. In the pause Sarpedon could hear the creaking as the

melta-bomb's detonation seared through the
machinery of the Galactarium and sent the huge
metal construction sagging. The image twisted and
flickered, and suddenly the star field was gone, to
be replaced with the marble architecture of the
temple. Sarpedon quickly scanned the edge of the
roof around the opening to the courtyard – no
Arbites waited there, but they would appear soon,
to keep the Soul Drinkers pinned down while the
other officers engaged them through the rubble.

Gunfire erupted between Squad Krydel and
Arbites using the fallen chunks of marble to close
with the Marines. Sarpedon saw Sergeant Krydel,
power sword flashing, wading into the fight. Squad
Hastis was backing them up, snapping bolter shots
into the Arbites who ducked out of cover to loose
off shotgun blasts.

Sarpedon holstered his bolter even as a scattering of blasts scored the floor armour him. He
gripped his nalwood force staff with both hands
and felt the psychic fire spiralling around him,
forming a circuit of power that ran from the heart
of his brain to the squirming nalwood in his fist.
He was still a little nervous of the power inside
him – he had always been strong but since the terrible events on the unnamed world and the
Brokenback his psychic powers boiled hotter than
ever, bubbling away in his subconscious and
demanding a release.

A release like this. Like the Hell.

He focused his psychic power and forced it outwards, trained by the lens of his mind into images created to inflict pure terror. Shrieking, bat-like shapes dropped from above to tear through the Arbites on trails of crimson fire. Sarpedon concentrated and forced more from his mind until a whole swarm of them coursed through the Galactarium temple.

'Daemons!' someone yelled. The Inquisition probably suspected the Soul Drinkers were worshippers of Chaos, and had warned the Arbites to expect a daemonic threat. If they feared daemons, that was what Sarpedon would give them.

The Hell, the psychic power that had caused Sarpedon to enter the ranks of the Chapter's librarium, ripped into the Arbites. It was a storm of nightmares, drawing images of terror from the minds of its targets and sending those terrors swarming around them. Sarpedon was a telepath who could transmit but not receive, and his power had been honed by the librarium and his own willpower into a mental weapon the likes of which few Librarians had ever possessed. Physically it was harmless, but psychologically it was devastating. In the wreckage of the temple the effect was magnified, as Arbites out of sight of their fellow officers were pounced on by flying horrors that howled as they whipped their coils through the air above them.

Arbites were firing into the air. Many were panicking – Arbites were ideologically trained to a degree that the best Imperial Guard units could not boast, but few of them had faced daemons. Or, for that matter, a psyker as trained and powerful as Sarpedon.

'Graevus!' yelled Sarpedon 'Attack!'

Squad Graevus ran through Squads Hastis and Krydel, and Sarpedon went with them. Sarpedon had seen to it that all Soul Drinkers had been trained against the Hell through simulated battlefields on the *Brokenback*, so they would not be broken by it as their enemies were. Graevus sprinted into the enemy, power axe flashing in his mutated hand. His Assault Marines sent sprays of bolt pistol fire into the Arbites that was followed up with their chainblades, cutting through riot armour as if it wasn't there.

Sarpedon was in a split second later, his altered legs carrying him over a chunk of fallen marble and into the Arbites sheltering behind. He focused his power into the force staff and swiped the weapon through the first knot of Arbites he saw. He saw himself reflected in the black glass visors of their riot helmets as he sliced right through two of them at once. One officer still stood – Sarpedon impaled him with his forward leg, the bionic one, punching through his chest and flinging him back over his head.

Sergeant Graevus darted round the slab of marble and cut down the officer trying to bring his shotgun to bear on Sarpedon. All around bolter shells were blazing, cutting orange traces of fire through the air.

The din of battle was hot in Sarpedon's ears – he could hear Arbites officers yelling, trying to find one another, give orders, or just scream at the monsters hurtling at them from the air.

Squad Graevus cut through the Arbites savagely. Arbites on the roof fired down not into battered, pinned Marines but into Squad Hastis, who returned fire instantly and sent the broken bodies of launcher-armed Arbites falling to the floor of the courtyard. By the time Squad Graevus reached the front of the temple, well over a hundred Arbites were dead, wounded, or hopelessly scattered.

The Soul Drinkers followed the fleeing Arbites out of the temple and into the grounds, knowing there were still enough officers left to regroup and attack again if they were given the chance. Squad Graevus quickly disabled the Arbites APCs with krak grenades while Squad Krydel took pot shots at the Arbites scattering into the gardens.

'Leave the crews,' said Sarpedon. 'I don't want more dead than there have to be.' He spotted the command APC on the slope near the ridge and quickly crossed the bullet-scarred earth. He holstered his force staff and ripped the side hatch off the side of the APC.

Inside sat the astropath. The old man showed no fear.

'You have one more message to send,' said Sarpedon. 'Tell Inquisitor Thaddeus that we are not what he thinks we are. I know he cannot let us go free, but ultimately he and I are on the same side. If it comes down to it, I will have to kill him in order to continue our work. He will understand what drives us, because it is the same thing that drives him.'

The astropath nodded silently. Sarpedon left him in the APC and voxed his squads in the temple.

'The fighters cannot reach us in the dome. We need to get out onto the surface for pickup. Follow me.'

Sarpedon let the lifesign runes for the three-squad force flash onto his retina. Squad Krydel had lost two Marines, while Squad Graevus had lost one in the thick of the fight with the Arbites. Three more that could not be replaced within the foreseeable future. Sarpedon knew that many more would be lost before the harvest could begin and the Soul Drinkers could rise again.

But now they knew, at least, where they had to start. Stratix Luminae. With that information, they were one step closer to survival.

THE MAP OF the empire was an arrangement of precious stones, torn from the necklaces and earrings of Stratix's wealthy and handed as tributes to the court of Teturact. They were set out on the floor of south-western dock three, which had been appointed as the seat of Teturact's rule. South-western dock three was several layers down into one of Stratix's hive-stacks and was draped in tapestries of gauze torn from infected wounds, their patterns of gore and pus a gift from the legions of grateful plague-ridden. The corners of the cavernous space, beneath the docking clamps and control towers, were crammed with huddled figures that had made pilgrimages into the very presence of their lord and yet were so awed by him they could not approach. The floor was heaped with the bodies of those who had died of that awe, and pure liquid pestilence wept from the walls and dripped in a fine drizzle from the ceiling.

Teturact leaned forward on his palanquin. The four brute-mutants, so muscular even the features of their faces were obscured by folds of brawn, tilted the platform forward so Teturact could get a better look at the map. Stratix, in the centre like the star in the middle of a system, was a single blood-red ruby the size of a fist. The forge worlds were sapphires, blue as dead lips. The worlds of the front line, where Imperial Guard regiments were pouring into killing grounds swarming with Teturact's followers, were fiery yellow-orange opals. Loyal worlds were diamonds, hard and clear in their devotion to their saviour. There were hundreds of gemstones, each one a major world under Teturact's control, each crammed with souls who owed their lives to him.

Teturact had been dead for several years. His heart was just a knot of dried flesh somewhere in his dusty ribcage. Only his mind was truly alive, pulsing away beneath the tight skin of his skull and behind the rictus face with its horrible dried-out eyeballs. His body, thin and wizened with jaundiced yellow skin, was animated by will alone – his muscles had long since wasted away. Teturact was, in a very real sense, a being of pure willpower. He dominated those around him directly. Take the simple bovine minds of the brute-mutant bearers – he barely had to think to control them. Others he controlled by manipulating their circumstances until they had no choice but to obey his every wish.

The diseases – and there were many, to keep any one cure from harming his cause – were just a part of it. They were the catalyst. It was the force of Teturact's will that was his real weapon. And that force of will had won him a mighty empire such as the Black Crusades themselves had rarely won.

Many of the worlds on the chart were emeralds, green with potential. They were worlds that had only just begun the traumatic process of bending to Teturact's will. On some, the plague was only just making itself known, spread by Teturact's agents devoted to bringing enlightening disease to governors and hive-scum alike. Others were nearly ripe, and Teturact would soon leave the seat of his power on Stratix to bestow life upon the infected through the sorcery he could wield over disease.

One emerald caught his eye. It was near the front line, and would provide a great strategic advantage in anchoring a stretch of space that could easily be turned into a massive warzone if he wished it.

Colonel, he spoke to the shadows, his voice a rich psychic boom since he could not speak with his own rotted vocal chords.

A human form shambled towards Teturact, and bowed before the palanquin. It was draped in bloody bandages but beneath them tattered crimsons showed, with the glints of silver bullion trim and a chest full of campaign medals. Colonel Karendin had been little more than a butcher even before the plague had taken him – Teturact had left his mind mostly intact and he served to oversee the military situation in the empire.

What of this world? Teturact pointed a spidery finger at the strategic emerald.

'Eumenix?' replied Karendin, voice hissing thick with spittle. 'It is nearly ready to fall. The governor is dead, they say. The Arbites have fallen. No ship has left for many weeks. A billion have drowned in blood and bile already.'

Then I will go there next, said Teturact. *I want this world, and with as little delay as possible.*

'If you leave now, saviour, the planet will be ripe when you arrive. I could have your flagship prepared at once.'

Do so. Teturact settled back into the upholstery of the palanquin. *Our empire grows, colonel. Like the disease, our worlds multiply. Do you see how we infect?*

'Oh yes, saviour!' hissed Karendin. A faint gaggle of agreement came from the pilgrims huddled in the shadows. 'Like the plague itself, a plague on the stars!'

See to it that the court can be embarked within the day, said Teturact, losing interest in the colonel's blandishments.

Eumenix. A fine world to take, a hive world teeming with infected who would rise up and worship him when he promised them release. Such a fine world, indeed, that would greet him as a saviour, and die for him as a god.

SISTER BERENICE AESCARION was sixty-three years old. She had spent fifty-three of those years consecrated as a daughter of the Emperor, her body conditioned and her mind purified with diligence and atonement so she could serve as a soldier of the Emperor's church. She had been taken from the Schola Progenium where orphans of Imperial servants were raised, then brought into the presence of the preachers and confessors of the Adeptus Ministorum. They had filled her mind with the revelations of the Emperor, but she had not been afraid. She had heard of the horrors of apostasy and unbelief that opened the doors to sin and corruption, but she had not despaired.

The hellfire confessors had not reduced the girl to tears. The words of the preachers had left her inspired, not cowed. She had the willpower to join the ranks of the Sisters, and during her novicehood amongst the Orders Famulous it had become apparent that she also had the physical endurance and zeal to join the Orders Militant.

Her faith had never left her. Never, though she had fought across the galaxy, following the banner of the Order of the Ebon Chalice from the abbey on Terra itself to the edge of Imperial space. In her later years she had tracked down and killed the Daemon Prince Parmenides the Vile, and in doing so had acted in a precarious alliance between the Sisters of Battle and the Inquisition. She had acquired a reputation as one of the few Sisters who could navigate the tangled question of church and Inquisitorial authority without losing sight of the ultimate enemy – Chaos, the darkness the Emperor still fought with the strength of his spirit. So when Inquisitor Thaddeus had requested a taskforce of Sisters to be assembled from a number of Orders Militant, it was Sister Aescarion he had asked to lead it.

Canoness Tasmander had asked Sister Aescarion to take on leadership of the Ebon Chalice, but she had turned down the office of canoness. Aescarion had fought her whole life, and she was too old to do anything other than keep fighting. It was the only way she knew her faith could become something more than mere words – that same faith that had made her a Sister in the first place, that had driven her to vanquish Parmenides and countless other enemies of humanity. It was the same faith that was being sorely tested in the depths of Eumenix.

Eumenix. If ever the Emperor's light had been taken from a world, it was this. She had never seen a world so utterly desolate of hope, and she had seen some terrible things. Eumenix was a grim illustration of what could happen in the absence of faith.

Aescarion watched as Interrogator Shen, his massive bronze carapace armour tarnished by the week-long trek through the filth and horror of Hive Quintus, moved warily down the steep shaft that led deeper into the lower layers of the hive. The air was infernally hot for the geothermal heatsinks were nearby, and everything stank. On the surface Sister Aescarion and her squad had seen mouldering mountains of corpses and their diseased reek seemed to permeate the whole planet – sweet and sickening, pure rot and corruption.

Down here, the heat made it worse. For several days Shen and the Sisters had been moving into the depths of the hive and now they were dozens of levels down, near the last possible Imperial institution in Hive Quintus. The Arbites and the governor's palace had fallen, the cathedral was a burned-out shell and the offices of the Administratum had been the first to fall when the madness began. The Adeptus Mechanicus geological outpost in the lower reaches of the hive was the last possible nugget of resistance, and last place where the reports of escaping Soul Drinkers might be confirmed.

That had been weeks ago. Thaddeus had passed on the news as quickly as he could, but had entrusted the actual investigation to Interrogator Shen while he himself sifted through the *Brokenback* and the wreckage of House Jenassis. Both Shen and Aescarion held out little hope for finding anything alive in Hive Quintus – at least, not alive in the normal sense.

The architecture this far down was cramped and twisted: the compressed, distorted relics of the settlements on which Hive Quintus had been built. Discoloured moisture ran down the walls, filtered down through a hundred floors of decay. Ruptured power conduits covered everything in a dank mist. Plague-rats the size of attack dogs writhed through the twisted metal. The groaning of the settling city was punctured by the screams of yet another life being snuffed out, one amongst billions on the nightmare of Eumenix.

The corridor angled downwards and bent sharply up ahead. Shen drew his inferno pistol from its holster and moved up to the corner, the boots of his carapace armour crunching through the crystallised filth that encrusted the floor. Sister Aescarion followed, bolt pistol drawn, as did the Seraphim she had chosen to accompany her on the mission. One of them, Sister Mixu, had been at her side for over a decade. The others had been supplied by their own Orders, and all fought with twin bolt pistols in the tradition of the Seraphim squads.

Shen led the way round the corner. The corridor flared out into a ragged cavity, like a hole torn by a bomb blast clean through layers of the warren-like lower levels. Murky water pooled on the uneven floor and pale vapour gouted from ruptured pipelines overhead.

'Geothermal must have gone up,' said Shen as he scanned for targets. His inferno pistol was an exceedingly rare weapon that packed the power of a melta gun into a relatively small pistol, and at short ranges it could carve through anything. 'Without maintenance half the hive is probably ready to explode.'

Sister Mixu pointed up at a symbol, half a stylised metallic skull and half a square-toothed cog, grinning lopsidedly down from the mass of twisted metal. 'The symbol of the Mechanicus. Looks like we're close, sister.'

'Movement!' shouted one of the Seraphim. Sister Aescarion turned to see one of the Sisters opening fire into the shadows. Shen followed her aim, firing a bolt of superheated matter that briefly lit the twisted, sub-humanoid shapes that were massing in the gloom.

The enemy weren't bandits, because they didn't steal anything. It was as if they pounced on anything living just for the novelty of killing something alive. They were the shambling remnants of the underhivers who had been reduced to walking corpses by the plague, and they had dogged the heels of Shen and the Seraphim for whole hellish journey to the underside of Hive Quintus.

In the brief burst of light, Aescarion counted fifty plus of them. The inferno pistol claimed three, scorched to cinders, and bolt pistol fire stitched a bloody path through several others.

'Fall back!' called Aescarion and drew her Sisters around her, adding her bolt pistol fire to theirs. The hive-scum surrounded them, clambering from the ragged walls, moaning their death-rattles. She could see their peeling skin and the runny whites of their eyes, their lolling jaws and the gnarled, blackened fingers that held crude clubs and blades.

If there was proof that Eumenix was cursed by Chaos, it was this. A disease that not only killed, but turned the bodies of its victims into mindless predators to stalk the survivors.

The Seraphim backed off slowly, pumping bolts into the shambling wave of the dead that was pouring in ever-greater numbers into the cavity. Shen's inferno pistol was recharged and sent out another hissing lance of fire that tore through a dozen scum at once.

'We're surrounded,' said Shen with a calm that struck Aescarion as most admirable. He indicated the Mechanicus symbol. 'We'll have to cut our way out. Head that way and we may hit the outpost, it'll be easier to defend.'

Aescarion nodded in agreement and drew the power axe from its holster on her back. She had fought with that same axe for decades, always refusing more refined weapons because the brutality of the axe was a befitting tool to bring down the Emperor's unflinching justice.

The weapon's blade hummed to life and a shimmering blue power field played around it.

'With me!' yelled Shen and fired his inferno pistol into the knot of plague-scum beneath the Mechanicus symbol. He charged into the remainder, barging their rotting bodies aside. The Seraphim behind Shen blew bodies apart with their twin bolt pistols. Sister Aescarion ran past Shen into the underhivers, hacking at the wall of flesh in front of her. Gnarled hands reached towards her and she hacked them off with her axe, punching her gauntleted fist into the mutilated faces behind. She stamped down and felt bodies crunching beneath her feet. Bolt pistol fire raged past her into the plague-dead, thinning them out around her as she and Shen barged their way through their attackers and out of the explosion site.

They plunged deeper into the darkness, snapping off shots at anything that moved. At Shen's lead they kept moving, knowing that if they stopped, their slower but massively more numerous attackers would be able to surround them and cut them off in the narrow, twisting tunnels below.

Age-darkened brass and heavy gothic mechanical architecture began to surface amongst the grime of the underhive. Massive industrial cogs lay here and there and the symbols of the Machine-God were tooled into every girder. The Adeptus Ministorum were privately wary of the Adeptus Mechanicus – the tech-priests worshipped the Omnissiah, the

Machine-God, which they claimed to be an aspect of Emperor, but the Ministorum had their secret doubts. That said, Sister Aescarion was grateful that at least they knew how to build.

The Mechanicus outpost was a solid cube of brass, its surface knotted with pipes, strong enough to survive the crushing weight of the hive above it. The entrances were massive blast doors sealed tight and Shen stepped back warily when he saw the sentry guns and the bullet-riddled bodies of plague-dead that had been unfortunate enough to shamble into range.

The squad scouted around the outpost, finding scores of dead – most of them infected but some in the rust-red coveralls of Mechanicus menials, along with one or two servitors hurriedly refitted for combat. Corpses lay draped over makeshift barricades, set up to funnel the shambling hordes into killzones now choked with their bodies. The outpost must have held out for weeks as Hive Quintus slowly turned into hell.

One door was not sealed. The underside of the outpost was blackened with scorch marks from a massive explosion that had ripped the lower hatch open. Jagged metal ringed the opening overhead like torn skin around an open wound.

Shen waded through the knee-deep murky water that filled the tunnels beneath the outpost. The opening overhead was dark and the walls were riddled with bullet holes.

'Bolter fire,' said Aescarion. She had seen the results of bolter weapons more often than she could remember. 'Disciplined. Tightly grouped.'

The final reports off Hive Quintus had been of the last shuttle out being stolen by purple-armoured monsters, leaving the wealthy Cartel Pollos on the hive to die. Shen and Aescarion had been sent to find out if there was any truth to them, but the outpost was the only place on the planet where Imperial personnel might survive to verify them. Now it seemed that not only had the outpost fallen, but that the Soul Drinkers might have been the ones who attacked it.

Shen reached up and grabbed the edge of the wrecked blast door above him. He hauled himself up through the opening and switched on the light mounted on the collar of his armour.

'Nothing,' he said. 'There must have been a hell of a firefight here. Small arms and grenades. There are bodies everywhere.'

'Follow me,' said Aescarion to her Seraphim, then followed Shen into the body of the outpost. She was reminded of her age as she clambered up beside him – it would have been much easier with the jump packs Seraphim usually fought with, but they had left the packs behind since a hive city was hardly the most appropriate terrain for their use.

Shen was right. The straight, metal-walled corridors of the outpost had seen ferocious fighting. Blade marks on the floor and walls told of hand-to-hand butchery, the bullet-riddled walls of massive weight of fire. The corpses of menials lay where they had fallen defending the breached entrance.

The rest of the Seraphim climbed up into the corridor. 'No life signs,' said Sister Mixu, who carried the squad's auspex scanner. 'But there's a lot of interference. This place is pretty solidly built.'

'The underhivers didn't do this,' said Shen.' And if the Soul Drinkers didn't then it was somebody capable of bringing down a similar level of firepower. We need to find out what they wanted with this place.'

'Agreed,' said Aescarion. 'Could the Mechanicus have been working on something here? A weapon?'

'We'll find out. This outpost will be built along standard template construct lines. There'll be a control post at the centre and a testing bay not far above us. We'll try those first, then scour the rest.'

The outpost was a combination of massive industrial workings and the sort of oppressive gothic architecture that Aescarion was familiar with from the convent prioris on Terra. Fluted columns separated banks of cogs like giant clockwork, frozen by the outpost's shutdown. Turbines lay beneath vaulted ceilings. Shrines to the Machine-God were everywhere, stained with libations of machine oil, scrawled with prayers in binary. Everything the Mechanicus did needed the correct rites enacted to the Machine-God – and judging by the abundance of offerings and prayer-tablets in the empty armoury, it seemed that included fighting.

The testing bay held hundreds of geological samples in various stages of examination under powerful brass-cased microscopes, or lying in chemical baths now dried out. There was nothing there that suggested anything valuable enough for the outpost to be attacked. The control room that overlooked the bay was empty, too, its cogitators ritually sealed with runes of inaction to appease the machine-spirits as they were shut down.

'We should take what information they still hold,' said Shen. 'At least we'll have some idea of what work they did here and who was involved. They might even have pict-recordings from the sentry guns, so we could see who attacked them.'

'I am no tech-priest,' said Aescarion. 'Do you know how to operate all this?' She indicated the banks of cogitators that covered the walls of the control room, with blank readout screens.

'We'll just take the memory units,' said Shen. 'Thaddeus has men who can open them up.'

'Movement,' said Mixu, glancing at the auspex screen. 'Somewhere above us.'

'Probably more underhivers,' said Shen, drawing his pistol.

A hand plunged down through the ceiling of the control room, grabbing Shen by the collar of his armour and dragging him up sharply, slamming him into the metal ceiling. The hand was encased in a gauntlet of purple ceramite.

'Fire!' yelled Aescarion and bolter fire ripped up into the ceiling beside Shen, who was trying to bring his inferno pistol to bear. Before he could get a shot up he was dragged through the ceiling completely, the metal tearing as his armoured body disappeared from view.

Sister Aescarion was the first after him. The hole in the ceiling led to what must have been the outpost's main shrine, where ranges of pews carved out of solid carbon faced an altar formed from the casings of a giant cogitator. Pipes and valves knotted the walls so the chapel was contained entirely within the body of the cogitator, and when operational its readouts would have bathed the shrine in a glow of information. Now it was dark, so the scene in front of her was lit only in the flashes from the light mounted on Shen's armour.

It was a Space Marine. Its armour bore the chalice symbol of the Soul Drinkers on one shoulder pad. It carried no weapons.

Aescarion caught a glimpse of its face. In life the skin had been dark but now it was pasty and mottled grey with disease. The eyes were gone and dark ragged holes stared blindly. The lower part of the face had been gnawed away and the bleached white of jawbone and teeth grinned out. Nothing living could look like that, and nothing dead could stare with such blind madness and hate. Sister Aescarion only had the briefest glimpse by the swinging light on Shen's armour, but in an instant there was no doubt.

A Soul Drinker, claimed by the plague. The bullet scars on its armour suggested that it had been mortally wounded in the battle for the outpost, that it had been left behind by its colleagues, and succumbed to the terrible plague that had savaged Hive Quintus. It was the first time Sister Aescarion had actually set eyes on a member of the Chapter.

As she watched, trying to get a clear shot, the dead Soul Drinker tore Interrogator Shen's arm off at the shoulder in a crimson crescent of blood. The arm holding the pistol was flung to one side of the chapel and the rest of him to the other, his armoured body crashing limply into the wall.

Sister Mixu was beside Aescarion, firing her twin pistols. She snapped off two rapid head shots, blowing a hole in the Marine's forehead, but the Soul Drinker seemed not to even notice the massive wound. Aescarion couldn't claim to know a great deal about fighting the living dead but she hazarded a guess that it would take more than just a killing wound to fell the Soul Drinker – nothing but dismemberment would stop it. And dismemberment was something at which Aescarion excelled.

She drew the power axe and charged the Marine. It was a full head taller than her but she was much quicker. Her blade flashed down and she hacked deep through the Marine's collar and into his torso, the axe's power field splitting his fused ribcage and carving through dead organs.

The Marine gripped the haft of the axe, pivoted, and flung Aescarion into the brass-cased altarpiece-machine. The casing buckled beneath the impact and components rained down as Aescarion slid to the floor. Telltales flashed on her armour's retinal display and a brief flash of pain dulled to an ache as painkillers flooded her system.

The Soul Drinker stood above her, staring blindly down with its dried-out eye sockets. Bolt pistol fire ripped into its back from the Seraphim emerging into the chapel behind it, punching through the tarnished armour and kicking chunks from its skull. Its broken face grinned down as it reached for Aescarion.

Aescarion tried to roll out of its way but her body wouldn't respond – she must have shattered a shoulder and maybe a hip. The Soul Drinker picked her up by the shoulder joins of her breastplate and began to pull, trying to crack her open like a predator opening up armoured prey to get at the flesh inside.

Aescarion could feel her armour coming apart. Her good arm still held her axe and she felt its power field humming. As the telltales flashed red on her retina she dragged the blade into the waist of the Soul Drinker. She used every ounce of her strength to cut through the ceramite power armour, but she had no leverage and her system was struggling to cope with the pain.

One of the Seraphim wrapped an arm around the Marine's neck from behind, trying to saw its head

off with her combat knife. The Marine turned and
drove an elbow into the Sister's midriff, knocking
her backwards. It let go of Aescarion with one hand
as it did so. She planted one foot onto the floor of
the chapel and swivelled on it, ripping the axe blade
through the waist of the Space Marine, cutting clean
through the ceramite and the Marine's spine.

Aescarion slumped to the floor. The upper part of
the Soul Drinker's body fell beside her. Its legs
stood for a moment, then fell to one side, clattering
against the metal of the chapel.

The Seraphim picked herself off the floor and
stood over the upper half of the Soul Drinker. It
looked up at her, head jerking as the end of its severed spine flopped like a beached fish. Aescarion
handed her the axe, and without switching on the
power field, the Seraphim cut off the Soul Drinker's
head.

Mixu was on the other side of the room, tending
to Shen.

'He's dying, sister,' said Mixu. Two of the
Seraphim helped Aescarion over to where the interrogator lay. Gore pumped from the torn shoulder
socket, forming a thick pool beneath him. His eyes
were open but they couldn't focus on anything and
though his jaw worked no sound came out. Mixu
opened up the breastplate of the carapace armour
and Aescarion saw right away that the interrogator
was beyond hope. The ribs had been broken and
separated by the force of his arm being torn off, and

then crushed when he hit the wall. The organs inside must have been torn to shreds.

As Aescarion watched, Shen died.

'He was a soldier of the Emperor,' said Aescarion, grimly aware of her own injuries. 'We cannot let him rise again.'

The Seraphim carried Shen's body down to the turbine floor, where they placed a long-fused krak grenade in his mouth and reduced the corpse to a rain of ash.

Aescarion was no tech-priest and only knew enough of the Machine-God's dogma to maintain her own battle-gear. She had the Seraphim lever off the casings of cogitators in the control room and remove what she took to be the datacores inside. Aescarion herself removed a plaque on the wall of the control room that recorded all the adepts who had ever worked in the outpost – hundreds of names inscribed in tiny letters on a sheet of brass. As an afterthought she took the head of the dead Marine, and sealed it in a specimen box from the lab, along with the Marine's bolt pistol that was still in its holster with its golden chalice symbol.

There was nothing else of value in the place. She only hoped that she had found something worth Shen's life. Mixu saw to Aescarion's injuries as best she could and Aescarion gave her the authority to lead the squad out to their extraction point.

It had been difficult for Shen to arrange for a naval salvage craft to pick them up from the wastes outside Hive Quintus – the Officio Medicae had banned all travel and few crews wanted to risk the polluted wastes. Inquisitorial authority had barely cut through the red tape in time to get Shen and the Seraphim onto Eumenix in the first place. If the squad wasn't there for the pick-up, the crew would abandon them there, and they would never escape. It was a good few days' travel to reach the barren inter-hive wastes and with Aescarion injured it would take even longer than she had feared.

Sister Mixu took them off as quickly as she dared, through the darkness and danger of Hive Quintus.

FAR ABOVE THE polluted wastes, a ship from the dockyards of Stratix approached the thinly-stretched quarantine line around Eumenix. Orbital batteries fell silent at its approach, crews suddenly riddled with the most virulent plagues. Officio Medicae craft fled from it like shoals of fish before a shark as their survival instincts set alarms ringing. Plague and madness had come, concentrated into the force of one being.

For the plague-damned of Hive Quintus, their saviour was almost upon them.

FIVE

A SHADOW, LIGHT years across, was cast like a dark halo around the warzone. The Imperium had quarantined the tortured worlds under Teturact's rebellion, establishing a firebreak of locked-down star systems. Whole worlds were under house arrest, their fleets grounded, their populations prevented from leaving without permission from the warzone's military command and the Officio Medicae. Cathedrals of the Imperial Faith offered up prayers for deliverance, begging the Emperor in his wisdom to let victory come to the Imperial war effort before the plague visited their worlds. Dark rumours circulated about Teturact, and the horror that would unfold if he ever broke through the Imperial fleets that were massing around his rebellious empire.

Governors reassured their people that the Navy and the Guard would soon blaze into the warzone and puncture the heart of Teturact's pestilent realm. They were also in the throes of preparing hermetically-sealed bunkers in case the plagues reached them.

The Imperium was, in many ways, constantly at war – but around the empire of Teturact, war was a stifling, sinister shroud draped over hundreds of worlds and billions of people. Fear swamped the minds of billions. They said that Eumenix had fallen, so who knew where would be struck next?

Interstellar traffic was quiet and the space lanes heavily monitored. Travel between systems had to be sanctioned by the Imperial authorities, with no exceptions. But there were always those who tried to make themselves exceptions – smugglers running supplies between quarantined worlds that they would sell for a huge mark-up, deserters escaping from the warzone, and the usual criminals and degenerates who fled from the Imperium during routine times. Most were picked up or destroyed, but some as ever got through.

And some were almost completely invisible. It was difficult enough to catch massive cargo ships slipping in and out of the warp in the quarantined systems. It was next to impossible to see them when they were fighter-sized craft – a fraction the size of the smallest Imperial warp-capable ship. But the shoal of craft that slipped through the darkness around the Stratix warzone were not Imperial.

They were alien fighters; their faintly sinister organic lines contained powerful vortex reactors that could push them into and out of the warp. It was dangerous, there was no doubt about it. No one really knew which xenos species had built the fighters, and the handful of captured Navigators who directed the squadron through the warp were, through necessity, not the best. But it was worth it. If they achieved what they set out to do, the risk was worth it.

Sarpedon looked out on the star-scattered darkness from the first fighter's cockpit. He wasn't even sure it was a fighter – when Techmarine Lygris had shown Sarpedon the fleet of bizarre craft on one of the *Brokenback's* many flight decks, the ships were empty of any ordnance or weapons save those that could be extruded from the ships' hulls. Instead, Lygris had fitted out the ships with grav-couches so each could carry a payload of Marines. It was an enormous risk, transporting almost the entire Chapter on ships that traversed the warp by means the Techmarines couldn't begin to understand. But it was the only way – the *Brokenback* couldn't have hoped to slip into the warzone.

Inside the fighter the cold, bulbous forms of the bridge were an odd silvery colour with a sheen of sinister purple. The Chapter serfs at the controls – some of the few survivors of the Chapter's break with the Imperium and the battle on the *Brokenback* – worked the fighter's instruments by moving their hands through pools of molten metal like strangely-hued quicksilver. The basic readouts had been translated from amorphous alien runes, but most of the information that ran across the irregularly shaped readouts was indecipherable. The ship was almost crushingly non-human – corridors twisted and the mysterious vortex generators were strange organic shapes like seed pods or the shells of sea creatures. The air was only breathable because of the filters and purifiers that pumped oxygen through vents that had once held gases toxic to humans. The inhabitants had evidently been taller but thinner than humans, as the ceilings were high and everything was narrow.

'What are our coordinates?' Sarpedon asked the Chapter serfs.

The serf at the navigation controls didn't look round as he replied. 'We're on top of the meeting point, Lord Sarpedon.'

'Give me the fleet vox.' Another serf dipped a hand into a shimmering pool of metal and Sarpedon was connected to the other nine fighter craft. 'All craft, be on the lookout for Dreo. We cannot wait here long.'

Somewhere in that band of stars across the sky was the corrupt heart of Teturact's empire. Somewhere far more distant was Terra, the equally corrupt heart of the Imperium. The galaxy out there was utterly immense, and beyond it was the warp, a whole dimension of horror that bled into real space every time mankind jumped between the stars. Against it all the Soul Drinkers stood, utterly alone, a little less than seven hundred warriors who were, even after all their alterations and training, still ultimately men. It was almost liberating for Sarpedon to look on the sheer vastness of the fight, and to know that he had made a conscious decision to go on fighting.

'Signals, commander,' came a voice over the vox. It was Techmarine Lygris, who had managed to activate some of the strange sensor devices that jutted from the prow of his fighter. 'It's weak. They must be low on fuel.'

'Do you have a visual?'

A few moments passed, and then a film of liquid metal bled across the air and an image swam onto it. A shuttle limped painfully through space, one of its engines flaring as it died. Its hull was pitted with corrosion and streaked with burns from laser fire. It was a private craft designed for short hops between planets – not agonising hauls between systems. It must have taken months to get this far from Eumenix. There was no guarantee that any normal human could survive such conditions.

'Lygris, direct us in. I'll dock with them.'

'Understood. You realise any one of them could be infected.'

'If they're infected then the prisoner will be dead, and we might as well be. Besides, I need to debrief them myself.'

Lygris directed the serfs on Sarpedon's fighter to fly towards the battered shuttle. A section of the fighter's hull bulged outwards and burst like an ulcer; globules of liquid metal flowing into one another until they formed a smooth tunnel that latched onto the side of the shuttle like a hungry leech.

The metal formed a sharp, biting edge and began to bore through the hull of the shuttle.

A pressurised pocket formed in the hull of the fighter as the metallic bridge became airtight, and the wall formed an airlock. Sarpedon was there as soon as it had fully formed. 'Squad Hastis, Squad Karvik, meet me at the airlock. You too, Pallas.'

The smell of stale sweat exhaled from the flower-like airlock as it opened and the two Marine squads joined Sarpedon. The air inside the shuttle must have been barely breathable.

'Any communication from them?' voxed Sarpedon.

'None,' replied Lygris from his own craft. 'They're not receiving, either. Their comms must have gone down.'

Sarpedon peered into the darkness at the end of the airlock tunnel. A figure moved from the shadows, and slowly limped into the tunnel.

It was Sergeant Salk. His face – usually youthful compared to the Chapter's battle-scarred veterans – was now sunken-eyed and emaciated. His armour was tarnished and he walked as if it weighed him down.

'We lost Captain Dreo,' he said hoarsely. 'Karrik and Krin made it. Nicias died in the shuttle. We lost Dreo and the rest on the planet.'

Sarpedon had seen dozens of good Marines die, but his heart still sank. Captain Dreo was perhaps the best shot in the whole Chapter, and a fine level headed soldier. It was his nerve that had held in the confrontation with the Daemon Prince Ve'Meth, and his command that had riddled Ve'Meth's host bodies with bolter fire. That was why Sarpedon had trusted him with the Eumenix mission. Now he was gone, and another Soul Drinker would never be replaced.

'And the prisoner?'

'Survived.'

Salk waved forward another Marine – Sarpedon recognised it as Krin, who normally carried Squad Salk's plasma gun. Now he carried the sleeping body of a woman, tiny in his arms. Her clothes had once been the rust-red robes that signified the rank of a Mechanicus Adept but now they were charred and filthy. She was short and boyish with a square face mostly obscured by the pilot's rebreather unit she wore.

Apothecary Pallas took the limp body from Krin. He consulted the medical readouts on the back of his Narthecium gauntlet, the instrument that would enable a blood transfusion and, if necessary, administer the Emperor's mercy to those beyond help. Now it gave him an overview of the woman's condition.

'She's badly malnourished,' he said. 'Semi-conscious. We have enough of an apothecarion on Karendin's ship to help her.'

'Can she speak?'

'Not yet.'

Sarpedon recognised her as the much younger woman from the Stratix Luminae files. In them she could be seen ducking in fear from the bolter fire as the Soul Drinkers of a decade ago stormed the labs to drive out the eldar pirates. Now she was much older, with lines around her eyes and her hair shaven at the back of her neck to accommodate the sockets drilled into her skull.

Somewhere in Captain Korvax's mission reports there was a staff roster for the installation, and from these records Sarpedon had learned the woman's name – Sarkia Aristeia. She was then an adept inferior, just one step up from a menial but one of the only staff members that the Soul Drinkers could locate. It was strange to finally see her when acquiring her had cost so many lives – she seemed such a small and inconsequential thing. Sarpedon had fought daemons and monstrous aliens for over seventy years as a warrior, but she was a vital part of Sarpedon's plan, and without her the Chapter was lost.

Was Sarkia Aristeia worth the deaths of Captain Dreo, of Aean, Hortis, Dryan and the giant Nicias? If a hundred other vital victories were won, then yes. But there was so much still to do, and the hardest fights were always ahead.

'Stabilise her and take her to Karendin,' said Sarpedon to Pallas. 'I need to question her as soon as possible.'

'Perhaps it would be wisest if Chaplain Iktinos…' began Pallas, with slight awkwardness.

'Of course,' said Sarpedon, realising the Apothecary's point. 'She must have seen enough monsters on Eumenix, there is no need for her to see another.' Sarpedon had been imposing enough before he had become a mutant and the sight of him now would probably have knocked Aristeia unconscious again. 'Let Iktinos talk to her.'

Pallas carried the woman to the crew compartment so he could examine her properly. Karrik emerged from the shuttle, his armour charred black. His face was burned badly and, like Salk's, emaciated in a way that was uncharacteristic of a Marine.

'How was Dreo lost?' asked Sarpedon.

'Sentry gun,' replied Salk. 'He blew open the lower entrance of the outpost and was the first in. The Mechanicus had stepped up their security, the whole planet was on the slide by then.'

'And the others?'

'Nicias died on the way here. He had multiple internal injuries and there were only emergency medical supplies on the shuttle. We used those for the woman. Nicias went into half-sleep and never woke up. The rest were killed in the assault or lost when we broke into the spaceport.'

'How long have you been adrift?'

'Three months. According to the mission plan it should have been longer, but Eumenix went downhill fast and we had to get off. Then again, I don't think she'd have survived the shuttle any longer. The food ran out a week ago. The air had been excessively recycled so she couldn't breathe properly and we were down to our last rebreather filter.'

'The astropathic traffic we have seen suggests there was a plague on Eumenix. Do you or your Marines show any symptoms?'

Salk shook his head. 'Nothing. The conditions were bad there but we haven't brought anything back with us. And it was more than a plague, commander. It was something that rotted the mind. The whole hive had gone mad. Maybe even the whole planet. The dead were walking the streets and the living were butchering one another. It was as well we moved when we did. We would never have got Aristeia off the planet otherwise.'

'You have done well, Salk. With Dreo gone your chances were very slim.'

'I cannot help but feel his death was too high a price to pay, commander.'

'High, but not too high. I cannot tell you what we are fighting for, Salk, but you must trust me when I say it is worth anything we sacrifice. Dreo will be remembered for his part in our coming victory, but if we do not win it then none of us will be remembered. You and your men should transfer to

Karendin's ship with the prisoner. He and Pallas will fix you up.'

The two squads returned to their quarters and the ragged remains of Squad Salk headed for the docking bay where they, along with Aristeia would be transferred to the infirmary.

Maybe Salk was right. Perhaps Sarpedon's mission was impossible and he was throwing away the lives of his men. But he could not falter now, when so much was at stake. They trusted him completely, even when he could not tell them what they fought for. To give up would be to betray that trust, and with the whole galaxy intent on wiping out the Chapter their trust was one of the few advantages Sarpedon had left.

The next stage could be the riskiest of all. While Pallas and Karendin tended to Aristeia's health and Iktinos interrogated her, the makeshift fleet would have to puncture the dark heart that lay past the Imperial cordon. The Soul Drinkers would be lucky to ever come out again.

'Piloting?' he voxed.

'Commander?' came the voice of the Chapter serfs on the bridge.

'Wait until the transfer is complete, then take us to the next waypoint. Cut the shuttle free. Report any contacts and have the other fighters keep formation.'

Sarkia Aristeia would have to know the information Sarpedon needed. The fleet would have to make it to the next stage and every Marine would have to fight harder than ever before. The Inquisition would have to stay a step behind for just a little while longer. So much could go wrong, but Sarpedon would have to accept those risks. It was enough that he would fight until the end and never turn his back on his mission. Everything else was down to the grace of the Emperor and the strength of his battle-brothers.

Sarpedon turned on his eight chitinous legs and headed back towards the bridge. They were close enough now that the fleet would not have to make another risky warp jump. However in real space there were sharp-eyed battleship captains and pirates to avoid.

The strange alien fighters lanced through space in formation, carrying a cargo of the Emperor's finest warriors, with one of the most dangerous places in the Imperium as their destination.

TETURACT'S FLAGSHIP WAS a vast flying tomb. Billions had died on Stratix before Teturact saved the survivors and bound them to his will. That had left mountains of corpses heaped from the undercities to the palaces and cathedrals, a festering monument to the power of Teturact's disease and the fate of those who opposed him. Such a volume of death was an end in itself – a great and glorious reminder of how Teturact could wield death like a king's sceptre. He wanted to surround himself with death at all times, to take it with him when he left Stratix so he would always be immersed in it.

The dark, heavy sensation of being drowned in death was an inspiration to Teturact and a reminder to all in his presence that he was not just their leader, he was their god. He decided who would die and who would live, and the form those lives would take.

The flagship itself had once been an Emperor-class battleship, a wedge-prowed slab of a ship that had rained fire on the enemies of the false Emperor. It had been taken to Stratix for refitting and was a stripped-down hulk in the naval dockyards when Teturact saved the planet. It was as if the planet had presented the ship to its new lord as a gift, and Teturact had accepted it. It had been refitted with masses of weaponry and shielding devices, replacing the life support systems and accommodation decks that were of no use when the crew needed neither air nor rest.

Then the dead had come – wrapped in their shrouds. They were entombed in their thousands, along the walls of the corridors and the cavernous spaces of the fighter decks. Teturact's loyal servants had broken bodies apart and used the bones to decorate the bridge and Teturact's own chambers. They had flayed skin off corpses to cover the walls and hang as curtains. The instrument panels were inlaid with human teeth. Columns of vertebrae ringed the bulkhead doors. The corridors leading to the bridge were paved with fragments of skulls. The ship was a magnificent monument to death, and death coursed through it like lifeblood.

The circular hall in which Teturact now stood had once been a briefing theatre, where the ship's captain would deliver his battlefield command to his underlings. Now it saw something far greater – a conclave of Teturact and his wizards.

Every system had its rogues. Amongst these were psykers, the witches and shamans that were hunted by inquisitors, Arbites, witchfinders and law-abiding Imperial weaklings. When Teturact's empire began to spread he had sought out these psykers and made them the most loyal of all his followers. Through them, his mastery of disease was complete. Their powers could let him raise a plague on a world light years distant – so it had been on Eumenix, where his touch had made the world ripe for conquest even while he was on distant Stratix.

The wizards were from a hundred worlds and they now all wore the filthy robes of Teturact, and were cowled like monks of an order devoted to him. Beneath their robes their bodies had changed: some had become bloated, others emaciated, and many sported tentacles or segmented clawed limbs. Each one was a receptacle of immense psychic power, and they were so subjected to Teturact's will that they couldn't even remember what names they had carried before he found them.

The seating of the auditorium had been replaced with benches of carved bone. The spotlight that fell on Teturact at the centre was tinted yellow by the corruption that seeped through the ship. The wizards were shambling, seeping things, and yet in the eyes that peered from underneath their cowls Teturact could still see their devotion.

None of them dared to be leader, so they all spoke in turn.

'Eumenix is ready,' one of them slurred.

'We have seen it,' said another. 'The only living things are nomads in the wastes, and they will be gone soon enough.'

Have any others visited my world? asked Teturact, speaking with his mind rather than his rotted vocal chords.

'Few, my lord. There were some fanatics who came to spread the word of their Emperor, but they did not survive. There were others who looked like the Emperor's warriors, but they carried the taste of rebellion and anger with them. But there were few and they were the last to escape the world.'

Teturact plucked an image from the head of the wizard who had spoken. It had been gleaned by the wizard from the collection of dying minds of Eumenix. Space Marines had visited his world – probably to find out what was happening on the planet. He saw them sprinting across one of the spaceports in Hive Quintus, swapping fire with the desperate citizens of the hive as they headed for the last off-world shuttle. They had fled like frightened children when they had seen the scale of death – such was Teturact's power he could even send the vaunted Space Marines running.

How long until my arrival? he asked.

'The warp looks on you with favour, my lord. Seven days more and we will return to real space.'

Good. Make them seven days of very particular suffering.

The wizards bowed as one. Then one of their number shambled forwards. It was a horribly misshapen, bloated creature with a bundle of dripping tentacles where its face had once been. The wizards began to chant, a low, atonal drone that filled their air with the sound of a billion plague-flies. The wizard's body opened up, it was a hideous tentacled maw of miscoloured flesh, with internal organs pulsing. A thousand eyes were set into its innards and they rolled madly, seeing across the warp all the way to the depths of Eumenix.

As the wizards worked their magic, Teturact could see the images the central wizard projected. Endless layers of hive were knee-deep in gore. The dead had risen and were wandering, waiting for a purpose. The view panned across battlefields where factions fought in the vain hope of securing supplies or transport, or just to give voice to their horror through combat.

The wizards drew more and more dead from their graves. Whole mounds of mouldering bodies writhed like nests of worms as the corpses dug their way out. In the barren toxic wastes between the hives, nomads watched in horror as columns of the dead marched from the cities. Soon there would be no trace of life left on the planet to spoil the pure magnificence of death.

For a moment, Teturact could feel the whole planet simultaneously, projected into his mind through the wizards. It was a beautiful thing – it was as if the whole of Eumenix was composed entirely of suffering and fear, an imprint so intense that it still drove the walking dead to prey on one another in desperation. He had seen a hundred worlds reduced to such a state, but it still filled him with pride.

The images faded as the wizards finished waking all the dead they could muster. Eumenix seethed to new levels of horror as it disappeared from Teturact's mind, and its aftertaste was like pure victory.

Teturact mentally ordered his bearers to take him back to his quarters to wait out the rest of the journey. There was much to contemplate before he became the god of yet another world.

THE INQUISITORIAL FORTRESS on Caitaran would, in saner days, have served to coordinate the efforts of the Ordo Hereticus for several sectors around, so the ordo could effectively face threats that spanned worlds and systems. But now it formed the wartime headquarters of the Inquisitorial effort against

Teturact, with a quarantined halo around it. It was now the gathering point for information submitted by inquisitors and their agents throughout the warzone.

Lord Inquisitor Kolgo had assumed overall authority, having rose to high favour after coordinating the Lastrati Pogrom decades before. Up to three hundred inquisitors and interrogators answered directly to him and his staff, with many more forming a secret network even the Inquisition itself could not unravel.

Many were embedded in the Imperial Guard units sent to claim back disputed worlds; others tried to determine which planets would be the next to fall. Some were even reporting back from worlds that now belonged to Teturact. They sent brief transmissions hinting at unimaginable horror, of the building-sized piles of corpses and plagues that rotted men's minds. The Ordo Malleus searched for daemons and the taint of Chaos amongst the thousands of reports from across the warzone. Even the Ordo Xenos, whose authority extended to the activities of aliens within the Imperium, examined the possibilities of xenos technology in Teturact's methods.

The Inquisitorial fortress was carved into the peak of the tallest mountain on Caitaran, so high the clouds rolled past below the fortress's spaceport. It was a remnant of a civilisation the Imperium had absorbed thousands of years before. It had been a martial society with kings, lords and barons, one of whom had expended untold fortunes to carve an impregnable palace from the mountains that no army could take. He was right – no invader took its walls, but the Imperium dropped a virus bomb on it when he refused to pay fealty to the explorator units that arrived on Caitaran when the world was on the frontier of Imperial space. The planet fell almost overnight once word spread that the fortress was now protected only by a legion of corpses.

It was a good story, the sort told to initiates in the Adeptus Terra about how a concentration of effort on one selected target could do more than a massive assault on all fronts. Perhaps it was even true, and it was certainly relevant here – the majority of the Inquisitorial effort was devoted to locating Teturact and killing him so that, just like the indigenous primitives of Caitaran, the empire of pestilence would crumble in short order. Unfortunately no one knew who, what or where Teturact might be, let alone what might kill him.

Strictly speaking, it wasn't Thaddeus's problem. He was lucky Lord Inquisitor Kolgo had given him use of the facilities on Caitaran. Thaddeus had little more than pure instinct to suggest that the Soul Drinkers might be in the warzone, or at least heading for it. The Soul Drinkers had been on Eumenix, of that there was little doubt, but Eumenix had only recently become off-limits through the plague and there wasn't even definite proof that Teturact was involved – worlds had fallen to disease before without agents of Chaos being responsible.

But it made a strange sort of sense in Thaddeus's trained mind. The Soul Drinkers might even be serving Teturact. But perhaps it was more complicated than that since the forces of Chaos fought one another as often as they fought the Imperium. Though the Soul Drinkers could be anywhere, there seemed a likelihood that they were tangled in the hideous mess of Teturact's fledgling empire. So that was where Thaddeus would look for them.

Thaddeus would soon try to push his luck by receiving an audience with Lord Inquisitor Kolgo himself. But for the moment, he was just trying to eke some comfort out of the quarters the fortress staff had given him. The outer parts of the fortress had not been modernised and the mountain cold blew through them with little resistance. The furnishings were sparse and the floor freezing. The view across the mountains was extraordinary, though, and Thaddeus had been lucky to requisition quarters for himself. The storm troopers and Sisters were in the spaceport barracks, and he had obtained an infirmary suite in which he could examine what Sister Aescarion had brought back from Eumenix.

It had been six months since he had landed on Koris XXIII-3, believing that he had run out of leads on the Soul Drinkers. Now he had part of one of their corpses, and the chalice symbol on the dead

Marine's pistol was testimony to his allegiance. Along with the reports from the survivors at House Jenassis, he had found the first concrete proof of the Chapter's activities since the Cerberian Field. To find it, he had paid with the life of Interrogator Shen and several dozen Arbites at House Jenassis. The inquisitor in him said that the trade had been worth it – he was surprised to find that the man in him agreed.

Thaddeus opened up the trunk at the foot of the chamber's four-poster bed. Inside was the meagre collection of hard evidence he had accumulated – a datacube and viewer containing a copy of the pict-file from the *Brokenback*, a charred volume of Daenyathos's *Catechisms Martial* salvaged from the Soul Drinkers' scuttled fleet, and data-slates containing transcripts of witness interviews. The bolt pistol lay on top in its holster.

Thaddeus picked it up – the weapon was so huge Thaddeus could only hold it in two hands, but a Space Marine carried it as a sidearm. It had an ammunition selector and twin magazines, and its casing was chased in gold. The chalice symbol of the Soul Drinkers was stamped on the handle.

'A fine weapon,' said a grimly familiar, grating voice. 'Terrible that it should be used for such evil.'

Thaddeus looked round to see the Pilgrim entering the chamber. Instantly the bare stone of the room seemed to darken and the air became even colder. The Pilgrim bore such strong determination to see the enemies of the Emperor dead, that its hate infected everything around it.

'The medicae are ready,' the Pilgrim said, and left the room. Thaddeus dropped the pistol back in the trunk, and followed.

THE OFFICIO MEDICAE personnel stationed at the Caitaran fortress had been seconded to the Inquisition to study the various plagues that sprung up wherever Teturact cast his gaze. Thaddeus had secured the services of the Medicae pathology team consisting of two orderlies and an Adeptus Mechanicus Biologis adept. These individuals were waiting in the small infirmary when Thaddeus and the Pilgrim arrived, the faceless orderlies standing as if to attention. The adept – a stocky middle-aged woman with a very serious face and wearing a white lab suit – stood with folded arms at the head of the slab of polished granite that served as an operation table. There was a Space Marine's battered head lying on it like an offering on an altar.

'I apologise for the delay, inquisitor,' said the adept in a clipped, no-nonsense voice. 'We had to ensure the specimen was fully irradiated and quarantined.'

'Understood, adept. May we begin?'

'Certainly. The specimen is of an oversized male humanoid cranium, partially fleshed, severed at the axis vertebra…'

Thaddeus watched as the orderlies took scalpels and forceps from the implement trays by the side of the slab and began to pare away the rotten flesh from the skull. The adept recited the initial findings, confirming that the head was from a Space Marine and a veteran at that, judging by the single silver long service stud in the forehead. The bones of the face and cranium were scored with old scars from blades and bullets, and a bullet wound that had blown a chunk from the forehead had evidently been caused after death. The adept had the orderlies reveal tell-tale implanted organs: larraman's ear – the inner and middle ear enhancement that gave a Marine sharper hearing and perfect balance. The occulobe – the organ that sat behind the eyes and gave the Marine a heightened sense of sight. The remains of the gene-seed in the throat – the sacred organ that controlled all the Marine's other enhancements and bolstered his metabolism.

'The state of the specimen suggests accelerated decomposition followed by a suspension of natural decay, similar to other specimens recovered from worlds within the disputed systems around Stratix.'

An orderly turned the head onto its side and began to remove the jaw. He struggled to break the strengthened bone around the joint.

With a snap the jaw gave way, and like a fountain, a thin jet of glittering liquid arced onto the front of the orderly's smock.

The orderly began to scream as the liquid burned through the smock and into his chest. The other orderly pushed him to the floor and began to tear off the burning clothes as an eye-watering acid smell filled the air and grey smoke coiled upwards. The adept grabbed an emergency medikit from one of the infirmary's wall cabinets and began to work on the orderly, washing down the hissing wounds with an alkali solution before it ate into his lungs.

'Inquisitor, you must leave,' said the adept sharply as she pulled a field dressing from the kit. 'We have possible contamination.'

'There is no contamination,' said the Pilgrim, its grating voice cutting through the orderly's gasping for air. 'The acid is a weak solution designed only to blind; your man will survive. It is produced by the Betcher's gland.'

'That's impossible,' said Thaddeus, watching the trail of greenish liquid spluttering on the granite surface. 'The Soul Drinkers are a successor Chapter of the Imperial Fists Legion. The Fists' gene-seed never allowed Betcher's gland to develop, it was only a vestigial organ.'

'Exactly,' said the Pilgrim, reaching towards the dissected head with a bandaged hand. It plucked the scrap of knotted flesh, the gene-seed, from the throat. 'Corrupt,' he said, holding up the gene-seed. It was mottled and discoloured. 'The Soul Drinkers carry the stain of mutation upon them. The gravest mutation of all, for their very gene-seed is degenerating and the organs implanted in them are themselves being changed.'

'Mutation,' repeated Thaddeus.

The survivors from House Jenassis had reported a monstrous creature leading the Soul Drinkers, with legs like a giant spider and vast psychic powers. He had been sceptical about such talk, but now he could not dismiss the image so easily. The Soul Drinkers were mutants, and with their gene-seed affected they would slide downhill fast.

That made them desperate. And desperation bred atrocity. Whatever their plans, the Soul Drinkers were heading faster and faster towards a state where they were mutated beyond all semblance of humanity.

Thaddeus had always known that his patience would have its limits. But now time had suddenly begun to press on him more strongly. Everyone was running out of time.

And Thaddeus had next to nothing to go on. But he would have to make it do.

He left the infirmary at a jog, heading towards his chambers through the cold, draughty stone corridors of the fortress. He heard the Pilgrim following him but had lost the strange creature by the time he reached his room. He flung open the chest again and pulled out another piece of evidence. It was something he had thought useless when Sister Aescarion had presented it to him – a thin brass plaque with the names of hundreds of adepts tooled into it, the adepts who had worked at the Hive Quintus outpost for the last few decades. There were hundreds of names in tiny, precise type, from the overseers of the menials and servitor engineers to the series of adepts senioris who had commanded the outpost.

The Pilgrim arrived at the door. 'Inquisitor? You have found something?'

Thaddeus looked round. He wished very much that he could have conducted this investigation without the Pilgrim, but he had to tolerate the creature for the insights it had into the renegade Chapter.

'Perhaps,' he replied. 'The Soul Drinkers were at the outpost for a reason. They left at least one of their own behind. Why? Why go to a planet consumed by plague, and journey into the heart of its worst city to fight a battle? Why break into a Mechanicus outpost that produced nothing of any real interest or importance? The rock samples were worth nothing. They had no specialised equipment or weapons. What *did* they have, Pilgrim?'

The Pilgrim tilted its head slightly, and Thaddeus had an unpleasant feeling that it might be smiling somewhere under there. 'They had people, inquisitor. A hundred Mechanicus adepts. Adepts who had not always worked at that one outpost.'

Thaddeus sat back onto his bed, still holding the plaque. 'One of them knew something. And it was enough for the Soul Drinkers to go down there and capture them. If they took a prisoner and got them off the planet they could have everything they need to know.'

Thaddeus stopped. The Imperium was so immensely vast, and the Adeptus Mechanicus such an insanely complicated organisation – from the Fabricator General on Mars to the lowliest menials and servitors labouring on forge worlds and in workshops across the known galaxy. How could he ever hope to track a single adept, even with the resources of an inquisitor? One tiny, meaningless worker who was no Chaos cultist or rogue secessionist, but a nobody in a galaxy of nobodies?

'No,' he said out loud to himself. 'I'm not letting this lead slip.' He flicked on the vox-bead on his collar. 'Colonel Vinn? Assemble your best infiltrators and scouts, ready for review at the spaceport in half an hour. See what you can do about commandeering us a shuttle for loading into the *Crescent*, it doesn't need much range but it will need stealth and assault capabilities. The best crew, too. Pull strings if you have to. Out.'

Thaddeus had not been in the warzone sector for long, but had done basic research into the sector's power structures. He knew that the information he needed might just be available if he was fast, skilled and lucky. It had been some time since he had last used a weapon in execution of his duty as an inquisitor, and he was mildly surprised to find that he was looking forward to doing so again.

SIX

It was quiet to the galactic west, a wasteland tract of space where few but hardy prospectors and driven missionaries bothered to go. The thick band of stars that marked out the galactic disk was empty for light years ahead, and pilot second class Maesus KinShao knew that without staging posts or space-ports there was little chance of an assault coming from that direction. But it was his duty to be here – he was a servant of the Emperor cocooned in the cockpit of his Scapula-class deep space fighter, a member of a squadron with orders to defend the western frontier of the warzone.

The Scapula had a six-man crew – KinShao, a navigator, three weapons officers and an engineer. There were seventy such craft spread out across this section of the frontier, each armed with sophisticated intruder detection sensors and a bellyful of ordnance.

KinShao called up the HUD screen to show an overview of his squadron's positions. Twenty fighters, each the size of a small cargo ship, hung in space with their sensor fields overlapping so nothing could get through. If any craft tried to escape from the warzone, or to break into it, the craft would be spotted and challenged. If it was remotely suspicious, it would be destroyed with a hail of guided munitions. The Scapulas were some of the most complex and valuable assault craft the sector naval command could muster, and KinShao loved the feeling of the massive metal structure all around with him. For now, though, everything was quiet, and the blazing war a few light hours to the galactic east seemed much further away.

'Squadron, sound in,' came the crackly voice of the squadron commander over the comms. The commander was young and aristocratic, but he seemed solid enough. KinShao hadn't flown under him in anger yet.

'KinShao, red seven. What's the problem?'

'Blue five is reading anomalies. Anything else on anyone's scopes?'

KinShao relayed the communication to his navigator, Shass.

'Nothing here,' she replied. 'All dead.'

'Keep alert, squadron,' said the commander, and signed off.

'You don't want to lose your nerve out here,' said Korgen from in the missile control pit amidships. 'Blue five had better not be getting the jitters. I've seen it happen, and when you can't think straight in deep space they blow you up just to be safe.'

'Stow it, Korgen,' said KinShao. Korgen had been a weapons man on deep spacers for decades, and had seen firefights at Patroclus Gate and St. Jowens's Dock that KinShao (though he wouldn't admit it) never tired hearing about. But he was also full of portentous stories of how crews went mad in deep space, light years from any support craft and with only their fellow crews for company.

'Wait, wait,' crackled another voice on the all-craft channel. 'This is red five. I've got something too.'

Red five's navigator was the squadron's best. He wouldn't have his captain jumping at ghosts.

'It's a small signature,' continued red five's pilot. 'Probably just junk. But it's emitting something, could be a rogue satellite or–'

A thin film of static, then silence.

'Red five?' came the commander's stern voice, as if admonishing red five for disappearing. 'Come in red five.'

KinShao kicked the ship's systems into combat alert almost as a reflex. 'Korgen, stand by to get me targets. Lovred, I want intercept speed on my mark.' Somewhere in the stern Lovred, the ship's engineer, would be readying the Scapula's engines to burst into intercept speed.

'Red five is off the map,' said Shass from the navigator's helm beneath the cockpit, with almost improper calm.

'Visual!' cried a voice on the squadron channel, 'I've got vis–'

'Blue ten's gone,' said Shass.

'Targets, Korgen, get me targets! Waist gunners, are you charged?'

'Check,' said a voice in one ear from the Scapula's starboard pulse laser battery. 'Check two,' said another in the other ear, from the port guns.

'I've got nothing,' said Shass. 'Just the remains of red five.'

There was a terrible pause. Pilots gabbled on all channels and the commander's voice tried to cut through it all and organise a proper sensor sweep as Scapulas disappeared one by one.

'Wait,' said Shass. 'Red five, it's moving.'

'Fire! Full spread!' yelled KinShao, and the fighter juddered around him like a bucking horse. Korgen sent half the fighter's missile payload in a glittering stream towards something that looked like red five's remains on the scanners. But it was moving towards KinShao's red seven faster than intercept speed.

Then he saw it. Lancing from the velvet black of space: a dart of silver that trailed a spray of stars. It rippled like mercury, shifted shape and widened, and a score of pure white laser bolts spat from the front edge of its glistening wings.

Red seven lurched and KinShao knew right away it was a hull breach. The artificial gravity kicked out of kilter and KinShao felt himself pressed against one side of his restraints.

'Count off! Damage report!'

'Nav, OK,' said Shass.

'Engineering, OK.'

'Ordnance, OK.'

'Gunnery? Gunnery sound off!' KinShao realised he was shouting. The silver streak flashed past, leaving a searing afterimage against the blackness of space.

'The shot took us amidships,' said Korgen. 'Waist guns gone.'

'I've got a target. It's faster than us. It's turning back to finish us,' said Shass.

'Korgen, give me everything. Short fuse, I want us screened.'

Korgen emptied most of the remaining torpedoes into space, their fuses cut so they detonated in a spread in front of the Scapula. A screen of electromagnetic radiation and debris was thrown up between red seven and the intruder, enough to screen the fighter from any attacker of Imperial-equivalent technology.

But the attacking fighter could see them. It darted up to red seven and stopped impossibly suddenly, hanging in space right in front of KinShao's cockpit.

It was a shard of liquid metal with sharp edges that rapidly flowed into one another, reconfiguring the whole fighter. It was probably smaller than the Scapula but its highly reflective liquid surface shone so brightly it seemed to fill KinShao's sight completely. A dark slit towards the ship's knife-like prow looked in onto the bridge but KinShao couldn't make out anything inside. He was almost completely dazzled by the light, and the graceful effect of its delta wings folding in on themselves to become multiple fins rippling along the fighter's hull.

KinShao kicked the Scapula's retros on, but the engines were still geared to intercept speed. Too late he realised his mistake and the Scapula lurched forward before its retros could take effect. The screen of debris pummelled red seven's hull and billowed an brief orange flame across the viewscreen.

A storm of light ripped through the Scapula. KinShao could see the pure white lances as they seared past the cockpit. He could feel them tear through the hull as if it wasn't there. A booming sound was followed by a sharp silence, that told him the ship's midsection had explosively decompressed. Korgen was dead, probably the engineer, too.

Smoke and the chemical stink of burning plastics filled the cockpit, and heat billowed up from beneath. Shass was probably dead, too, incinerated down there.

The engines collapsed with a crump that washed through the Scapula's superstructure and the fighter lurched backwards as the retros gained a purchase. KinShao could see the enemy fighter wheeling, its body flattening like a manta ray's as it swam through the void, bolts of light spitting from it in an incandescent spray.

Every warning light on the instrument panel lit up. KinShao knew he was going to die, but the screaming sirens and roaring heat around him seemed to blot out any panic. He jammed his thumb onto the manual fire control and the twin gatlings spattered gunfire from beneath the Scapula's nose. They wouldn't hit and they didn't have the range, but KinShao had to go down fighting.

Warning lights winked in desperation. One of them was for the saviour pod behind the cockpit that KinShao was supposed to use if the Scapula was lost. The heat around his feet was unbearable, and flames licked from the instrument panels. The viewscreen started to blacken.

The silver wings rippled again as the fighter wheeled around and twin dark eyes opened up in its leading edge. Bolts of silver lightning burst from the apertures and punched through the cockpit of red seven, spitting the Scapula on a lance of light.

THE CONTROLS AROUND Sarpedon's hands squirmed as he sent fire ripping from the fighter's primary weapons, and punched ragged holes through the wounded craft in front of him.

The cold liquid metal seeped into his gauntlets and connected him with the ship. He only had to think and the fighter's weapons would fill the void with bolts of laser and plasma. The craft in front – a deep-space fighter, part of a cordon around one of the warzone's quieter frontiers – came apart in a blossom of shimmering debris. Sarpedon's fighter flew right through the clouds of wreckage; the fighter's liquid surface absorbing the thousands of impacts.

Beside Sarpedon two serfs still held the flight controls. But Sarpedon had taken over the weapons helm himself – none of the serfs understood weaponry and destruction like a Marine who had been a warrior for more than seventy years.

Karraidin's ship had gone in first and taken out three of the fighters. Sarpedon's had just destroyed two more. The deep space fighters seemed unwieldy compared to the Soul Drinkers' alien fighter fleet, even though the Scapula-class were actually highly sophisticated by Imperial standards. It was a sign of how much the Imperium had stagnated – the development of their technology had slowed to a crawl. Soon it would be at a standstill and its enemies would race past it, conquering and burning.

Sarpedon called up the fleet display. The ten Soul Drinkers' fighters had got through unscathed and had left the cordon well behind them. Sergeant Luko's ship, with the infirmary and Chaplain Iktinos on board, was safe in the middle of the formation since it carried the prisoner Sarkia Aristeia. The fighter at the rear was captained by Tyrendian, one of the Chapter's few remaining Librarians, apart from Sarpedon. His ship flew through fields of spinning debris and never took a shot.

Sarpedon always felt a faint pang of remorse when he was forced to take the lives of Imperial citizens. He had even felt it when Phrantis Jenassis died. The tragedy of the Imperium wasn't that it provided a breeding ground for the galaxy's evils – it was that the untold billions of people locked in its authority fought as if it was their only salvation. The people were the Imperium, and if they could only understand the error of that tyranny they could dissolve it overnight and make it into something that could truly eradicate the darkness of Chaos. But they could not. People were too blind to look beyond what surrounded them. Sarpedon himself, and every single Soul Drinker, had once been the most fervent defenders of the Imperium, believing its existence to be part of the Emperor's great plan to shepherd humanity towards something better.

But in truth the Emperor hated corruption, sin, and Chaos, and all those things were made possible by the Imperium. That was why the Emperor had given the Soul Drinkers a chance of redemption. They answered to no one but him, and Sarpedon knew that he wanted nothing more from them than to fight Chaos wherever they found it. Perhaps the

Emperor was dead and was now no more than an idea – but that idea was still worth fighting for. And fighting was all the Soul Drinkers could do.

But the Soul Drinkers had to survive. And that was the purpose of this mission – survival. It seemed a petty thing alongside the war against Chaos, but it had to be done before the Emperor's commands could be fulfilled.

The alien fleet slipped through the void, leaving behind a squadron of vaporised fighters. Silently they slid into the Stratix warzone, into that place of death on a mission of survival.

LORD INQUISITOR KOLGO was an old man. It was all but impossible to rise to any position of authority within the Inquisition without having weathered decades of persecuting the Emperor's foes. Kolgo's rise within the Ordo Hereticus had taken a relatively short time – about eighty years.

Lord Inquisitor Kolgo was like a giant of a man, wearing the impossibly ornate ceremonial power armour that rivalled the Terminator armour of the Space Marines in size. Gilded angels danced across the barrel-like chest plate of ceramite. A power fist adorned each massive arm, with litanies of faith on the knuckles to symbolise how faith itself destroyed the Emperor's enemies, not simple raw strength. Sculpted friezes on each shoulder depicted infidels crushed beneath the boots of crusading knights. Red purity seals studded the armoured limbs, trailing ribbons of parchment inscribed with prayers.

Lord Kolgo's face, with nut-brown wrinkled skin and tiny inquisitive eyes, seemed utterly out of place on such a gilded monster. But the armour was the ceremonial garb of the lord inquisitor of the Stratix sector, and Kolgo could hardly hold audience without it.

At that moment he was giving an audience to one Inquisitor Thaddeus, in relative terms not long out of his interrogator training. It was something of a stretch for the man to have asked for an audience at all, since he was not directly involved with the warzone effort to which Kolgo had dedicated his waking hours. The circular audience chamber with its deep scarlet carpet and oppressively huge chandeliers was designed to remind everyone of Kolgo's authority, but to his credit Thaddeus didn't seem to be cowed by Kolgo's presence.

'Inquisitor Thaddeus,' began Kolgo. 'You understand that, given our current situation, I cannot allocate any real resources to you. It is fortunate that there is enough room in this fortress for you and your staff.'

'I understand,' replied Thaddeus. 'But my mission does intersect with yours. The Soul Drinkers may well be in league with Chaos, and a renegade Chapter in the employ of the enemy would be a major factor in Teturact's favour. The Soul Drinkers' presence within the Stratix warzone is surely a matter of some concern.'

'Perhaps you are right. But you must understand my priorities. Teturact has killed billions already, and if we do not maintain our focus on destroying him the sector may be lost for good.'

'The favour I have to ask you, lord inquisitor, is not a great one.' Thaddeus was following the correct form for an audience with a lord, but he was not obsequious. Kolgo was quietly impressed. 'My staff and I are very close indeed to cornering the Soul Drinkers. What I need now is information. The Adeptus Mechanicus will have records of all their staff members that were on the outpost on Eumenix when the Soul Drinkers attacked…'

Kolgo held up a hand, the massive power fist whirring with servos. 'What you ask I cannot deliver.'

'But my lord, the Mechanicus must bow to your authority. It is not much that I ask. I regret only that my own authority does not stretch as far as to force the hand of the archmagi. If I could learn what I needed by myself I would have gladly done so, but your word carries far more weight than mine so I must ask that you do this for our mutual good.'

Kolgo sighed, as if weary. 'Thaddeus, the Mechanicus supply the ordinatus which inquisitors under my remit will use to destroy the targets they identify. The Mechanicus maintain our ships and the weapons we carry. Most importantly, it is their magi biologis who are being used by us to examine all aspects of the plague and the horrors that follow them. This operation requires closer cooperation with the Adeptus Mechanicus than any I have commanded before.

'When this Inquisitorial command was formed, I had to ensure that cooperation would not fail. Archmagos Ultima Cryol met with me to confirm that we would do all we could to help one another. He promised me the ordinatus, weapons and support we desperately needed. I promised him in return that the forge worlds of Sadlyen Falls XXI, Themiscyra Beta and Salshan Anterior would not fall to Teturact.

'Salshan Anterior is already gone. We believe its servitor stocks were infected and were scrapped rather than incinerated – they returned to life, rose up and killed every living thing on the planet. This is bad enough, I am having to make concessions I cannot afford just to keep Inquisitorial warships in space. But Themiscyra Beta is showing signs of infection, too. I have flooded the place with inquisitors and their staff, but they cannot find the source of the infection and are having precious little success in stopping its spread. You understand, Thaddeus, that I simply cannot ask for any more favours from the Mechanicus.'

Thaddeus shook his head, more sad than angry. 'Lord Kolgo, we are so close. The Soul Drinkers are a step ahead of us but I could stop them if I could

only pre-empt their next move. I could do that with
your help. If we could get the Mechanicus to allow
me just a few minutes' access to their databases...'

'Thaddeus, if what you want is information con-
cerning Eumenix then it is more difficult than that.
Eumenix would have fallen under the jurisdiction
of the subsector command on Salshan Anterior,
which is impossible to access if indeed it even exists
any more. The only repository for the information
you seek will be the Mechanicus sector command
itself, and the archmagos ultima considers the
information it contains to be a sacred relic. At the
best of times it could take years of politicking to get
an inquisitor inside. As you are no doubt aware,
these are not the best of times.'

Thaddeus was silent for a moment. Then, he
spread his hands as if utterly resigned. 'I fear, then,
that I will have to look for some other way to find
the Soul Drinkers. I appreciate your audience, Lord
Kolgo. It has taught me a great deal that I did not
expect to learn.'

'I am a politician, Thaddeus. I accepted that role
when I took the title of lord inquisitor. It is my task
to ensure that the holy orders of the Emperor's
Inquisition are able to do their jobs, and sometimes
that requires some reciprocity. I have the authority
to have Archmagos Ultima Cryol executed and the
Mechanicus command raided for the information
you need, but then who would repair the warp
engines on our ships? Who would find us a cure for

Teturact's plagues? It is this cooperation that holds the Imperium together, Thaddeus. If you are lucky you will never have to deal with it, but someone must and that someone in this instance is me. I wish you the best of luck, inquisitor. Continue with the Emperor's work.'

Thaddeus bowed slightly, and turned to leave.

'I do hope,' added Kolgo, 'that you are not planning on doing anything rash.'

'I would not dream of it, Lord Kolgo. You have made your position clear, and it is my duty to see that your commands are respected.'

Thaddeus left the audience chamber, head held a touch too high. Kolgo smiled and considered how Thaddeus had a great future ahead of him, if he survived.

SARKIA ARISTEIA WAS forty-three years old. She had been born in the hives of Methalor, a dark, hot place where generations lived out pointless lives in machine shops or sank into the nightmare of the underhive. Sarkia broke out. She had a keen mind and a keener sense of duty. The Imperium needed every single nut and bolt that Methalor produced, but Sarkia could do more for her Emperor. She was quietly religious, intelligent, and terrified of a life of mediocrity. She needed the Adeptus Mechanicus as much as they needed her, and recruits like her.

Sarkia was taken in by the temple of the Machine-God on Methalor and told the first truths about the Omnissiah, the spirit that permeated all machinery whose thoughts were pure logic and whose worship was the gathering of knowledge. She made a competent and useful adept, and by the time she had been transferred to the Stratix sector she was considered a potential tech-priest, on the verge of completing her apprenticeship as an adept inferior.

Then she had been given a post on the research outpost on Stratix Luminae, a tiny cold planetoid barely even visible above the dockyards of Stratix itself. The work suited her; it was away from the immense masses of humanity, and from here she could begin to believe that she was a part of something meaningful. In the rarified environment of the labs she could achieve something that would have some impact on the Imperium. She began to touch on the mysteries of the Omnissiah, and the religious power of unadulterated knowledge gained for its own sake.

Then the eldar marauders had made a daring raid into the Stratix system, running the gauntlet of the sector battlefleets in a cycle of attack and flight that seemed closer to a game than to war. The eldar, in their lighting-quick ships that sailed the solar winds, chose Stratix Luminae for the next round of their game. But this time, the Soul Drinkers Space Marines were in their way. The distress signal from Stratix Luminae found a Soul Drinkers strike cruiser at Stratix for repairs and the result was the mission which had been recorded in corrupted, incomplete files in the Chapter archives.

Sarkia Aristeia had lived through the eldar raid and the brutal reply by the Soul Drinkers. She had seen what had happened at Stratix Luminae and the horrors that followed it. Then, along with the few other survivors she had been granted a quiet posting at Eumenix. She had seen Eumenix die, too, die screaming around her until the same purple-armoured warriors of the decade before came and whisked her away. It was no wonder she had been found near-catatonic with fear and shock.

The room set aside for her interrogation had been made as comfortable as possible. The walls were draped in fabric to cover up the strange alien architecture. She had been given fresh clothes – loose-fitting Chapter serf garb, but at least it was clean. Pallas had examined her and fed her intravenously until her health was recovered and her cheeks less hollow. But she was still on an alien spacecraft, about to be interrogated. And it was still Chaplain Iktinos who was doing the interrogating.

Iktinos, as a guardian of the Chapter's faith and spiritual strength, had been at the heart of the Chapter war when Sarpedon led the Soul Drinkers away from the Imperium. He had sided with Sarpedon, for he had witnessed the treachery of which the Imperium was capable and watched as Sarpedon defeated Chapter Master Gorgoleon in ritual combat. The terrible events of the Chapter war had been orchestrated by the Daemon Prince Abraxes who had nearly turned the Soul Drinkers over to the purpose of Chaos – but the Soul Drinkers' faith had held nonetheless. Iktinos was one of the reasons. Even when doubt had been sown in the heart of every Marine, Iktinos had remained resolute. The Chapter followed the Emperor, not the Imperium, partly because of Iktinos's spiritual leadership.

He was sitting across a table from Sarkia Aristeia, dwarfing the woman completely. All Space Marines were intimidating to a normal human – and a chaplain's black armour and skull-faced helmet were more intimidating than most. Sarpedon watched from the shadows beyond the drapery and wondered if Sarkia was too deep in shock to be useful. Could anyone open up to an armoured monster like Iktinos? If Sarkia were to see Sarpedon it would probably kill her, but the skull-faced chaplain couldn't have been much better.

Iktinos reached up and released the collar catches on his helmet. He lifted it off his head and felt the breath of stale spacecraft air on his face for the first time in days. He hardly ever removed his helmet, and never in front of witnesses. Faith should be faceless and the battle-brothers should consider him the Emperor's hand guiding them, not a human being. Sarpedon had very rarely seen Iktinos's face, and it surprised him to see it now.

His face was the colour of dark polished wood. It was slim and open compared to most Marines, with large dark eyes, and was completely hairless. There were two silver studs in his forehead and two ebony studs, to represent twenty years of service as a battle-brother and twenty as a chaplain. Faith and confidence seemed to radiate from him, and Sarpedon understood why he kept his face covered. He wore the skull-helmet because he wanted the battle-brothers to follow him as a faceless icon of faith, not as a man. He could have been a charismatic leader, but that was not his job. He was there to guard the souls of the brethren – the leadership he left to Sarpedon.

'Sarkia,' said Iktinos in a deep, sonorous voice that was normally a mechanical drone inside his helmet. 'You understand why we have brought you here.'

Sarkia was silent for a moment. 'Stratix Luminae,' she said quietly.

'Ten years ago my battle-brothers came to your lab on Stratix Luminae. Now we need to go back there, and we need to go soon. You were an adept, you had access to the upper levels. We need that access.'

Sarkia shook her head. 'No, that was ten years ago…'

'The Stratix Luminae lab was abandoned. You know that. Everything will be the same. We know what happened afterwards, Sarkia. There would have been no recovery teams sent. The same protocols that you knew will still work today and we need to know them.'

'Why?' Sarkia looked up suddenly, right into Iktinos's eyes. 'Why would anyone want to go back there?'

'We have no choice and neither do you.'

'It won't be enough. I was just an adept, only the magi knew how to get onto the containment levels and they never came out. We never saw them, we didn't even know a fraction of what they were doing down there. I'm useless, don't you understand? I only know the upper support and lab levels, there's nothing there…'

'We know all we need to, Sarkia. Just tell us, and when this is over, you will go free.'

Sarkia choked back a sob. 'You're renegades. You'll kill me.'

'You don't know what we are. At the moment the only thing you have is my word as a soldier of the Emperor. Tell us what we need to know and you will eventually go free.'

Sarkia shrugged. 'I am going to die. Stratix Luminae will kill you, too.' She paused, staring at the table. 'The grids are keyed to phrases from the revelations of the Omnissiah. There's a copy in every workshop and laboratory. There's an algorithm that'll pick out the code words, I can write it down. That'll open up the first level. The hot zone you'll have to get through yourselves.'

'You have been very helpful, Sarkia.'

She smiled bitterly. 'Are you trying to be comforting? You're a monster. You all are. You can't make this any easier. You're going to kill me, Marine.'

'You can call me Iktinos.'

'I won't call you anything. I've only told you what I have so you won't have to break me for it, now I'm worth nothing to you. I'll be lucky if you just throw me out of an airlock.'

Iktinos stood up and picked up his rictus-faced helmet from the table. 'I say again, Sarkia, you have my word that when our work is done you will be freed. We have no interest in harming you. If we were still at the beck and call of the Imperium we would probably be required to hand you over for mindwiping. But we do not play that game any more.'

Iktinos strode out of the room, leaving Sarkia at the table. In a while the serfs would bring her something to eat and drink, and show her to the bunk that had been squeezed into one of the corridors they were using as a dormitory.

To anyone else, the successful questioning would have been a triumph. But Sarpedon was all too aware of the further risks the Chapter would have to take to survive, let alone succeed. In many ways it would have been a relief if Sarkia had known nothing. At least he would be able to banish any hope, and direct the Chapter's efforts elsewhere. Instead, Sarkia had just opened the gate for the Chapter to head into the heart of corruption and face both the horrors of Teturact's empire and the wrath of the Imperium. It would almost have been better if Sarkia had never been found, but Sarpedon had to lead his Chapter to do the Emperor's work, no matter what the risks.

Sarpedon watched her for a moment. She wasn't crying or trembling. She just looked very tired, and he imagined that facing up to an alien environment and the very real possibility of interrogation and death had been draining for her.

Sometimes, Sarpedon thought, watching unaugmented humans was like observing members of a different species. The Soul Drinkers were so isolated from the Imperium that the only normal humans Sarpedon saw regularly were the Chapter serfs: men and women so conditioned and loyal that they were more like intelligent servitors than people. Sarkia was Sarpedon's only contact with an Imperial citizen for a very long time apart from the short-lived Phrantis Jenassis, and no matter how curious he was about her he could not speak to her himself because she would probably go insane at the sight of him.

Sarpedon walked away from the shadows back towards the bridge, leaving Sarkia to the Chapter serfs. If she heard the talons of his arachnoid legs clattering on the metallic floor, she didn't look up.

ONE OF THE things that Thaddeus had begun to notice was that the Soul Drinkers were becoming officially nonexistent. His requests for astropathic traffic monitoring had been more and more difficult to implement, even when he brandished the small Inquisitorial symbol that carried the weight of immense authority. The warzone had been divided into military administration zones so the Departmento Munitorum could have a hope of wrestling with the logistics of such an immense operation, and Thaddeus had ordered alerts if astropathic transmissions were made with certain keywords – Astartes, renegade Marines, purple, spider, psychic and dozens of others. But there were several sectors that had not cooperated as Thaddeus had expected.

Imperial monitoring was impossible in areas completely controlled by Teturact, such as the space around Stratix that had been designated target sector primary, so Thaddeus could not expect much reply from the scattered recon ships and Inquisitorial operatives skulking between the plague worlds. But the Septiam-Calliargan sector had replied to Thaddeus's requests with red tape and misdirection. Aggarendon Nebula sector hadn't replied at all, yet there was little military activity around the nebula's scattered mining worlds. Subsector Caitaran, a tiny tract of space but one that included the Inquisition fortress and several Imperial Guard command flotillas, was worst of all: the communications Thaddeus received from the astropathic monitoring stations seemed stilted and contrived, and he had little doubt they were doctored.

That was only one symptom. Thaddeus's previous attempts to access historical records from worlds the Soul Drinkers had once fought on had yielded no information at all about the Chapter. The cathedral of heroes on Mortenken's World, for instance, no longer held the carved stone mural depicting Daenyathos, the Soul Drinkers' legendary philosopher-soldier who drove the alien hrud from the planet's holy city. Almost all the Soul Drinkers' marks since the Cerberian Field had been erased. Only Inquisitorial sources retained any cohesive history of the Soul Drinkers and their glorious history – glorious, at least, until the betrayal at Lakonia and the Chapter's excommunication. If there were aspects of their history not held in the Inquisition archives on the fortress-worlds in sectors where the Soul Drinkers had fought, then as far as the Imperium was concerned that history never occurred.

Thaddeus had never seen a deletion order in action before. He had heard of them of course, and been a part of some operations where they had been enforced. But he had never been aware of such a stain of ignorance across the Imperium, that burned books and wiped data-slates. Perhaps mind-wipings were being carried out on people who had encountered the Soul Drinkers. Thaddeus, as an inquisitor must, understood the importance of information, and how knowledge could rot the souls of those unable to cope with it.

Renegade Chapters were not unknown – how many children had been told the grim stories of the Horus Heresy, when half the Space Marine Legions were corrupted by the great enemy? But that it could happen now, and without any great Chaos presence to blame for it, could cause disillusion and panic; a situation the Imperium could ill afford. And the Soul Drinkers' disappearance from the memory of the Imperium made Thaddeus's job a damn sight harder.

He didn't know which sub-ordo of the Inquisition enforced the order. Neither did he know which operatives in astropathic nexus outposts and planetary archives were fuddling communications about proscribed topics. But they were effective, and without the authority of an inquisitor lord Thaddeus felt he could do little to get round them. He was feeding on scraps, and it was getting worse. He only hoped that his last remaining lead – an investigation of Eumenix outpost and the reason they had attacked it – would lead to some breakthrough. Otherwise his investigation would be starved of information until it died.

The Inquisition could be obsessed with blinding one part of itself to the activities of another, and Thaddeus sometimes wondered if it could one day push back the darkness and learn to trust itself. But there were enough dark rumours of Inquisitors who had become dangerous radicals or gone mad in their pursuit of corruption, so perhaps keeping members ignorant was the only way to stop it from rotting inside.

'Inquisitor?'

Thaddeus looked up from the data-slate. He had been reviewing the potential hits on the astropathic traffic, but there had been nothing promising, yet again. He saw – inevitably – the Pilgrim waiting at the door to the cold stone chamber. It was night on Caitaran and the filmy pale blue light from the cloudless night sky coloured blue and grey. Thaddeus had been so intent on sifting through the paltry astropathic data that he had failed to notice Caitaran's twin suns going down.

'Pilgrim.'

The Pilgrim bowed slightly, as if in mockery. 'Colonel Vinn has assembled his men and has them ready for review.'

'Good. What do you think of them?'

'Me?' The Pilgrim paused. 'They are mostly veterans of reconnaissance formations or counter-insurgency on primitive worlds. They are skilled and determined soldiers. They will probably die well, but not much else.'

'You think this is insane, don't you?'

Thaddeus had the feeling that the Pilgrim, if it possessed a face, was snarling under its cowl. 'When you have seen the things I have seen, inquisitor, insanity has no meaning. I think it will fail, if that is what you mean. Better soldiers than your storm troopers have tried such ventures before and have not made it past the laser grids.'

'I haven't actually told you what I need the troops for, Pilgrim. You seem very certain I will fail, so you must know what I am going to attempt.'

'You are going to Pharos, inquisitor. There is no other way. And if I can guess it, Lord Kolgo can.'

'Lord Kolgo,' said Thaddeus, rising from his bed and dropping the data-slate into one of the trunks he had nearly finished packing, 'would like nothing better than to see me try. If I fail, I will have tested the defences for him. If I succeed, he will know how to crack that particular nut and will probably try to put me under his direct authority so I can do it again if needs be.'

'Perhaps. But you are going to Pharos, inquisitor, that much is so obvious to me there is no reason for your secrecy. If you are found out and survive you could make enemies who will never forget.'

'Are you trying to discourage me, Pilgrim? Don't you want to see the Soul Drinkers found?'

'More than you do, inquisitor. More than you. Never forget that.' A note of irritation crept into the normally inscrutable mechanised voice. 'You asked my opinion. I believe you will die. But if I were in your position, I would choose probable death too, for otherwise the chances of ultimate success are nil. I am simply saying that your mission is impossible.'

'The Emperor slew Horus at the dark one's moment of triumph. That was impossible, too.

They say Inquisitor Czevak saw the black library and lived. Impossible, again. Protecting the Imperium from a galaxy of evil is impossible, too, but it is an inquisitor's duty to try. My duty. The only weapon I have now against the Soul Drinkers is information, and if I must do the impossible to gain it then that is what I will do.'

'Of course, inquisitor.' The Pilgrim, as ever, was being obsequious. 'Colonel Vinn has his men awaiting inspection.'

'Tell Vinn I trust his judgement. If his men are as dead as you think then I hardly need to inspect them. Have them embark onto the *Crescent* and make sure it's fuelled up. I'll be at the spaceport in an hour.'

The Pilgrim melted into the darkness beyond the door. Even though he was essential to Thaddeus's hopes of ever finding the Soul Drinkers, there was a constant nagging voice that told him he shouldn't have brought the Pilgrim along with him. Treachery seemed to ooze from him like a stink – and it lingered in the chamber after he had gone. But then again, inquisitors had always dealt with the foulest of mutants and aliens as long as they were useful. But the Pilgrim at least was no heretic or daemon, so Thaddeus would have to endure his company for a while longer.

Thaddeus finished throwing his few clothes and possessions into the trunk. He travelled light, and had not followed the holy orders of the Inquisition long enough to build up a library or collection of artefacts as longer-serving inquisitors had. His only possessions of note were the *Crescent Moon* itself, his copy of the *Catechisms Martial* and the heavily modified autopistol he kept on the ship. The pistol had been given to him by the citizens of Hive Secundus on Jouryan after he had wiped out the genestealer cult in the depths of the hive's heatsink complex. He had felt like one of the heroes from the Imperial epics then: a crusader crushing corruption and evil wherever it broke through to threaten the blessed Imperium. He felt very different now.

Had the Ordo Hereticus chosen the right man? Thaddeus was certainly good, there was no doubt. He was intelligent and tenacious, and had the patience to marshal his resources until he could execute a final, critical strike against his opponent. But there were so many inquisitors with more experience. There were some who even specialised in dealing with the Space Marine Chapters – which though they were amongst the Imperium's greatest heroes – possessed an attitude of individuality and autonomy that meant they had to be constantly watched. Was Thaddeus up to the task of finding the Soul Drinkers? Had he been picked for some political reason, by an inquisitor lord like Kolgo who had to balance a million interests against one another?

It didn't matter. He had the job, and he would do it. A thousand inquisitors were working in the warzone on a hundred different missions, and even agents of the Officio Assassinorum were creeping across the stars towards targets in Teturact's empire. And that included Teturact himself. Thaddeus had his own mission, and it was no less important than any of the others. He would hunt down the Soul Drinkers or die trying. Was there any greater devotion than his? No, there was not, he told himself.

He called for one of the fortress staff to take his trunk to the *Crescent Moon* and left the cold, draughty fortress quarters for the spaceport. He would leave for Pharos as soon as possible – that was where the final pieces had to lie. He would find what he needed there. Because if he did not he would fail, and that was not going to happen.

SEVEN

FOR THE MOMENT, the fleet was silent. The fighters had paused in a quiet system, waiting for a break in the heavy traffic of Imperial warships and transports between them and their objective. The system was dark and silent, its sole human structures the mine heads on a burned-out mineral world, its star mottled and dying.

The alien fighters hung in orbit around the system's gas giant, the blue-white strata of gas swirling beneath them in an unending storm. The star's sickly light cast the other half-glimpsed planets and moons in a faded greyish glow. The light muted the bright silver of the fighters, so they looked like just one more handful of mining debris thrown into orbit and left behind when the humans departed.

It was only after the rebellion of the Soul Drinkers that Sarpedon had begun to appreciate the galaxy. In some ways, it was a marvel – every remote corner held something new and extraordinary. Even in this washed-out system there were sights of beauty, like the constant torments of the gas giant below or the endlessly complex orbits of the planet's moons. But it was also a terrible and dark galaxy. In every one of those corners darkness and corruption could be waiting, hidden and frozen, ready to wake and ravenously hunt the stars.

Chaos could be anywhere, and by its very nature it was never in the open but hidden in the galaxy's corners like filth that could never be washed away. That was why the Imperium was such a malevolent thing – it was a part of the galaxy that provided so many hiding places for the Enemy, and most of the best places were within the corrupt structures of the Imperial organisations themselves.

When Chaos had most threatened mankind, it had not sent a tide of daemons from the warp, but had corrupted its greatest heroes – fully half of the Space Marine primarchs – and ripped the galaxy apart in the wars of the Horus Heresy. It had only been men like Rogal Dorn, the Soul Drinkers' primarch and hero of the Battle of Terra, that had kept mankind from falling completely. Now Sarpedon saw what Rogal Dorn really was – a heroic man created as such by the Emperor, but a hero who found himself trapped in the decaying hypocrisy of the Imperium when the Emperor was confined to the Golden Throne and the Adeptus Terra turned His master plan into a mockery of humanity.

The porthole looking out onto space was located amidships on Chaplain Iktinos's ship, where Apothecary Karendin had set up the apothecarion. Pallas, the Chapter's most senior Apothecary, and Karendin worked here tirelessly, because the Soul Drinkers needed their expertise now more than at any time in their history. Pallas had just completed an examination of Sarpedon himself, the Soul Drinkers' first and most obvious mutant.

'Commander?' came a voice from behind him.

Sarpedon snapped out of his reverie and turned to see Apothecary Pallas reading analysis off a data-slate connected to an autosurgeon. The apothecarion set up in the fighter was comprehensive but cramped, packed into what had probably once been quarters for the alien crew. The autosurgeon, servitor orderlies and monitoring consoles were crammed in alongside the bulbous organic ripples of silvery metal. Wires and equipment hung from the abnormally high ceiling.

Pallas looked up from the data-slate. 'You are getting worse,' he said.

'I know,' replied Sarpedon. 'I felt it at House Jenassis. The Hell is... changing. If we do not succeed, the day is coming when I will not be able to control it any longer.'

'Nevertheless,' continued Pallas, 'you're not the worst. Datestan from Squad Hastis has increasing abnormalities in his internal organs that will kill him, or turn him into something different. We've had to take two Marines from Squad Luko off-duty entirely – one has claws that can't hold a bolt gun and the other is growing a second head.'

'And you?'

Pallas paused, put down the data-slate and removed one gauntlet and the forearm of his armour. Ruddy scales had grown from the skin on the back of his hand and spread up past his elbow. 'They go up to my shoulder,' said Pallas, 'and they're spreading. Marines like yourself and Tellos have the most obvious mutations, but there's hardly a Soul Drinker left who isn't changing in some way. Most of them are getting worse quicker and quicker.'

Sarpedon looked down at his spider's legs. There had been a time when, his mind clouded by the Daemon Prince Abraxes, he and his fellow Marines had thought his altered form to be a gift from the Emperor. Now he knew he was just another mutant, no different in many ways to the numberless hordes of unfortunates who were enslaved and killed in the Imperium to protect mankind's genetic stability. Sarpedon had killed enough mutants himself and, if any servant of the Imperium were to so much as look at him, they would try to kill him, too. 'How long do we have?' he asked.

Pallas shrugged. 'Months. Certainly not more than two years before the Chapter ceases to exist as a fighting force. We're already losing Marines to unchecked mutation and that number will only increase. I don't know what you're planning, commander, but it must be our last chance.'

Sarpedon knew what happened to the Soul Drinkers who could no longer function properly. Most were put down when they lost their minds, taken in chains to the plasma reactors on the *Brokenback* to receive a bolt round through the brain before being incinerated. There had been few so far, but Sarpedon had felt every one as keenly as the needless deaths of the Chapter war. 'Our last chance in more ways than one,' agreed Sarpedon. 'Teturact's empire is sustained by forcing the Navy and the Guard into battles that neither side can win, because Teturact has the numbers and the capacity to raise the dead. And we're heading right into the middle of it. From the information Salk brought back from Eumenix it'll be a meat grinder wherever Teturact's armies fight. This Chapter won't die out to mutation, Pallas, it'll die in battle or it will be cured.'

'We can't carry on like this, can we?' said Pallas unexpectedly. 'We have no support. The Imperium will destroy us if it can and Chaos will see us for the enemy we are. No Chapter can survive like this.'

'Carry on with the tests, Apothecary,' said Sarpedon. 'Let me know of any changes.' He turned and left the apothecarion, eight talons clicking on the metallic floor as he headed back towards the bridge.

THE SHUTTLE COCKPIT was bathed in eerie blue-grey light. It shone on the brass fittings of the servitor-pilot and turned the deep red upholstery a velvet black. The viewscreen swam with swirls of white, blue and grey as the servitor applied a touch of pressure to the engines, nudging the shuttle forward. Many of the cockpit's alarm readouts were incongruous beads of red on the instrument panels – the shuttle had not originally been designed for these conditions, but Thaddeus knew it would hold together. Colonel Vinn had pulled a few of the right strings with the Guard units seconded to the Caitaran command and acquired an exceptional craft for the mission. The shuttle had been fitted with reactive armour plates that even now were flexing under the abnormal pressure and cold, and the stealth mode of the engines worked on a jet propulsion principle that enabled the shuttle to be propelled underwater.

Or, in this case, under liquid hydrogen.

'Surface?' asked Thaddeus quietly.

'Three hundred metres,' came the mechanised voice of the servitor-pilot. The armatures plugged into its shoulder sockets eased into the controls in front of it and the shuttle's steering fins were angled upwards a touch, sending the craft on a gentle upwards arc through the unnaturally cold ocean.

Thaddeus switched on the ship vox. 'Lieutenant, to the bridge,' he said. A few seconds later the door at the rear of the cockpit slid open and Lieutenant Kindarek looked in.

'Inquisitor?'

'We'll hit the shore in about seven minutes. Are your men ready to go?'

'Standing by, sir.'

'Keep the grenade launchers slung until we get well away from the edge. There'll be dampening fields to prevent the liquid exploding but we'll still have a hell of a bang if it goes off. I don't want us losing anyone to accidents, it's dangerous enough in there.'

'Yes, sir. Hellguns only until your order.'

'Good.' Thaddeus paused, watching the liquid swirling in front of him. 'What do you think of this mission, Kindarek?'

Kindarek barely thought for a second. 'High-risk and vital, inquisitor. Our kind of operation.'

'And why do you think that?'

'Because Colonel Vinn selected us, inquisitor. He doesn't risk his recon platoon without a good reason, and good reasons always involve risk.'

'No one has ever done this, Kindarek. Some have tried, but no one's ever succeeded.'

'I'd imagine no one has ever tried taking this way in, sir.'

Thaddeus smiled. 'You're quite right, Kindarek. I hope.'

'Two hundred metres,' said the servitor.

'Prepare your men, lieutenant. I want men on point as soon as we hit the shore.'

Kindarek saluted briskly and headed back towards the crew compartment. Since Thaddeus wasn't an officer the gesture was inappropriate, but Thaddeus didn't point it out. It was probably force of habit. Kindarek seemed a soldier who learned his habits early and never strayed from them – it had made him a soldier trusted by Vinn to lead his recon platoon, as professional and unshakeable a body of men as the Ordo Hereticus could make out of mundane troops.

Shapes loomed past, half-glimpsed through the near-opaque liquid, picked out briefly by the floodlights mounted under the nose of the shuttle. Leaning columns and shadowy, submerged structures, set in precarious shapes by the extreme cold, formed a lattice of obstacles for the servitor-pilot to negotiate.

The light became paler as the shuttle ascended. An undersea shelf composed of drifts of silvery machine-shavings rolled out of the gloom – where it broke the surface was a shining horizon, the beach on which the shuttle would land.

Perhaps the shuttle had already been spotted. Perhaps combat servitors were writhing their way through the ocean or were waiting for the shuttle on the shore, ready to turn the liquid hydrogen into a localised, short-lived inferno that would incinerate the shuttle and crew. But these were the risks you took when you tangled with the Adeptus Mechanicus head-on.

PHAROS WAS AN asteroid, part of the remains of a world that had been destroyed millions of years before. It hung in a broken necklace around a dead, blood-orange star. Across those asteroids were scattered mining colonies and hard-bitten missionary outposts; the system was almost completely forgotten.

A thousand years before, the Adeptus Mechanicus had followed their complex fate-equations and tech-priest divinations and arrived at the asteroid chain. They selected the region to be the seat of Stratix sector command, which in an emergency would serve to coordinate Adeptus Mechanicus troops, spacecraft and expertise. But information was most critical of all – the Adeptus Mechanicus was a priesthood, and its religion was knowledge. Information was the stuff of holiness, and the sector command had built a cathedral to learning that would hold all the information generated by the many adepts throughout the sector.

The cathedral jutted from the surface of one of the largest asteroids, the iron-heavy Pharos, bored out by giant tunnelling machines and plated in sacred metals – purest iron, solid carbon, bronze and zinc.

It took the form of a cluster of immense cylinders, arranged like the pipes of an organ, connected by thousands of glass bridges.

Several floors were below the surface of the asteroid, rooted into the super-dense core. Endless floors of knowledge and chapels of unfettered learning filled the cavernous spaces, and a regiment of combat servitors were hardwired into the structure to keep out the ignorant.

The delicate datastacks had to be kept cold to ensure their stability and the immutability of the information they contained. A whole ocean of liquid hydrogen flooded the lower levels, drowning the underground portion of the cathedral in the impossibly cold depths, fed by giant intakes that opened onto the asteroid's rocky surface. The captive ocean was regularly refilled by Mechanicus tanker craft in the never-ending cycle of holy maintenance that formed an act of worship for thousands of adepts and menials.

Inside, galleries of data-cubes were arranged above the freezing lake, almost alive with the immense volume of information they contained. A small body of tech-priests was permitted to live inside, sharing the cathedral with the maintenance servitors, bathing in the holiness of so much knowledge. They were adepts blessed for their devotion and service to the Machine-God with the opportunity to live out their extended lives in the icy splendour of Pharos.

When circumstances required, Pharos was a repository of vital knowledge that sector command could plumb for the good of the Imperium – the archives of its medical tower were at that moment being combed for solutions to the terrible plagues erupting throughout the Stratix warzone. But only tech-priests understood its real purpose – holy ground, created by the Mechanicus as a monument to the Omnissiah and a model of the Machine-God's ideal universe where immutable knowledge was the only reality.

There was no Chaos here, no evil randomness to pollute the sacred knowledge. And the Adeptus Mechanicus intended to keep it that way. No one was permitted access to Pharos except on the express order of the Archmagos Ultima, and he was known as a man not to be hurried. Only a handful of the Emperor's most trusted servants had been given access to the holy ground of Pharos, and then for the briefest periods of research under strict supervision. Some misguided souls and outright heretics had tried to force their way in, of course, but the holy ground had been kept inviolate with combat servitors and monitor ships.

No one had successfully stolen information from the cathedral of Pharos. But then again, no one had tried going in through the liquid hydrogen vents before.

* * *

'THE SEAL IS loose. Let me.' Lieutenant Kindarek reached over and adjusted the seal between Thaddeus's helmet and the neck ring of his hostile environment suit. Normally issued to explorator pioneers or engineers working on ships' hulls, the suit could keep extremes of temperature or noxious atmospheres from harming the occupant. All members of the recon platoon wore them, their faces appearing subtly warped through the square, transparent faceplates and their bulk increased by the thick, spongy dark grey material of the suits.

There was a hiss as the seal tightened and Thaddeus felt the air around his face turn cold and chemical.

'My thanks, lieutenant.'

The suited-up platoon was crammed into the rearward deployment airlock in front of Thaddeus, hellguns at the ready. Four storm troopers had grenade launchers slung on their backs and heavy garlands of frag grenade rounds looped on their belts. Neither the HE suits nor the fatigues underneath bore any Inquisitorial insignia, and Thaddeus himself didn't carry his Ordo Hereticus seal of authority – if the mission failed, there would be little to suggest that the Inquisition had been behind the infiltration.

None of them spoke. Thaddeus's own voice had sounded unwelcome and incongruous. How many battles had these men fought in? How many times had they waited in a Chimera APC or a Valkyrie airborne transport, not knowing if they would be dropped into a fire-fight?

Thaddeus knew several of these men had been at the Harrow Field Bridge where daemons of the Change God were emerging from the ground with the summer crops. Many had been part of the path-finding force that had found the tomb of the Arch-Idolator on Amethyst V. Some had scars and low-grade bionic eyes visible through their face-plates – all were silent and grim. Thaddeus's own nerves were tempered by his faith in the Imperial vision and the critical nature of the mission. Each man coped with the tense last few moments in their own way.

The shuttle tilted as the servitor-pilot in the cockpit turned it around. There was a metallic grating on the underside of the hull as the shuttle beached itself, braking jets pushing it up onto the shore.

'In position,' came the servitor voice over the vox.

'Open us up,' ordered Thaddeus. There was a squeal of hydraulics and the back wall of the pas-senger compartment dislocated, hissing downwards as the deployment ramp lowered.

Bright, cold, fluorescent light flooded in. The hydrogen lake filled the lower levels of this particu-lar cylinder of the cathedral, and heaps of metallic cast formed piles under the surface that became sandbanks of silvery filings. It was against one of these that the shuttle beached. The beach glowed silver in the light and the ripples on the surface of the lake were as bright as knife blades.

The pointmen jumped onto the beach before the ramp was down, the huge boots of the HE suits splashing in the liquid hydrogen at the shore's edge. The photoreactive faceplates darkened in the glare as they panned the barrels of their hellguns over the area.

Kindarek's head tilted to the side for a moment as he received their voxes. 'All clear,' he voxed on his squad frequency. 'Move out.'

The platoon poured rapidly from the shuttle, boots kicking up the drifts of metallic shavings as they moved. Thaddeus followed, autopistol heavy in his hand and his mouth and nose already raw from the treated air. The light surrounded him as he stomped down the ramp onto the shore and he saw that the far wall was a single vast light source, phosphorescent gases trapped behind panes of transparent crystal, wrapping around the inside of the cylinder.

This cylinder of the cathedral was three kilometres across and perhaps ten high, with the lit section a hundred metres high. Access ladders wound their way in double helixes up to the first gallery levels. Columns hung from the distant ceiling, matt-grey so they drunk the abundant light. Between them were webs of glass walkways and platforms, thousands of filaments that turned the light flooding from below into a bright shimmering forest. It was like being inside a polished diamond, with a million faces looking up at the broken light of a new star. Clustered around the pillars and forming starbursts of light at the intersections of the web were intricate crystalline sculptures in complex geometric shapes, mathematical prayers coded into the angles and faces, each sculpture a crystal information repository holding enough information to fill a hundred cogitator engines.

Further up, the curved walls were hung with banners, rust-red cloth embroidered with binary prayers in gold thread. The brightness gave way to shadows towards the ceiling, incense-stained darkness swallowing the cathedral's light where Thaddeus could just make out the control structures looking down on the cathedral, where tech-priests might even now be watching intruders violating the Omnissiah's temple.

The technology of this place was the old kind, the kind they couldn't make any more, salvaged from the forgotten madness of the Dark Age of Technology and put to a new use in the worship of the Omnissiah. This was a sacred place indeed, where the Adeptus Mechanicus kept technology they could not – some said would not – replicate.

To Thaddeus, it was beautiful. To Lieutenant Kindarek and his men it was just another warzone. Kindarek barked an order and the platoons fanned out behind the pointmen, who were rapidly scanning the ridges of the metal sandbar. The platoon dissolved into its component squads, each overlapping fields of fire.

'What's our entry point, sir?' came Kindarek's voice.

Thaddeus glanced around. They couldn't spend more than a few moments down here, where they had no cover and where gunfire could make the hydrogen lake erupt. There were several maintenance stairwells hanging down from the columns above, where adepts or servitors could descend to the lake surface. Thaddeus pointed towards the closest. 'There. Keep it simple.'

'Sir.' At Kindarek's order the platoon jogged towards the stairwell, a spindly spiral of pale silver metal that seemed impossibly fragile against the sheer size of the cathedral cylinder.

The pointmen ascended rapidly, taking two of the grenade launcher troopers with them. The squads went up after them, Thaddeus jogging alongside them as they took the stairs two at a time in their hurry to get out of such a vulnerable position. Thaddeus glanced down and saw the rear of the shuttle disappearing from view as it slid back under the surface to minimise the chances of detection.

The webs of light above fractured and reformed as Thaddeus ascended, as if the whole cathedral had been constructed to appear radically different from each possible angle, mirroring the billions of facets of information it contained. He almost stumbled as he stared up at the sight and remembered that he was a soldier, too, just like these men who were ignoring the splendour, their minds only on the mission.

The pointmen were at the first level of the web-like walkways, picking their way warily along the transparent crystal. The base of one of the suspended columns was nearby and they gathered there, one consulting an auspex to check for movement, others checking cautiously around the giant smooth pillar.

Kindarek waved the first of the platoon's squads onto the walkways. They spread out into a mobile perimeter, hellguns ready to fire, moving around the abstract geometric shapes that formed the crystalline information vaults.

Several men carried bundles of equipment slung at their waists or backs – basic interface equipment, guaranteed to survive the intense cold, that would enable the user to jack into a simple information system. Many of the more technically-minded storm troopers had been quickly trained in its use, and Thaddeus himself could perform the vital task if need be.

Kindarek himself had got to the walkways. For a moment he paused and looked towards the troopers by the pillar – Thaddeus saw one of them, one of the pointmen with an auspex, mouth a single word as he voxed the lieutenant.

Movement.

That was all the warning Thaddeus had.

The trooper turned as he tried to gauge the source of the movement signal on his auspex scanner. He faced the pillar behind him and dropped the scanner to bring his hellgun to bear as he realised the movement was inside the pillar.

The pillar's surface fractured into hundreds of dark grey ceramic tiles. The column broke apart and the tiles were revealed as the flexible armoured carapaces of giant metal-limbed beetles that hung in the freezing air as a host of glowing metal eyes lit up on the scanner arrays jutting from their thoraxes.

The lower half of the pillar had broken into more than twenty combat servitors, each three times the bulk of a man, highly advanced and hovering with in-built grav-units. Metallic limbs folded into multilaser barrels and circular diamond-toothed power saws emerged on metallic armatures. In the few seconds before the servitors were battle-ready Thaddeus realised they had indeed been observed as soon as they had made it to the shore – the cathedral's defences had waited until the storm troopers were spread out between the walkways and the stairwell, vulnerable and out of formation.

Stupid. How could Thaddeus have believed he could succeed in infiltrating the Pharos archives when it had been proved impossible so many times?

No. That was the thinking of someone without faith. Fight on, for death in service of the Emperor was its own reward.

'Open fire!' yelled Kindarek over the squad vox. 'Launchers, now!'

The frozen air erupted into laser fire, searing red streaks from the overcharged power packs of the hellguns lashing from every trooper able to shoot, multi-lasers pumping volleys of white fire through the bodies of the troopers closest to the pillar. The screech and hiss of laser fire filled Thaddeus's ears and the vox was suddenly a mess of static and din, men shouting as they opened fire or screaming as they died. Men were shredded, their blood freezing into a hail of red shrapnel, chunks of flesh shattering against the crystal. One fell backwards as his leg was sheared clean off by the slash of a power saw, beads of frozen blood glittering as he tumbled off the walkway down towards the hydrogen lake. Another was picked up by the razor-sharp mandibles of the beetle-servitor and pulled apart, his body erupting in a shower of crimson shards.

White-hot laser fire slashed through the stairwell and the man directly above Thaddeus was hit, his torso shattering as a laser bolt punched through his chest. White fire screeched through the stairs beneath him and the structure came apart, metal steps raining down along with half of the last squad.

Thaddeus reached out and grabbed the railing as the steps under his feet disappeared. The bulk of the dead man above buffeted him as it fell, and Thaddeus was dangling one-handed nearly a hundred metres above the lake. The blinding light swallowed the men as they fell, reducing them to ripples in the silvery surface as they hit the lake.

Grenade rounds exploded above, sending clouds of shrapnel ripping through the servitors. The damage was minimal but the explosions scrambled their sensors, and one of the insectoid servitors fell wreathed in strange blue flame as a dozen high-powered hellgun shots tore up into its underbelly.

'Paniss! Telleryev! Make for their flank, pin them down!' Kindarek was yelling – Thaddeus saw Kindarek, back against one of the information-sculptures, firing with his hellpistol as he shouted orders over the vox.

A hand reached down and Thaddeus grabbed it – a trooper hauled him up onto the still-stable top end of the stairwell. Thaddeus was about to breathe a word of thanks when a laser shot seared through the air between them and sliced a deep furrow through the trooper's faceplate – Thaddeus saw him choke as the cold air he inhaled turned his lungs to chunks of ice. The man's eyes froze into white crystals and his body turned rigid, the heat fleeing from inside his suit and his muscles turning solid.

Thaddeus pushed the dead man to one side and let the corpse fall. He stumbled forward a few steps and pulled himself onto the walkway, the dizzying drop still yawning beneath him. The passage was only wide enough for a couple of men abreast and troopers were scrambling for the junctions where they could gather in gaggles of three or four, using sculptures as cover and concentrating hellgun fire on one servitor at a time.

Thaddeus drew his autopistol, feeling it click as an executioner round chambered itself in response to his hand around the grip. He sprinted the few steps towards the closest sculpture as laser blasts scored deep gouges into the crystal of the walkway beneath him.

He slid into cover beside two storm troopers, one of them hefting a grenade launcher and using it to lob occasional shots over the sculpture towards knots of servitors.

The trooper with the hellgun nodded curtly at Thaddeus as the inquisitor scrambled to a half-sitting position, back against the crystal.

'Musta lost half the lads!' shouted the trooper, voice muffled by the HE suit's faceplate. 'Do we have extraction?' Thaddeus recognised Trooper Telleryev, one of the platoon's sergeants.

Thaddeus shook his head. 'We break out the hard way.'

Telleryev spat a word from his homeworld that Thaddeus assumed was profane, then flicked his hellgun onto full power and sent a bright lance of laser into the body of a servitor drifting ominously over to flank them. Thaddeus took aim with his pistol and loosed off three shots, the microcogitators in the rare executioner rounds sending the bullets curving as they flew, punching into the servitor with mechanical accuracy.

The servitor juddered and listed suddenly as one of its grav units burst in a shower of sparks – Thaddeus sighted down the barrel at the bundle of sensors that made up its head and pumped the rest of the autogun's ten-round magazine into it. Like swift metal insects the rounds looped towards their target and shattered the servitor's metal face, sending arcs of electricity spitting from the broken machinery and exposing the biological core of the machine, the part that had once been human.

Without anything to guide it, the servitor yawed aimlessly, exposing the underbelly to which its jointed limbs were attached. The other storm trooper swung the barrel of his grenade launcher around and fired a single frag grenade into the servitor's belly, ripping it clean open and spilling machine parts and pulped flesh down towards the lake.

The grenade trooper allowed himself a grim smile of triumph as he racked another round into his weapon.

'Get us to Kindarek!' shouted Thaddeus. Telleryev nodded and the two men broke cover at a run. The grenade trooper waved them forward, pumping a volley of grenades into the walkways above them to send hot shrapnel bursting through the air and momentarily blinding the servitors as Thaddeus and Telleryev ran.

Kindarek was trying to organise a strongpoint around a couple of sculptures and a length of walkway that had fallen down from above, with seven or eight troopers keeping up fields of fire and preventing the servitors from surrounding them. There were still a dozen of the machines left, spraying multilaser fire across the width of the cylinder – but they were avoiding blasting directly at the sculptures, and so they had to close to use their power saws while keeping the walkways between clear. Kindarek was trying to punish the servitors that drifted towards them and, though he would probably not succeed, he was at least buying time.

Thaddeus reached Kindarek's position, Telleryev beside him.

'We need to get men upwards,' voxed Thaddeus breathlessly. 'We have to get a link set up.'

Kindarek paused as his soldier's mind rifled through the possibilities – stay here with at least some cover and a plan, or throw men through the gauntlet in an attempt to drag some information screaming from the cathedral's archives.

'We're dead here anyway,' he replied. Then, on the squad frequency – 'Suppression fire and break cover! Head for the upper walkways and concentrate fire:. Move, move!'

Thaddeus slipped a single shell from one of his waist pouches into the breech of the autopistol. A single heavy shell, it was more expensive than many spaceships and a handful of them had cost

Thaddeus a lot of favours. Now, he was immensely grateful he had shown the prescience to have brought them along.

Thaddeus ran alongside the storm troopers and fired once at a servitor turning to spray fire at them. The autopistol barked and a glittering trail followed the bullet. Its armour-piercing tip and micro-guidance systems let it punch repeatedly through the glossy carapace of the servitor before running out of propellant. Its concentrated explosive core detonated in the heart of the servitor and blew it apart in a shower of frozen flesh and shimmering metal.

Adeptus Mechanicus specials, the pinnacle of personal armaments technology. Now Thaddeus was using them to get him out of a spot where it was the Mechanicus that wanted him dead. There would be a moral in there somewhere if Thaddeus survived long enough to work it out.

Thaddeus managed to spend two more priceless rounds of ammunition blowing another servitor out of the air, and the frantic hellgun fire accounted for three more as the storm troopers ran to the closest junction that would lead them upwards towards the next levels.

'Telleryev!' yelled Kindarek as the storm troopers made it to the next level and took cover behind a huge sculpture. 'Take three men and keep them occupied! The rest watch the boss's back!'

Thaddeus nodded at the lieutenant and took the hook-up equipment from a hip pocket of his suit. It was a simple portable cogitator linked to a data-slate by a thick bundle of wires, with various interfaces leading off on yet more wires. Thaddeus fumbled with the device as he crouched by the sculpture feeling the sudden hot flashes of laser blasts passing close by.

He couldn't find an interface. He passed his hands over the clear, angular crystal surface but there was no way in. Would he fail here because he had been stupid enough to assume the Mechanicus would use standard interfaces?

No – there was something, at the base of the crystal. A metal panel was bolted to the surface, an ugly flaw in the crystal. A data-thief probe extended from the plate into the body of the crystal and provided a low-tech way in. The data-sculptures were technology from a previous age and the Mechanicus had obviously lacked an equally elegant way of using them – they had been forced to make do with the technology they had, and that was the same technology used across the Imperium.

Thaddeus plugged one wire into the crude interface. There was a pause and suddenly the data-slate was full of solid information, dense columns of binary pouring across the screen.

The program loaded onto the cogitator had been almost as expensive in its own way as the bullets in Thaddeus's gun, taken from a tech-heretic that Thaddeus had helped capture back in his interrogator days. The Hereticus had ordered that the heretic be left alive so the Inquisition could make use of his skills – the man had escaped and Thaddeus had been a part of the mission that had finally killed him. The program he had given the Inquisition before his escape was a decoder, powerful enough to crunch through the encryption of just about any secure information source but simple enough to fit onto almost any computation device.

Skrin Kavansiel had been the man's name. A madman who had turned servitors and industrial machinery into rampaging monsters across half-a-dozen worlds in the Scarus sector, all in the name of the Change God. Thaddeus had shared the kill himself with two other interrogators on an agri-world near the galactic core. That Kavansiel had been allowed to live the first time had sowed the doubts in Thaddeus that Lord Inquisitor Kolgo had confirmed – the Inquisition was not the single, focused instrument of the Emperor's justice that he had learned of when he was first groomed as an interrogator. Half the time, it might as well be fighting itself.

The cogitator broke the mass of information down into categories and homed in on the records of Adeptus Mechanicus installations and personnel throughout the Stratix sector. There were still trillions of scraps of information in there – at least, thought Thaddeus as laser fire spattered around him and short, gargled screams told of troopers dying, the information vaults were all connected.

He only hoped that the sculptures shattered below them had not contained the information he needed.

'Gak me sideways!' someone shouted. 'Company!'

Thaddeus glanced upwards. There were lights now in the darkness at the top of the cylinder, powerful spotlights swinging through the shadows. The lights picked out ropes coiling downwards and figures rappelling down them, troopers in rust-red jumpsuits, guns slung on their backs.

'Frag, tech-guard!' said Kindarek.

Half the storm troopers were still pinned down by the servitors. Thaddeus didn't hold out much hope that those who remained could deal with crack tech-guard troops firing on them from above.

He spotted a couple of tech-priests directing the tech-guard, robed and hooded adepts armed with shimmering power axes and exotic weaponry that sent bolts of power burning down at the storm troopers.

The data-slate began to sort through the information according to the same codewords that Thaddeus had used to filter astropathic traffic – Soul Drinker, purple, Marine, spider, a host of others.

As the screen seethed with information Thaddeus switched to the vox frequency he had reserved for the shuttle.

'Thaddeus to shuttle. Target above us, multiple hostiles. Make it count.'

'Received,' came the servitor's mechanical voice, the signal warped by the intervening liquid hydrogen. 'Shuttle out.'

A fountain of hydrogen burst out of the lake and with a roar the shuttle's stealth engines kicked in, ripping it out of the lake and sending it hurtling upwards like a bullet from a gun. Once clear of the lake the main engines erupted and the shuttle rose on a plume of flame, past the lowest walkways and upwards.

The data now rushing through the uplink device still poured through the cogitator in awesome amounts. Every Mechanicus outpost from the present day back to the time of the Great Crusade was listed, with staff lists, schematics, work rotas, research reports, accounts, tech-prayers, and all the ephemera of the Mechanicus's immense operation.

Thaddeus keyed in the last command he had – the order to sort the data by the staff list Sister Aescarion had recovered from the outpost on Eumenix. A few hundred names that represented the last hope – maddeningly, everything Thaddeus needed to know was probably streaming past in front of his eyes, he just had to pick it out from the ocean of information.

The datastream thinned. A blinking green light on the frame of the data-slate told Thaddeus that the information was concise enough for the cogitator to hold. Thaddeus pressed a switch and the information was seared onto the cogitator's memory.

Maybe it was enough. Maybe there was nothing there but trivia. Thaddeus would have to take the chance, if he survived. That was a big if.

The shuttle soared upwards shattering its way through walkways as it went. Mounted guns on the half-glimpsed structures above pumped a stream of shells into the shuttle, ripping through the armour plates and sending sudden, shocking gouts of flame bursting from the engine housings.

The first tech-guard were landing on walkways high above, sending down hails of rapid-firing autogun shots. The freezing air was full of shrapnel and vapour. Thaddeus saw Sergeant Telleryev ripped clean in two by one of the last servitors, his insides turning to a mist of crimson shards even as two of his men were shot off the walkway by tech-guard fire. Thaddeus blasted twice, three times, and three tech-guard were picked off their rappel lines by ammunition they could only have dreamed of using one day.

The shuttle's engine blew and clouds of vapour bloomed around it. Its rise peaked and it began to fall, just a few metres beneath the levels the tech-guard were now landing on.

The servitor-pilot, working to hardwired protocols Thaddeus himself had installed, switched the shuttle's fuel cells into reverse, pumping high-grade prometheum derivative backwards until it flooded through the ignition chambers.

The fuel ignited and incinerated everything in the cockpit and crew compartment in an instant. The servitor-pilot was atomised, metal components melted to gas, flesh disappearing.

The hull of the shuttle failed under the stress of the explosive forces within. With a thunderclap and a flash of flame that turned the crystal cathedral a blazing orange, the shuttle exploded, and boiling flame filled the top half of the cylinder.

Vapour, like a falling sky, billowed downwards and washed over the storm troopers. Thaddeus was blinded, bright white turning dark.

The vox was a mess of static. For a few seconds he was alone, encased in cold and confusion, fumbling blind as he tried to stuff the data-slate into the pocket of his HE suit. The shadowy shape of a storm trooper stumbled by then fell out of view, slipping over the edge of the walkway as random autogun fire spattered down through the darkness.

Something huge was falling. The sound of shattering crystal cut through the din, a high fractured crash growing rapidly closer. Shards of crystal, like huge glass knives, plunged through the darkness and the air was full of filaments. Spikes of icy cold jabbed at Thaddeus as fragments of crystal punctured his suit and cold air jetted in before the fabric tightened around the tiny wounds.

The huge burning hulk of Thaddeus's transport ripped down from above, trailing ribbons of flame, carving through the dense vapour like a comet. It took half the walkways with it, countless strands of the crystal web snapping, information vaults shattering into a blizzard of fragments. Men were screaming as they fell. Thaddeus expected any second to be dragged down with them, or to have his HE suit sliced open and his muscles turned to slabs of frozen meat.

The transport impacted far below, and a fraction of a second later the top layer of liquid hydrogen ignited.

The containment fields, designed to divert the energy of any ignition away from the information vaults above, compressed the heat and shockwave downwards and outwards. But the hydrogen kept burning as the transport plunged through it and then its plasma drive imploded. Without the containment fields, the whole lake would have burned and turned the cathedral into a column of flame, incinerating everything inside. Instead, the explosion was forced down into the root of the cylinder, where the ferrofibre walls met the rock of Pharos.

The walls of the cylinder fractured catastrophically, great black fissures rippling up the walls. The air shrieked out into the hard vacuum beyond, sucking men and debris with it. Thaddeus grabbed the data-vault beside him as razor-sharp crystal shard whipped past. Storm troopers and tech-guard tumbled past, flailing hopelessly.

The hydrogen lake, designed to keep the information vaults stable, had instead led to the whole cathedral being destroyed. The Adeptus Mechanicus, in their obsession with technical perfection, had missed the obvious danger. It had never occurred to them that anything hostile could survive the extreme cold and the servitor-warriors, or that anything could detonate the lake with such ferocity that the confinement fields could not cope. It was holy ground, and holy information was inviolable.

The upper echelons of the Mechanicus could not imagine that a desperate, lone inquisitor would invade the Omnissiah's sanctum and would bring with him all the random, chaotic factors that could destroy it.

The irony was momentarily lost on Thaddeus as the columns broke away from the ceiling and swung around him, churning up the broken crystal into a storm of razors. Thaddeus's section of walkway broke away and suddenly the cylinder was whirling around him. The fissures tore on upwards and suddenly the whole top half of the cylinder boomed open, the stresses in the structure building up until the whole cylinder split like a seed pod.

Thaddeus tried to control his movement but he couldn't. He kicked fruitlessly against nothing, and glimpsed surviving storm troopers and tech-guard doing the same. The fires from below went dark as the air rushed out and there was nothing but darkness now, the ruins of the cathedral below him and the blackness of space above. The tide of escaping air carried him upwards and out of the cylinder and, as he span out past the limits of Pharos's artificial gravity field, he saw the damage inflicted on the rest of the cathedral. The fires had burst up into the neighbouring cylinders and flames boiled around the base of the cathedral.

Thousands of years of priceless information was burning together with the menials and adepts trapped inside. Thaddeus saw one or two storm troopers and tech-guard who were suffering the same fate as him, struggling helplessly as they were thrown further and further into space. Ejected crystal debris glittered like shooting stars, streams of bright silver fragments spinning against the blackness. Bodies and body parts span amongst the debris, broken and helpless.

Thaddeus's mind raced through the situation. He tried to think objectively, like a good inquisitor should when first presented with a problem. His HE suit could survive hard vacuum but the air filters would fail soon without an atmosphere from which to draw oxygen and nitrogen. He had no means of propulsion and nowhere to go even if he could move.

The data-slate was in his pocket. That, at least, was something. With luck, he had completed his objective. Now he just had to survive.

There was nothing around him now but space. Pharos was a brightly-lit city-temple behind him, the remnants of the cylinder a darkening mass of twisted metal. The searing unblinking eye of the dying red star burned to one side, and to the other was just cold vacuum. Thaddeus had seen space only through viewscreen or portholes, or as the night sky from the safety of a planet's surface. He had never been surrounded by it. For the first time, he realised just how delicate the Imperium truly was – an infinitely thin layer of tenacious life clinging to the dead rock that made up a minuscule fraction of the galaxy. No wonder mankind had to fight. No wonder it saw extinction around every corner.

The Soul Drinkers were out there somewhere, between those stars. Thaddeus might even now have the information he needed to find them, but he was cruelly aware of just how close his death was. An inquisitor was not afraid of death, but he was afraid – and proud to be afraid – of dying with his service to the Emperor left incomplete. As Thaddeus drifted, that fear grew and grew, until it surrounded him as completely as the uncaring galaxy itself.

EIGHT

SEPTIAM TORUS WAS a garden world. Its two main continents were covered in temperate grasslands and deep, lush forests. The faint rings around the planet lit up the sky in shimmering rainbows, with sunsets of a million colours. Crystal-clear rivers wound their way through breathtaking country-side and plunged down spectacular waterfalls before joining a great shining ocean teeming with coral reefs. The planet's ecosystem had never evolved far beyond plant life, and so there were no animals to act as predators or scavengers save for the species introduced to pollinate the planet's small crop of soulfire flowers – flocks of birds with green and blue plumage that streaked across the skies like comets.

Soulfire stamens were the source of some of the most potent combat drugs the Imperium issued to its penal legions and more expendable Guard regiments, and so Septiam Torus was accorded special status. Its tithes were paid in the soulfire crop alone and the ruling family – descended from the first rogue trader to find the planet and annexe it in the name of the Emperor – was granted perpetual rights over the world.

Septiam Torus remained unsettled and unspoilt apart from its sole city, a sprawl of marble, like a vast colonnaded palace, with a barracks and brig for its private law enforcement regiment and endless tile-roofed streets housing the crop workers.

One day a ship's lifeboat was glimpsed in the upper atmosphere, its distress beacon bleating that it contained a sole occupant severely injured. The pod thudded home into the middle of a field, kicking up a plume of purple-black petals. The Septiam Torus Enforcement Division sent a paramedic team to recover the occupant and bring him for treatment to the city. They found a body badly charred but alive, and brought it back to the infirmary in the shadow of the senate house.

For three weeks the infirmary staff tried to coax life from the victim. Eventually they caused their patient – they couldn't even tell if it was a man or a woman – to flicker an eyelid in recognition.

At that moment one of Septiam's senators was visiting the facility. It was the sort of duty expected of all senators, representing as they did a loose family group expected to outdo one another in service to their world. The senator disliked the infirmary but it was crucial to keeping the crop workers secure and happy on Septiam Torus, and she blandly absorbed the facts and figures the medical staff handed out as she followed them around the wards.

She rounded a corner and saw the charred form of the crash victim, suspended in a wire harness and wrapped in bandages that were yellow and stained even though they had been changed barely an hour earlier. Monitoring equipment blinked and chirped. The perfumed curtains that hung around the patient couldn't mask the faint odour of cooked meat.

'Ah, our visitor.' The senator smiled – ostensibly to show a friendly face to the unfortunate, but really because the seeping raw body was the first interesting thing she had seen all day. 'Our stranger. How long before you can tell us who you are? We are much concerned to find out about you and your ship.'

'The patient has only just awoken, my lady,' said one of the orderlies. 'We hope for a return to consciousness very soon.'

The patient stirred and stared out at the senator with pained, rolling eyes.

Then, as the senator watched, the patient dissolved, bandages unravelling as skin sloughed off, looping entrails slithering and hissing to the polished floor, organs bubbling away into a foul brackish pool. The spine came apart and the skull plopped onto the floor, brains liquefying, eyes running down the cheeks, teeth bleached cubes in the stinking mess.

The senator was hurried out of the infirmary and the orderlies hosed the gory mess into the drains. But the senator had breathed in a good lungful of noisome gases from the dissolving patient, and in this way contracted a disease which she then transferred to the senate house at the next meeting.

Within two weeks, the senate and half the population was wiped out. The tens of thousands of dead were heaped into pits and the beautiful sky of Septiam Torus turned dirty grey with fatty smoke from the pyres. The survivors tried to set up a sterile zone within the walls of Septiam City but charred skeletal fingers tore down the barriers and the dead walked again, the perfection of the garden world turned into a bloodstained nightmare of shambling corpses.

The few living dead that could speak spoke the name of Teturact.

GUARDSMAN SENSHINI COULD swear he heard the crunch of bone beneath the tracks of the Leman Russ Executioner as the tank lurched over a wooded ridge, churning up the cratered mud that stretched across the land where once fragrant fields of soulfire flowers and lush woodlands had thrived. Beyond the main cannon's targeting array Senshini could just pick out the jumble of shapes on the horizon, past the broken lumpy landscape of chewed-up forests and churned mud. Septiam City was dug in against the landscape, pockmarked slabs of marble and log-jams of toppled columns forming huge barricades and rows of tank traps ringing the city's outskirts.

Senshini knew enough about the short history of the conflict on Septiam Torus to guess this was the big push. The first attack on the planet had taken place just a few weeks after Septiam Torus had been confirmed as having been tainted by Teturact. A regiment of Elysians had dropped onto the world from Valkyries by grav-chute. They had died almost to the man, finding themselves surrounded by masses of walking corpses where they had expected a handful of rebel private troopers. The Elysian Drop Troop regiments were considered elite formations but no amount of training would make a lasgun shot kill something that was already dead, especially when some of those living dead were former comrades.

The Imperial Guard had pulled out those Elysians they could and had sent in a regiment of more conventional ground-pounders, the Jouryan XVII. They besieged Septiam City. The Stratix XXIII, hard-bitten hive ganger conscripts itching for a chance to avenge their dead world, had been sent in to support them once it had become clear that the twenty thousand Jouryans couldn't take Septiam City themselves. The governor's own Gathalamorian Artillery were brought in to soften up the entrenched defenders prior to the inevitable assault.

In total, including the support and supply formations, Army Group Torus numbered just shy of a hundred thousand men.

Senshini, if he were being honest, didn't think it would be enough.

He had been with the Jouryans on Septiam Torus for three weeks. During that time he had heard some of the stories that patrols and kill-sweep teams had brought back. There were dead men out there, walking like the living. Some of them had once been Elysians. Some of them now were Jouryans. At least now the waiting was over, but, like everyone else in the armour section, Senshini feared what they might find inside the city.

He saw foot troops at the edges of his target viewer, figures hurrying past in the dark grey fatigues of the Jouryan XVII, black helmets and body armour already spattered with mud, lasguns held close to their chests.

The armour and infantry were to support one another as they closed in on the perimeter, the tanks breaching the walls and the infantry swarming through the gaps. Demolisher siege tanks were rumbling towards knots of shattered trees where they could scrounge some cover as they opened up at long range. Leman Russ tanks would close in, their medium-range guns shattering masonry and throwing defenders from the walls. The Executioners, of which there were only a handful amongst the Jouryans, would have to venture in further so their guns could fill the breaches with liquid fire before the infantry went in.

The Executioner was armed unlike any other Imperial Guard tank. Its Leman Russ-pattern chassis was topped with a massive plasma blastgun, most of the crew compartment crammed with the hot, thrumming plasma coils that fuelled the gun. An Executioner was a rare beast, hardly ever seen outside the forge worlds where the Adeptus Mechanicus jealously guarded the secrets of their manufacture, and the Jouryan XVII was fortunate indeed to have acquired any at all. It was Senshini's duty to fire the blastgun, and he knew that it would light up the tank to enemy spotters like a firework display.

Still, it could be worse, thought Senshini as he spotted broken figures moving between the shattered columns that broke the jumbled silhouette of the walls. He could be riding a Hellhound, the notorious and often ill-fated flamethrower tanks with external tanks full of promethium, which had to go into the teeth of the enemy to support the infantry with waves of fire.

Kaito, the Executioner's commander, swung open the top hatch and hauled himself up so he could see out. The awful battlefield smell rolled into the tank, cutting through even the electrical stink of the plasma coils – a stench of sickly rotting flesh and the heavy, charred smell of burning bodies.

'Hang left, Tanako!' called Kaito, 'Keep them beside us!'

Senshini, like Kaito, was well aware of the need to keep the infantry close alongside the tank. The Executioner had no sponson weapons to cover its side arcs, and it needed supporting infantry to minimise the chance of a lascannon or krak missile punching through the side armour.

Tanako, in the cramped driver's compartment below Senshini, swung the steering levers and the tank swerved to the left – Senshini could see through the targeter as the tank crept closer to the hunched Jouryans hurrying over the cratered mud.

Kaito dropped back into the tank and pulled the hatch down. 'Artillery's coming over,' he said. Senshini saw that already the tank commander's face was streaked with engine grime and the shoulders of his officer's greatcoat were spattered with kicked-up mud. Kaito was a veteran who had lost his previous tank, a Vanquisher tank hunter, to enemy fire on Salshan Anterior and had only taken over the Executioner a week before. To both Senshini and Tanako, the man was a mystery – quiet and reserved, rarely speaking without reason, with a calm face that showed little sign of having witnessed the fiercest action on Salshan Anterior.

Even with the hatch down Senshini could hear the first salvoes of the artillery attack shrieking overhead.

The Gathalamorians' guns fired heavy, armour-cracking shells to shatter the walls, and high explosive rounds to wreak havoc in the city behind them. Senshini watched them as they hurtled over the advancing Jouryan line like falling constellations. The first of them hit home a split second later. He felt their impact through the lurching hull of the tank as they detonated with a sound like an earthquake, a dozen shells ripping into Septiam City, lighting up the walls and throwing the makeshift defences into harsh silhouettes against the flame.

Manticore artillery tanks to the rear of the Jouryans' armour added bright streaks of rockets, like claw marks against the dark sky, and one of the Gathalamorians' Deathstrike launchers sent a fat missile thudding into the city just beyond the wall where it erupted into a blue-white ball of nuclear flame.

Answering fire spattered back from the walls, a dusting of glitter that was distant small arms fire, autoweapons and lasguns.

'Squadron Twelve is giving us a ranging shot,' said Kaito through the tank's intercom, his voice punctuated by explosions growing closer.

'Understood, sir.'

Squadron Twelve was a few hundred metres to the left, consisting of two Leman Russ tanks with lascannon sponsons and a Vanquisher tank hunter; the squadron functioning as a nugget of anti-armour firepower in the infantry line.

Senshini swivelled the targeter to get a view of Squadron Six's Vanquisher tank firing a tracer shell towards the walls. It fell just short of the walls in a crimson starburst.

'Squadron Twelve, this is Squadron Six gunner,' said Senshini into the tank's primitive field vox unit. 'We got that. Make it three hundred metres to blastgun range.'

'Squadron Six, this is Squadron Command,' came the voice of the artillery's command section, mounted in a Salamander command vehicle a few hundred metres back. 'You have the short range, move forward for combined long range firing.'

'Yes, sir. Squadron Six out.' Kaito flicked off the vox. 'Get us closer, Tanako. We need to get into range the same time as the Vanquishers.'

'Let's just hope some of those footsloggers follow us up,' said Tanako bleakly as he gunned the Executioner's engines and accelerated.

The Jouryans in front of them would be in the first wave to hit the walls. Senshini had heard that such a thing was a great honour to many soldiers, but then he had also heard that there were a lot of crazy men in the Guard.

The thin, dark line of Jouryans crept closer to the city outskirts as the fire from the walls increased and the next waves of artillery hit home. Somewhere on the other side of the city the Stratix XXIII would be doing the same, gang-scum conscripts hurrying to get to grips with the defenders in the close-quarters butchery at which they excelled. And inside the city, defenders would be manning the walls even as they died, then rising from the dead again, if there was enough left of them.

Two hundred metres. Senshini could see barely human silhouettes, some limbless or even headless, many toting weaponry looted from the Enforcement Division armouries, others just shambling along the broken stone. Whole marble-tiled roofs had been tipped on edge to form walls, stacks of toppled pillar sections made huge obstacles. Whatever had been knocked down in the previous shelling had been carted to the edge of the city and piled into treacherous slopes of pulverised marble and brick, with fire points on the top to rake troops with gunfire as they struggled upwards.

One hundred metres.

Small arms fire was spattering in the mud around the troopers – the Jouryans knew better than to try to engage in a fire-fight at this range but one or two still fell, the steel rain cutting them down as they advanced. A couple of shots rang off the hull of the Executioner, sharp steel dints against the grinding of the engine and the crunching as the tracks rode over the remains of previous assaults. There were dead men in the mud below them, Elysians and Enforcement Division troops mixed with gnarled Septiam limbs, along with weapons and equipment dropped by dead hands. No matter what happened, there would be a new layer of Jouryan dead added to it before long.

Fifty metres.

If this had been a normal city the fleet would have obliterated it from orbit. But previous experience with Teturact's followers had shown that would just have given them a ruined warren of hiding places for the corpses to rise from. It had to be done the old-fashioned way, with troopers on foot bayoneting every one of them and burning the remains.

Senshini could just make out the yells of frontline officers as they lined their squads and platoons up with their designated attack points on the defences. Some would try to climb vertical marble rooftops with ropes and had climbing gear slung over their shoulders. Others would slog their way up crumbling slopes. Sapper units would try to go through or under, their task considered the most dangerous of all.

The targeting reticule showed the range in the bottom corner. Senshini knew he was close enough. For a second more he let the Executioner trundle on, bringing a few more metres of wall within the blastgun's reach.

'Squadron Six gunner, in range,' said Senshini.

'This is Squadron Six command,' echoed Kaito into the vox. 'Ready to fire.'

'Squadron Six, fire,' came command's response.

'Fire!' yelled Kaito, and Senshini slammed the firing lever down.

The reticule was filled with light, streaming from above and behind as the coils emptied their massive charges through the blastgun barrel. The energy was focused into a compacted bolt of superheated plasma, white-hot and liquid, which was spat with tremendous force towards the wall of column sections in Senshini's sights.

Huge column drums toppled, forming a landslide of carved stone, the sections rolling into the mud at the foot of the wall, kicking up great crescents of filth. Liquid plasma burst into a storm of lethal droplets, seething through the gaps between the stone. Figures tumbled down the ruined wall, bodies breaking or dissolving as the plasma hit them. Shells from the other squadrons nearby, and the longer-ranged tanks behind, slammed into the stone, splintering the marble and kicking more column sections down into the mud.

The troops to either side sped up, squads holding back to cover the advancing units. Lasgun fire spattered up towards the walls and heavy weapon units sent frag missiles and airburst mortars filling the air on the battlements with shrapnel.

The enemy took just a few moments to recover. The column stacks were broken but not completely breached. Senshini could see dozens and dozens of small dark figures dressed in rags, like insects swarming from under the bark of a tree.

The coils behind Senshini thrummed as they recharged and the tracks groaned in complaint as

Tanako forced the tank over the churned earth by the walls, following the units that were running for the cover of fallen masonry as autogun and lasgun fire rattled down towards them. Shots were spattering off the Executioner's front armour, and components were sparking and shorting out in the crew compartment.

Tanako spat an ancient Jouryan curse as tiny flames licked from his control consoles. A cold chemical smell filled the compartment as Kaito smothered the fire with a handheld extinguisher.

Senshini watched as a vicious, swirling fight was born amongst the fallen stone of the broken wall. The enemy had the numbers, hundreds of ragged pasty-skinned men and women clambering over the blocks and taking cover amongst the crevices, but each Jouryan carried better firepower and had far better discipline than his opposite in the city. Officers formed fire lines to support the units advancing into the rubble. Assault teams hurled demo charges into knots of enemies, before charging with bayonets and feeding a brutal, swirling, close-order scrap that swelled at the base of the wall.

The old-fashioned way. No matter what the Mechanicus could cook up or the Navy could send into orbit, when it came down to it you needed a bayonet and some guts to win a war. For the briefest moment Senshini wished he were down there in the heart of the fighting, lasgun in his hand – but he could see men stumbling with limbs severed or entrails spilling, and he knew he should be glad there were several layers of armour between him and the hail of fire raking down into the Jouryans.

'This is Squadron Command,' crackled the vox. 'I need a visual on Squadron Twenty.'

'Twenty?' replied Kaito. 'This is Squadron Six, they won't be this far up front yet.'

'We've lost contact with Squadron Twenty. Report in a visual, we need them deployed at the wall.'

It made no sense. Squadron Twenty was a rear echelon squadron, consisting of three stripped-down Chimera transports crewed by medical corps officers. They would race up to the front line when the first wave of the attack had gone in, picking up the wounded and taking them back to the casualty stations to the rear of the Jouryan lines. Senshini hated to think what would go through the minds of the assaulting troops if they knew their only hope of any kind of rapid medical attention had been lost somewhere in the rearward echelons.

'Gunner! Emplacement, thirty degrees high!'

Senshini yanked on the vertical lever and the viewpoint swung upwards, framing a precarious section of the wall where several enemies were loading shells into a field gun that fired almost point-blank into the Jouryans battling to get a foothold in the rubble below. Senshini took a ranging, correcting up a few metres, and fired. The plasma discharged with a roar and the emplacement disappeared in a bursting blister of plasma.

Armour was coming up beside the Executioner, a Demolisher to help crack the wall open further and an Exterminator, twin autocannons barking rapidly as they sent shrapnel bursting amongst the enemy scrambling down the rubble slope. A pair of Chimeras streaked by, tracks kicking up sprays of dirt, and a Valkyrie roared overhead, belly compartment full of storm troopers to exploit a full breach further up the wall.

'Gak me sideways,' said Tanako from below. 'That's Squadron Twenty!'

Senshini swung the targeting array down to catch sight of the rear of a Chimera as it drove headlong for the walls, the staff-and-snake symbol of the medical corps stencilled on its rear ramp. A third Chimera with the same markings drove by a moment later, its driver recklessly gunning the engine and crunching through the gears as it rode over the crest of a shell crater.

'Take us closer, Tanako,' ordered Kaito. 'Senshini, close support fire, they're pinned down. And get onto command, tell them we've found Squadron Twenty.'

The Executioner lurched forward. The stink of the recharging coils surrounded Senshini, and he could feel the greasy grime caking on his bare hands and face. The viewpoint swung violently and he caught a glimpse of the top hatch of Squadron Twenty's closest Chimera swinging open.

Heavy-calibre fire spattered from the open hatch. Senshini spotted dark figures tumbling down the rubble slope. The volume of fire was massive and shocking, ripping into the Septiam's on the slopes. It was accurate, too, and Senshini saw Septiam's fall. No lasgun could blow a man apart like that, not even the hellguns of the Guard elites.

'That's not medical corps,' said Senshini, mostly to himself.

The Executioner was within easy small arms fire of the wall and shots rang loudly off the upper plates, kicking chunks of armour from the hull. Senshini caught glimpses of the closest enemy, sheltering in the cover of fallen column sections as they swapped fire with the Jouryans – dressed in rags, skin pale and torn, covered in old open wounds that didn't bleed. He saw tatters of finery and Enforcement Division uniforms. Opaque grey eyes took aim. Hands with missing fingers held hunting rifles and salvaged Elysian lasguns.

Every single dead man was walking again, and fighting too – the whole of Septiam City and half a regiment of butchered Elysians, lost Jouryan patrols, workers from the now-ruined soulfire fields. The commanders had expected a fraction of the city's inhabitants still to be waiting at the walls. But now Senshini could see there were thousands of them, streaming down the breach into the advancing Jouryans like bloodants from a nest.

A storm of laser fire was like burning red stitches between the fallen blocks. Lascannon shots streaked from Jouryan armour moving up and explosions stitched the rubble slope where mortar and anti-tank volleys hit home.

The Executioner juddered to a halt. Senshini lined up another shot, paused to check the coils had charged, and sent another blastgun shot ripping into a knot of Septiams huddling in the cover of a fallen marble block. Two squads of Jouryans, no longer pinned down by the enemy fire, ran forward through the falling debris.

The Chimeras of Squadron Twenty skidded to a halt in a slew of mud. The top hatches and rear ramps swung open and the occupants leapt out, guns blazing.

'Looks like we got some glory boys,' said Senshini. 'They must've given Squadron Twenty to the storm troopers.'

But they weren't storm troopers, Senshini realised. They were huge figures, much larger than a man, and in the few seconds before grime and flying mud turned them into a spattered dark grey he saw that they wore purple, not the dull fatigues of the Jouryans.

'Shenking gakrats,' swore Senshini. 'Marines.'

Kaito opened the observer hatch and dared to poke his head up into the shrapnel-filled air. He pulled a pair of field glasses from inside his coat. Senshini was sure he heard a cheer go up from the Jouryan attackers, even over the din of gunfire, as the Space Marines charged into battle beside them. Every Guardsman had heard of the Adeptus Astartes and some even claimed to have seen them on the battlefield, superhuman warriors who could strike like lightning into the heart of the enemy, wore massive powered armour and had the best weapons the Imperium could provide. Preachers extolled them as paragons of humankind. Children swapped stories about their exploits. They decorated a million stained glass windows and sculpted friezes in temples and basilica across the Imperium, and now they were here on Septiam Torus.

After a long couple of seconds Kaito dropped back into the tank. 'Right, Command have sent us some Space Marines. It's the first and last time we'll see these buggers so we're going to close in and support them. If that breach can fall, they're going to be the ones to take it. Tanako, as close as you can. Senshini, I want plasma at the top of the wall, give these freaks nowhere to run. Fire at will, Now!'

The Executioner roared into the shadow of the walls, rumbling past the fallen column sections and crunching through the dead of the assault, heading for the maelstrom of the breach where the Space Marines were weaving a new kind of hell amongst the Septiams.

Jouryans were rallying all around, following the Executioner into the storm of fire, officers yelling at their men to follow in the Marines' wake. Senshini sighted the heart of the breach where the corpse-like Septiams were massed, thrown back by the shock of the renewed assault.

Senshini fired the blastgun and plasma erupted as if from beneath the rubble. He spotted the Marines scrambling up the burning slope, boltguns chewing through the swarming Septiams, and he knew the battle for Septiam City was on.

EVERYTHING WAS COLD. Thaddeus couldn't feel his hands or feet. For a horrible moment he thought he might have lost them to frostbite or shrapnel flying from the disintegrating cathedral, but then a prickly, electrical pain flashed through the nerves of his arms and legs and he knew that he was whole.

He tried tensing the muscles he could feel, expecting a sunburst of pain to tell him of a broken limb or a ruptured organ. He couldn't find any obvious injuries, but he was constricted. He thought he might be lying down but he couldn't sit up or turn his head. Although the numbness from the cold kept him from being sure, it felt like his hands were encased in something that stopped him even moving his fingers.

He smelled chemicals. Preservatives, disinfectants, a substance that smelled rusty and metallic like something distilled from blood. Ruthlessly clean and sterile.

At first he thought there was no sound – but gradually he picked out layers of soft noise, fluorescent buzzing, the faint irregular ticking and scratching from some machine near his head, a faint dripping of liquid.

Finally, he tried to pry his eyes open. A slash of light burned across his vision and it was several minutes before he could begin to see – he must have been unconscious for some time and his eyes were barely able to adjust to the light. He seemed to be looking up at a square of pure light, until gradually a pair of glowstrips coalesced in the centre of a white-painted ceiling.

The walls were also white. The floor was polished metal with channels leading to a central drain to bleed away unwanted fluids – this alone told Thaddeus he was in a medical facility. The machine by his head was a medical servitor, a biological brain somewhere in its chromed casing telling the armatures jutting from its front to scribble Thaddeus's life-signs onto a long strip of parchment that spooled from the machine. Several cylinders were racked on one wall, thin transparent tubes feeding odd-coloured fluid into the gauntlets that covered his hands and wrists. The gauntlets were medical contraptions that kept veins in his hands and wrists open to keep medication flowing into him. The pains he had felt were the occasional probing of neurosensors adhering to his skin, triggering pain receptors intermittently to check his nervous system was still working.

Thaddeus listened harder. Beneath the faint thrum of the lighting and the ticking of the medical machinery, there was a distant rumbling, like a thunderstorm over the horizon. Engines – he was on a spaceship, then. It made sense, seeing as the last place he remembered being was in space.

There was a faint chiming as the light on the life signs machine blinked in response to Thaddeus's waking. A few minutes later the room's single featureless door slid open and Lord Inquisitor Kolgo walked in.

Kolgo seemed weak and wizened outside his ceremonial armour. He wore shapeless dark robes like a monk's habit, and the neuro-interfaces were red and raw on the back of his head where his armour was normally connected. To anyone else he would just look like another old man – but Thaddeus could see the authority Kolgo still carried with him, the indefinable quality that made even fellow inquisitors accept his command.

Kolgo pulled a chrome-plated chair close to the bed, and sat down.

'You are most determined, Thaddeus,' he said. 'I confess we really didn't anticipate you going this far.' There was a faint note of amusement in his voice.

'The Hereticus gave me a job to do,' replied Thaddeus, his voice raw and painful in his throat. 'Any inquisitor would have done the same.'

Kolgo shook his head, almost sadly. 'Our mistake was both underestimating and overestimating you, Thaddeus. Underestimated because we thought that your skills were not yet well developed enough to allow you to pursue the Soul Drinkers as closely as you have. Overestimated because we thought you would be quicker to develop a sense for the consequences of your actions. The Inquisitorial remit is theoretically limitless, but Thaddeus, for the Throne's sake – Pharos? After I told you how delicate our situation with the Mechanicus was. The damn place only blew seventy-two hours ago and already sub-battlefleet Aggarendon has lost three ships to the withdrawal of tech-priest support. Ordinatus units on Calliargan and Vogel are about to fall silent. The Mechanicus are convinced that Teturact somehow got at Pharos and the tech-guard presence there has been tripled.'

'You have your objectives, Kolgo, I have mine.'

'Ah yes, the Soul Drinkers. Presumably you know why you were given the task of tracking them down.'

'Because I could do it. And because I work differently from Tsouras.'

Kolgo reached up to the life signs machine and made an adjustment. The medi-gauntlets around Thaddeus's hands cracked open and there were several pinpricks of pain as the sensors and needles were withdrawn. Warmth seeped back into Thaddeus's body and he felt he could move again – he flexed his fingers and arms, and gradually sat up. He was aching and tired, but there was no more pain than there should be.

'We chose you, Thaddeus,' said Kolgo with an unforgivable twinkle in his eye, 'because we knew you would fail. We knew you would keep your distance, tailing the Soul Drinkers and gathering information without actually striking. You are a watcher, Thaddeus, a listener. A good one, too. But not a victor.'

'You didn't want them stopped.'

'Oh, we did. I and the inner circles of the Ordo Hereticus recognise the Soul Drinkers as a grave threat and it is entirely our intention to corner and destroy them. But not just yet. Think about it, Thaddeus. We estimate the Soul Drinkers Chapter is between half and three-quarters strength, with no chance of reinforcement. That gives us a maximum of seven hundred and fifty Space Marines with barely a handful of surviving Chapter serfs if the evidence from the scuttled fleet is anything to go by. My household's own staff numbers more than three times that. The storm troopers attached directly to my command outnumber the Soul Drinkers tenfold.

'Space Marines from preachers' sermons can take on entire armies on their own but the truth is rather different. Without the support of other Imperial forces, or hordes of cultists or secessionists, or legions of daemons, they are alone and vulnerable. There is no point being the head of the spear if there is no haft or driving hand to back you up. The Soul Drinkers are dangerous but compared to someone like Teturact, they really are of little consequence. And there are many creatures like Teturact loose in the galaxy, I am afraid to say.'

'So you sent me after them because they aren't important.'

'On the contrary, Thaddeus. They could be very important. Regardless of the truth, Space Marines are legends. Traitor Marines are a nightmare. There is something so inherently heretical in the very concept that it carries with it far greater power than the actual Marines in question.'

Thaddeus should have felt betrayed and used. But he felt neither in particular – he just felt small, like a tiny wheel in a huge machine. It was a strange, dry feeling, as if his blood had been drained and replaced with dust. All his life he had worked for the Inquisition, battling against the vastness of the galaxy in a quest to make a difference. But now, with Lord Inquisitor Kolgo sitting next to him and explaining how he was just a pawn in better men's games, the galaxy seemed vaster than ever.

'They are a weapon,' said Thaddeus, his voice tired. 'A political weapon.'

Kolgo smiled, almost like a father. 'I knew you would realise it eventually. It surprised me you didn't get it more quickly. The Soul Drinkers are political capital – an enemy with the symbolic power of a renegade Chapter is not to be destroyed lightly. There will be times when the Ordo Hereticus must fight its corner against the rest of the Imperium, for the Imperium is almost as likely to harbour enemies as the ranks of the heretic and the alien. When that happens, we need the power of such symbols to prove our worth in the eyes of the lesser-minded of the Emperor's servants. The Soul Drinkers are to be destroyed when it would bring us the most benefit, and when that time comes we will bring more and better minds to bear than yours.'

'I understand,' said Thaddeus. 'I am expected to track the Soul Drinkers but not to move on them until you give the word.'

'It will be a long time before you really understand.' Kolgo stood up and, as if on command, a pair of valet servitors trundled in, their low bodies sprouting long, thin manipulators that held the simple, dark leather bodyglove and blastcloak of an interrogator. 'You will be taken back to the fortress at Caitaran and reassigned. We need competent minds like yours in the warzone. The trip will take about three weeks – I'm afraid I can only offer clothes such as these and few comforts, I keep a very simple ship.'

'The data I collected. It was in a data-slate in a pocket of my HE suit. Do you have it?'

'Everything you were wearing was lost. Only your sidearm was robust enough to survive. A very nice piece, if I may say, particularly the ammunition. I have it in my armoury here.'

'No matter,' said Thaddeus, hoping Kolgo couldn't tell when he was lying. 'It didn't contain anything important.'

But in a way it was true. Thaddeus only remembered two names from the reams of data he had salvaged, but they were the most important information of all. The first was Karlu Grien, a Magos Biologis who was the only surviving adept to have worked in a certain isolated genetor facility. The second was the name of the facility itself: Stratix Luminae.

SEPTIAM CITY BURNED. The Gathalamorian artillery had lobbed incendiary charges into the presumed hotspots of defenders – the palace quarter, the senate buildings, the Enforcement Division barracks – and raging firestorms had engulfed the flammable hovels that crowded against the city's once-grand buildings. But far worse were the fires the defenders themselves had set. They didn't need to breathe as normal men did, so tottering piles of plague dead were lit to fill the streets with banks of greasy, stinking smoke. Ammunition and fuel dumps were rigged to blow and the first elements of the Stratix XXIII through the defences to the north found themselves in a nightmare of booby-traps and flaming debris. The Jouryans entered through the southern quarter, which was composed of the more spacious gardens and townhouses of Septiam Torus's middle classes, so they moved faster and further when the breaches were taken.

At their head were their unexpected allies, the Space Marines who had arrived at the largest breach at the critical moment and punched through the defences like a dagger. Few Jouryans asked what had happened to the crews and medics of Squadron Twenty – all they saw were purple-armoured warriors a head taller than any Guardsman, who charged ahead with insane speed and seemed almost desperate to come to grips with the enemy face to face.

The Stratix XXIII found themselves bogged down in the sprawling dwellings to the north. The homes of dead soulfire harvesters became room-to-room battlegrounds where dug-in weapons teams shredded Stratix troopers at intersections and in open spaces, where tripwires rigged with demo charges blunted assaults long enough for the Septiams to counter-attack.

But the Stratix XXIII had all lived out childhoods in the vicious underhives of their lost homeworld, and were happier fighting with bayonet and guile than out in the open. For many of them it was like coming home, and the Stratix were slowly, savagely, bleeding the Septiams dry, drawing more and more enemies from the south of the city into a meat grinding killing zone. Most of their officers were dead – but they had mostly been outsiders brought in by the Guard to tame the savages, and the Stratix fought this battle better on their own.

The Jouryans made good speed through to the palace quarter, which had formed the elegant marble core of the city before death and disease turned the place into a charnel house mockery of splendour. Grand buildings stripped of their roofs formed sheer-walled canyons of priceless marble, often with gilded decorations still coiling gracefully along the scorched stone. Tanks rumbled through the broader streets and blasted the ill-disciplined Septiam snipers off the tops of the walls.

A brutal jungle fight erupted between several Jouryan platoons and the blood-streaked retinue of a corrupted Septiam noble in the lush botanical gardens of a senator's villa. The noble hunted Jouryans with a silver-chased groxrifle in his rotting hands while the Jouryans waded through a tiny square of death-world terrain. One of the city's forums became a critical objective for staging armoured thrusts towards the senate-house, and Guardsmen fought almost toe-to-toe with thousands of Septiams over a space barely a hundred metres wide. Leman Russ tanks formed mobile strong-points to hold courtyards and gardens as Jouryan platoons leapfrogged from one shattered residence to the next. Wounded men drowned in ornamental pools. Shells airburst in the boughs of trees in the city parks and killed dozens with splinters of exotic hardwood.

And at the front of the slowing tide of Jouryans were the Space Marines, charging into labyrinthine villas with bolters blazing and chainswords sparking on the stone, flushing concentrations of walking dead out into Jouryan fire-zones and taking strong-points for the Guardsmen to occupy behind them.

The Jouryans followed them, because any man who valued his life chose to consolidate the path of destruction they blazed rather then venture into the enemy-held quarters.

When the Marines veered to one side and began to fight their way towards the Enforcement Division barracks instead of the senate house, the Jouryans backed them up with little argument from senior officers who were having trouble following the rapid advance anyway. The smooth, towering walls of the barracks formed a formidable barrier between the attackers, and the plan had been for the Jouryans to bypass the fortified compound entirely, leaving it to elements of Gathalamorian artillery to move up and hurl high explosives over the wall until the barracks were dust.

The Space Marines had other plans. When they went into direct assault against the most fortified structure in Septiam City, the Jouryans began to wonder why the Space Marines were actually here.

'OVER THE WALL! Now!' yelled Captain Karraidin, a huge tank-like figure in his Terminator armour, waving the Assault Marines forward with his enormous power fist.

Tellos knew that was his cue. He wasn't a sergeant any more – he had no rank at all, not even battle-brother, officially. But the Assault Marines of the Soul Drinkers followed him anyway, because to them there was no better symbol of the resolve that had taken the Chapter so far. Tellos was more severely mutated and crippled than any of them, and yet he loved nothing better than to be at the forefront of the assault where he could do the Emperor's work in destroying His enemies. He was an inspiration. He was the very tip of the spear.

Tellos broke cover and sprinted from the shadows of the collapsed Administratum building across the corpse-littered road from the barracks wall. He wore no armour on the upper half of his body and the wind was hot and grimy against his skin, sharp and painful against the stumps of still-red flesh where his hands had once been. He had lost both hands during the betrayal when the Soul Drinkers had first been forced to turn against the Imperium. Now he had replaced them with twin chainblades from the Chapter armoury, old-pattern chainswords with broad, curved blades like machetes.

Gunfire spattered down from the Septiams manning an autocannon post on the wall, surrounded by razor wire. Shrapnel and a couple of shots hit Tellos but they passed right through his shockingly white, strangely gelatinous flesh, cutting through skin and muscle that knitted itself back together again leaving scores of tiny white scars.

A burning Leman Russ tank had crashed into the wall, its blazing form reaching halfway up the wall. Tellos ran through the rain of gunfire and leapt onto the tank, scrambling quickly up onto its turret, chainblades scoring gouges in the armour. He could hear the footsteps of twenty Assault Marines as they followed him and they felt exactly what he did – the enemy were just a few steps away, crowded into the barracks, practically begging for the Emperor's justice.

Tellos leapt onto the crest of the wall. It bulged outwards at the top to prevent anyone climbing it but Tellos's chainblades dug deep into the plasticrete and he hauled himself up onto the crest of the wall.

Two autogun shots punched through his abdomen. He felt the pain, but he welcomed it, because that meant his body was healing as quickly as it was wounded. Bolt pistol fire crackled from the Marines beside him and the fire point on the wall fell silent. Tellos barely glanced at the Marines following him up, and he jumped into the compound.

The main barracks was an imposing building of black metal with gun-slits for windows, surrounded by a wide plasticrete plaza criss-crossed by fire points on the building and on each corner of the compound's walls. A makeshift village of hovels and tents had grown up around the building and there were scores of Septiams here, massed near the main blast-doors in the opposite wall, ready for the Jouryans to blow the doors and try to take the compound.

If the Soul Drinkers hadn't been there, perhaps that was what would have happened. But with Tellos leading the assault from an unexpected direction, every one of those Septiams was dead.

Tellos hit the ground running and twenty Marines followed him. Every second he spent here was a second when the enemy were beyond his reach and so he charged headlong through the jerry-built shanty-town. He ran heedlessly through the walls of flimsy dwellings and brushed hovels aside with his chainblades, barely breaking step to slice through the few defenders who managed to turn and face him.

The Septiams – several hundred of them, clustered around barricades to form a killing zone inside the blastdoors – barely had time to notice the assault charging in behind them.

Tellos was a good dozen paces ahead of the assault squads. When he hit the Septiam lines, he didn't stop to fight. He dived into the mass of Septiams and kept going, carving deep into their ranks, twin chainblades swinging in great arcs that severed limbs and head with every stroke. The Septiams turned and tried to counter-charge but they just ran straight into the storm of death.

Tellos strode deeper into the Septiams, leaving a gore-soaked channel of broken bodies that gave the Assault Marines a crucial gap to get a foothold against them.

Rotting faces lolled as they died a second time. Knobbed, grey-skinned limbs swung clubs and knives uselessly. Short-range lasbursts and autogun shots spat from the throng but Tellos ignored them, absorbing the ill-aimed shots with his mutated flesh and slicing off the hands that tried to bring weapons to bear too close.

It was the purest butchery. The rage came on Tellos again, the same rage that had first been sparked in him when he lost his hands on the Geryon weapons platform, and had continued burning inside him as he stormed the beaches of Ve'Meth's stronghold and battled daemons on the deck of the *Brokenback*. It took hold of him and pushed him further than any Marine could go. It was the fuel that fed his mutated flesh and the impossibly fast, deadly strikes he made with the improvised weapons thrust into the stumps of his wrists.

Tellos didn't live for much else – the rage was the only thing that could make him feel worth anything. Killing in the name of the Emperor was the purest form of service, and when His spirit took over Tellos there was nothing that could stop him.

His chainblades were clotted with blood. He was covered in gore from head to toe, occulobe organs secreting fluids to wash the blood out of his eyes, blood raw on his pale skin and slick against the armour on his legs. Hundreds of faces merged into one as he thrust in every direction, the Septiams trying to surround him just walking into the killing zone that radiated from him.

The more mindless Septiams were driven forward to surround and swamp him. He batted them aside or cut them in two, clambering onto the rampart formed from their bodies to hack down at the tainted troopers from above. Scores died around him, hundreds, every cut ending an undeserving life. The Assault Marines pushed the Septiams back against the gates and forced them into Tellos – those who tried to counterattack found themselves trying to duel with superhuman warriors whose armour turned away bayonets and rifle shots and whose chainblades cut through flesh, bone, and salvaged Elysian armour alike.

Tellos saw Jouryan helmets, Elysian fatigues, senators' finery and Enforcement Division uniforms, all wrapped around subhuman corpse-creatures, faces twisted with hatred and disease. Their desiccated tongues moaned and gurgled as they died. Their bones cracked and skin split, muscles ripped to rags by the chainblade teeth. It was the purest slaughter of all, corruption and decay vanquished by the Emperor's strength, Tellos's rage a link to the Emperor like a vox-line to the Golden Throne.

A heavy hand clapped down onto Tellos's shoulder and only the reflexes hard-wired into Tellos's brain kept him from driving his chainblades into the body of a fellow Marine.

Captain Karraidin's leathery, battered face snarled out of the hood of his Terminator armour. 'Damn it, Tellos! The enemy's broken! Blow these doors and get to the brig entrance!'

For a moment Tellos was enraged that the Emperor's work had been so rudely interrupted.

Didn't Karraidin realise they were surrounded by slavering, corrupted enemies?

Then he saw what Karraidin saw – Tellos was just a few metres from the inside of the compound wall, standing on a pile of bodies twenty men high, with the Septiams broken and cowering around him.

Karraidin was right. The rage could wait a while before taking over again.

He waved the two assault squads forward from where they had formed a line of steel backing him up. All carried frag and krak grenades and several had melta-bombs designed to melt through armoured hulls. The Assault Marines sprinted across the blood-slicked ground to the huge double blastdoors and attached bundles of grenades to the hinges and bolts.

Meanwhile, Karraidin's command squad swapped bolter fire with the fire points on the walls and in the barracks buildings, covering the Assault Marines as they rigged the doors and fell back before blowing them.

The blastdoors fell open in a shower of sparks, sheets of steel crashing to the rockcrete ground.

Squads Luko and Hastis entered under Karraidin's covering fire. With them was Sarpedon. 'Good work Karraidin, Tellos,' he voxed. 'We've cleared out the buildings around the perimeter. The Jouryans are holding them. The Septiams are trapped between the Stratix and the Jouryans and they'll try to break out at any moment, so we have no time to waste.

Hastis and Luko, you're with me into the holding cells. Karraidin, hold the doors. Tellos, you're reserve. Cold and fast, Soul Drinkers, move out.'

The small strike-force Sarpedon had managed to smuggle into Septiam City split in two, Karraidin and Tellos to take up positions in the compound amongst the broken bodies of the Septiams, Sarpedon and the two tactical squads heading towards the barracks building from which intermittent fire still spattered down from roof and gun-slit windows.

Somewhere beneath that building were the holding cells, where the criminals of Septiam Torus had been held before the plague took a hold. If they had not been emptied in the chaos that gripped the city, and if there was anything left alive down there, then somewhere in those cells was Adept Karlu Grien.

NINE

From the observation deck of the yacht, the war-zone seemed calm. The stars were as hard and cold as they were anywhere else in the galaxy, and had Thaddeus not been so familiar with the torments of Teturact's rebellion it would have been easy for him to assume that all was right in the heavens.

But he knew that one tiny winking red star was actually the forge world of Salshan Anterior, where half a million Guardsmen had been surrounded and butchered on the oxide-rich plains and where the Navy was now primed to bomb the hardened workshop-bunkers into dust. One constellation was composed of unnamed dead xenos worlds where Guardsmen and tech-guard warred with tens of thousands of Teturact's cultists, battles flowing like water over planets of frozen oxygen. Gigantic fleet actions were being enacted right in front of his eyes, the blackness between the stars scattered with battleships maintaining blockades and forming up from orbital barrage runs.

The yacht's observation deck was a crystal hemisphere blistered out from the upper hull, providing an unbroken panorama of space. Several drinks cabinets and reclining couches rose from the floor and a trio of personal servitors waited attentively in case their masters showed any signs of needing something. It was an easy place to forget about war.

But Thaddeus could not forget. Lord Kolgo was probably right – he was far more experienced an inquisitor than Thaddeus would probably ever be. However, Thaddeus still had a job to do. He had made a private vow, and he could not betray himself by breaking it now. No matter what the cost.

A circular hole hissed open in the floor and a platform rose up. On the platform was an impossibly slight figure, a man so insubstantial it seemed he hardly cast a shadow. He wore a cobalt uniform trimmed with silver bullion and his frail body was topped with a curiously featureless face, smooth jet-black skin almost unbroken by eyes, nose and mouth. A length of white cloth embroidered with High Gothic devotionals was tied around his head, and the blistered, charred skin just showing on the man's forehead indicated the stresses regularly placed on the warp eye underneath.

'Navigator,' said Thaddeus. 'I am glad you could join me.'

The Navigator smiled. 'Your invitation took me by surprise, my master. I am not much used to social functions. I hope I am not found lacking.'

'Not at all,' replied Thaddeus with his friendliest smile. 'There are trillions of souls in this galaxy, it is only right that you should get to meet a few of them. Amasec? Assuming you're not on duty, of course.' He held out a decanter and glass.

The Navigator accepted a glass of the rich, treacly amasec, which Lord Inquisitor Kolgo had probably had imported at a cost Thaddeus couldn't imagine. The Navigator took a tentative sip and seemed to appreciate the nicety.

Thaddeus looked up at the starscape. 'What do you see, Navigator?' he asked. 'Does it look anything like this in the warp?'

It was a risk. Navigators rarely spoke of what they saw when they led ships through the dreams and nightmares of the warp and there was an unspoken taboo against asking them about it. Thaddeus reasoned that this meant Kolgo's Navigator had probably never been asked, and that it would be a relief for him to tell someone.

'It... sometimes. At first. We want it to look the same, you see. Everyone knows what space looks like, everyone who has ever seen the night sky. But after the first few moments you have to let it change. You have to begin to see the warp as it truly is. There are no rules to it – half of it is inside your head – but that doesn't make it any less real. Just by looking at it, you change it. The Astronomican is the only constant and even then it can flicker and leave you alone. All the things you see when between sleeping and waking, those are real in the warp. There are colours you can't make with light and every now and again, something... looks back at you...' He smiled again, taking another swallow of amasec. 'And you can call me Starn. Iason Starn.'

'And you can call me Thaddeus, Starn.' Thaddeus placed the decanter back into the gold-plated hands of the servitor that glided silently over to him as he sat down on one of the couches. 'I imagine Kolgo places great value on you.'

'Indeed. I have been with him for twenty-three years.'

'It sounds like we are both prisoners of a sort.'

'There are worse things.'

Thaddeus sat up suddenly, as if in surprise. 'Starn... isn't the Starn clan related to House Jenassis?'

'We are a sub-clan,' replied Starn. 'We are proud to be one of the constituent parts of House Jenassis. Few outsiders know much of our Houses, Thaddeus, you must be most learned.'

'I'm sorry, I didn't realise you counted House Jenassis as your patrons. You must all be mourning your patriarch.'

Starn nodded, looking mournfully into his amasec. 'Yes, a terrible thing. Chaos Marines, they say. The Enemy, in House Jenassis itself. Many of us do not believe it, others know it must be true but cannot fully understand it.'

'And you?'

'This is a dark galaxy, Thaddeus. Terrible things do happen. The Emperor knows I have seen enough of them with Kolgo over the years.'

Thaddeus let the silence mature. The subtle mutations that accompanied the Navigator gene hid the fact that Iason Starn was more than eighty years old, and he had probably been in service since adolescence. How often had any non-Navigator talked to him like this? Let alone an inquisitor, someone with authority, even if he was very much subordinate to Lord Kolgo.

'Phrantis Jenassis was not the best of leaders,' said Starn at last. 'But without him the House has no leadership at all. There will be another round of politics, and how we hate it. Some of us will die, inquisitor, though we are forbidden to admit it. Even Navigators have their factions.'

'So do inquisitors, Starn. But we are forbidden to mention it, too, so don't tell anyone.'

On cue, a servitor hovered up to Starn and refilled his glass. The beauty of amasec was that it didn't taste strong, but it was.

Starn was not a stupid man. He accepted the refilled glass almost resignedly, as if he had worked out what his part was to be and he was just going through the motions until it was over.

Thaddeus knew his role, too. 'If there was someone who knew who had killed Phrantis Jenassis – imagine that! Perhaps it was something slightly more complicated than a raiding force of Chaos Marines. It would almost be comforting to know that Phrantis wasn't just a random killing, wouldn't it?'

Starn took a deep swallow. 'I should have guessed this wasn't a social call. Why would a man of your station associate with me out of choice?'

'Why would a man of your quality associate with your master's prisoner? That's what I am, Iason, and you are well aware of it. You don't want to spend the rest of your life flirting with madness. Perhaps you were once content, but not any more. You find yourself dreaming of the life of a common citizen. You wish you could be something more than you are, because what you are is a piece of someone else's machine. Lord Kolgo considers you a part of this ship. Why shouldn't he? You've never claimed to be anything more. But if you could do something meaningful, something that would affect the whole of House Jenassis – that would be worth something far more.'

'I have heard… stories.' Iason Starn's eyes were suddenly alive, as if he were finally aware of himself. They formed an incongruous focus in his featureless face. 'Inquisitors can have a man skinned alive with a word. They can kill thousands, millions if they think they have to. It would be nothing for

Lord Kolgo to have me killed if he thought I was betraying his trust.'

'It is too late for that, Iason. Kolgo has this place bugged, of course. He knows every word we have said. If he wants to have you liquidated he will have made the decision already, no matter what you do. You know I am right, Iason. And you should consider yourself fortunate – now you can make your decision without worrying about what Kolgo will do, because he will have made up his mind already.'

Starn was shaking, and almost unconsciously bolted the rest of the amasec to calm his nerves. 'I can see why you inquisitors are so feared.'

'You should see Kolgo in full flow. He does the same thing to fellow inquisitors. Now, the choice.'

'The choice.'

Thaddeus reached inside the plain clothes he had been given in the infirmary. He took out a small, folded letter. 'This document is in.cipher, you need never know what it says. All I need is for you to make sure it is transmitted to the correct astropathic duct. Nothing more. I have no access to Kolgo's astropaths but you do. Kolgo will consider me a potential ally for the future and will let me get away with this, because crossing me now could come back to haunt him in the unlikely event I rise to a similar rank as he. He will not let me get away with a blatant abuse of his hospitality, however, since that would hardly be playing the game. So I must use you.

'Kolgo cannot get rid of you immediately since that would leave him in largely uninhabited space without a Navigator and his work within the warzone is too important for him to spend months marooned. Once he has returned to the fortress you will be surrounded by fellow Navigators and can doubtless organise some protection from other members of your House. This game is not without its risks, but you see how you have a relatively low-risk part to play.'

Starn waved away the servitor that came to refill his glass once again. 'What a complicated game.'

Thaddeus smiled, genuinely this time. 'Politics, Iason. I'm just learning myself.'

The Navigator stood, smoothed down the flawless uniform of Clan Starn and took the letter from Thaddeus's hand. 'I am afraid, inquisitor, that my time is short. There are charts to be drawn up and courses to plot, you know how it is.'

'Of course, Navigator Starn. I wouldn't want to keep you from your work. The Emperor protects.'

'That he does, inquisitor.' Starn stepped onto the platform and disappeared back through the floor. If Thaddeus was lucky, he would soon be delivering Thaddeus's message which, if again he was lucky, would reach the *Crescent Moon* shortly.

Not only would his strikeforce be able to act on the information he had recovered from the cathedral, but it would also demonstrate to Kolgo that keeping Thaddeus a virtual prisoner on his yacht served very little purpose. Kolgo couldn't visit anything outrageous on Thaddeus – the Inquisitor Lord had only as much authority as his fellow inquisitors let him have and he needed lesser men to defer to him. Thaddeus could be one of those lesser men, which meant it wasn't in Kolgo's interests to have him imprisoned, killed, or anything else.

Thaddeus hated the idea that infighting and point-scoring should be as large a part of the inquisitor's world as fighting the Emperor's foes. But the game was there to be played, and if he had to play it to fulfil his vows, then play it he would.

And no matter what Kolgo wanted, Thaddeus had a critical advantage. He had Stratix Luminae. Very soon, he felt that little else would matter.

THE MESSAGE HAD been simple. There were two locations – the first was Stratix Luminae, a location which was absolutely not to be approached without Inquisitor Thaddeus himself. The second was Septiam Torus, last recorded location of Adept Karlu Grien, which could be the last chance the strikeforce had to intercept the Soul Drinkers before Stratix Luminae, after which they might be lost forever.

Colonel Vinn and the storm troopers, minus the recon platoons lost at Pharos, were waiting in deep system space for Thaddeus's next communication. Septiam Torus, meanwhile, belonged to the Sisters.

Sister Aescarion slipped the restraints of the grav-couch and reached up to grab the handrail mounted onto the ceiling of the Valkyrie's passenger compartment. Aescarion had bullied the three Valkyrie aerial transports plus crews out of the rear echelon Jouryan forces, knowing that fifty battle-ready Sisters and the mention of Inquisitorial authority was more than enough to secure anything she might need.

By the time she had made it to the surface of Septiam Torus the battle for Septiam City was almost a full day old and she needed to get into the thick of it quick. They said there were Space Marines spearheading the Jouryan assault, and even if they did not turn out to be the Soul Drinkers, it seemed the Imperial forces could do with a force of heavily-armed battle-sisters fighting alongside them.

The Valkyrie lurched as it switched to defensive manoeuvres. Aescarion couldn't see out of the passenger compartment but she could hear the anti-aircraft fire punching up past the Valkyrie from enemy-held sections of the city, and knew the ruins of Septiam City would be streaking by below. One good hit now and the twenty Sisters with her would die in an instant, regardless of training, armour, or even faith. But that was the way war went. Aescarion had taken a vow long ago to wait for death and welcome it, when the time came.

Her battle-sisters felt the same. She had her own Seraphim squad and two more squads, Retributors carrying three heavy flamers led by Sister Aspasia and a ten-strong unit under Sister Superior Rufilla. Two more Valkyries carried similar complements – whether it would be enough to face the Soul Drinkers would be in the hands of the Emperor.

'Black Three's lost an engine, ma'am,' came the tinny voice of the pilot through the ship's vox. 'Says he's going down.'

'Can they land?' replied Aescarion, the image of a score of valiant dead Sisters flitting through her mind. Black Three was the lead Valkyrie in the formation, heading for the plaza near the senate-house which the Jouryans had just liberated from the enemy.

'They can bring her down but they're well short. They're going to hit the slums.'

'We can't be spread out. Follow them in and prepare for deployment. From the Enemy will the Golden Throne deliver us, citizen.'

'Whatever you say, ma'am,' replied the pilot. 'Hold on.'

Bad news. The designated landing zone would have put the Sisters behind the last reported location of the Marines, in a position to assault them if they were the Soul Drinkers or reinforce them if they were loyalist Marines. The situation in the city was fluid and confused, but from what Aescarion understood the slums were seething with close-quarters battles between the benighted Septiams and the Stratix XXIII. Aescarion wasn't sure which would be more dangerous to her Sisters.

'Coming down, ma'am. Doors away,' said the pilot, his voice strained as he fought to pull the Valkyrie's nose up after a steep descent.

'Sisters!' yelled Aescarion. 'Prepare to deploy! Aspasia, I want fire before we hit the ground! Rufilla, secure our zone and cover us!'

The Sisters Superior saluted in acknowledgement, and then the rear ramp juddered open.

The Valkyrie was swooping down an avenue of shattered slum buildings, little more than shacks piled on top of one another until they spilled into the road and crushed the lower layers into strata of rubble. More solid buildings were pocked and scorched by small arms and artillery. Greying tangles of bodies lay clustered around intersections and barricades. Smoke plumed up from below, filling the compartment with the stink of fuel and las-burned air. Tracer fire streaked from every other window and explosions crumped beneath the sudden roar of the Valkyrie's engines.

Black Three was already down, one engine billowing black smoke, the bulk of the ship laid crossways across the road where it had crash-landed and skidded to a halt. The black-armoured forms of Sisters were deploying rapidly from the stricken transport, using the hull itself for cover or sprinting through a shower of enemy fire into the ruins at the side of the road.

Aescarion saw they were coming down almost on top of Black Three. The Valkyrie dipped lower, downward thrust driving up thick clouds of dust and debris. Without waiting for the pilot's signal, she ran onto the ramp and jumped.

She flicked a switch and her Seraphim jump pack kicked in. Useless on Eumenix, she and her squad had equipped with the jump packs knowing how useful they could be deploying from the air. Her squad followed, Sister Mixu right behind her, all with bolt pistols drawn and cocked.

Aescarion hit the ground and managed to keep her feet. She was about thirty metres from Black Three, a smouldering dark shape through the swirl of dust. The engine roar was suddenly replaced with gunfire, crackling from all directions. The distinctive report of bolt weapons told her that the Sisters were leaving Black Three and returning fire from the ruined buildings that lined the road. Smaller-calibre weapons blazed down from the buildings all around and Aescarion knew that while they didn't have the discipline of the Sisters, they had far greater numbers. She glimpsed muzzle flashes and oddly twisted, loping humanoid forms through the chaos.

A single report sounded and a las-flash, white-hot, speared through the air next to her. Aescarion glanced behind her in time to see one of her Seraphim fall, shot through the throat by a long-las shot.

Snipers.

Aescarion loosed off a few shots at the closest attackers and ran for the nearest cover. She couldn't get pinned down here. She had to get clear, then gather the Sisters and break out. If she paused for a moment they could be surrounded and bogged

down, and not get out of here until the whole city
was won. That was not an option.

The collapsed building offered scraps of cover,
half-toppled walls and piles of rubble. Aescarion
dived for cover as a volley of shots tore down from
the other side of the street. Autogun and las-fire
kicked up sprays of broken stone and wood around
her as she hit the ground.

More fire followed, this time from directly above.
Sister Mixu skidded in beside her, twin bolt pistols
drawn, and both Sisters returned fire into the
remains of the ceiling overhead.

They had taken cover directly beneath an enemy
fire point. Through the ragged hole twisted faces
leered down, rotten jawbones hanging, skeletal
hands aiming their rusted guns down at the Sisters.

Shots rang off Aescarion's armour. She and Mixu
returned fire, pumping bolt shells through the ceiling into the attackers, sending showers of debris
falling. Aescarion felt a shot crease her cheek. The
fire fight drew more attackers in, sharpshooters
picking shots through the swirling dust and more
Septiams crawled through the ruined buildings to
face this new threat. Mixu fired upwards with one
hand and sideways with the other. Aescarion drew
her power axe but even her power armour could be
overwhelmed by the sheer weight of fire coming at
her if she were to stand up and charge.

A sheet of pure white flame tore through the
building at head-height, then swung upwards to fill

the building above with billowing flame. Burning skeletons fell down from above, and the gunfire was replaced with the strangled screams of burning men.

Aescarion looked up to see Sister Aspasia directing her Retributor squad's heavy flamers as they hosed the building around Aescarion's Seraphim with fire.

Aescarion saluted Sister Aspasia as the Retributors and Sister Rufilla's squad moved in to secure the ruins.

'Seraphim,' she yelled, 'with me! Forward!' Aescarion charged through the rubble, towards where the Sisters from Black Three were holed up. She and her Seraphim blasted the Septiams who rounded a ruined doorway in front of them at close range, shattering half-a-dozen diseased bodies before Aescarion lunged through the door and laid into the Septiams beyond. A sharpshooter, long-las still clutched in his gnarled hands, fell headless to the rubble. Aescarion's axe cut the arm off another Septiam and her boot shattered his spine as he fell. One of her Seraphim vaulted over the wall beside her, grabbed the closest Septiam and hauled him off his feet, shooting two of his comrades through the man's stomach.

Aspasia's squad followed Aescarion through the ruins. 'Rufilla's secured a landing zone for Black Two,' voxed the Sister Superior as she hurried over the rubble. Aspasia was a true veteran, older than Aescarion who was no young woman herself. Her power maul steamed with the caked blood burning in its power field, and her armour was pocked and smouldering with bullet scars.

'Casualties?' asked Aescarion.

'Three Sisters lost, commended to the Emperor. Tyndaria lost a hand. We can fight on,' replied Aspasia.

'Good.' Aescarion voxed all the Sisters within range. 'When Black Two is down the whole strike-force will advance southwards! This area is held by the Septiams and we will have to go through them first. Aspasia, I want you to the fore. With flame shall the unholy be cleansed.'

Aescarion switched her vox-receiver through the Guard frequencies, tapping into the tangle of transmissions blaring from all over the city. It was a chaotic mess, with two major regiments in the city and a third, the Gathalamorians, trying to coordinate artillery strikes that more often than not killed as many Guardsmen as Septiams.

Snatches of battlefield communication filtered through static. The Stratix regiment were pushing hard, butchering their way through the ruins of the residential areas in a tide that swept towards the centre of the city, the senate-house and temples.

The Jouryans, Aescarion knew from the sketchy reports she had got from the Jouryan rear echelons, formed a massive wedge thrust deep into the heart of the city as far as the Enforcement Division barracks. It was a wedge tipped by the Space Marines, who had arrived so suddenly nobody knew who they were or why they were here. To reach that position the Sisters had to get through the battle lines to the cluster of temples that cast a shadow onto the edge of the residential district, then through the heart of the Septiam defence to reach the Arbites precinct.

The roar of engines drowned out the transmissions as the shadow of Black Two passed over the road. It turned and descended, back ramp dropping and squads Tathlaya and Serentes jumping into the edge of the ruins. The Valkyrie swivelled to bring its chin-mounted guns to bear and blasted hundreds of rounds into the buildings opposite, scouring the upper floors clean of the sharpshooters. Boltguns blasted at the few Septiams still in the area, the return fire scattered and feeble. The Sister carrying Squad Serentes's heavy bolter paused at the threshold of the ruins and sent a volley of shots across the road, and Aescarion spotted broken figures flailing in a ground-floor window.

'Move out!' ordered Aescarion. Squad Aspasia broke cover under Rufilla's fire, sending sheets of flame in front of them as they moved off through the ruins, aiming to flush waiting Septiams into the teeth of Rufilla's guns.

Black One and Black Two were gone, soaring up away from the vulnerable position over the road. The Sisters were alone – but that was when they always fought the best.

* * *

THE UPPER FLOORS of the barracks building were infested with the enemy, toting weapons stripped from the precinct's armoury, many wearing patchy ill-fitting armour over their hunched bodies. Sarpedon didn't care about them. Everything he cared about was beneath the building.

Blue-white light flared in the confined basement stairwell as Sergeant Luko's lightning claws leapt into life. Squad Luko was in the front with Sarpedon, and Squad Hastis would form the rearguard to see off any Septiams coming down from the upper floors.

The door at the bottom of the stairwell was of massive plasteel, with a huge mechanical lock. Septiam City was like any other place in the galaxy, with its own criminals and petty heretics. This was where they were kept, and such people could not be allowed out.

'Mine,' said Luko with some relish. 'Back me up, men.' The sergeant lunged forward and punched both sets of claws into the metal of the lock, the talons sparking as they bored into the metal. He planted one foot against the base of the door and tore the whole locking mechanism out, ripping a ragged hole in the door, spitting with molten metal.

The door swung open and Squad Luko trained their guns into the darkness behind. Sarpedon hung back as they moved into the darkness beyond the doorway, keeping his force staff drawn. His autosenses peeled away the dark to reveal the grim grey plasticrete walls of the cell block beyond, glowstrips on the ceiling burned out, floor and walls stained with age and blood.

'We're in, no contacts,' came a vox from Squad Luko. Luko himself followed, his lightning claws casting flickering lights across the walls.

There was no sound from inside, just the rumble of battle from above. But the place stank: of sweat, decay, rotted filth. Sarpedon's engineered third lung kicked in to filter out the worst of it but it was still the stench of pure death.

The prison held two hundred inmates, mostly in solitary confinement, in cells fronted with tarnished steel bars. The first rows of cells were empty – they must have been released when the plague's madness had first gripped Septiam City.

Karlu Grien was probably among them. But Sarpedon had known that before he had come to Septiam Torus, and he had come anyway. There was always hope, no matter how slim.

'Kitchens up ahead,' voxed one of the Marines from Squad Luko.

'Move in,' said Sarpedon. Nothing moved in the shadows. The Marines trained their guns over the insides of filth-spattered cells. Sergeant Luko pushed through the large double doors into the kitchens, with long benches and tables beneath a high ceiling. Lines from Imperial psalms were carved into the plasticrete of the walls and ceiling and a pulpit stood at one end of the room where the preacher of the Enforcement Division would inform the inmates of the gravity of their sins as they ate. Like the rest of the prison the place was empty, with the kitchens ransacked and pages of devotional texts torn up and lying around the pulpit.

Luko glanced at the auspex scanner he carried, checking the layout of the brig. The Enforcement Division barracks were based on a Standard Template, the same as thousands of similar buildings on frontier and low-population worlds. 'Cell 7-F,' he said. 'Through this room and to the left, in the moral criminal wing.'

Karlu Grien was a moral criminal, a tech-heretic, guilty of making forbidden technology. He had been stationed on Septiam Torus to oversee the refining of the Soulfire crop, but what he had seen on Stratix Luminae had driven him to dabble in dark things and the Enforcement Division had locked him up. If he was still down here, he would be in cell 7-F.

'We've got movement,' voxed Sergeant Hastis from outside the kitchens.

'Karraidin?' voxed Sarpedon to the squads on the plaza above. 'Do we have hostiles coming in behind us?'

'None, commander,' replied Captain Karraidin. 'We've got them pinned down.'

'Hastis, get your men into this–'

Sarpedon was interrupted by a terrible sound, a dozen voices screaming at once, and a hideous cracking like hundreds of breaking bones. Hastis yelled an order and bolter fire roared, but the screams grew louder in reply. Luko rushed up to the door into the area, ready to take on anything that came through the door that wasn't a member of Squad Hastis.

Three Marines burst through the door at once, running backwards and firing into the corridor on full auto. They were followed by something Sarpedon could only think of as a wave of flesh, a tide of melded human forms, dozens of bodies welded into a single wall of muscle and breaking bone that erupted through the door. Twisted faces leered from the mass, hands reached and organs pulsed through rips in the taut skin. Every mouth was screaming, an atonal keening that cut through even the roar of gunfire. The stench it carried with it would have been enough to knock out a lesser man, and even Sarpedon felt it driving him back from the beast.

Sergeant Hastis was half-swallowed by the mass, too, bones snapping as the mass extruded limbs to drag him face-first into it. The Marines of his squad already swallowed were still fighting back, the flesh splitting and ripping as bolters and combat knives slashed at it from inside.

Bolt shells pumped into the mass as Squad Luko and the remaining members of Squad Hastis fell back into the dining area. Sarpedon held his force staff tight and felt the force of his will flooding into its psychoactive nalwood, the wood hot and thrumming in his hands as it focused the psychic power flowing around his body.

The mass already filled half the room and there seemed no end to it. Bolt shells seemed to have no effect.

'Mine again,' said Sergeant Luko. He spread his lightning claws and dived into the mass, the claws slashing deep scorched furrows in the flesh. Sarpedon reared up on his hind legs and leapt across the room, following Luko into the mess of melded corpses. He clambered up the front of the roiling mass and tore deep gouges with his front legs, before plunging his force staff and letting all his psychic force rip through it and into the flesh. Skin and muscle boiled away leaving a huge scorched pit beneath Sarpedon, burned deep through layers of melded bodies, sending a shower of ash bursting from the wound.

Luko ripped the slabs of flesh apart and hauled Sergeant Hastis out of the gory mass – but the front of Hastis's head had been dissolved and a bloody skull's face stared blindly out, long service studs still embedded in the bone of the forehead. Luko threw Hastis's remains behind him and slashed away the tendrils of muscle trying to entwine his legs.

The mass surged forward again and filled the room. Bolter fire poured into it and didn't seem to slow it down – tainted blood was ankle-deep in the room and chunks of shredded flesh were spattered across the walls and ceiling.

Sarpedon could feel the disease inside it, like a ball of white noise somewhere deep in the heart of the corpses. It was dense and evil, something he saw with the psychic eye inside him and felt through the skin of his mutated legs where they touched the unholy flesh. Here the supernatural disease that infected Septiam City had taken the prisoners in the cells and, in that confined space, it had worked its corruption on them until they had gathered around the carrier into this ball of melded corpses.

The carrier – the first to be infected down here, now the host for the disease – lay in the very centre of the mass. Sarpedon felt this with his mind's eye, the seething knot of disease sending out a mindless psychic scream as it powered the exertions of two hundred bodies melted into one.

Sarpedon raised his force staff and cut downwards, opening a three-metre slash in the skin. With his front legs he pulled the wound wide open, drew his bolter with his free hand, and with his hind legs powered himself into the wound. Sarpedon heard Luko yell something as he dived in. But the room would soon fill with the mass and only Sarpedon stood a chance of stopping it in time.

He couldn't see, but he could feel. Corruption flowed through the veins around him. Walls of flesh pressed against him and he held his breath to keep from inhaling the foulness of the beast's innards. He tore his way through towards the carrier, pulling himself forward with his front legs and free hand. The wound closed behind him, so he was encased in a cocoon of muscle. Bones snapped as limbs turned inward and reformed to grasp at him. The heat was intense and the darkness complete.

But he could feel the carrier, the still-human shape hunched and foetal in front of him. He gouged and clawed his way closer to it until its seething corruption was bright against his mind. With two legs he speared the body and dragged it closer to him. With one hand he grabbed it by the back of the neck, and with the other he put the bolter against the forehead and fired.

The body spasmed and the flesh surrounding it shuddered in unison as the monstrous intelligence inside was shattered. The mass released its grip on Sarpedon and he pushed himself backwards. The flesh liquefied behind him until he burst back out through the skin again, sliding to the floor on a wave of gore.

He still had the body of the carrier in one hand. It was mostly intact, save for the gaping bolter wound in its forehead and the severed arteries extruded through its skin where it had been connected to the other bodies. The prisoner's electoo was still on the back of the neck, with the prisoner's name, number, and bar code.

Somehow, it didn't come as a surprise that the carrier had been Karlu Grien.

'Take the gene-seed of the fallen,' said Sarpedon, dropping the deformed body to the ground.

One of Squad Hastis – Brother Dvoran, the youngest – removed his helmet and drew his combat knife. He kneeled down by the ruined body of Hastis and began to cut out the gene-seed organs, the twin glands in the throat and chest that controlled all a Space Marine's other augmentations.

Sergeant Hastis had been at the forefront of the assault of Ve'Meth's fortress, one of the Marines who had joined Sarpedon after the catastrophe of the Lakonia mission and Sarpedon's defeat of Chapter Master Gorgoleon. He had been as loyal as any Marine, one of the solid veterans Sarpedon relied on as much as they relied on him. Now he was dead, and so went another man who could not be replaced. They would have to cut off Hastis's head when the gene-seed was taken, to stop him from turning into a walking corpse like those that infested Septiam City.

Of course, Hastis's gene-seed couldn't then be implanted into a novice, as the Chapter traditions required. Not now. But it was still a powerful symbol, and it was symbols that held the Chapter together – so Dvoran cut the sacred organ from the sergeant's throat for transport back to the Chapter.

'It was always a long shot, commander,' said Luko, looking down at the body of Karlu Grien, the only man who could have told them the information they needed.

'Secure this area,' said Sarpedon, heading for the doors beyond the pulpit.

He tore the doors off their hinges and strode into the corridor beyond. This was where the prisoners had gathered as the madness first took them – deep gouges marked the walls where the prisoners had tried to claw their way out. Teeth and bone shards were embedded in the plasticrete and everything was stained brown-black. Bars on the cells were bent out of shape. Sarpedon could feel the madness imprinted on the walls. He could still hear the screams.

Cell 7-F was a pit of stained darkness, blood and filth crusted up the walls, the bars so corroded that they shattered as Sarpedon tore them aside. The pallet Karlu Grien had used as a bed was a slab of decay and Sarpedon's talons sunk into the caked filth on the floor as he entered the cell.

It was barely two metres square and into that space was packed so much malice and despair that Sarpedon could taste it, acrid and metallic in his mouth. Karlu Grien had probably been insane before he ever came here – Stratix Luminae had seen to that. When the plague came it sought out the most receptive carrier and found the mind of a mad heretic.

Sarpedon reached up and scraped away the hardened gore. Beneath were deep scratches in the walls, like in the corridors outside – but more ordered, forming patterns against the plasticrete. Sarpedon scraped the wall clean, revealing a pattern of straight lines and arcs that covered the whole back wall.

'They've taken Hastis's gene-seed,' said Luko. Sarpedon turned to see the sergeant standing in the corridor behind him. 'His was the only seed intact.'

'Good,' said Sarpedon. He pointed at the image gouged into the back wall. 'Record this on the auspex. Then get ready to move out, there's nothing left for us here. Send the message to Lygris to bring us out.'

'Yes, commander,' said Luko, and headed back to join his squad.

Sarpedon stared for a moment at the image, carved by a madman using the bloody stumps of his fingers. Techmarine Lygris would know if it meant anything. It was these tiny hopes that kept Sarpedon going, and the Chapter with him. They all looked to him for leadership, even born officers like Captain Karraidin or Chaplain Iktinos. If he gave in to despair then the Soul Drinkers would all give in, too – but they had followed him through the Chapter's greatest crisis and embarked with him on a mission which forced them to give up almost all they had – he owed them more than failure.

AESCARION SUSPECTED DeVayne wasn't a genuine officer. Like almost all the Stratix troopers he didn't wear the jacket of his fatigues, the loaded ammo webbing taut over a bare torso covered with gang tattoos. He wore several desiccated scalps on his belt and carried a pair of ivory-handled hunting laspistols that surely more properly belonged to a real officer. But his platoon of near-savages evidently had enough faith in DeVayne's leadership and, on the ground, that was enough for Sister Aescarion.

'Storm 'em, you sons a' hrud-lovers!' yelled DeVayne as he directed the men of his platoon into the shattered temple grounds and towards Septiam City's forum, where public buildings clustered around a wide marble-tiled plaza broken by gilded statues of Imperial heroes. The forum had become the focus for a brutal Septiam counterattack against the foremost Jouryan forces – most of the statues lay toppled by explosions and the tiles had been hurled up by artillery strikes to fall back down in a lethal stone rain. Basilica and shrines were burning shells. Jouryans and Septiams were dug in on either side, the blasted expanse of the forum a no-man's land for which thousands of men were dying.

The largest concentration of Septiams were in the grounds of the Macharian Temple, where a giant porphyry statue of Lord Solar Macharius looked out over ornamental gardens, now a mess of dug-in fire points and trenches swarming with corpse-like Septiams. It was this position that the Stratix forces were assaulting from the rear, with Aescarion's Sisters lending bolter and flame to the Stratix lasguns.

The Stratix broke cover from the tangle of minor devotionals and shrines behind the temple, heading for the rear wall of the temple grounds. They sported several exotic, salvaged guns – hunting rifles, hellguns, well-worn shotguns with hive ganger kill-marks – alongside their standard issue lasguns, and they wore a patchwork of salvaged, stolen and patched-up fatigues and body armour.

They looked more like feral world savages than Guardsmen, but after Aescarion had linked up with DeVayne's men she had watched them carving their way through the Septiam defences with the added firepower of the Sisters. They ripped their way out of the slums at last and made a massive push to link up with the Jouryans in the centre of the city. Now they were assaulting the last strongpoint between the two forces.

'Seraphim, to the fore!' yelled Aescarion and followed the Stratix out of cover and up to the wall.

The Stratix were clambering over the sagging brick wall. Aescarion glanced back to ensure her squad was with her, then thumbed the inhibitor switch on her jump pack and let it propel her clean over the wall. She landed in a roll, crashing through the woody plants at the base of the wall. She glanced around her, trying to build up a rapid picture of her surroundings – a pair of ex-Enforcement Division field guns had been manhandled hurriedly into position leaving deep gouges in the turf, and a gang of Septiams were loading massive shells into the breaches.

Aescarion broke into a run, a round clunking home into the chamber of her bolt pistol, her Sisters landing and following her. The Seraphim were on the gun gang before they knew they were even under attack, Aescarion blowing holes through one before beheading another with her power axe, Sister Mixu unleashing a volley that stitched bloody ruin through three more. The Sisters killed so quickly and efficiently that by the time the Stratix caught up with them the fire point was denuded of Septiams, bodies draped over the gun emplacement and the makeshift barricades.

DeVayne took one look and ordered a detail of his men to man the guns. Within minutes the field guns were blasting at near point-blank range into the Septiam trenches and dugouts. The shells ripped huge plumes of pulverised earth out of the ground, raining debris and bodies back onto the temple gardens.

'Nice work, Sisters,' called DeVayne as he led the rest of his men into the shattered Septiam lines. Aescarion followed him, Sisters at her side, the air filling with lasblasts and autogun rounds as the Septiams tried to return fire.

Aescarion and DeVayne charged into a Septiam position that, facing fire from both directions, rapidly disintegrated into chaos.

SARPEDON LEAPT OVER the pedestal, which had once held a monumental statue of Ecclesiarch Pulis XXIXth, landing squarely in the middle of the Septiams dug into a shell hole in the middle of the forum. He lashed his force staff into the midriff of one even as Tellos dived in beside him, twin chainblades ripping arcs of gore from the Septiams. Rotted jaws dropped in horror as Tellos's Assault Marines followed, bolt pistols and chainswords spattering the Septiams across the torn marble.

'Tellos!' yelled Sarpedon. 'Take the autocannon!' He pointed towards a quad-mounted autocannon dug in just inside a shattered basilica – it was pounding fire into the Jouryan positions, but it could easily be re-sighted to bring down any ship trying to land on the forum and that was why it had to go.

Tellos seemed not to hear, intent on butchering the Septiams he had beaten down to his feet.

Sarpedon grabbed Tellos's shoulder and picked him up, holding him level with his own face.

'Take the autocannon,' he snarled. 'Now!'

Tellos glared at him through a mask of Septiam blood and found his feet, sprinting through a hail of fire, taking shells and lasblasts to his body as he ran for the autocannon mount. His assault squad followed, just as Squad Karraidin and the survivors of Squad Hastis vaulted into the shell hole.

'Karraidin, spread your men out and keep some heads down.'

'Can Lygris land here?'

'It's hotter than he'd like but he'll do it. Now get to it, Soul Drinker.'

Karraidin sprayed with his storm bolter at the source of the heaviest Septiam fire, and led his squad out of the shell hole to cut down the enemy crossfire as much as possible. Squad Luko had spread down one side of the forum and were exchanging fierce fire with the Septiams cowering in the law courts, and the Jouryans behind the Soul

Drinkers were adding what fire they could to cover the Space Marines.

If the Guardsmen had known the Space Marines were securing a landing zone for extraction, they might not have been so enthusiastic about supporting the Soul Drinkers' drive for the forum. But Sarpedon wasn't here to fight their battle for them – the success of his mission depended on what fate dealt to them, and getting off Septiam Torus was the only objective left.

A vicious gun battle erupted at the Septiam-held far end of the forum and spilled out onto the forum itself. Septiams broke cover as gunfire and flashes of flame chased them out of their positions. Sarpedon snapped off shots at a couple of unwary targets. Luko's guns chewed through several more. It was a counterattack – Sarpedon saw that some of the troopers vaulting over barricades and struggling with each other at close quarters were not Septiams, but soldiers from the Stratix XXIII that barely resembled Guardsmen at all.

'Tell Lygris to move it,' called Luko over the vox, 'We're taking fire!'

'From the Septiams or the Stratix?'

'Neither,' came the reply. 'Adeptus Sororitas!'

SISTER AESCARION DUCKED into the cover of a column as a spray of fire spattered against the front of the basilica. She paused for a second and charged out again, firing as she went, the boltguns of her Sisters covering her as she led the way to the next patch of shelter. The Stratix and the Septiams were locked in a mad, swirling melee behind her, two sets of savages getting to grips with knives and rifle butts, and if she and her Sisters got dragged down into it they would never get out.

'Marine!' yelled Sister Mixu behind her. Aescarion glanced and saw a flash of deep purple as a Space Marine blasted at them with his boltgun, ducking back in time to avoid the return volley of bolts that shattered the marble around him.

It was the first living Soul Drinker that Aescarion had ever seen, the first glimpse of an enemy her faith required her to fight. More fire lanced from the sheltered Marine squad and Aescarion heard a scream as one of her Seraphim died, drilled by a bolter round through the abdomen that found a weak spot in her armour and blew out her lower back.

'Aspasia! Get the flamers to the fore and pin them down!' ordered Aescarion as her Sisters dived for cover, a whole Space Marine squad now blazing away at them. The dying Seraphim was dragged into shelter and Aescarion threw herself against the closest column, feeling bolter shells impacting against the other side of the stone.

She could see across the forum from where she sheltered, and she quickly scanned the expanse of broken marble for more Marines. She spotted some battling amongst the ruins of a shattered basilica, swarming over an autocannon artillery piece, cutting through the Septiams defending it. Another was in massive hulking Terminator armour, something Aescarion had never seen before, and more were moving out of a shell hole by a statue plinth to find better cover as Septiams tried to push onto the forum away from the assaulting Stratix.

Mutant. The glimpse she got of it was so fleeting she couldn't believe it was real – but when the Soul Drinker dodged from cover again her suspicions were confirmed. The Marine's legs were like those of a huge and monstrous spider, insectoid and tipped with long talons. The Soul Drinker's armour was more ornate than that of his battle-brothers, and from the force staff he wielded Aescarion recognised a Librarian, keeper of the Chapter's psychic lore and power.

The Sisters of Battle despised witches, and regarded even those in the employ of the Imperium with suspicion. Aescarion had never seen the psyker's art result in anything other than corruption and Chaos. The Librarian would be a target even if he wasn't who Aescarion suspected: Sarpedon. Commander of the Soul Drinkers, leader of the rebellion, and the primary target of Strikeforce Thaddeus.

'Rufilla, Aspasia, give us cover!' yelled Aescarion over the din of gunfire and the whistle of bullets. Sister Mixu dived down to Aescarion's side.

'That him?' she gasped.

'Do not pause to rescue me if I should fall. He will not fail to kill me and we need lose no more Sisters here than we have to.'

'Can you take him?'

'Probably not. Keep the other Marines away, the only chance is for me to catch him alone.'

Aescarion charged, firing at Sarpedon with her pistol in her left hand, her power axe in her right. Sister Mixu and the three remaining Seraphim charged out behind her, twin pistols blazing at anything that threatened their Sister Superior as flame from Squad Aspasia washed over the Marine squad in the ruins. Rufilla's Sisters sent sheets of rapid fire across the forum. On the other side of the battlefield, the autocannon mount was shattered by krak grenades and the Soul Drinkers assault squad fell back from the collapsing artillery piece as Aescarion sprinted the last few paces through the bullets to reach Commander Sarpedon.

SARPEDON SAW THE shimmering diamond of the power axe before he saw the Sister herself. He knew no Septiam, and precious few Guard officers, would ever have a power weapon – the charging figure was a Sister of Battle, a soldier of the Imperial Cult, fanatical and fuelled by pure faith.

If he was lucky, she would think he was a Chaos Marine, mutated by exposure to the magics of the Enemy. If he was unlucky, she would be a part of the Inquisitorial taskforce that Sarpedon had known was following the Soul Drinkers since their assault on House Jenassis.

He dug a talon into the ground and pivoted, his great weight – Marine, armour, altered legs – swivelling on a pin. One hand gripped the force staff and he let it swing out in a wide arc. The staff met the axe in a huge flash of sparks.

The Sister was a true veteran, with a lined, strongly-featured face and red-brown hair streaked with grey. Her armour was glossy black with no order markings, free of ornamentation. She swung away from Sarpedon, reversing the swing of her axe and trying to bring the butt of it into Sarpedon's ribs. He raised a leg and deflected the blow but the leg's joint folded under the impact and he lurched to one side, almost forced to put a hand down to the ground to steady himself. He rolled with the motion and lashed out with two legs, catching the Sister with a glancing blow, and knocked her back a pace. There was a pause, a fraction of a second, as the two sized one another up and tried to anticipate the next move.

'Traitor,' hissed the Sister, hefting her axe from one hand to the other, her pistol holstered and forgotten.

'No traitor,' said Sarpedon levelly. 'Just free.'

The Sister struck first, an easy feint, striking at Sarpedon's head in the hope that he would raise his guard and open himself up to a chop to the legs. He deflected the high blow with the head of the staff and the low blow with the other end, handling it like a quarterstaff. He struck back with a leg, stabbing at the Sister's throat with a blow she dodged with enough speed to instil some respect in Sarpedon. She was a born fighter, this one, with her instincts honed across scores of battlefields until she had the faith to take on a warrior like Sarpedon.

Faith was power. Faith was the straitjacket that had held the Soul Drinkers prisoner since the days of their founding, and faith was the force that kept them fighting now even when so much of their world was gone. Sarpedon had learned long ago to respect faith, and to treat it as the deadliest weapon there was.

There was a roar overhead and Sarpedon didn't have to look up to know it was Lygris in the fighter craft. The Sister hacked down at him with a lack of finesse that was well beneath her, driving the shimmering axe blade down at the Soul Drinker. She stamped down on Sarpedon's front foreleg – the one that wasn't bionic – with her foot and Sarpedon felt the joint wrench, ligaments torn inside the chitinous exoskeleton. Sarpedon parried her next blow and reached out with his free hand, grasping her armour at the collar. With strength even a normal Marine didn't have, he picked her up and swung her over his head, smashing her body into a huge chunk of fallen masonry.

The glistening, metallic fighter craft above sent incandescent lances of energy burning into the buildings along one side of the forum. It dipped low, openings forming in the side and a tongue of metal flowing from the hull to let Marines of Squad Luko scramble on board. Sarpedon spotted the Assault Marines following Tellos from the wreckage of the autocannon mount as the fighter swooped low again, close enough to the ground for the Marines to run onto the lowered ramp. Small arms fire rattled along the hull of the fighter and bolter fire ripped back from inside the passenger compartment.

The Sister crashed to the ground, winded but not broken. Sarpedon swung the force staff round and drove it, head-first and double-handed, towards the woman's midriff. She rolled aside and grabbed one of Sarpedon's legs, using it as leverage to swing herself up and ram an armoured elbow into the side of Sarpedon's head.

Sarpedon reeled. For a moment he was open and vulnerable, and a quick blade would have taken his head off. But instinct took over and he jabbed forward and down with one of his powerful hind legs. The axe blade whistled past his face, blistering the skin of one cheek with its power field, as he fell backwards. One hand planted on the ground to support him as the talon of his hind leg sheared through the Sister's armour and impaled her through the muscle of her thigh.

Two more legs stabbed into the ground to give him leverage and he flung the Sister across the forum, the talon ripping out of her leg as she flew through the air trailing an arc of blood.

'Sarpedon! Karraidin!' came Lygris's urgent voice over the vox. 'We've got Guardsmen coming your way, you need to get on board now!'

Sarpedon looked away from the Sister's prone body and saw the troopers – Stratix XXIII, tattooed hive-scum to a man – pouring through the Septiam lines and over the ruined forum. There were hundreds of them, and in Sarpedon they saw a mutant who had just defeated one of their Sororitas allies.

Lasgun fire ripped towards Sarpedon and Karraidin, whose squad was taking cover in ruins a hundred metres away. Sarpedon vaulted over the closest statue plinth but fire was coming from everywhere, scoring deep scars in his armour, several lasbursts burning through the chitin of his legs. One Stratix followed him into cover, combat knife clutched in his hand. Sarpedon punched him hard in the face – his head snapped back and he flopped brokenly to the ground. Sarpedon fired twice with his bolter, blowing the torso of one Guardsman apart, before impaling another on his force staff as he fell.

'Damn it, taking fire! Get us some support!' voxed Karraidin over the chatter of his storm bolter, but Lygris's fighter was yawing upwards as Stratix anti-tank teams got into position and started sending lascannon blasts up into the gleaming hull.

Without warning there was a titanic flash and a searing wave of heat. Sarpedon saw charging Stratix reduced to ashen skeletons as his own autosenses

forced his pupils almost shut against the glare. The
blistering wave of energy washed over him, scalding
the skin of his legs and peeling the paint from the
edges of his armour.

He glanced behind him and a saw the source of
the blast – a Leman Russ Executioner tank, huge
plasma blastgun glowing from the sudden dis-
charge of power, white smoke billowing from the
energy coils.

For a moment there was silence as the glare on
Sarpedon's retinas died to reveal a huge hole blown
in the Stratix attack, dozens of charred bodies filling
a massive scorch mark across the stone.

A huge Jouryan attack filled the vacuum, grey-
fatigued troops rushing to blunt the Stratix charge.
Guardsmen or no, they had seen the Soul Drinkers
as allies and the Stratix as the enemies of their
friends. Many of them could probably not tell the
difference between a Septiam and a Stratix in the
heat of battle anyway, and though some saw Sarpedon's deformities and faltered in their charge most
hurtled into the fray.

A brutal close-quarters fight erupted in the forum,
Stratix against Jouryan, looted knives against bayonets. Heavy weapons teams opened up against the
Executioner but other front-line tanks, Extermina-
tors and Leman Russ battle tanks, rolled through
the rubble to support the infantry.

Lygris saw his opening and the fighter lurched
downwards again, hull opening up to let Karraidin

drag his massive armoured frame on board followed by his squad. The fighter turned and dipped low enough for Sarpedon to leap up on his powerful legs. He grabbed the edge of the opening and pulled himself up into the passenger compartment. The fighter aimed its nose upwards and Sarpedon could see the huge swirling melee filling the forum, Stratix and Jouryan Guardsmen killing each other, the surviving Septiams caught up in the butchery.

Something flared below the fighter and Sarpedon looked over the edge of the doorway to see the Sister he had beaten, rocketing upwards on her Seraphim jump pack. She came up just short and grasped the edge with one hand, the other holding her power axe.

Sarpedon saw she was was streaked with grime and blood, her face set with faith and zeal.

He had to admire her determination.

'For the Emperor, Sister,' he said, and with a flick of his powerful bionic foreleg he kicked her off the edge of the ship to fall helplessly into the heart of the battle.

'Get us out of her, Lygris,' he voxed, and felt the fighter tip back as the metal flowed back over the opening. The last impression he had of Septiam Torus was the mingled cries of thousands of men as they fought, killed and died. Just as it had been for thousands of years the Imperium was destroying its own, although Sarpedon had rarely seen the idea so vividly come to life.

'Did you see the image we sent you from the aus-pex?' voxed Sarpedon as the engines kicked in and he strapped himself back into the grav-restraints. He looked around the passenger compartment and saw that the Marine force on Septiam Torus had lost over a quarter of its number, with almost all of Squad Hastis gone. Had it been worth it? Was anything?

'Received intact,' replied Lygris from the cockpit.

'Do you know what it is?'

'Looks like a cogitator circuit, something to recall information from a mem-bank. Probably the key for a security system.'

The main engines took over and the sound of the atmosphere rippling on the hull dropped away as the fighter passed out into space.

It had been worth it, Sarpedon told himself. It had to have been. Otherwise, not one of them would survive Stratix Luminae.

TEN

FOR THADDEUS, SPACE travel was the most frustrating part of his work. The time spent between the stars was time wasted, and even when the warp meant a century's worth of travel took only days those were still days he wouldn't get back. Patience was perhaps his greatest strength but space travel, more than anything, made it wear thin.

He knew the *Crescent Moon* was fast, that was one of the reasons he used it. But he had no way of knowing how quickly the Soul Drinkers could move. Presumably the alien fighters Aescarion had reported were warp-capable, since they would be the perfect way to sneak past the warzone's blockades with the minimum of risk – perhaps they were already on Stratix Luminae, and Thaddeus was already too late. Perhaps they had to enact some other part of their plan before they could reach the planet. Perhaps Stratix Luminae was already lost – Stratix, after all, was in the same solar system and Teturact could have decided to despoil and garrison the planets bordering his homeworld.

At least Thaddeus had some idea of what the place looked like. He had Captain Korvax's pict-recording playing on a personal holo-servitor. The image was paused as Korvax looked across the defences towards the outpost – a simple, low plasti-crete building with massive blast doors and fire points on the roof. It didn't look like much but, for whatever reason, Sarpedon had risked his own life and the lives of his Chapter to get there.

Lord Inquisitor Kolgo had released Thaddeus without actually admitting he had ever been held prisoner, simply docking his ship for refuelling and maintenance and letting Thaddeus walk out. It was just the next stage in the game, a favour done to secure a favour in the future when Thaddeus might be worth something. However, Kolgo and Thaddeus would never be allies, because Thaddeus would destroy the Soul Drinkers or die trying. Neither option would endear him much to Kolgo.

Thaddeus had used the time he had spent waiting to meet up with the *Crescent Moon* researching Stratix Luminae, but there hadn't been much to find out. It was an Adeptus Mechanicus Genetor facility, where biological experiments had been carried out by adepts seeking to delve further into the secrets of genetics and mutation. Such outposts were usually isolated and Stratix Luminae was no exception, being a world of frozen tundra with no population aside from the outpost staff. Ten years ago eldar pirates, who had plagued the Stratix system intermittently, were fought off by a force of Space Marines who responded to the Adeptus Mechanicus's distress call. There was, of course, no record of who the Chapter involved might have been, which led Thaddeus to conclude that it had been the Soul Drinkers well before their break with the Imperium.

What had Korvax found there that had interested Sarpedon so much? Thaddeus could only hope he got there in time to find out.

'Inquisitor?' came a polite voice from the door.

Thaddeus looked up to see Sister Aescarion in the doorway. Thaddeus's quarters on the *Crescent Moon* weren't spartan but were still towards the simpler side of what an inquisitor could become accustomed to – there was little more than a bed, his trunk, a couple of chests of clothes and belongings and his desk with its shelves of books above. The large viewport looking out onto space was one of the few obvious luxuries – hidden in the room were also a poison-sniffer servitor, an anti-transmission field generator and a small void safe in which Thaddeus could transport sensitive or potentially tainted items.

Aescarion wore the simple white robes of the Sisters – without her armour she seemed half the size, little more than an ageing woman with an unusually proud bearing. So puritanical was the aura she seemed to project that she made Thaddeus's rooms seem positively decadent.

'Sister,' said Thaddeus. 'I hadn't expected you to leave the infirmary so soon.'

'I have had worse wounds that this,' replied Aescarion, limping slightly as she walked over to take a seat at Thaddeus's desk. That she chose to sit at all illustrated her discomfort, but she refused to show it otherwise. 'The bone was broken but there was little muscle loss. And I have learned to heal quickly.'

'I can imagine.'

'I wanted to speak with you, inquisitor. Something has been troubling me.'

'About Sarpedon? He is a Space Marine Chapter Master and a powerful psyker. There is no point in chastising yourself for not defeating him.'

'It is not that, inquisitor. I have lost in battle before, it is part of what makes us strong. It is just… he could have killed me, and he did not. The ways of the Enemy are many and strange and heretics might spare those who they think will suffer more from living than from a quick death – but he had no idea who I was. I was just another soldier in a city full of soldiers.'

'Do you believe he knew you were part of my strike-force? That he let you live to send a message to me?'

'Perhaps. I just think that Sarpedon is no normal enemy. The Guardsmen genuinely believed that the Soul Drinkers were Imperial Marines and fought alongside them, even against their fellow Guardsmen. I fought Brother Castus and Parmenides the Vile, inquisitor, I was at Saafir and the Scorpion Pass. I know many of the forms of the Enemy, but the Soul Drinkers are the subtlest yet. They are not just animals to be hunted. This pursuit could cost us more than just our lives.'

'Sister, you have done what I have not. You have seen the Soul Drinkers up close and you have fought with their leader. You must be at the forefront on Stratix Luminae. As always, you may be required to give up your life and you will very probably have to face Sarpedon again. Be honest with me, Sister – does this scare you?'

Aescarion smiled, a rare thing. 'I am terrified, inquisitor. The Enemy has always terrified me. It is through faith that I live with this fear. If I was not afraid, then what would there be to believe in? I know the Emperor is with me because without Him I would be paralysed with fear. But with him, I can fight the Enemy in spite of it.'

'Very enlightened, Sister.'

'It took me most of my life to understand, inquisitor. And it has not been a short life.'

Thaddeus reached down and adjusted the holoservitor's controls. The image flickered and changed to an old Mechanicus file. Once he had known the name of Stratix Luminae he had been able to find some rudimentary information on the place, and the newest layouts dated from a few months after the Soul Drinkers had driven off the eldar there. The surface building was a simple one-storey entrance to the lower levels. Hastily-improved defences ringed the outpost entrance, consisting mostly of plasticrete blocks placed on the frozen, broken earth.

'The entrance is just one floor, probably no more than security station,' said Thaddeus. 'Assuming the installation is on Standard Template Construct lines there will be at least two levels below the surface. Probably a laboratory level, maybe containment on the lowest floor where it's easiest to isolate. Apart from that we know nothing, except that somewhere in there is an objective that Sarpedon considers important enough to risk the life of his whole Chapter.'

'Unless we get there first,' said Aescarion.

'We may not have that luxury. The Soul Drinkers have a head-start and they know what they are looking for.'

'I and my Sisters are ready. I know that Colonel Vinn and the storm troopers would say the same. I have just one question, inquisitor.'

'Ask, Sister.'

'Stratix Luminae is evidently deserted. Do you know why it was closed down?'

Thaddeus shrugged. 'No, Sister, I don't. Aside from these final schematics Stratix Luminae will cease to exist as soon as the Soul Drinkers turn up. I have noticed they seem to have that effect.' Thaddeus picked up the decanter that stood on a side table. 'I would offer you a glass of devilberry liqueur, Sister, but I would imagine you abstain.'

'The human form is the form of the Emperor and to poison it willingly is a sin,' said Aescarion.

'We are all sinners, Sister,' replied Thaddeus, pouring himself a measure.

Aescarion stood, smoothing out her simple robes. 'There are some things that it is pointless to lecture on,' she said. 'Many are the times I have extolled the virtues of abstinence to the laity. Few are the times I have been listened to. In this case it is enough that I follow my vows myself.'

'I am glad I do not offend your sensibilities.'

'You know as well as I do there are far graver sins you could sink to. Now, I should minister to my Sisters, I have not led their prayers for several days.'

'Say a few words for me, Sister. We must all prepare as best we can.'

Thaddeus watched Aescarion leave, seeing for the first time not a warrior but an old woman who had seen rather too much of the universe.

He switched the holo-servitor back to Korvax's pict-recording, reviewing for the hundredth time the same file that had perhaps sent Sarpedon deep into the warzone. As it had done every time before, the file cut out just before Korvax entered the installation, but the original file must have shown the

inside of the installation and the work the Adeptus
Mechanicus had done there. Whatever it was, Stratix
Luminae had been closed down soon afterwards
and of the two known surviving staff members one
had gone insane and the other had been relocated
to an outpost almost hidden beneath a hive city.

Thaddeus switched off the holo. He knew as
much about Stratix Luminae as anyone could now.
He poured the liqueur back into the decanter and
headed up to the bridge.

It would only be a few more days before the *Crescent Moon* reached the Stratix system, but in the
back of his mind Thaddeus knew every intervening
moment was wasted.

THE SPACE AROUND Stratix was diseased. A miasma
of pestilence hung in the space between planets,
like an almost imperceptible gauze turning the distant stars sickly colours and colouring the worlds of
the Stratix system strange hues of decay. Stratix's sun
was paler, and anyone who looked at it through the
right filters would see sunspots, like black scabs, festering on its surface. So strong was Teturact's
influence that it had even infected the star that
shone on his homeworld.

The system's blockade was a shoal of rotting
ships, launched from Stratix's dockyards and cannibalised from merchant and outpost fleets
throughout the system, or brought in from the fleets
of worlds conquered in Teturact's name.

Squadrons of escorts were fitted to function as fire-ships, rigged to burst like seed pods in huge clouds of space-borne spores that would eat their way through portholes and bulkheads and infect enemy crews. Larger cruisers teemed with crew who needed neither heat nor air to work, making for ships that could only be disabled by complete obliteration, while other near-derelict cruisers had massive armour plates welded to their prows so they could act as suicidal ram-ships like giant hypodermics loaded with disease. Monitoring stations and orbital defence platforms turned weaponry outwards, cyclonic torpedoes and magnalasers now hard-wired into crewmen whose minds were the only parts of them left alive.

Stratix itself was a giant gnarled ball of charred blackness, studded with glowing spots like embers where hive-forges still burned. The hives covered almost the entire surface of the planet and were charred with exhaust fumes, and whole swathes of city were obscured by thick streaks of toxic cloud. Here and there low-orbit docks broke the atmosphere like tarnished metal thorns.

The other worlds were just as touched by Teturact. The whole system had warped according to his will. Locanis, closest to the system's star, had a thick greenhouse of an atmosphere that had turned from pale grey to rotten black overnight. Callicrates was rich in the ores that Stratix used in its industries, but the silvery metallic surface was now pockmarked with patches of rust hundreds of kilometres across. St Phal was a graveyard world now, so thick with walking skeletal dead that from space its surface seemed to squirm as if covered with maggots.

Stratix Luminae was even colder and whiter than ever. The gas giant of Majoris Crien was covered in swirling storms of sickly browns and purples where once it had been vibrant green, and its many moons were drifting away in erratic orbits as though the giant world was too weak to hold onto them any more. The Three Sisters, the tiny, far-orbit ice worlds of Cygnan, Terrin and Olatinne, were pulling further and further from the distant sun as if trying to escape from the infection spreading across the system.

Teturact's tombship dropped back into realspace; it was like a home-coming. The comforting glow of disease surrounded the planets with haloes of pestilence. Somehow, space smelt different here. It was redolent with life. Even through the many layers of armour between the void and the bridge of the tombship, the stench was there: the stench of home.

The crew of servitors and menials who had been jacked into the bridge had degenerated to the point where only fragments of their minds still worked. So the crew had brought more in, plugging their minds into the consoles and heaping more and more bodies against the banks of readouts and controls until the bridge was a single charnel pit, three deep in writhing corpses like a carpet of skin and muscle.

It was the ultimate slavery, for these near-dead to surrender their very humanity to Teturact. No one else was allowed on the bridge aside from Teturact and his bearers, because it was a place where anyone in control would be worshipped and that honour was only permissible for Teturact himself.

The front of the bridge gave way to a massive viewscreen through which Teturact could see the beauty of the Stratix system stretching in front of him. Stratix represented more than just another world, it was the first, the heart of his corruption and the first proof that he truly had the power to rule worlds. He had done much good work on Eumenix and the place would be as solid a bastion as any in his empire, but the Stratix system was home.

Wordlessly, he urged the bridge crew to turn the ship towards Stratix. The bodies writhed beneath his feet and moaned as their minds were connected through the bridge cogitators to signal the main engines and thrusters.

Teturact let his mind sweep out. With every new world he became stronger, and his consciousness was no longer bound to his wizened body. He let it flow through the tombship, washing over the bright, roiling pits of corruption that were the minds of his wizards. He felt the fractured pride of the Navigator above the prow, still trying to hold on to the idea of the old naval aristocracy even as his flesh melted off his bones.

He could see beyond the ship, past the ripples it left in realspace as it passed out into the void. It was warm and welcoming, tinted with disease, and he could hear, like the echoes of a distant choir, the voices clamouring for him to come and save them all over again. He could drink that feeling, their desperation and their gratitude, and the pleading that followed as they came to realise they would always need him to keep their slow deaths at bay. It was what fuelled him. It was why he had built a war machine out of his empire and engaged Imperial forces in grinding campaigns of attrition that only he could win.

He felt the desperate dimming of Stratix's star and the warping of the gravitational web between the worlds – so powerful was the concept of Teturact as a god that it deformed the universe around it. He could taste the dark, rich taste of corruption so pure it could bleed across the void in a stain that would eventually cover his whole empire.

Stratix itself was a glorious beating heart of suffering, St Phal a suppurating wound in reality, Stratix Luminae a hard white pearl of dead ice, Majoris Crien a bloated spectre. Teturact could feel them distorting space around them, so powerful was the taint he had left on them. Spacecraft like swarms of locusts or huge lumbering monsters patrolled the system, and Teturact could hear them calling his name.

The beauty of it all still had the power to astound him. Teturact had seen extraordinary things and become immune to all of them but this – these billions of souls in pain and rapture, pleading for his touch and singing praises in gratitude, all forming a psychic tide that flowed into Teturact's mind.

But there was something else here, something that wasn't here before. Something pure and untouched by Teturact. Different, yes, shifted sideways from reality – but not diseased.

Teturact focused his will on the intrusion. Tiny and metallic, they were like needles sewing a wound back together, piercing the gauze of suffering and driving deep into system space. There were several tiny craft, faster than any Imperial ships of comparable size.

Teturact felt a cold, affronted anger. These were his worlds. The Imperial spearheads that had tried to punch into the Stratix system at the start of the rebellion had paid for their boldness with madness followed by servitude in Teturact's armies. No one had dared poison this cauldron of disease with their cleanliness since then.

Teturact could smell a hot, bright bolt of psychic intelligence in one of the ships, something subtly different than a normal human psyker. It was taut, focused, and very, very powerful.

Teturact pulled back from the shoal of bright slivers and let the whole system fill his mind. He could see the trails of near-normality that the ships left behind them and estimated the course they were taking, straight as an arrow into the heart of the system.

Their route would take them to Stratix Luminae.

Teturact's consciousness snapped back into the confines of the bridge. The bodies piled up around him shuddered as even they felt the resonance of their lord's anger. He spat out an order with his mind to switch the tombship's course towards the frozen planet and intercept the intruders.

Stratix Luminae – no, thought Teturact, that could not be allowed.

KORVAX SLAMMED *a new magazine into his bolter and heard half his squad doing the same. He glanced at Sergeant Veiyal – the sergeant's helmet had been damaged and he was bare-headed, his breath coiling white in the cold.*

'The others have our backs,' said Korvax. 'Sergeant Livris, your squad has the point. Veiyal, with me. Advance.'

Korvax levelled his bolter and followed the Assault Marines as they charged into the darkened heart of the outpost...

The air was close and Korvax recognised the smells that got through his helmet filter – gun smoke, blood both alien and human, unwashed and terrified men. His autosenses adjusted quickly to the darkness and Korvax saw tech-guard bodies lying where they had taken up fire points near the blast doors. Automated guns hung limp and shattered from the ceiling, and a gun-servitor lay dismembered on the makeshift defences.

The blast doors led into a single large, low room with a smouldering rectangular hole in the floor where a cargo elevator had once been. The security stations that covered the blast doors and entrance chamber were heavy constructions of ferrocrete with firing slits and automated guns – Korvax saw tech-guard bodies slumped at the fixed heavy stubbers and blood spattered across the walls and floor.

'They've been shredded, captain,' voxed Livris, who was moving rapidly into the entrance chamber with his assault squad.

'Shuriken fire?'

'Something else.'

Korvax's squad moved in behind the Assault Marines, training bolters on the dark corners that pooled where glowstrips had failed.

Livris peered over the edge of the cargo lift, auspex scanner in hand. 'Do we move in, captain?'

'Go, Livris. Cold and fast.'

Livris dropped down the smoking hole, followed by the assault squad. Korvax could still hear the gunfire from outside as Squad Veiyal held off the remains of the eldar forces from the blast doors. If the xenos had got inside, they were doing a good job of hiding it – hardly any sound seemed to filter from the outpost's lower floors.

'It's a lab floor,' said Livris. 'Wait, the auspex is…'

Gunfire erupted below. Chainblades chewed into metal.

'Squad, with me!' yelled Korvax and followed Squad Livris onto the floor below, power sword hot in his hand.

The darkness below was punctuated with strobing muzzle flashes. Heavy gothic architecture was crammed into the low-ceilinged lab floor, with ornate workstations covered in complex machinery and webs of glass tubing. Korvax saw tech-guard and lab personnel still living, and many more lying dead slumped on seats or consoles. Tech-guard were taking cover and firing almost blindly with lasguns.

Korvax couldn't see the enemy. Squad Livris were sending out suppressive volleys of bolt pistol fire and Korvax's tactical squad lent their own fire, spitting explosive bolts in all directions.

A battle-brother's scream ended in a choked-off gurgle, and in the flash of gunfire Korvax saw him fall, a shining web of silvery filaments billowing over and through him, slicing through armour plates, coiling into armour joints and unravelling to shred the flesh and bone inside.

Korvax got a glimpse of the aliens – they had heavier armour suits than the warriors Korvax had fought at the barricades, with a large carapace over the back and large, thick forearm plates that helped support massive weapons with spinning barrels that wove spirals of bright threads. The eldar aimed and a bolt of filaments shot out, bursting against one of Livris's Marines and reducing his pistol arm to a mess of loose armour and shredded muscle.

Korvax fired but too late, the eldar had disappeared, winking out of existence with a clap of air rushing into the space he left behind.

'Teleporters!' yelled Korvax as gunfire continued to spatter across the darkened lab floor. A surviving tech-guard screamed as an unseen enemy shredded him with a monofilament burst. Something flitted into view and disappeared, almost catching Sergeant Livris with its lethal web.

Korvax kept his head down and moved past his battle-brothers, trying to gauge the angle he would take if he were trying to kill as many of them as possible. He had to trust the alien attackers would be too distracted by the other Marines and their gunfire to notice him until it was too late.

He backed up against a pillar, listening carefully, trying to filter through the din of bolter and lasgun fire. He heard, very close, the burst of air as something materialised on the other side of the pillar.

He lashed round the pillar with his power sword and felt it cut through something, armour plate and flesh, not deep but enough to impose a split-second of pain and confusion. The eldar warrior turned in surprise, the emerald eyepieces of its conical helmet staring out at Korvax as the Space Marine grabbed it by the throat with his free hand.

He hauled the alien off its feet and slammed it hard into the pillar, then powered it up into the ceiling so the carapace on its back hit the low fluted roof. The carapace fractured and blue flashes of escaping energy confirmed Korvax's suspicion that the carapace housed the teleport-jump device. Korvax lifted the xenos again and, before it could bring its flailing gun to bear, plunged his power *sword through its chest. The flashes of the sword's power field illuminated the several warriors who jumped in to surround Korvax, perhaps half-a-dozen of them, moving to kill the Soul Drinkers' obvious leader and avenge their fallen.*

Livris's Assault Marines jumped the eldar from behind, chainblades glancing off carapaces. Livris himself beheaded one and Korvax took another, breaking its leg with a stamp of his foot and cutting the alien clean in two. The surviving xenos jumped again, flitting out of reality not to surround the Marines but to flee.

Korvax pulled his sword from the remains of the eldar at his feet. He saw a couple of surviving tech-guard still hunkered down amongst the equipment. There was a technician, too, a woman in an adept's robes, peeking terrified from beneath a lab bench, doubtlessly not knowing whether to fear the aliens or the Soul Drinkers more.

Korvax walked over to the closest tech-guard and hauled him to his feet. The man's face was laced with blood where he had caught the edge of a filament burst and the barrel of his lasgun was warped, overheated from continuous firing.

'Are there any more?' asked Korvax sternly.

The tech-guard nodded and pointed to the far end of the lab floor, where a set of doors had been blown off their mountings leading to a dark corridor beyond.

Korvax dropped the tech-guard and led his Marines into the corridor. It was low and close, too narrow for two Marines to stand abreast. The air stank of something rotting and biological, and his helmet pre-filter was flashing up warning runes to mark the toxins it was keeping out of his system. The corridor sloped downwards and curved sharply back on itself, leading towards the next floor down.

Korvax looked down to see the floor ankle-deep in milky fluid, swimming with scraps of muscle tissue. It reflected the wan light from ahead, filtering weakly from the entrance to the next floor down. Normally security doors would have sealed off the lower floor, but they were open now.

Through the doorway Korvax glimpsed drifts of shattered glass and thick ribbed cables lying across a floor awash with the fluid, the drainage channels clogged with clotted wads of flesh. Glass cylinders three metres high stood in rows along the length of an enormous hangar-like room, some intact and full of fluids, others shattered.

Korvax slowed, edging towards the entrance, ready for that shuriken shot or energy blast. The eldar down here would have heard the battle above, they would know the Soul Drinkers were coming.

'Any movement on the auspex?' he voxed.

'Nothing,' came the reply.

The first body Korvax saw was slumped over the shattered remains of a cylinder, its abdomen impaled on jagged shards of curved glass still stabbing up from the cylinder's base. It was an eldar, in a blue armoured bodyglove with the helmet removed. The features of its slender, angular face were slack in death, its large dark eyes open. A shuriken pistol lay by its limp hand.

Another body lay nearby – or most of it at least, Korvax saw. This eldar's body had been bisected at the waist, and the lower half lay mangled several metres away.

Korvax waved his squad forward and cautiously they entered the room, Livris alongside him. There must have been five hundred of the cylinders here, arranged in rows like standing stones, with a clearing in the middle where cold vapour coiled off a huge hemispherical machine.

'Spread out!' ordered Livris, and his Assault Marines broke formation as they entered, moving between the cylinders in ones and twos. Korvas kept his squad closer, and as he advanced towards the centre of the room he saw more and more eldar bodies, mostly warriors but also one or two xenos in elaborate robes whose enclosed helmets had complex crystalline arrays built in. The eldar leadership caste, all psychic, the guides of their species on the battlefield and off it. The Imperial studies of the eldar named them warlocks, and several had met their end here beneath Stratix Luminae. One body was full of shuriken discs – this was not the result of a tech-guard last stand. Something else had happened here.

'Something's alive,' voxed Livris curtly. Korvax looked across to see the sergeant consulting his auspex scanner.

'Where?'

'Everywhere.'

There was a strange, faint buzzing in the air now, like a failing lumoglobe, almost imperceptible but coming from everywhere at once.

Bio-alarms flashed on Korvax's retinal display. Toxins were building up in his blood now. His armour integrity was in the green so it was as if the poisons were spontaneously appearing in his organs. His oolitic kidney kicked in to filter it out but if it kept increasing...

'I see him,' voxed the point Marine of his squad. Korvax looked through the cylinders and saw what the Marine was indicating – in front of the huge metallic hemisphere was a figure, kneeling as if in supplication, its warlock's robes spattered with blood.

'In position,' voxed Livris. Korvax knew he could give the word and the assault squad would be on the stranger in a heartbeat.

'Hold,' he replied. 'Squad, cover me.'

Korvax stepped slowly towards the figure. The area around the hemisphere was like a clearing in a forest of glass, and thick cables ran from ports all over the curved panels. The tingling, buzzing sound grew stronger and Korvax could feel the strain on his internal organs as more and more exotic poisons synthesized themselves in his bloodstream.

The figure stood. It was tall and slim, and even from behind Korvax recognised the elongated skull of the eldar. It turned around. Its long face was mournful and its eyes were weeping black blood. Korvax levelled his bolt pistol at the alien's head. 'Why are you here, xenos? What do you want?'

The alien spoke a few hushed syllables, then as if suddenly remembering the Marine could not speak its language–

'I could not hold it, brutish one. I thought... we could take it with us and keep it from you. We could destroy it.

But we were too late, you have let it grow for far too long.'

'What? What did you come for?'

The eldar smiled. The skin of its face was taut and it split hideously, weeping watery gore. Korvax saw blood running down its wrists to drip off its fingers and realised the alien was coming apart under some great force.

'You tell me, low creature. It was your kind that made it.'

As Korvax watched, the eldar's skin turned mottled and dark, tendrils of blackness tracing out its veins. It slumped back down to its knees and its body sagged grotesquely, its skeleton coming apart under the same forces that were starting to prey on Korvax and his Marines.

'Squad Veiyal?' voxed Korvax, 'get onto the crews on the Carnivore. Have them prep the infirmary, we'll need every man checked out. Inform the Chaplain there is a potential moral threat on Stratix Luminae.'

'Understood,' came Sergeant Veiyal's voice, filtering down through the sound of static and muted gunfire.

'Marines, fall back!' ordered Korvax as the eldar warlock collapsed in a welter of blood.

The eldar was dead, its remains twitching inside its stained robes. The plates of the hemisphere were pulsing in and out like a ribcage drawing breath, cables popping from the sockets.

Korvax turned and jogged with his squad as they fell back, then broke into a run as a terrible creaking roar began from the hemisphere and the floor and walls began to warp. The remaining cylinders shattered one by one, filling the air with showers of liquid and glass, spilling malformed humanoid shapes out on the floor. A plate burst off the hemisphere, spinning across the huge room and embedding itself in a wall.

The buzzing became a scream and warning telltales flashed all over Korvax's retina. He saw battle-brothers flagging as they ran, the terrible influence of whatever lurked in the centre of the room working on their systems. The eldar warlock had held on with his mind, the Marines had their bodies, but the eldar had been defeated and so could they.

Korvax was one of the last through the doorway. Livris, beside him, slammed a palm into the door controls and the massive security doors began to yawn closed.

'Move!' yelled Korvax. 'Get to the surface, this battle is over!'

Before the doors shut Korvax saw the hemisphere erupting in a huge gout of cables and machinery like metallic entrails, biomechanical equipment pouring up from a lower level and bringing a force with it that Korvax could feel in his very bones. The gene-seed organs in his throat and chest burned, his third lung and second heart were like lumps of molten metal in his chest.

Korvax just had time to see a human form rising from the middle of the destruction.

The eldar had come to Stratix Luminae to kill it. They had been too late. As Korvax rushed towards the surface, he hoped the Imperium would not make the same mistake...

* * *

THE IMAGE FROZE, with Korvax's pict-recorder looking out on the destruction of the lab floor.

'This,' said Sarpedon, 'is all we have. Stratix Luminae was closed afterwards and forgotten about. There are no plans or records within our reach. Captain Korvax's record is the only visual of the facility that exists. So this is what we will use.'

Sarpedon stood on a pulpit looking out on the Marines of Squads Luko, Karraidin and Graevus. In front and below him was the focus of the briefing sermon – the projected pict-recording that Captain Korvax had taken during the first assault on Stratix Luminae. The image, and Sarpedon's voice, would be transmitted to the other ships in the tiny fleet, where the Soul Drinkers would be stood as here in the cargo bay of the alien fighters.

'It is a testament to the strength of your will, brothers,' continued Sarpedon, 'that you have fought alongside me though very few of you know our ultimate goal. The truth is, we are fighting for survival. We are fighting for the Great Harvest, when the Soul Drinkers will take novices and begin the process of transforming them into Marines. The Harvest should be underway already, with our Chaplain and our Apothecaries forging another generation to take the fight to the Enemy. It has not happened.'

Sarpedon spread his arms, indicating his mutated legs. 'This is why. There is not one Marine that has no mark of mutation upon them. Many are stronger because of it, as am I. But the blood of Rogal Dorn is poisoned.

'Our blood, the gene-seed taken from Dorn's own body, is corrupted down to its basest elements. The Chapter is a chalice of that blood, and each drop poured out is the seed of another battle-brother. But the chalice is bleeding dry of Dorn's blood and soon there will be only corruption left. Our gene-seed is tainted, it cannot be used to create new Marines.'

The image rewound suddenly, flitting through the moments of destruction as Korvax retreated. Then it paused again, looking out on the glass cylinders and their obscure contents, as Korvax saw them when he first entered the lower floor.

'The adepts at Stratix Luminae were trying to control mutation. They were growing mutated flesh and trying to make it whole again. I, and the highest officers of this Chapter, believe they succeeded. The evidence Korvax gives us shows that the experimentation was in its final stages and was only halted by the deaths of the adepts at the hands of the eldar. It is waiting there to be recovered and used. Used by us, brothers, to reverse the poison that is killing the Soul Drinkers.'

Karraidin stepped up to the pulpit, the boots of his huge Terminator armour clunking on the metallic floor. The Soul Drinkers Chapter had never possessed many suits of the advanced armour and Karraidin's was one of the few left. He had earned it, though – a resolute and fearless assault leader he had proved himself capable of leading the hardest ship-to-ship attacks. He had joined Sarpedon in the heat of the Chapter war and there were few veterans in the Chapter that Sarpedon trusted more.

'The first force will be under my command,' began Karraidin. 'Our objective is the lower floor of the facility. The force will consist of my squad along with Squads Salk and Graevus. The mission is to recover experimental material and data – Techmarine Lygris and Solun and Apothecary Pallas will go in with us as support. You do not need to be reminded that whatever Korvax found may still be there.'

'The second force,' said Sarpedon, 'will be commanded by me. We will secure the surface and the exterior of the facility, and hold it until the assault force is extracted. Stratix Luminae is located in one of the most heavily enemy-infested systems in Imperial space and we will be seen, if we have not been located already. It is likely the facility will be attacked and we must ensure the facility and our landing zone remains secure at all costs. Luko, Krydel, Assault Sergeant Tellos and myself will be in command on the ground. All Marines not in the assault or the ground force will remain on the fighters as interception and reserve.'

Every Marine would know what that meant. Up until now Sarpedon had not risked the whole Chapter at once – Marines could not be replaced and there would be no edict from the Adeptus Terra to resurrect the Chapter if it was all but destroyed. The mission was about survival, and the future of the Chapter could be risked because it was that future they were fighting for.

Sarpedon took out his battered, well-thumbed copy of Daenyathos's *Catechisms Martial*. 'Emperor, deliver us,' he began, 'so that we might deliver creation from the Enemy…'

Together, solemnly and all aware that it could be for the last time, the Soul Drinkers began to pray.

STRATIX LUMINAE WAS pale as a cataract stricken eye, several thousand square kilometres of frozen tundra broken only by rare rock formations and the single incongruous structure of the Adeptus Mechanicus Biologis installation. From above, it was barely a pinprick of artificiality in an infuriatingly dead world. But Teturact could feel the life within, a life rather like himself that seethed with potential.

He pulled his consciousness back through the hull of the ship and into the ritual chamber. Deep in the heart of Teturact's ship, this was a secret place he had forbidden anyone to enter.

It was the only part that was clean and free of the corpses that littered the rest of the ship. Lacquered, decorated panels of exotic hardwood covered the walls and ceilings. Tapestries hung from the walls, covered in images of Imperial heroism that seemed desperate and comical now so much of that Imperium had turned into Teturact's nightmare. The floor was tiled with mosaics of devotional texts, and the air was perfumed by censers that swung slowly from the ceiling.

Glow-globes concealed in chandeliers produced a light that made the shadows harsh. The light glinted off relics assembled in alcoves set into the walls – the finger bones of a saint, the hereditary power axe of Stratix's priesthood chased with silver and set with gemstones, the furled banner of the Adepta Sororitas, sacred works of art from the distant Imperial past and powerful symbols that had seemed vital to its future. Teturact had gathered them from Stratix itself and holy places his forces had conquered. Their influence was a painful veil over the brightness of his power, as if some new gravity was dragging his mind back down to mortality – it pained Teturact to enter the room, but it existed for a reason.

This was the only place that Teturact had ordered kept pure in his entire empire. Its components had been looted from luxurious upper spires and sacred conquered places, and assembled here into a place of purity that Teturact had ordered kept inviolate. The reason was simple – the most powerful magics required something to be defiled as part of the enactment, and nothing was so powerful as the defiling of purity.

Teturact's wizards were ranged before him, hooded and deformed, their heads hunched down in reverence because it was to him that they owed everything. This unholy nugget of purity must have been painful for them, too, a sharp painful obstruction to the complete corruption of the ship, but they were bound to Teturact's will and took the pain as he demanded.

You know what you must do, he thought at them. *Make it happen.*

One wizard shambled forward. He pulled down his hood and Teturact saw he had not one face but several, melded together as if they had melted into one. Several malformed eyes blinked in the light of the chamber's chandeliers. One of its mouths opened and began to keen, a low, buzzing drone. Its other mouths joined in, weaving a grotesque harmony that would have reduced mortal men to tears.

Gnarled limbs reached out from beneath its tattered robes, some arms, some pincers, some tentacles. Each hand made a different sign of blasphemy in the air, trails of red light spelled out symbols of heresy.

The other wizards shuffled into a circle around the singer. Teturact's brute-mutants carried him back out of the circle and each mutilated mind began to enact a separate part of the spell. One was a pure stab of rage, a bright red spire of burning hatred that provided fuel for the ritual. Another took that hatred and wove it into a tapestry of suffering, the chamber resonating with psychic after-images of torture and despair.

The lacquer on the walls began to peel. Images of the Emperor's sacred armies tarnished and were obliterated. The tapestries began to unravel and a patina of age and corruption spread across the gleaming relics. Even the light changed, gradually becoming dimmer and yellower, making everything in the room seem older.

Shapes began to appear, broken spectres drawn by the ritual's power, shadowy forms that stood hunched over the circle. The magic was drawing curious warp-creatures like blood draws scavengers. Monstrous things were watching. Perhaps the gods themselves, who would look down on Teturact with jealously that he had achieved what they could not and built an empire of suffering in the heart of the Imperium.

He could taste it, like old blood. This was one of the oldest magics, and it was his to command.

The keening rose, becoming louder and higher. Another wizard entered the circle and drew a knife of blackened iron from its robes. This wizard was larger than the rest, broad-shouldered with a musculature that showed even through its robes. It threw its head back, revealing a face with shredded skin that hung like ribbons over the red wet features beneath, and plunged the knife into its stomach.

Ropy purple entrails slithered out and where they hit the floor a dark stain spread like rust, warping the mosaics until the devotional High Gothic texts were squirming symbols of disease and death. The wizard sank to its knees and scraped the point of its knife through its spilled entrails, divining the course of the magic now coursing around the room. It carved a final sigil in the floor and the symbol lit up.

The walls themselves were peeling away in layers, revealing what lay beyond. The room had been set up in one of the ship's fighter decks. Where once hundreds of attack craft had been parked on the wide expanse of rusted metal, now heaps of thousands upon thousands of bodies festered. Pasty, desiccated limbs lay across dead faces staring blindly. The heaps were dozens deep, mountains of death, harvested from the hives of Stratix and heaped as an offering to Teturact's mercy.

Teturact had been glad of them, not just as a symbol of his own power. They had a practical purpose, too, as did all the bodies crammed into every spare corner of the tombship.

The walls of the room fell away and its ceiling broke into flakes of rust that fluttered away. The spell was all but complete. The chanting grew higher and the air burned with power, black sparks leaping from the cowls of the wizards, half-formed shadowy observers flickering in and out of sight.

The first of the bodies stirred, dragging itself from the side of one of the corpse-mountains and tumbling down the slope. It knocked other bodies down with it and they stirred, reaching out dumbly with gnawed fingers. Limbs reached from the slopes until whole mountains were stirring and the first of the bodies struggled to its feet and began to walk.

Teturact could feel the seething as the whole ship began to awaken. The people of Stratix had pleaded, begged, for him to save them from death, and he had done so in return for their souls. Now he was extending the bargain to those he had not saved the first time round, the dregs of Stratix's charnel pits. The tombship was more than a place of worship for Teturact – it was a weapon of war, the deadliest he could create. It was the vessel for an army that did not need to eat or sleep, that would follow unquestioningly, that would never flee and could fight to the death because they were already dead.

Teturact's master plan, the infection and salvation of an empire, could only go so far. Sometimes, he had known all along, he would have to intervene directly and take the fight to the enemy. The tombship was his means of doing so. Now his enemies had struck closer to home than even he had imagined, driving into the Stratix system itself, daring to defile Stratix Luminae – and Teturact had created the tombship for just such an offence.

The mountains were now shifting heaps of human beings, struggling to clamber from beneath one another, teeth and nails gouging, brackish blood running in streams across the fighter deck floor. Many of them shambled closer, dressed in the rags of workers' overalls, regal finery, soldiers' fatigues and everything in between. Teturact's brute-mutants raised him high and his vast mind took in the faint pinpricks of guttering light that were the minds of the dead.

He took every one of those points of light and snuffed them out one by one, replacing them with the unblinking black pearls of his own mind. The final phase of the ritual was Teturact's own – to make these awakened dead answer solely to his will. They were now no more than his instruments, to be controlled as if they were his own limbs. He stretched his mind out and did the same to the bodies waking throughout the ship, until he felt tens of thousands of mind-slaves connected to him like parts of his own shrivelled body.

The pitiful resistance of the Imperium seemed more laughable than ever. How could anyone claim Teturact was not a god? He had created an army and controlled them utterly. He was master of billions and billions of worshippers. There was no greater calling. Soon, when his empire stretched across the stars, it would be complete and Teturact would take his place in the pantheon amongst the gods of the warp.

A tiny part of his mind reached out to the controllers on the bridge. His orders were the last they would ever receive.

He commanded that the tombship be taken into low orbit around Stratix Luminae. Then he demanded that the shields be dropped and the hull of the tombship be allowed to disintegrate in the planet's atmosphere. He already knew how the ship would break up, the parts that would land intact and the remaining fighter craft and shuttles that would fly out of the wreckage. He knew which parts would split open and rain down an army on the frozen surface.

It was a beautiful thing, his tombship. But it was just a single building block in the immense cathedral of his empire. It was a small thing for it to be sacrificed, when the prize would be the sanctity of the world where Teturact himself was born.

ELEVEN

'EMPEROR PRESERVE US,' said Sister Aescarion. 'That's the ugliest thing I've ever seen.'

Inquisitor Thaddeus had to agree. The long-range sensors on the *Crescent Moon* were transmitting a visual composite directly onto the viewscreen on the bridge, and it was not pretty. Stratix Luminae was in the background, looking like a huge eye without a pupil. In the foreground hung a truly hideous thing, a ship that was as diseased as any of the unfortunates on Eumenix. Pustules the size of islands spat plumes of bile out into space. Hull plates oozed out of the superstructure, straining under the ship's corpulent mass. Lance batteries were rusted gun barrels sticking out of orifices ringed with scabs. The engines bled pus and the entrances to the fighter decks had deformed into lipless drooling orifices that mouthed dumbly and vomited clouds of debris, corpses and filth.

The ship was huge, larger by magnitudes than the *Crescent Moon*. It had to be a full-scale battleship – there might have been an Emperor-class under there somewhere.

'Bridge, do we have this profile stored?' asked Thaddeus.

The servitors at the consoles spent a moment calculating, wire fingers clattering on the keyboards of their mem-consoles.

'Battlefleet Stratix had three Emperor-class battleships,' came a tinny, synthetic voice. 'The *Ultima Khan* was reclassified heretic and reported destroyed at Kolova. The *Olympus Mons* and the *Dutiful* are unaccounted for.'

'It doesn't matter what it used to be,' said Colonel Vinn unexpectedly. 'It's orbit is too low. It'll be breaking up within the hour.'

'Maybe so, colonel,' said Thaddeus, 'but this is too much to be a coincidence. Bridge, what do we have following us?'

Another moment's pause. Then, 'Two light cruisers, designation unknown, heretic probable. Cobra-class escort squadron, again heretic. Unknown attack craft and merchantmen.'

'If we're being trailed by that many and we're still this far out,' said Thaddeus, 'then the Soul Drinkers will have been spotted, too. They're on Stratix

Luminae already and the Enemy is close behind them.'

'Let them fight one another?' suggested Vinn.

'Unless they're in league,' replied Aescarion with bitterness, spitting out the words as if she longed for the Soul Drinkers to be under Teturact's command so she could destroy them all the more justly.

'Agreed,' said Thaddeus. 'We will not have another chance to bring them to bear. But we can't land right on top of them. If they're landing troops we'll be blown out of the sky even if this ship has broken up by then. Bridge, get me landing solutions, far away from that battleship to get down in one piece. Colonel, how's our armour?'

'Enough APCs for the Sisters and remaining men,' said Vinn. Thaddeus felt the sting even through the man's expressionless voice – the best of his men were dead, shot or frozen stiff at Pharos. 'We weren't expecting to run a mechanised assault, inquisitor.'

'It'll do, colonel. We just have to get there, the rest we'll make up as we go along. Sister, colonel, you both understand the enemy we will be facing. The Soul Drinkers are probably under-strength but they are still Space Marines. We cannot destroy them all, but we have an advantage in that they want something at Stratix Luminae and must make themselves vulnerable to get it. They will probably be engaged by other forces so we will have the luxury of picking our targets.'

'The first of those targets,' came that familiar half-machine voice from the rear of the bridge, 'is Sarpedon.' The Pilgrim emerged from the bridge entrance. Thaddeus didn't know how long he had been there – though every member of the strikeforce had to be fully briefed, he had privately wished to have this talk with Aescarion and Vinn alone. But the Pilgrim seemed able to shadow everything he did.

'Sarpedon is the key,' continued the Pilgrim. He walked slowly up the bridge until he stood between Aescarion and Vinn, and Thaddeus saw the repulsion pass over Aescarion's face. 'Sarpedon is their weakness, and he knows it himself. Without him there will be no purpose. Without him, even if he is the only one to die here, the Chapter will fragment to be hunted down one by one. All other targets are secondary.'

'I have command here, Pilgrim,' said Thaddeus sternly, more as a show to the others than in any real hope of reining in the creature. 'We know there will be other key Marines. Any specialists or officers are to be considered vital targets. But agreed, Sarpedon is high on that list. At least he should be easy to spot.' Pict-recordings from House Jenassis had been issued to every Sister and storm trooper – every one of them knew that amongst the Soul Drinkers was a monster with spider's legs who was to be destroyed at all costs.

'There is a good chance the Soul Drinkers will be fighting another enemy when we engage,' repeated

Thaddeus. 'This is the best advantage we have, and we will use it. They will not know we are coming and we will strike as hard and fast as the Soul Drinkers themselves. Have your troops pray, both of you, and never forget we are here to do the Emperor's will.'

The strikeforce's leaders left the bridge and suddenly the whole area was bathed in a red glow. The engines below roared into life, immense plasma turbines grinding into action as the primary engines fired.

The motley flotilla tracking them was left behind as the *Crescent Moon* powered away from them. The thruster solutions took over and the ship began the descent to Stratix Luminae.

THE FIGHTERS SCREAMED into the planet's upper atmosphere, the surface a frozen desolation beneath them, Teturact's flagship a still vaster slab of pure rotting malice above them. The xenos fighters slid through Stratix Luminae's atmospheric envelope like knives through silk, forewings flowing into shining blades that cut through the strong, freezing air currents.

The ship – and it had to be Teturact's flagship, nothing else could radiate that aura of corruption and evil – didn't fire on them. Perhaps its crew and systems were too far gone to be able to track them and fire effectively. But it had certainly seen them – every Marine, even those with no psychic ability, felt the dark eye of something within focusing on them as if they were samples on a microscope slide.

The ten fighters carried the whole of the remaining Soul Drinkers Chapter, down to barely six hundred Marines and a handful of Chapter serfs. Sarpedon along with Squad Krydel and Squad Luko were in one craft, with one given over entirely to Tellos and his Assault Marines who Sarpedon suspected wouldn't follow anyone else. Another carried the force that would strike directly into the facility – Squads Karraidin, Graevus and Salk along with Techmarines Lygris and Solun and Apothecary Salk.

Apothecary Karendin and the Chapter Infirmary took up a fighter craft along with Techmarine Varuk. Chaplain Iktinos had a craft of his own along with those Marines whose squads had lost their officers and chose to follow the Chaplain into battle. One fighter held Tyrendian, the Librarian who was effectively the Chapter's chief psyker after Sarpedon himself. The remaining three contained the squads earmarked to form a mobile reserve – Sevras, Karvik, Corvan, Dyon, Shastarik, Kelvor, Locano, Preadon and the Librarian Gresk.

When assembling the force it had been brought home to Sarpedon just what a state the Chapter was in. Less than half the Marines were still organised into squads along the old Chapter lines – Marines whose squads had lost their officers joined other squads or formed around leaders like Iktinos, Tellos or Karraidin. The Chapter had always had a more fluid organisation than the Codex Astartes had set out but it was now in a constant state of flux. There had simply not been enough time to organise it properly, not when every passing hour made their irretrievable genetic corruption more likely.

It was Techmarine Varuk who noticed the disintegration first. The scanner signature of the flagship above began to become more indistinct, as if there was some kind of interference covering it. Rapidly the truth became apparent – the ship was coming apart, shedding hull sections like scabbed skin. Whole decks peeled away and began to fall into the atmosphere, bloated hull sections rupturing and spilling clouds of debris. The rearmost fighters began to report near-collisions with chunks of debris streaking down from above. The scanners on the fighters, even though they were advanced xenos tech, were quickly blinded by the mass of signals suddenly pouring into orbit.

Teturact's flagship was coming apart above them. Varuk voxed Sarpedon to tell him, and Sarpedon knew better than to assume the death of the ship was good news.

TETURACT WATCHED HIS ship rupture and it tasted good. The ship had once been a mighty battleship, carrying enough firepower to raze a city to the ground. Teturact had not only corrupted it until it served him, but had proven he could destroy such a thing with a thought. A symbol of Imperial might had been captured, deformed, and then destroyed, all because Teturact wished it.

If anyone had needed proof that Teturact was a god, this was it.

He felt the plasma reactors overloading and breaking up, sending shockwaves through the hull that fractured the stern and sent the engines spiralling downwards towards the surface. The tang of escaping fuel plasma was a metallic, chemical taste of Imperial doom.

Already sections of corridor and gun deck were falling, packed with the living dead. Some would not make it to the surface intact but enough would to disgorge an army onto the ground. He reached out with his mind and felt the wizards, held in a near-indestructible plasma conduit, waiting in the belly of the ship to be vomited onto Stratix Luminae. Teturact, as was proper for the master of the dying ship, waited on the bridge. The bulkheads nearby had already failed and hard vacuum had turned the slave-bodies beneath his feet rigid and cold, but Teturact kept himself and his brute-mutant bearers intact with a barely-conscious effort. The hardness of space was a reminder of the purity of death he would leave at Stratix Luminae.

The gods were watching. Teturact could feel their eyes on him, both curious and jealous, and fearful that he would rise and join them. The gods were no more than ideas made real in the warp, and Teturact had created ideas of his own – servitude through death, purity and corruption made one, the subjugation of souls through suffering and deliverance. Those concepts would be coalescing in the warp even now, and when they became strong enough Teturact's mind would be divorced from his body completely and he would join the kingdom he had created in the warp as its god.

He could feel the universe flickering at the edges of his consciousness, like an endless harvest of souls begging to be enslaved, delivered from their suffering by the servitude and oblivion Teturact offered.

But there were matters closer at hand. He drew his mind back in, the sensation almost painful. He watched the first wave falling towards Stratix Luminae and the hard bright darts of the intruder craft flying through the first curtain of debris.

His army would be on the ground waiting when the intruders landed. If they ever got to land at all.

THE FIGHTER LURCHED suddenly, throwing Sarpedon against the curved metal wall. The instrument panels flared brightly as damage signals from the fighter's systems flooded into the controls. The viewscreen flickered and was suddenly full of debris shooting down past them, chunks of blackened metal and showers of torn corpses.

'Keep us straight!' yelled Sarpedon to the serfs wrestling with the alien controls. 'Get us down!'

Comms runes flickered on Sarpedon's retina. Several Marines were voxing him at once.

'...Karvik's down, sir, lost its engines...' the voice was Lygris, whose craft was closest in the formation to the fighter carrying Squads Sevras and Karvik.

There were thirty Marines on the fighter. They would not be the last to fall – Sarpedon could see the life sign monitors going haywire in the confusion and guessed that the falling storm of wreckage was Teturact's way of landing an army.

'Sarpedon to all squads,' he voxed. 'Break formation and take evasive action. Do whatever you have to.' He turned to the serfs at the controls of his fighter. 'Find Karvik's fighter, I want to know if anyone could have made it.'

Another jolt and the fighter banked to avoid a falling torrent of wreckage, slabs of hull plate streaking past the viewscreen. Karendin's craft, which housed the infirmary, would be busy even before the fighters landed, guessed Sarpedon.

'Crash us if you have to,' said Sarpedon to his crew. 'Just bring us down.'

'Crash-land in thirty seconds, commander,' replied the serf at the navigation helm.

'Do it.' Sarpedon switched to the channels for Squads Krydel and Luko in the fighter's passenger compartment. 'We're coming down hard, sergeants.'

LUKO CHECKED THE restraints on his grav-couch, his hand dextrous in spite of the massive lightning claw gauntlets he wore. 'You heard the man,' he shouted to his men over the din of wreckage slamming off the fighter's hull. 'Buckle up.'

KARVIK AND SEVRAS'S fighter hit the ground too steeply, one wing catching in the frozen earth and flipping the fighter end over end. It came to rest upside-down within sight of the facility, spewing strange alien fuel onto the tundra.

Theirs was the first down, though not intentionally. Even as the craft was still slewing to a stop the first elements of Teturact's army were picking themselves from the fallen chunks of wreckage and piles of bodies, their flesh burned and frozen by the fall, bones broken, minds jelly. The will of their master demanded that they stand on broken legs and take up twisted shards of wreckage as weapons. Their master had shown them salvation, even holding back death itself – so what could they do but serve?

Their master, their god, demanded service in return for everything he had given them. There was no reason for them to resist as they shambled towards the fallen fighter and towards the landing spots of other silver craft now streaking towards the ground, nothing remaining in their ruined minds but the resonating order to kill.

SERGEANT LUKO'S RESTRAINTS only just held as the fighter slammed into the ground, the frozen surface scraping agonisingly against the hull, the alien entrails of the craft shaking loose under the impact. He was thrown around in his restraints until he thought his reinforced ribcage would collapse.

He knew how important this mission was, and that to die during it was a more honourable death than any of the billions of Imperial citizens could hope for – but he did not want to die like this, out of sight of the enemy, the victim of chance and gravity.

The howling stopped. In the moment of silence that followed Luko checked his autosenses and tested his muscle groups for injury. Bruises, strains: nothing he couldn't ignore.

'We're down,' came the vox from the bridge.

'Soul Drinkers, move out!' ordered Sergeant Krydel from the other side of the compartment. The metal of the hull flowed and peeled back from an iris that opened in the fighter's side. Freezing air flooded in.

Krydel was out of his restraints and already leading his Marines out. Luko snapped off his own restraints and the power fields of his lightning claws were alive before he hit the ground.

'Look lively, men, it's not a happy welcome!' he voxed as he saw the first enemies scrambling towards him. Bolter fire snapped and several of the living dead came apart.

Sergeant Krydel set off headlong to secure the fighter's landing site. Luko ran to the nearest cover – a gigantic fallen chunk of machinery – and sliced the first few corpses that crawled out of it to ribbons with his lightning claws.

Good. He was blooded. Now the real business could begin.

Debris was still falling. Some was recognisable, landing craft or jerry-built drop pods, more was just random chunks of the diseased flagship. Bodies were falling, too, and very few stayed lying down where they landed. Luko could see the facility, smaller than some of the fallen wreckage, a single-storey building pockmarked and scorched by small arms fire.

'Get me a fire point here! I want fire arcs covering the approach, Karraidin's coming in on our tail!' Luko's Marines scrambled onto the wreckage, forming a hard point where they could find cover and form a disciplined fire point to keep the approaches to the facility clear of enemies.

Luko glanced up and saw the sky dark as if a thunderstorm was brewing. A bright streak of light was another fighter coming in and dark specks were more of Teturact's army coming down.

The first wave was just a harrying force to keep the Soul Drinkers from getting dug in. What followed would be the real test. Vermin like this had killed Dreo, they said, a man Luko had served alongside as a brother and who he could not imagine dying. The heart of that corruption was above them, and Luko hoped that whether the Chapter succeeded or failed, they could do some damage to that heart.

Maybe even stop it from beating. But for the moment Luko had more immediate concerns.

'We're clear to thirty metres,' voxed Krydel over the chatter of bolter fire.'

'We've got you covered. Start the push on the facility,' replied Luko, barely flinching as a building-sized chunk of engine crashed to the ground nearby.

Luko glanced round to see Sarpedon emerging from the craft, moving swiftly on his eight legs, beheading a corpse-mutant that loped towards him without breaking his stride.

'Karraidin, we're down. What's your position?' Sarpedon was voxing. Then a scream and the descending silver dart of a fighter cut through the air overhead in answer, the craft banking sharply and looping down into a perfect short landing between Sarpedon's position and the facility.

Sarpedon hurried into cover beside Luko, snapping off shots with his bolt pistol as he went. 'Hold this position, sergeant,' said Sarpedon. 'Cover Krydel and Karraidin's force.'

'Where will you be, commander?'

'Everywhere. Same as the enemy.'

Luko nodded and clambered onto the smouldering wreckage where he could direct his squad's fire. Already, thick swarms of enemies were pouring from fallen landers, their numbers denuded by disciplined fire from Luko and Krydel. But there were so many of them...

And there would be more. It was raining corpses, and not one of them would stay dead for long.

EVEN FROM THE *Crescent Moon's* landing site the fall-out was clearly visible, a dark torrent pouring onto the horizon like a storm of black rain. The blurred black smudge in the sky that was the enemy battleship was fragmenting even as Thaddeus watched, sections of the hull peeling away to reveal the ship's skeleton.

The cargo ramp of the *Crescent Moon* touched the ground and Colonel Vinn, in the lead APC, gave the order to roll out. The column of vehicles – refitted Chimera transports with reinforced armour and overcharged engines, along with a couple of Sororitas Rhino APCs – roared out of the *Crescent Moon* and onto the surface of Stratix Luminae.

Thaddeus, from his Chimera towards the back of the column, looked out from the commander's hatch as the vehicle rolled down the ramp. The air was freezing and he was glad of the heavy blastcoat he wore – he could see his breath coiling in the air. Every planet, he had learned in his short Inquisitorial career, had its own smell, and Stratix Luminae smelled empty and secretive like an abandoned house. The colourless landscape of endless tundra seemed to hold something more than just desolation, as if something had happened long ago, or was sleeping beneath the surface, that resonated through the air and the barren earth.

'Rein in the front vehicles if you have to,' Thaddeus voxed to Colonel Vinn. 'I don't want us blundering into someone else's fire fight. Halt at the first contact and keep me posted.'

An acknowledgement signal was Vinn's only reply. He was a man of few words, perhaps because he knew that even if he survived he would probably be mind-wiped and unable to remember any conversations he had had.

Thaddeus ducked back down into the body of the Chimera, where the Pilgrim sat in the darkness, filling the passenger compartment with its aura of menace. Thaddeus would rather not have travelled with the creature but he didn't yet trust it to be out of his sight.

'We can kill them, inquisitor,' grated the Pilgrim. 'You know that, don't you? We are not just here to find them and report back. We are soldiers. We can kill them with our own hands.'

'I am not here for your revenge, Pilgrim,' said Thaddeus darkly. 'I have vowed to do my duty. I will bring the Soul Drinkers to justice but that doesn't mean I'm going to get this strikeforce destroyed in the attempt. If it takes me decades then I will wait.'

'There will not be another chance.'

'If I cannot finish it here then I will make another chance.' Thaddeus sat back in the juddering APC and checked the load in his autopistol. He had very few of his custom bullets left but if there was ever a time to use them it was on Stratix Luminae. If the

Pilgrim was right then one of those fearsomely expensive shells would be enough to kill Sarpedon and behead his Chapter. If the Pilgrim was wrong, and Thaddeus had to admit it tended to be right, then just getting close enough to take the shot would be enough to get Thaddeus killed and end any hope of the Inquisition ending the threat.

'Vehicle on point reports small arms fire,' came a vox from Vinn.

'Any hostiles?'

'Not yet.'

Good. At least it seemed the strikeforce wouldn't be heading into a combined force of Teturact's followers and Sarpedon's Marines. Thaddeus suspected this would be the only good news he got that day.

KARRAIDIN'S POWER FIST ripped through two enemies, blasting their rotting bodies apart in showers of spoiled meat and bone. Bolters chattered and chewed through a dozen more as Sergeant Salk blew another apart. What had been a barren wasteland minutes before was rapidly turning into a landscape of twisted, blackened metal, stinking smoke billowing off the fallen wreckage, enemies clawing their way towards Karraidin's spearhead from every angle. Bodies fell from the sky, thudding into the ground, and more often than not something ragged and broken rose up to carry on fighting.

Salk couldn't even see the facility now, with towering engine stacks and hull segments embedded in the ground in front of him.

'Salk! We need to split the force, get through any way we can and rendezvous at the blast doors!' bellowed Karraidin, storm bolter blazing away at a knot of creatures that had once been Guardsmen, some still holding lasguns and combat knives.

Salk nodded and waved his Marines forward, Trooper Krin blasting into the shadows with his plasma gun and being rewarded with a shower of broken bodies illuminated by the plasma flash. Small arms fire – lasguns, autoguns, stub pistols – was spattering against the wreckage around them. Salk knew they had to keep moving or the sheer numbers now being thrown against them would trap them.

'After me! Krin, pick your targets and go for clusters!' Salk drew his chainsword and jogged forward, slashing at the emaciated faces that loomed through the wreckage and smoke. The fight was getting closer by the second, limbs reaching out for him, bolter fire spattering from behind him into anything that moved. A lasgun shot speared past his head and another burst against the ceramite of his chest armour – he stamped down on a corpse-soldier crawling in front of him and rammed his chainblade through the abdomen of another who fell gibbering down at him from above.

A plasma blast roared overhead and incinerated half a unit of enemies, dressed in the tatters of Naval

Security uniforms, emerging from a crashed lander. They were more intact than most of the enemies Salk had faced so far, the cold hatred still legible on their faces, assault shotguns in their hands. Salk snapped off bolter shots at them then dropped into the cover of a hull section as shotgun fire ripped back at him, filling the air with a storm of shrapnel.

Bolter counter-fire tore back and Trooper Karrick dived into the fray, charging into the security troopers followed by the rest of the squad. Salk clambered to his feet and joined the melee, beheading one enemy and crushing the ribcage of another with the pommel of his chainblade. Karrick, a tough veteran with more experience than Salk but who seemed to accept the younger man's authority without question, grabbed one trooper by the wrist and hurled him against the hull plate with enough force to break his back.

The surviving troopers tried to fall back but Squad Salk never left the front foot, and in a final volley of bolter shots the Naval Security unit lay shredded and smoking on the ground.

'Keep going,' voxed Salk. 'There'll be more.'

Salk led the way through the labyrinth of wreckage, heading towards where he knew the facility should be. He checked the squad icons – a couple of battle-brothers were wounded but it was nothing they couldn't fight through.

Salk got his first glimpse of the facility building and it was nearly his last. The single-storey building was swarming with enemy troopers of higher quality than the shambling corpses that had fallen so far. They were not resurrected dead but fanatic troopers, scores of them manning the fire points on the roof and clambering up the walls. They fired from behind the makeshift barricades still remaining from the assault ten years ago. Heavy bolter shells tore down from the roof and Salk ducked rapidly back into cover, hearing the too-familiar report of shells through ceramite as one of his brothers lost a limb to the large calibre fire tearing through the wreckage.

They had to get out. The first line of defences would be a safer place to fight from than here, but the squad had to get there first.

'Grenades!' called Salk and the Marines who could do so pulled frag grenades from their belt pouches. 'Krin, give us a covering shot!'

Plasma fire erupted over the closest barricade, white-hot liquid fire rippling over the barbed wire and into the trench behind. Several Marines hurled grenades a split-second afterwards, multiple reports adding to the plasma shot and throwing plumes of pulverised earth into the air.

'Now!' ordered Salk and led the charge, sprinting the few metres over the ruined barricade and into the same trench that Captain Korvax had taken from the eldar a decade earlier. This time it was not xenos but corrupted heretics the Soul Drinkers were fighting, still wearing the uniforms of their original units, Imperial Guard and PDF troopers, even private militia – Salk recognised the emerald uniform of Cartel Pollos before he cut the man wearing it in two. Teturact's army had come from all over his empire, and doubtless every world he had visited had provided a tithe of armed worshippers to their master.

Karrick was at Salk's side in the trench, hauling an ex-Elysian Guardsman towards him and cutting his throat with a combat knife.

Salk glanced down the trench and saw other Soul Drinkers doing what they did better than almost any other force in the galaxy – close-quarters battle, cold and fast, toe-to-toe with the enemy where they were safer than anywhere else in the battle.

Salk checked the icons again – it was Brother Vaeryn they had left behind, his life-icon flickering to show great blood loss and trauma.

'Vaeryn, come in,' voxed Salk.

'Lost a leg, sergeant,' came the crackly reply.

'Can you fight?'

'Fight but not move. I'll have to do my bit from here.'

'Fates be with you, brother.'

'The Emperor protects.'

Maybe they would be able to pick up the stricken Marine on their way back out of the facility, but Salk doubted it.

Heavy bolter fire was still streaming down, throwing up chains of explosions along the rear parapet of the trench. The sudden whine of a heavy weapon and a bright orange explosion on the roof of the facility told Salk that his was not the only Soul Drinkers squad moving on the facility. Salk took the brief respite in firing to look up over the parapet at the facility – one corner was down but there was still a dual heavy bolter mount facing them, along with the small arms fire streaking down from either end of the trench where heretics were trying to win back their defences by firing blindly down from both corners.

A plasma shot ripped down the trench on cue and blew another three men into the air at one end of the trench, Krin's shot freeing half the squad to fire up at the remaining weapon mount. Bolter shots spattered against the plasticrete of the building and a gunner's shattered body tumbled off the roof.

Salk led the charge over the rear of the trench and into the next, vaulting over makeshift barricades to cut down the few cultists huddling for cover from the bolter fire. Salk could see the blast doors now, through the web of tracer fire and the gauze of falling earth from the explosions now bursting all around the facility.

The towering form of Karraidin appeared as the captain strode towards the facility, storm bolter firing. Small arms shots bounced off his thick armour as the Marines around him snapped off shots at the roof, bringing down more and more shooters. Salk ran forward again and his squad met Karraidin's in the shadow of the facility as the last fire point was cracked open by a well-aimed frag grenade. Salk saw that Apothecary Pallas and Techmarine Lygris were with Karraidin's squad – Lygris, Salk remembered, had suffered severe wounds early in his career and now wore a near-expressionless mask of synthetic flesh instead of a face.

'Well met, brother,' said Karraidin with a grin creasing his battered features.

Salk drew his squad up in cover around the blast doors. 'I'll get grenades. We'll blow the door.'

Karraidin just walked up to the doors and, the power field around his gauntlet flickering to life, punched his power fist into the metal. Arcs of light spat as the field ripped through the metal and Karraidin tore great strips from the door until he had gouged a hole large enough for even him to walk through.

'Squad Graevus, where are you?' voxed Karraidin.

'Got tied down, we're on your heels. Solun's with us.'

Salk saw Squad Graevus heading through the wreckage of the defences, the white diamond of Graevus's power axe blade shining.

Karraidin switched to the vox for all the squads and specialists under his command. 'Spearhead, we've made the facility. We're going in.'

The captain ducked through the ragged hole and into the facility. Salk followed, chainsword drawn.

The first thing that hit him was the smell, a stench so awful that it almost made Salk reel. It would have been enough to drive back a normal man and even with a Marine's constitution Salk felt his additional organs and filters kicking in to prevent the stench from leaving him nauseous and dizzy.

His autosenses rapidly adjusted to the darkness. The first floor was the security station he remembered from Korvax's pict-recording, the shattered automated defences spilling metal entrails onto the floor, stark plasticrete construction pocked with bullet scars.

Where the cargo elevator had been there was now a solid metal slab with a security console nearby, blocking the way down.

'Can you get through it?' asked Salk.

Karraidin shook his head. 'It's wired. Probably to blow if it's tampered with. Get a techmarine up here.'

Lygris came to the fore and began to work with the security console. 'Time to see what Adept Aristeia taught us.'

Squad Graevus and Techmarine Solun were entering through the breach. Solun hurried up to help Lygris input the complex code that Aristeia had provided them with. Solun's mem-gear made quick work of the complicated algorithms that generated the entry code, but even so there was a painful delay as the techmarines worked on the interface.

The few minutes were agonising. Cultist counter-attacks came to the breach and were swept away by pin-sharp bolter fire from Squads Karraidin and Salk. Lasgun shots spattered in from ex-Guardsman cultists and Salk drew his men up in front of the console to shield its delicate working with their bodies from any stray shots. This could be it – Sarkia Aristeia could have been mistaken or lying and everything would end here, on this Emperor-forsaken snowball of a planet which had nothing to give them.

A Space Marine never gave in to despair, but in those moments Salk felt the enormity of the task weighing on him – the Soul Drinkers were finally free after thousands of years of servitude to the Imperium, and now a tiny thing like Aristeia's memory would decide if they survived to use that new freedom.

'Done. Stand back!'

A spiral crack appeared in the slab and slowly it opened, segments fanning open like an iris. Half the Marines pointed their bolters into the growing hole in the floor as corroded motors strained to open a hatch that had been sealed for ten years. A thin, stinking fog coiled up from below and Karraidin held up a hand to fend it off while his sensors adjusted. Salk glanced at his squad's auspex to see what was beneath them, but there was just a mass of static swirling. They knew it was a four metre drop into the floor below, but that was it. There could be anything down there.

'Graevus, do you object to having the point?'

'It's what I'm here for,' replied Graevus. He hurried up to the opening with his squad. It was absolutely pitch black inside.

'Cold and fast, we get in and we secure whatever we find. Karraidin, get the specialists in afterwards, if there's anything in here I don't know how long we can hold it off. Squad, move!'

Graevus holstered his bolt pistol to hold his axe two-handed, then dropped into the hole. His assault squad followed him rapidly, each man dropping into the unknown with weapons drawn.

'Damnation!' came a vox almost immediately, half-scrambled by interference but definitely Graevus's voice. 'What is… Get down here, everyone, I can't…'

Static howled over the vox. Without pausing Salk jumped in after the squad, knowing that his squad would be right behind him.

He landed on something hot and soft, squirming and undulating beneath him. Something twisted past his face and his autosenses picked out a tentacle, as thick as a Marine's waist, squeezing the life out of one of Graevus's Assault Marines before cramming the remains into a giant circular maw big enough to swallow a tank. Yelled orders and cries of pain were everywhere, along with the roaring of something inhuman that seemed to be coming from everywhere at once.

Salk's squad were dropping in all around him. He flicked the selector on his bolt pistol to full auto and dived into the fray.

SARKIA ARISTEIA GULPED *down the pure, freezing air, trying to get the stink of mutation and burning flesh out of her lungs. She stumbled from the open blast doors and fell to the ground, grazing her palms on the frozen earth. It was ruination outside the facility, with the tech-guard defences reduced to rubble and heaps of pulverised earth. Barbed wire was wrapped around broken bodies of men and eldar. Corpses lay everywhere, their blood already freezing hard – Sarkia even saw the armoured form of a fallen Marine. Plumes of smoke rose from craters and, as Sarkia looked up at Stratix Luminae's pale blank sky, she saw the twirling contrails of the Soul Drinkers Thunder-hawks as they returned to their ship in orbit. She had seen them fight, and by the Omnissiah they were awe-some, a head taller than the tallest normal man, fast and ruthless, deadeye shots and ferocious in hand-to-hand. Truth be told they had scared her more than the quick, skilful eldar. She supposed that the Soul Drinkers had saved her life from the alien menace, but it was a hollow feeling.*

The Marines hadn't bothered with the survivors. An Adeptus Mechanicus ship would probably come, carrying adepts that would use Sarkia and the other survivors to seal the facility and label it Interdictus. The work they were doing there had been revolutionary, even Sarkia knew it. But it had been dangerous, and even if the eldar raid had been a coincidence (it couldn't be, the aliens had to have known what they were doing here and come to stop or steal it) the mutagenics could easily have got out of hand. Now the containment around the primary samples had been breached – Sarkia might be killed and incinerated to prevent contamination, or she might be interrogated until she gave up what little she knew about the program in an investigation into possible corruption or incompetence. It all depended on the unknowable logic of the Archmagus in charge.

Something stirred in the entrance, moving out of the shadows. Another survivor? A few tech-guard and adepts had survived, Sarkia was sure she had seen old Karlu Grien hobbling out of the wreckage below. But no… it was a survivor, perhaps, but not one she wanted to see.

It was naked, humanoid but not human. It was so emaciated it couldn't possibly be alive – pallid skin stretched taut over a vestigial ribcage and a stringy abdomen. Its limbs were too long and it had too many fingers and toes, which had too many joints apiece. It looked too weak to stand but it strode confidently out of the blast doors and into the light. Its face was no face but a knot of hanging skin, with a pair of stern triangular eyes that glowed faintly. It looked at her, once, and Sarkia could feel the menace, like a lasgun beam right into her soul, burning those eyes and that nonexistent face into her mind forever.

It looked at her like she looked at cells under a micro-scope. In that moment she knew what it was – one of the experiments from the lowest level, perhaps a success, *perhaps a failure. The adepts had been trying to unlock the human genetic pattern so they could halt, reverse, or create mutations at will – this was one of the things they had made. By the way it moved without enough musculature to support itself, Sarkia presumed that it was one of the psychic creations she had heard rumoured darkly by the menial staff.*

A wave of revulsion rolled over her and she scrambled away into a half-collapsed trench as the creature walked by, forgetting her as it looked out over the remnants of the defences and the gory relics of the battle. She could feel its hatred and corruption, she could feel her very soul becoming filthy with its presence. She fought the urge to vomit, to grab sharp chunks of frozen soil and scrape herself bloodily clean.

She tried to tear her eyes away but couldn't, as the creature lifted off the ground and shot towards the sky, leaving behind an invisible but powerful stain of hatred and corruption that Sarkia Aristeia would never be able to wash off.

HE WAS BORED *by this world, where the sum of living things wasn't even worth the effort of killing. Filled with the hatred of life that was hard-wired into a soul that should never have been born, Teturact looked up at the darkening evening sky, took hold of his feeble body with his awesome mind, and flung himself up towards the heavens.*

He could feel life out there. And life meant death, and death meant power, and power was the closest thing in the universe to the sacred. For Teturact had known, since the moment he had been born in a test tube crammed with mutating clone-cells, that he was a god, with a god's power and a god's ambition. Now he just had to let his worshippers know they had to worship him, and as he plunged through the vacuum towards the teeming life-light of Stratix, he knew exactly how to make them kneel.

THE HELL WAS lighting up the sky. The psychic circuit raged around Sarpedon's body, cold fire against his skin, and he felt as if his blood would boil trapped inside his armour. He poured every last drop of his willpower into the Hell, the unique power that had brought him into the fold as Chapter Librarian a lifetime ago. The same power was now drawing stern spectres of order and justice in the sky, throwing down lightning bolts of purity at the hordes pouring from crashed landers and fallen piles of bodies. The nalwood force staff was hot in his hand and Sarpedon had to force back the Hell, rein it in before it demanded all his focus and blocked his capability to lead his Marines.

He let the psychic fire die down to a bearable level and clambered up onto the pile of wreckage he was using for cover, climbing to a vantage point where he could get some overview of the battle-field. A short distance away Squad Dyon was taking ranging shots at distant groups of enemies, and nearby Librarian Gresk was leading the prayers of Corvan's assault squad as they prepared for the counter-attack they would soon drive into the heart of the enemy. Sarpedon looked out over the battlefield at the force his Marines were facing and though he did not accept despair, he got some idea of the sheer scale of the fight to come.

Traitorous Guardsmen jumped from Valkyrie transports so twisted with corruption that they looked like huge flying beasts. Shambling dead groped their way from drifts of broken bodies and were whipped into advancing waves by cadaverous taskmasters. The sky was thick with falling debris, and Sarpedon knew the force had already lost Marines to the wreckage dropping from orbit. He could not begin to estimate the numbers of Teturact's army. He knew that a battleship could hold upwards of twenty thousand crew, but there was no telling how many cultists and living dead could be crammed into the same space.

The Hell was throwing some of the enemy back, forcing the still-sentient troops of Teturact's horde to falter as they charged. But the dead and the fanatics kept coming, and with each passing moment a hundred more emerged, formed huge bloodthirsty mobs, and advanced.

The Soul Drinkers were drawn up in a rough defensive circle around the facility. The barren tundra had become a landscape of broken metal and dead bodies, where the Soul Drinkers' superior firepower mattered less than brutal close combat. Several squads were already fighting hard within the position, hunting down and crushing the pockets of attackers that fell close to the facility, and already there were tales of brutality and bravery being written in the bloodstained maze of wreckage.

Sarpedon held the front and Iktinos the rear, and it was from the far side of the facility that Sarpedon could see the flashes of psychic fire from the Librarian Tyrendian. Two fighters were still airborne and functioning as a mobile reserve, but Sarpedon knew they could not stay in the air much longer. All he could see of Sevras and Karvik's fighter was a pall of smoke hundreds of metres away. If anyone had survived, they would have to fend for themselves.

Sarpedon dropped back down to the ground as the first lasgun shots from the advancing horde spanged off the twisted metal around him.

'Range?' he asked of the closest sergeant, Dyon.

'Give the word and we can give them a counter-volley.'

'Let them get closer. I want rapid fire, we need to thin them out, not scare them.'

'Understood.'

The vox crackled with gunfire. 'Commander!' came Chaplain Iktinos's voice. 'The heathens have assaulted with armour. We are engaging.'

Iktinos was cut off before Sarpedon could reply, the sky past the facility flashing scarlet with Tyrendian's psychic lightning.

Sergeant Luko's voice came over the vox a second later. 'Tellos is counter-attacking, sir. We can't hold him back, we're advancing to give his men covering fire.'

'Do it, Luko. Just don't get cut off, they're coming in everywhere.'

'Understood.'

So battle was joined. Sarpedon knew the Hell would be little use against the mindless hordes at the forefront of the attack. He let the psychic circuit die down to a faint dull glow against his skin and holstered the force staff on his back.

'Dyon, bring your men forward and engage. We'll throw them against the men behind them. Pass the order on, give me solid rapid fire and cover the assault squads.'

Dyon ran forward through the growing storm of las-fire, his Marines snapping bolter shots off at the hordes that were even now breaking into a run as they began to charge.

Sarpedon followed, cycling through the vox-traffic, ready to intervene when a flashpoint erupted. He could feel the psychic feedback like a million buzzing insects as Gresk started to quicken the reactions and thought speed of the Marines around him and Tyrendian continued to fling mental artillery at the forces charging the rear of the facility.

This was where the future of the Soul Drinkers would be won or lost. He checked the magazine in his bolter, and drew the Soulspear.

* * *

TETURACT'S SHIP WAS a ragged skeleton around him, sheets of hull flapping uselessly like torn skin, the inner decks exposed like the cells of a beehive, bleeding the living dead into the upper atmosphere. The ship was shedding its last few scales, and Teturact willed his wizards down to the surface one by one where they could direct the battle and lend the power of their minds to the vastness of his horde.

There was a sudden flare of power far below, right in the heart of the growing battle. It coincided with a flare of hatred and grim determination as the two sides met, tinged with a delectable joy as someone who loved bloodshed charged into the fray. But the flare of power remained, hard and bright, something old and powerful and tinted by the taste of humanity. A relic, a weapon, the presence of which suggested that someone down there could be powerful enough to put a dent in Teturact's glorious army.

That could not be allowed. And furthermore, it was in itself a disadvantage. Because Teturact could see it, a bright black light on the surface of Stratix Luminae, and if he could see it then he could deal with it personally.

His brute-mutants, drifting aimlessly since the ship's gravity had given way, were drawn to him to act as bearers once more. They lifted Teturact's wizened body onto their broad shoulders and with a thought he willed them downwards, through the disintegrating body of the ship, and into the upper atmosphere of the planet.

The freezing, thin air whipped around him as he descended, extinguishing the fear flickering in the bovine minds of his brute-mutants. His senses flowed out and he saw the tiny force, just a few hundred Marines, surrounded by the legions of his loyal worshippers. Where the two forces met combat blazed and the hot, spicy taste of lives lost flooded the wreckage of the battlefield. The Marines could fight, but the fire of that combat would eventually consume them. With the wizards even now landing amongst their flock, Teturact had more than enough raw manpower to make it happen.

The hard nugget of raw power shone directly beneath him. Teturact smiled, if it could be called a smile, and plummeted downwards.

TWELVE

MUTATION HAD RUN unchecked through the stores of sample tissue for ten years. The lower basement had been full of refrigeration units containing sheets of cultured skin and cylindrical slabs of artificial muscle and, when containment broke down the unleashed half-humans absorbed it all. Now there was barely any difference between the individual organisms – several had joined into huge gestalt creatures and, aside from the strongest who had left them so long ago, they thought with one mind.

They had been starving for some time. Now, they were hungry. In the lab floor just below the surface, many were loose, and at last they had some new game on which to prey.

Sergeant Salk hacked down with his chainsword and severed a long, articulated tentacle-limb as it tried to wrap itself around Techmarine Solun's throat. The beast reared up twice as tall as a Marine, its head a writhing knot of tendrils surrounding a round muscular lamprey's mouth, its body a pulsating column of oozing muscle. Its head touched the low vaulted roof of the dark, nightmarish laboratory before it bellowed and crashed down on the spot where Solun had lain a moment before.

Salk dragged the techmarine aside just in time. Both Solun's legs were gone, chewed off by the same beast that had swallowed half of Salk's squad. The beast thundered in rage as it lumbered forward – Salk jabbed at the gaping maw and stabbing tentacles, keeping the thing at bay as Solun tried to fend off the claws of its lower limbs.

The lab floor was a nightmare. The vaulted ceiling was crusted and discoloured. Banks of corroded machinery and shorted-out command consoles provided scores of hiding places for mutant creatures and obstacles for the Marines. Bolter shells were zipping across the room and globs of brackish mutant blood spattered from gunshot wounds and chainblades. Salk's own chainblade was so clotted with gore that its motor whined and smoked angrily. The lights were out and the gauze of filth and corruption that lay over everything cut down the visibility like fog, so that all Salk could see were huge mutant forms looming all around and glimpses of his battle-brothers in muzzle flashes and the detonations of grenades. The din was terrible, gunfire and bestial howls, the crack of fractured ceramite and the cries of the dying.

It was all but impossible to keep cohesive. The vox was distorted and near-useless. Salk's own squad was scattered, many of them dead, others wounded. Brother Karrick would be lucky to keep the arm that had been mangled by something unspeakable that struck from above. Salk knew that any of them would be lucky to get out alive.

There was a flash of white armour and Apothecary Pallas was diving onto the beast from behind, punching his carnifex gauntlet through the mutant's hide. The array of chemical vials emptied through the gauntlet's injector spike and a black stain of necrotic tissue spread. The huge mutant convulsed, forcing Pallas to hold on to avoid being thrown across the room. Salk ducked forward and drove his chainblade into the mutant's head, again and again, feeling the weapon's motor straining under the weight of tissue clotted around its teeth.

The beast stopped thrashing. Pallas rolled off it and landed beside Solun, the white sections of his armour now dark and slick with corrupted blood.

'Thank you, brother,' gasped Salk.

'Don't thank me yet,' replied Pallas. 'We still have to get onto the containment level. That's where the samples will be kept.'

'Where's Karraidin?'

'Down. He and his squad are making a stand but they're trapped. Graevus is holding the way down but he can't make it without help. Lygris is with them, trying to get the blast doors open.' Pallas used one of his few remaining vials to inject Solun with powerful painkillers and coagulants, restricting the blood flow to his ruined legs.

'I'll take what men I can and help out Graevus,' said Salk. He looked down at Solun.

'I'll do what I can here,' replied Pallas.

'They'll need you down there,' said Solun, his voice weakening. 'There isn't much you can do for me, Pallas.'

'I can stabilise you so we can pick you up on the way out. We need you alive.'

'Good luck, brothers,' said Salk, knocking the worst of the gore off his chainblade before heading into the foetid gloom to gather the remains of his squad.

'Wait!' said Solun. 'What… what's yours?'

'My what?'

'Your mutation. We are all changing, that's why we are here.'

Salk thought for a second. To tell the truth he had been ignoring it. Pretending to himself that it wasn't real. 'Karendin says it's metabolic. My body chemistry is changing. I don't know the details.'

'And it's getting worse?' Solun was going into shock and his voice was faltering.

'Yes, brother. It is.'

'So is mine. It's my memory, you see. I can... remember things. I'm starting to remember things that I never learned. Ever since the Galactarium... please, we have to finish this. Even if we die trying, we can't turn into one of these creatures.'

'Don't speak, Solun,' said Pallas. 'Drop into half-trance, you're in shock.' He looked up at Salk – his face was streaked with mutant blood. 'Get to Graevus. Don't wait for me, I'll make it if I can.'

Salk nodded once and sprinted into the gloom, the deformed monstrosities of Stratix Luminae closing in from the darkness around him, and the secret of survival somewhere below.

THADDEUS HIT THE floor of the Chimera APC as it roared over piles of wreckage, storm trooper driver grinding the gears as the vehicle almost overturned trying to scale the unexpected obstacle.

'Tanks are ruptured,' said the driver from up front. 'Bail out!'

The rear hatch swung down and Thaddeus jumped out, followed by the Pilgrim, who showed agility beyond his ragged appearance as he scuttled down the wreckage to ground level.

Towering twisted piles of wreckage had turned the barren tundra into a maze. The sound of battle came from all directions: hellguns and bolters, the booming amplified voices of cultist taskmasters, storm trooper sergeants yelling orders. A couple of storm trooper squads were nearby trying to clear out a cordon to mount another push – the vehicle column had broken up completely, the APCs rendered all but useless by the rapidly changing, lethal environment.

Thaddeus snapped off a couple of autopistol shots, knocking down a couple of cultists who had taken up a firing position high up in the closest wreckage. He saw as they fell that they were Guardsmen, damned souls whose will had proven too weak and who had been corrupted into the service of Teturact. This was the worst kind of evil, the kind that took dutiful Imperial citizens and turned them into the tools of Chaos.

'Sister! Colonel! What's our situation?'

The vox was a mess of warped static. Sister Aescarion's voice came through first. 'We're not going to be able to break through here, inquisitor. We're facing some kind of... moral threat. Heresy and daemonology.'

'Sarpedon?'

'I think not. Witches, inquisitor. We have lost many already.'

'Fight on, Sister, I will see if there is another way.'

Thaddeus couldn't raise Colonel Vinn at all. The storm troopers were moving forward, battering their way towards the facility with volleys of hellgun fire, but they could not move fast enough to keep from being surrounded. Thaddeus recognised the advancing hordes from the battlefield reports that had come in from all over the warzone – vastly superior numbers, most of whom were barely sentient and so felt no pain or despair, who could be defeated only by killing them all. The same armies that had carved out Teturact's empire were here on Stratix Luminae, and they wouldn't be any easier to kill.

Thaddeus and Pilgrim ducked into cover as lasgun fire spattered towards them from ex-Guardsmen traitors duelling with the closest storm troopers.

'Do not feel sympathy for the Soul Drinkers,' said the Pilgrim, as if reading Thaddeus's mind. 'Evil will always fight with itself. Just because Sarpedon battles this same corruption does not mean he is our ally.'

Thaddeus looked over the twisted hull fragment he was using as cover. He saw heretics crouched in the wreckage, swapping fire with the storm troopers – hellgun blasts took off heads and ripped torsos apart but there were just too many of them.

'We cannot make it as one,' Thaddeus said.

'The strikeforce was never anything more than a decoy,' replied the Pilgrim. 'Though you may be loathe to admit it, it was only us who could face Sarpedon. Let them fight, it takes the eyes of our enemies away from us.'

Thaddeus looked at the Pilgrim, its hooded face as sinister as ever, its grinding voice like a warning in his head. 'Not without Aescarion.'

'Teturact's witches are here. There is much power in them, I can taste it. If Aescarion is facing them then she is lost. We are the only hope.'

Thaddeus gripped his autopistol tight, sweating in spite of the freezing cold of Stratix Luminae. Aescarion was as loyal a Sister as he could hope to have on his side, and the storm troopers were some of the best-trained troops the Ordo Hereticus could field. But men like Kolgo had taught Thaddeus that even loyal citizens like these were secondary to the ultimate goal of doing the Emperor's will. If they had known, they would have understood.

'Agreed,' said Thaddeus. 'We two can slip by when a hundred are halted. Lead the way, Pilgrim.'

The inquisitor and the Pilgrim moved quickly towards the facility, always keeping the wreckage between them and the concentrations of enemy troops, leaving the strikeforce to draw away the enemy while they searched for their true quarry.

Whatever Sarpedon wanted, it was in the facility. And that was where Thaddeus would find him.

PERHAPS KARRAIDIN WAS dead. Perhaps Solun was, too, trapped and all but helpless on the floor above. It didn't matter. What mattered was that the future was below them, trapped in the festering heart of an evil that had grown unchecked for a decade. Salk still lived, along with a handful of his squad. Graevus and many of his Assault Marines, too, along with Techmarine Lygris and Apothecary Pallas. It would have to be enough, because they had one chance and this was it.

Techmarine Lygris, covered by the bolters of his brothers crammed into the corridor behind him, had opened the control panel of the blast doors and was rewiring the security circuits. The data-slate showing the scrawlings from Karlu Grien's cell was his guide – the diagram was the most secret thing the mad adept had known, the key to the blast doors fitted to the containment floors after the facility had been hurriedly sealed.

A fountain of sparks burst from the door controls and the doors juddered open, smoke pumping from the corroded servos.

'Cover!' yelled Graevus and the bolt pistols of his squad were levelled at the opening doors as Lygris scrambled back and drew his own pistol.

Salk watched as he prepared to enter the place that had almost killed Captain Korvax ten years before.

The floor of the facility's second underground level was gone, eaten away as if by acid, a ragged ring of blackened metal all that remained. In the centre, where it would have been bisected by the floor, was suspended a huge sphere, corpulent and rotting, seething flesh pulsing between the rusting metal plates. It hung from the ceiling by a web of raw tendons and rained a steady shower of filth down into the lowest level below.

It was there, at the deepest point of the facility, that the containment had failed and where the worst of the corruption waited. The released mutagens had knitted the raw tissue into a thick pulsing mantle of flesh that lay over everything like a blanket, rippling like water, boils as tall as a man spurting hot pus like geysers, the remains of hulking biocontainment units like islands surrounded by bleeding scabs and writhing proto-limbs.

In the centre, breaking the surface of a small lake of brackish blood rained down by the sphere above, was a structure that Salk guessed was a control room or tech-shrine. Thick cables snaked away from it, and the windows now clouded with corrosion would once have looked out across the whole containment floor.

The Soul Drinkers looked down on the scene from a thin ledge of crumbling metal that clung to the wall just beyond the exit of the corridor leading to the floor above. The sounds of battle coming from the lab floor made it clear that they couldn't stay there – they could be trapped and butchered by the mutated beasts charging down the corridor from above.

Salk glanced across at Graevus. The veteran's power axe, clutched in his huge mutated hand, still fizzed and crackled as its power field burned off the blood crusted on its blade.

'One way,' said Graevus simply.

'Agreed,' said Salk. 'Lygris?'

Lygris nodded. 'You need me down there.'

'Pallas,' said Graevus, 'you stay here. Someone has to get to the surface if we don't make it. Get

Sarpedon to evacuate the force as best he can if we can't find anything or get back up. Whatever happens, we'll need you to fix us afterwards.'

'Just make sure there's enough left of you to patch up,' replied Pallas.

Graevus smiled, hefted his power axe in both hands, and jumped.

SARPEDON SAW THE dark star as it fell, a weeping open eye that bled malice as it plummeted down from the sky. It warped everything around it – with sight alone Sarpedon could tell it was something of terrible power.

But his mind confirmed it. Sarpedon was a telepath who could transmit but normally not receive – but even so he was receptive enough for the new arrival's sheer malevolence to burn itself into his mind. He felt filthy, as if some physical corruption were washing over him, and his mutated genes seemed to squirm inside him as if trying to escape. He heard screams as the traitor horde surrounding the facility keened in worship or despair, or perhaps both. The sky was turning dark and for a moment everything seemed to tilt as reality itself buckled under the strain of containing such a power.

The falling object landed a few hundred metres away in an explosion of shattered metal and earth. The Soul Drinkers firebases were holding well against the advancing masses of enemies, except where Tellos to the front and Iktinos to the back were embroiled in brutal swirling hand-to-hand combat. This would turn the tide, Sarpedon had no doubt – the leader of the horde had decided to take a personal hand in the battle. Sarpedon hurried through the closest cover, where several Marines had taken up firing positions. He didn't know which squad they were from – organisation was breaking down and officers were in charge of whichever Marines were in earshot.

'We need to put together an assault force,' he called to the nearest Marine. 'Round up as many brothers as you can and...'

The Marine turned to speak just as his head snapped to the side and a ragged hole appeared in his temple. A report sounded over the din, the sharp crack of an autopistol. Sarpedon ducked into cover as more pinpoint shots rang out, one punching through the chitinous armour of his leg, another zipping past his head far too close. He saw the attackers closing in from behind. There were two of them, one a hooded, hunched figure prowling forward like an animal, the other an unaugmented man in a long blastcoat with a heavily modified autopistol in one hand.

Sarpedon brought out the Soulspear and it responded to his grip, his genetic signature unlocking its pre-Imperial technology and sending twin blade-shaped vortex fields out from either end. The

Soulspear had served him well so far in this battle, but these new enemies were no traitors or mutants.

With sudden, shocking speed the cowled figure leapt forward, great strength propelling it as it pounced. Sarpedon slashed with the Soulspear but the cowled monster was too quick, ducking beneath the vortex blade and batting aside the front legs that Sarpedon jabbed up to fend it off.

Sarpedon was thrown back onto a mass of wreckage, the foul-smelling creature pinning him down with strength that Sarpedon had only witnessed in a fellow Space Marine. The arm that held the Soulspear was pinned – he reached round with his free left hand and tried to grab the attacker by the throat but it lunged back and drove an elbow into Sarpedon's face. His mouth filled with blood and he spat out a tooth bitterly, reaching out with two legs to get some purchase on the wreckage. He dug his talons into the torn metal and hauled himself over, rolling to the side and using the momentum to push the attacker off him. He grabbed a handful of the rags that covered it, and pulled.

The cowl tore away, and Sarpedon saw his attacker's face. Its skin was dead and pale blue-grey, red-raw where thick cables snaked into interfaces in the scalp. Its eyes were pure black. Its nose, mouth and throat were gone, replaced with brass-cased augmetics, metallic gills that fanned open and closed as it breathed and thick cylindrical filtration units where its throat should have been.

Sarpedon recognised that hate-filled expression, eyes burst black from the sudden pressure drop, twisted with loathing for the betrayal it felt. 'Greetings, Michairas,' said Sarpedon, and cracked a vicious head butt into his enemy's face.

Sarpedon had killed Brother Michairas once before during the Chapter war. When many of the Soul Drinkers had rebelled against Sarpedon's ascension to the post of Chapter Master, Michairas had been one of their leaders. He had been a young but excellent warrior, novice to Commander Caeon, and had even participated in the rites that followed victory on the Lakonia space fort. When Sarpedon had tracked Michairas down on the strike cruiser, he had torn out his rebreather implants, throttled the life out of him and hurled him out of an airlock. Those hate-filled eyes had stared at him from through the porthole even as they filled up with blood and turned black.

Sarpedon had a moment to admire Michairas's toughness and resourcefulness. He had no idea how the Marine had survived – perhaps the damage done to his rebreathers hadn't been enough and he had somehow managed to get his helmet on and drift until picked up. Probably he had clawed his way back on board the strike cruiser and stolen a saviour pod. It didn't really matter – it must have taken massive strength of will to not only survive, but set out on a path of revenge that had brought him to Stratix Luminae.

The blade of the Soulspear hummed through the air and Michairas ducked it as Sarpedon knew he would – he stabbed deep into Michairas's shoulder with his front leg and felt the talon slide through muscle, bone and augmetics.

But Michairas didn't feel the pain. He probably couldn't feel anything any more, with so many of his organs replaced with augmentics and bionics. Instead he grabbed hold of the leg embedded in his shoulder and used its leverage to throw Sarpedon clear over his shoulder, slamming him into the rock-hard earth.

Michairas leapt onto Sarpedon like a predator, fingers reaching out to gouge at Sarpedon's eyes. It was only when his limbs suddenly refused to obey him that he realised the blade of the Soulspear was stabbing through his stomach, shearing through his spine. Sarpedon kicked him off to roll onto the ground beside him, withdrawing the vortex blade of the Soulspear.

'The Soul Drinkers you knew are gone,' Sarpedon said grimly. 'That Chapter dies with you.'

The black eyes were still staring at him when the Soulspear sliced Michairas's head off. Augmetics shorted as the headless body fell back, bionics sparking and cables spewing black conductor fluid.

Sarpedon turned to the second attacker, the normal man who had hung back while Michairas attacked. Wordlessly, the man took aim and fired. The bullet hummed like an insect as it whipped through the air – Sarpedon ducked it but he could hear it as it zipped back towards him. A guided round, rare and lethal.

Sarpedon's wrist flicked and the Soulspear cut the bullet in half in mid-flight.

The man lowered his weapon.

'Inquisition?' asked Sarpedon, the Soulspear still alive and thrumming in his hand.

'Yes. Ordo Hereticus, sent to kill you.'

'Are you going to stand there wasting bullets on me, or are you going to fight an enemy worth fighting?'

The inquisitor stared at Sarpedon and paused for what seemed like forever. Sarpedon could see the tendons in his hand and neck tensing as he prepared for the next move – to attack or flee, to demand Sarpedon's surrender or to negotiate for his own safety.

Before the inquisitor could act a shockwave tore across the battlefield, tearing from the traitor leader's landing site through the wreckage and barricades. Sarpedon turned and saw showers of earth and shattered metal fountaining as something powerful and fast hurtled straight towards him, carving a furrow through the battlefield, throwing traitors and Marines alike into the air as it passed.

Sarpedon dived to one side as a wall of flying debris ripped over him, covering his legs with deep slash marks down to the muscle and knocking the inquisitor flying. Sarpedon hit the ground hard and rolled quickly, planting his leg under him to spring up and face whatever new monstrosity had sent itself against the Soul Drinkers.

Metal and soil fell like rain. In the centre of the destruction, in a zone of calm like the eye of a hurricane, was Teturact.

No descriptions existed of Teturact but Sarpedon knew straight away who he was facing. Sarpedon could feel his augmented organs straining to keep diseases from erupting throughout his body at the enemy's mere presence. Strange sounds rolled just beneath his range of hearing, the taste of rank blood filled his mouth. His autosenses could barely contain the sight in front of him.

Teturact was a thin, wizened humanoid form perched like a malevolent carrion bird on the shoulders of four immense, brawny brute-mutants. The faces of the mutants were swamped with muscle until their features hardly showed, and their trunk-like arms ended in fists as large as a man's torso. Teturact probably couldn't walk on his own, but even in that deformed, dried-out body Sarpedon could taste the vastness of Teturact's mind and the immense power it could bring to bear.

Teturact reached out and Sarpedon was held in a psychic vice that reached through his armour and began to crush his solid bone ribcage as it hauled him high into the air. A white wall of pain crushed inwards as he struggled against bonds that only existed in Teturact's mind. The battlefield whirled underneath him and Sarpedon could see the facility, the isolated pockets of Soul Drinkers holding back the tide, the vast swarms of traitors wading through the volleys of bolter fire and the piles of their own dead. He saw the snarled knots of slaughter where Tellos and Iktinos were engaged in savage hand-to-hand fighting on opposite sides of the battlefield. He could even pick out, through a whitening gauze of agony, the battle on the edge of his vision where black-armoured Sisters and Hereticus storm troopers were fighting tides of zombies and wizards whose corrupt magic Sarpedon could taste.

Sarpedon's ribcage fractured. A warm wave rode through him as internal organs ruptured and his insides were flooded with blood. He tried to reach through Teturact's grip deep into his own mind, to dredge out the power of the Hell that might distract Teturact long enough for Sarpedon to strike back. But Teturact was powerful, more powerful than anything Sarpedon had felt before, a vessel of pure hatred and corruption focused through an utterly malevolent mind.

With a flick of his will, Teturact threw Sarpedon down to the ground. Somehow, Sarpedon forced his legs underneath him and spread them enough to cushion his landing, otherwise his armour would have been cracked clean open by the impact. As it was he felt the muscles tearing in their armour of chitin and his single bionic leg shorted out with a flash of pain.

Teturact lifted him up again, legs dangling use-lessly, and brought Sarpedon through the air towards him. Sarpedon saw Teturact's ruin of a face, flaps of ragged skin for features, weeping raw pits for eyes.

'You are different,' said Teturact's voice in Sarpe-don's head, thick and treacly, like acid corroding his brain. 'My worshippers have faced the Astartes many times, but they tasted pure and misguided. You are tainted. You are like I once was, a man flawed down to the genes. Ah, but I took those flaws and made them my reason for being. You are afraid of them, however. You want to turn yourself back. How can you turn back when you are already so much more than a man?'

Teturact drew Sarpedon closer. It felt like his mind was on fire.

'If you could only see what is possible when your own body is no longer a prison, then you would really know what freedom is. That is what you want, isn't it, flawed man? To be free? Yet you search to rebuild the prisons of your flesh.'

Sarpedon knew he couldn't take Teturact on, not when the vast fortress of the mutant's mind stood before him and Sarpedon himself was, ultimately, little more than a man. But Sarpedon could taste somewhere in Teturact a single weakness, the same weakness that was killing the Imperium and which the Soul Drinkers themselves had possessed until Sarpedon had shown them the way out.

It was arrogance. Teturact believed he was a god, and his victims were worshippers. When he looked at the Soul Drinkers he saw more fodder for his worship, strong and skilled men but men nonetheless. Sarpedon was not much more than a man but he was more, and what set him apart was the strength of will that had seen him fight against his Chapter and his Imperium, accepting the hatred of the universe in return for a fleeting taste of freedom.

A white stab of psychic power was driving forth from Teturact's mind, boring into Sarpedon's own mind the same way it had done to untold billions of desperate plague victims, to plant in him the seeds of worship and bind him to Teturact's will. Sarpedon let him in, pulling back his psychic defences just enough to let Teturact think he was winning.

Cold horror washed through Sarpedon. He could feel the exultation of a god and the billions of minds united in worship. He could see a universe where stars were weeping sores and planets teemed with life like spores of a disease, all singing the name of Teturact. He could feel the Imperium he hated crushed beneath the weight of worship, the minds of its citizens liberated even as their bodies decayed and the armies of the Emperor died in their trillions...

Sarpedon opened his eyes. He could swear he detected rapture in that near-featureless face, the face of a god being fed the worship he craved.

With a strength he didn't know he had, Sarpedon snapped his mind away from Teturact, the images of glorious decay receding with impossible speed and leaving him dazed and near-blind with the effort. But Teturact was stunned, too, his mind losing its grip on Sarpedon and dropping him to the ground. Sarpedon landed hard on his back, exhaust gases hissing from the fractured power plant in his armour's backpack.

He fumbled with numb fingers for his boltgun. His hands shook as he brought it to bear on the indistinct shapes towering over him, and his trigger finger spasmed as he willed it to pull down on the trigger.

Half a magazine of bolts sprayed out. Every one ricocheted off an invisible shield of will, space warping where they hit.

The brute-mutants leaned down and Teturact leaned with them, his spindly form tottering directly over Sarpedon.

Traitor! it screeched into his head. *I am a god, you are vermin! Vermin! And you deny me, believer of nothing? I will give you something to believe!*

A red spear of psychic hatred shot down and held Sarpedon to the ground like an insect pinned to a board. Spite poured into him, hot and livid, the rage of a god denied. Just once it had been denied, once in its lifetime, and its response was to annihilate the mind that denied it in a tide of hatred.

Sarpedon was strong, stronger than a man, stronger than even any Marine. That meant he would survive a split second more before his mind gave way and his body became just another shell in service of Teturact the God. The last thing he would see would be the ruined mutant face, those bleeding eye-holes narrowed in hate. It gave him a strange satisfaction, in those last moments, that he could force even that unreadable face to give away its emotions.

'In the name of the Immortal Emperor,' cried a voice from nowhere, 'I dub thee Hereticus!'

A shower of blood and flesh was the head of a brute-mutant disintegrating. A falling shadow was the mutant's body falling and the spindly shape above it was Teturact falling with it, wizened limbs flailing.

Sarpedon forced himself to roll through the pain as Teturact and his mutant bearers fell to the hard earth around him.

INQUISITOR THADDEUS FELT the kick of the autopistol in his hand and was grateful that he could feel anything at all. He had been frozen in place as Teturact had seemed about to tear Sarpedon apart with psychic power, but whatever Sarpedon had done had worked and in the split second Teturact's attention was diverted Thaddeus had taken aim and blown apart the head of the closest brute-mutant.

He yelled out the protocol forms of the Inquisition as he fired. He was going to do this properly.

'By the edicts of the Conclave of Mount Amalath I claim your life as forfeit and cast your soul to the mercy of the Emperor!' Thaddeus pumped shells towards Teturact's spindly, momentarily vulnerable body but one of his mutant bearers got in the way and the explosive-tipped shells blew fist-sized lumps of flesh from its hide. Thaddeus had spent the last of his precious tracker-shells on Sarpedon, and seen it swatted out of the air before it hit – he had to rely on old-fashioned hand-aiming now.

Thaddeus ran towards Teturact, trying to draw a bead on his cowering mutant form, snapping shots between the brute-mutants sheltering him. The hammer fell on an empty chamber and Thaddeus holstered the pistol quickly, for he was out of ammunition and his remaining spare clips lay back in the storm trooper Chimera.

He still had one more weapon. He reached inside his flak-coat and drew out the massive, boxy bolt pistol Aescarion had brought back from Eumenix, its casing decorated with the golden chalice of the Soul Drinkers, half a clip of explosive bolts in its curved magazine. He had to grip it with both hands to take aim.

Teturact's wits were gathering and the cold, greasy feel of its deformed mind was evident in the air. The surviving mutants were rearing up to defend their master – Thaddeus's first shot missed high as the pistol's kick deceived him but the second hit, blowing a mutant's throat out. It fell backwards against its brother mutant and in a flash of strange black light the second mutant's body was sliced clean in two in a welter of strange-coloured blood.

Sarpedon, battering and bleeding, was back on his many feet, his armour scored and dented, the strange weapon with its twin shimmering black blades in one hand.

Thaddeus raised the bolt pistol. His opponent was battered, shocked and slowed, but would not remain so for long. 'By the authority of the Holy Orders of His Inquisition and the Chamber of the Ordo Hereticus,' he said, 'I execute the destruction of your body and the release your soul for judgement. May the Emperor have mercy on you, for His servants cannot.'

His trigger finger pressed down and his whole body shook as the bolt pistol juddered, hot cases spilling to Thaddeus's feet. The pronouncement of execution ringing in his ears, he emptied the rest of the pistol's shells into Teturact.

SARPEDON HAD BEEN ready to die. But the final shots were not for him. The inquisitor fired off the last of his bullets into Teturact who was sprawled on the frozen ground beside Sarpedon, showered in the blood of his brute-mutant retainers.

You couldn't kill something like Teturact just by destroying its body. Sarpedon could feel the malevolent mind reaching out even now, seeking for some other living thing to take up roost, so it could escape and begin its reign again.

Sarpedon reared up on his back legs. Forgetting the pain of his torn muscles and ruptured organs, he took one last look at the ruined non-face of Teturact.

I serve the Emperor, mutant, he thought, knowing full well that Teturact could hear him. *I need no other god.*

He stamped down on Teturact's head, talons shearing through the feverish brain, and the dark light of Teturact's soul was extinguished forever.

TECHMARINE LYGRIS TORE the mem-circuits from the archive console. There was no time for finesse, they would just have to trust that enough would survive. From inside the command room he could hear the vicious din of battle and he knew that every second here cost more battle-brothers their lives.

Beside him, Sergeant Salk plunged a hand through the window of the command structure and, bracing his legs against the plasteel wall, hauled Apothecary Pallas out of the pulsing sea of rotting flesh that pressed in on the structure from all sides. Pallas was covered in filth, smoke rising where his armour's exhausts were clogged with gore, and somewhere he had lost his bolt pistol in the mire.

He held up a hand, and it held a specimen cylinder with a clot of pink, uncorrupted flesh inside.

'Got it,' he said, almost out of breath. 'There was one containment unit intact. I think Graevus is still out there, he...'

That was all he could say before everything erupted in white noise. It was a scream so loud it filled the heads of every Soul Drinker, blocking out every sense. It was the death-scream of something vastly powerful, a keening of absolute rage and despair. The walls of mutant flesh shrunk back as they felt the death of one of their own.

Squad Graevus were revealed, hacking their way from beneath a web of flesh, where they had held position around the last functioning containment unit. The heaving mass of muscle and skin spat back Marines, some still alive, others half-digested. The mutant sea spasmed and the whole containment floor churned like a sea in a storm.

'Salk to all points,' yelled Salk over the vox, which was barely functioning any more. 'It's over, every man out!'

He clambered onto the roof of the command structure where he could see Graevus's squad battering a path across the floor. The survivors of Salk's own squad were fighting their way up onto the top of the rolling mantle of muscle. They had seen him and were forging their way towards him, slicing and shooting through the malformed limbs that reached for them.

'I don't know if this is getting through,' voxed Salk through the static on the command channel, 'but this is Squad Salk and we are withdrawing from the facility. If there's an army still up there we will need extraction in about five minutes. Salk out.'

NO ONE KNEW where Colonel Vinn was. Inquisitor Thaddeus and the Pilgrim hadn't returned. Aescarion now had command of the Inquisitorial troops and she was organising them into a withdrawal. The Soul Drinkers were on the other side of an immense mass of walking dead and fanatical traitors, led by powerful witches who threw lightning or turned men inside-out with a look. Many of the storm troopers were dead or cut off, but the Sisters had formed a formidable hard core of warriors against which wave after wave of enemies had broken, chewed up by bolter volleys or blasted into guttering valleys of fire by flamers and melta-guns.

'Squad Rufilla, secure the Rhinos and cover us as we embark,' voxed Aescarion as she snapped shots at traitors clambering over burning barricades of their own dead. She had personally led counter-attack after counter-attack into the shattered traitor lines, and her axe arm ached with the jarring of power blade against bone. Her Seraphim had fought as well as any troops on Stratix Luminae but in spite of the pride the warrior in her felt, the Sister saw only failure. The Soul Drinkers were on the other side of an army she could not hope to cut through, and no matter how many enemies of the Emperor fell here the strikeforce would not corner their quarry today.

The dead had not died for nothing. She would never forget that, for every one died in the service of the immortal Emperor and that was an end in itself. But the Soul Drinkers would escape their justice, and their treachery would stay an open wound in the soul of the Imperium.

Squad Rufilla was pouring fire over the heads of the Sisters and storm troopers as they ran back towards the Rhinos and Chimeras. Several of the vehicles were out of action, tracks ripped apart by sharp ridges of wreckage or hulls dented by collisions. The strikeforce crammed into the surviving transports, small arms fire spattering against the hulls, the traitorous hordes taking the opportunity to press on through Rufilla's fire.

Aescarion was on the front lines with the Sisters around her rapidly falling back. She followed them, snapping shots into the shambling dead tumbling down the valleys of twisted metal around her. A hand reached out and she sliced it off with a slash of her power axe.

'We have you covered, Sister, get on board now!' Rufilla's bold voice sounded over the vox and Aescarion picked up her pace, the vehicle convoy beginning to roar off back towards the distant *Crescent Moon*.

'Sister!' someone yelled, not over the vox but out loud, out of breath and close by. Aescarion paused and looked back to see Inquisitor Thaddeus struggling across the blasted battlefield, firing with a bolt pistol he held with both hands, shooting his way through the living dead of Teturact's army. His face was streaked with blood and his flak-coat was torn and burned at the edges. He broke into a run when he saw Aescarion and she thought for a moment that there were troops with him lending him covering fire as he ran towards Aescarion and the convoy, but Squad Rufilla's fire was soon ripping over his head and into the living dead.

'Sister,' he said as he got close, 'we are done here.'

'I am pulling the troops out,' she replied. 'We thought you were lost.'

'I was,' he replied. 'Teturact is dead, we have done enough here.'

'And the Soul Drinkers?'

Thaddeus reloaded his bolt pistol. Aescarion wondered where he had got it, and the ammunition for it. 'Teturact's wizards are still in command here?'

'They are. I have seen them, they are foul things indeed.'

'They command this army now. They are our target. Without Teturact they will have nowhere to flee to. If we can hunt them down quickly their armies will fall and the warzone will be cleansed.'

'But the Soul Drinkers will have to flee this planet too, inquisitor, surely we will never have a better opportunity to...'

Thaddeus blasted a volley of bolts into the closest few traitors as Rufilla's covering fire lanced down over his head and scoured a zone of safety around them. 'Aescarion, one day I will teach you about politics. But for now I must exercise my authority as an inquisitor and demand you do as I instruct. We can argue when it is all over.'

Rufilla yelled a final plea and Aescarion turned, leading Thaddeus back to the last Rhino where they clambered in beside Squad Rufilla and, still snatching shots at the enemy through the firing slits and hatches, roared bruisingly across the battlefield towards the *Crescent Moon*.

THE AIR WAS full of the stench of gunfire and rotting flesh, but Salk still gulped it down in relief as he led the bedraggled spearhead from the ruins of the facility. The sound of battle raged not far away and Salk knew that bitter close combat was waged just behind the facility, where the lives of Marines had bought the spearhead the time to snatch the Chapter's future. The facility smoked from thousands of small arms hits and the area around it was a dark twisted nightmare of wreckage and craters. Above, Salk could see the dark form of the battleship still ghosted against the sky, its skeletal frame disintegrating.

Behind Salk and the survivors of his squad was Graevus, supporting Karraidin with his mutated arm. One of Karraidin's legs was gone at the knee and his storm bolter hand was a gleaming red ruin, but he was alive, and his squad formed a cordon around him. Pallas and Lygris were with them – they had tried to find Techmarine Solun as they charged through the mutant-infested laboratory level, but he was gone.

'Soul Drinkers, this is Sergeant Salk. Mission fulfilled, get us out of here.'

Static. Then – 'Salk, stay in cover we're coming in.'

The seconds were agonising. Lygris and Pallas carried the only chance the Soul Drinkers had of genetic survival. A single well-timed assault or lucky impact could wipe out the future.

With a roar of engines and a flash of silver a fighter shot down from above, impossibly bright against the darkening sky. The lower portals yawned open and the fighter dipped so low its belly scraped the piles of wreckage.

Pallas and Lygris went first, dragged into the passenger compartment. Somehow, Graevus got Karraidin onto the top of a pile of wreckage and purple-armoured hands reached down to haul the wounded old captain aboard. Salk covered Graevus as he and his men went next, and finally Salk boarded, bolter chattering to the last. The portal began to bleed closed and the last Salk saw of Stratix Luminae was a blackened ruin, a twisted metal hell swarming with enemies that formed a writhing sea around an impossibly thin cordon of purple.

'Librarian Gresk to Commander Sarpedon,' someone was voxing, and Salk realised it was one of the reserve fighters that had picked them up. Gresk – one of the Soul Drinkers' pyskers, a Marine who could throw fireballs with a look – must have dropped off most of the Marines with him already as only his retinue and the survivors of the spearhead were in the passenger compartment. 'We have the spearhead. Mission concluded. Repeat, mission concluded.'

'Understood,' came the reply vox, which Salk could just hear over the growing whine of the engines. 'All squads, fall back and extract. All squads…'

Salk fell back against the grav-couch. He ached all over and, as his metabolism came back down to near-normal, he would feel a dozen new injuries he didn't know he had.

He was alive, and somehow it hardly seemed right. He could see Solun, as if he were there in front of him, lying crippled on the floor. He could see Marines pounded to bits by the tide of mutant flesh. He could see Captain Dreo lying mortally wounded in the Mechanicus lab on Eumenix, and he remembered the account of how Hastis had died on Septiam Torus. How many of the Chapter had died? He didn't dare think. Only the Chapter's true leaders, like Sarpedon, Karraidin and Lygris, would dare to comprehend the price they had paid, and Salk knew that it would weigh them down like death itself.

If it was worth it, though, if the Chapter had a future, then there was hope. Sarpedon had not cursed them with hope until he had known they had a real chance, and now that hope was all the Chapter had left.

The Marines struggled into their grav-harnesses and Gresk gave the order to the bridge. The fighter's engines kicked in and it shot through the atmosphere, out into the hard vacuum and away from Stratix Luminae at last.

THREE OF THE fighters were lost, the one that had crashed in the first moments of the assault and two more that had been brought down by fire from the ground as they swooped low for extraction. The rest picked up the Soul Drinkers even as they fought. With the squads of the cordon gone, the traitorous, leaderless hordes poured over the facility like a tide of hungry vermin, there to fight against the mutated inhabitants until there was nothing left at the facility but death.

Iktinos was one of the last to be picked up. He and the squads with him were surrounded, and he was still battering traitors back from the lower hatch with his crozius as the fighter lifted off. The fighters broke formation and swooped out into space, weaving through the remnants of Teturact's flagship and leaving the Stratix system far behind. They evaded the *Crescent Moon* as they went, as its weapons shot down the transports trying to leave Stratix.

As the squads counted off, Sarpedon estimated that about four hundred and fifty Soul Drinkers had got off Stratix Luminae, leaving the Chapter at less than half its original strength.

THE LAST FIGHTER, having picked up Iktinos and his men at massive risk, made one last pass over the battlefield. Iktinos himself called out over the vox as the craft searched for Tellos and his Assault Marines, last seen cut off and surrounded, taking on tens of thousands of mutants and traitors face-to-face.

The battlefield was in such chaos that it was impossible to find anything, let alone a last stand of so few men against so many. As the fighter was ordered to give up the search and escape before it was shot down, Iktinos found Tellos's vox-channel and tried to contact him one last time.

But all he could hear was screaming.

'NOT ONE AMONGST you does not know fear. If you say any different, then you lie. You are terrified. You are assembled on a space hulk, surrounded by rebel Space Marines, being lectured by a mutant and a witch. Yes, I am well aware of what I am, and I am also aware of what the Imperium would say if they knew what I was. They would find strong, young, free men like you and they would point me out as a warning of what you might become. Traitor, they would say. Heretic. Unclean. And so another generation would be poisoned against freedom and become a part of the corrupt, crumbling Imperium, a breeding ground for Chaos, built on the backs of slaves.'

Sarpedon gripped the pulpit. He felt the burning of pride on the back of his mind, and though it was pride that had cost the Soul Drinkers so much in the past, he knew that here he had something he could truly be proud of. The novice candidates, three hundred of them, were stood in ranks on the gun deck of a battleship deep in the heart of the *Brokenback*. They were all towards the older end of recruitment age, beyond which the implants and operations that turned a man into a Space Marine would fail. All were strong and fit, not necessarily great warriors but – much more importantly – youths who had proved their bravery and their willingness to face any odds for what they believed in.

Iktinos had selected them, with Sarpedon's approval. After Stratix Luminae the Soul Drinkers had taken back the *Brokenback*, taking their alien fighters close enough to activate the many combined machine-spirits and causing the hulk to break from its moorings and rendezvous with the fighter fleet again. It had been the best part of a year since then, during which time the hulk had visited hotbeds of rebellion and secession, finding those who had banded together against the might of the Imperium and selecting the bravest of their young fighters.

Many who fought against the Imperium were just bandits and tyrants. But some were driven by an all-pervading hatred of oppression, and it was those that had provided the recruits Sarpedon now addressed. Chaplain Iktinos had selected them for courage, intelligence and dedication, and so the Great Harvest had begun again.

'You will not all survive,' continued Sarpedon. Three hundred pairs of eyes watched him intently. 'The implant procedures alone will account for some. Training will account for more. But those who survive will be ready to understand some of the truths about mankind and the threats it faces. The Imperium is one of those threats, for it is too obsessed with its own tyranny to face what is truly dangerous to humankind. Daemons, powers of the warp, dark magics and gods you will be forbidden to name – these are the enemies we fight against. These, and no other. For this is the will of the Emperor untainted by the ambitions of the power-hungry. I can offer you a lifetime of battle and pain and the promise of a violent death, and I demand of you your every waking moment. But you will die knowing you have lived fighting for what the Emperor stands for, and that is more than anyone in the Imperium can claim.

'Soon the blood of Rogal Dorn will run in your veins and you will learn of your place in the unending defence of mankind. Until then, think on the unforgiving future I am showing you. If it was easy, it would not be worth doing. I trust that when you take on the mantle of novice and eventually the armour of a battle-brother, you will understand some of what I have told you, and the legacy of the Soul Drinkers will live on in you.'

They were afraid, and they had every reason to be. They were facing the long and trying process of becoming a Space Marine, and Sarpedon could not properly explain to them the constant hardship and pain combined with the ever-present fear of failure. But Iktinos had chosen well, and Sarpedon felt that few of them would fall before they took up the armour and boltgun of a Soul Drinker.

It was a miracle they were here at all. The existing mutations of the Soul Drinkers, including Sarpedon's arachnoid form, could not be reversed, but the accelerating mutation had been halted thanks to the tireless efforts of Pallas and the apothecarion, using the information they had found on Stratix Luminae. The gene-seed organs recovered from the many dead had been stored and eventually their mutations had been regressed, to the stage that they could now be implanted into the recruits who passed the first stages of their training. The carnage that culminated on Stratix Luminae had been for one reason, and that was to purify the Chapter's gene-seed and make the Great Harvest possible again – it would take a long time before the Chapter approached full strength again, but it would happen, and of that Sarpedon was proud.

Under Iktinos's gaze, the novices filed off the gun deck towards their first training sessions. Graevus would teach them hand-to-hand fighting while

Karraidin, who could do little else until the tech-marines and apothecaries fashioned some bionics to replace his lost hand and leg, would school them in the ways of Daenyathos and the sciences of war. Sarpedon wished Dreo was still there to teach them marksmanship, but there were enough crack shots still alive in the Chapter to do an admirable job. Sarpedon himself would have a role schooling that handful of recruits who showed some psychic potential, testing their mental resilience and training them in the use of their powers. And, of course, he would regularly expose all the recruits to the horrors of the Hell, so they would be able to face their fears and keep on fighting.

Sarpedon knew the Soul Drinkers were utterly alone, surrounded on all sides by those who hated them. The Inquisition would not give up hunting them and the daemonic foes they faced would only get more savage. There were doubtless forces more deadly even than Teturact out there, and the Soul Drinkers would have to seek them out and face them if they were to stay true to their purpose. But in spite of it all, Sarpedon knew how grateful he should be. How many men in the galaxy could claim they were truly free? Sarpedon could, and so could his Marines, and in time so would his novices.

In the end, there was nothing else that mattered. The Emperor's message was one of freedom – from the warp-spawned and the tyrannous alike.

mankind was in chains all across the galaxy, and Sarpedon swore to himself that the Soul Drinkers would free it.

Sarpedon stepped down from the podium and began the long walk through the body of the *Brokenback* towards the bridge. The hulk was to head for a silent sector, light years from habitation, where the training and slow rebuilding of the Chapter could begin.

Freedom. It had taken Sarpedon so long to find out that it was the only thing worth fighting for. Freedom was what both the Imperium and the warp feared more than anything. It would take thousands if not tens of thousands of years but if Sarpedon could wield that freedom like a weapon to destroy the enemies of humanity, then the Soul Drinkers might truly be victorious and the Emperor's will might at last be done.

ABOUT THE AUTHOR

Ben Counter has made several contributions to the
Black Library's *Inferno!* magazine, and has been
published in 2000 AD and the UK small press.
An Ancient History graduate and avid miniature
painter, he is also secretary of the Comics Creators
Guild. *The Bleeding Chalice* is his third novel.

INFERNO!

More Warhammer 40,000 from Ben Counter

SOUL DRINKER

GIVRILLIAN'S SQUAD HAD torn the first rank of mutants apart, and were now crouched in firepoints as return fire sheeted over their heads. Sarpedon strode through it all, ignoring the autoshells and las-blasts spattering across the shadowy interior of the hub.

He spread his arms, and felt the coil of the aegis circuits light up and flow around his armoured body. He forced the images in his head to screaming intensity – and let them go.

The Hell began.

THE SOUL DRINKERS have served the Emperor loyally for thousands of years, but their obsessive desire to retrieve an ancient relic throws them into conflict with those they are honour-bound to obey. Faced with an impossible choice, will this proud and noble Chapter back down, or rebel to forge a new destiny for themselves among the stars?